WHISPERINGS

WHISPERINGS

a novel

C. K. Bailey

Covenant Communications, Inc.

Cover image by Alan and Sandy Carey © Photodisc Green/Getty Images

Cover design copyrighted 2004 by Covenant Communications, Inc.

Published by Covenant Communications, Inc.
American Fork, Utah

Printed in Canada
First Printing: February 2004

10 09 08 07 06 05 04   10 9 8 7 6 5 4 3 2 1

ISBN 1-59156-418-2

CHAPTER 1

"Please, Daddy . . . It's dark down here . . . Please don't leave . . . The light, Daddy. Turn on the light!" Jessie awoke wet with perspiration. She embraced the moist feather pillow.

Sleep was a distant illusion.

Exasperated at the thought of another sleepless night, Jessie pulled herself out of bed and began her nightly ritual. She headed for the bathroom sink. She knew her effort to wash away the haunting dream with a few splashes of cold water would surely fail, so she then donned her favorite flannel robe, set off toward the kitchen and poured a cup of warm chamomile tea. In her younger days, something stronger—probably Jack Daniels—would have occupied the well-used mug. Having relinquished that vice, her taste buds had since found their way to herbal teas.

After carrying the tea down the almost nonexistent hallway to her study, she placed the cup on the edge of the desk. She slipped into the soft leather of her favorite chair, pulling her knees to her chest. A brightly colored, crocheted afghan carefully concealed any patch of skin still exposed to the cool night air.

Wrapping her cold fingers around the warm mug, she slowly began to sip. She drew in a deep breath and calmly allowed her eyelids to close. The little girl locked in the dark, musty basement inched her way back. Jessie's eyes flew wide open as her head jerked. The splashing tea descended to its usual spot on the table as she rummaged through the neatly stacked papers.

Reviewing the day's client profiles had become a necessary predawn diversion. While she'd often chided her associates for working too late at the office, she had recently acquired the same habit. Only the environment was different.

Blaring music jolted Jessie's head from the back of the chair. She had somehow managed a nap. Annoyed at the clamor of the alarm clock in the next room, she couldn't help but wonder what idiot had invented such a ridiculous way of awakening someone. Moving reluctantly, she reached the clock on the nightstand by her bed.

In the quiet, Jessie sat staring, contemplating the soft, inviting space that awaited just beneath those covers. Slithering into the cool sheets, she lay for several minutes. When her mind drifted to the image of the scared little girl, she quickly rose and stumbled, half-asleep, toward the shower. Her eyes were not yet capable of suitable focus. The light of the sun, inching its way through the bedroom curtains, offered no additional motivation to see clearly. She had envisioned a long, therapeutic shower, the soothing massage of the hot liquid cascading down her back. Within minutes, however, reality emerged and the warmth dissipated. The cold water began its usual interruption, forcing an early end.

Today would be the first time in four years she would arrive to the office late, but most likely, no one would say a word. It was, after all, common practice for partners to be late.

She glanced through her apartment. Any quest for cleanliness would have to be put on hold. The bed would go unmade, and clutter would linger until evening. She threw on her favorite teal knit suit, which fit snugly around her slender waist. Her long, naturally dark auburn hair would normally be braided, coiled, and pinned up into a more sophisticated look. Today, however, it was pulled back with a black barrette.

Choosing to speed at a minimal excess of five miles over the limit ensured Jessie's late arrival. A mere fifteen-minute tardiness was more acceptable than the prominent delay a speeding ticket would have created.

Pulling in next to Susan Steed's car, Jessie sighed. She knew Susan would be the one client to comment on her late arrival. Time-conscious Susan—as the office personnel referred to her—usually arrived fifteen minutes early, hoping for more time in therapy.

To avoid a confrontation in the lobby, Jessie slipped in through the back entrance. No revolving door, no digital keyless entry, and no welcoming committee. Just an ordinary key lock with a simple sign above the door that read *Stone, Welch, Arnold, Winston & Associates. Psychologists. Please use front entrance.*

Jessie had barely opened her office door when the receptionist's voice came over the intercom, "Susan Steed has been waiting."

"I'm on my way." Jessie didn't care for the newest receptionist. Tendra was the niece of the founding partner, Elliott, and made sure everyone knew it. At eighteen, her grades had barely allowed her to graduate from high school. Tendra's explanation for the purpose of schooling was to educate oneself on the "who's who" of society. She was petite, barely five feet tall, and had shoulder-length, curly, vibrant red hair. Jessie often felt the urge to ask if her bloodlines coincided with Little Orphan Annie's. Tendra packed a constant air of false sweetness. After thirty seconds of conversation with her, anyone endowed with even minor intelligence grew nauseated.

Jessie set her open briefcase neatly on the corner of the desk, leaving her access to the client files she had taken with her the night before.

Jessie's office was small in comparison to those of the other partners. She wasn't one to want to impress clients with expensive furniture, art, or knickknacks. The limited space sported a basic oak desk, a filing case, a coat rack, bookshelves, a couch, and a comfortable, high-back chair for clients. Her license to practice and a picture of a local mountain scene graced her walls. She was comfortable here.

Taking a deep, calming breath, she walked out to meet Susan. Meeting clients in the lobby often helped them feel more at ease. However, Susan, who was already walking toward Jessie, didn't care much for courtesy, protocol, or anything else that wasn't originally *her* idea. She pushed past Jessie and slumped into her usual position on the gray fabric couch in the corner. Jessie had barely closed the door before Susan started in on the frustrations that currently littered her life's path.

Jessie positioned herself behind her oaken barricade, retrieved Susan's folder, and laid it neatly on the desk. As Susan's voice droned on, Jessie moved to her briefcase and removed the files, placing them in the pile before her. She leaned back in her chair and placed her hands on the armrests. The hum of Susan's voice began to have its usual effect. Entirely void of any and all excitement, Jessie's eyes became dull and glassy. She lost herself in thoughts of the morning's nightmare.

"Jessie!" sobbed Susan. "Are you listening to me?"

Jessie blinked her eyes rapidly and turned her attention directly to Susan's unfriendly stare. "What? Oh . . . I'm sorry. Please go on."

"Go on? I've repeated my question twice now. Aren't you listening?"

"Of course I'm listening, Susan."

"Then what did I just ask?"

"Well, . . . you . . . ah . . ."

"Oh, what's the use! First you're late—"

There it is, Jessie thought silently.

"And then you don't even listen to me. What am I paying you for, anyway?" In one fluid motion, Susan was gone.

Jessie softly closed Susan's file, wishing that her frustrations could close with the same ease. *These nightmares are invading too much of my sleep. I can't seem to concentrate. I'm focusing on the wrong things. You'd think seven years as a therapist would supply me with a greater ability to hide my anxiety and stress from the outside world! I'll have to call Susan in a couple hours and apologize. I'll blame my behavior on the flu or P.M.S.*

Opening the file drawer to her right, Jessie put Susan's folder away and pulled out one marked *Karen Edwards*. Karen would most likely come in swearing this was the week she and the kids would leave home. How many times would she keep saying this until . . .

A slight shadow darkened the file, interrupting Jessie's thoughts. "Oh, hello, Elliott," she said, trying to appear calm. "I didn't hear you come in."

"Not surprised. Seems par for the course lately," rasped Elliott. Standing at just five feet nine inches, Elliott Stone had the ability to make even the tallest of partners and associates feel inferior. Approaching fifty, he was distinguished in appearance. Slivers of gray glistened throughout his dark hair as well as his neatly trimmed mustache and goatee. His eyes, though seemingly undistinguished in color or size, had a piercing quality. He always dressed impeccably and commanded instant respect. He took his work seriously, often being the first in and the last to leave, which made for an endless client waiting list.

"What? What's par for the course?" Jessie asked, silently chastising herself for not using the last few minutes to gain a more professional composure after Susan's abrupt departure.

Elliott rested on a small space on the side of her desk, his hands on his knees. "Oh, . . . not hearing, not listening, not understanding. At least that's the impression I get from your clients, not to mention the staff and everyone else with whom we are mutually acquainted."

"Listen, if you're talking about what just happened with Susan Steed, well, . . . that's just . . . I'm not feeling quite . . ." She searched for words, her face twisting in thought.

Elliott stood and quietly closed her office door. "It's not just this client," he said as he pushed the high-back chair closer and sat. His eyes closed momentarily as he leaned forward and searched for the empathy that he must surely apply. "Jess, I have someone I'd like you to meet. It's time you worked through things."

Jessie's pulse quickened. She felt a rush of blood soar to her head and a sharp pain pierce her chest. If she didn't know better, she would swear sweat was dripping from her entire body.

"I don't follow, Elliott."

"We both know the signs, Jess. I've tried to figure out what's going on inside that head of yours, but you push me away."

"Who am I meeting?" Jessie snapped, her calm veneer beginning to crack.

Elliott opened the door and motioned for his friend. Jessie rose cautiously. Feeling cornered, she leaned against the bookshelves behind her desk, slowly folding her arms across her chest, again sensing the perspiration build.

"Jessica Winston, meet Ryan Blake," Elliott said, watching her intently.

Jessie stared blankly. Her mouth felt heavy, as though it were filled with sand. She knew that name.

"This is by far the calmest response I've received yet. It's nice to meet you, Dr. Winston," Ryan said, extending his hand.

Jessie drew in a slow, deep breath, ignored Ryan's hand, and turned to face Elliott. "I would like to speak with you privately."

* * *

Ryan's six-foot-tall frame was unaccustomed to being shoved out a door, especially by a woman. However unbelievable, the door slammed, barely clearing his nose. He was one of Denver's most renowned therapists. During Ryan's college years, a near-photographic memory had established his reputation as a walking encyclopedia of psychology. If he didn't know the answer to a problem, there most likely wasn't one. Aside from that, his riveting blue eyes, black, wavy hair that fell to just above his shoulders, and skin tanned dark by the sun caused almost every female head to turn for a second look. Some simply stared. Ryan adjourned to the lobby and pretended to be engrossed in a magazine.

Ryan's practice had begun during his midtwenties. His client list contained not only the names of normal, everyday people, but also well-known therapists searching for their own path back to reality. After twelve years of practicing, however, he decided he had had enough. His deceased wife's inheritance, as well as his own bank account, had allowed him to put psychology behind him.

It had been a month since Ryan and Elliott first communicated about Jessie. Following a week of daily conversation, Ryan was forced to put his early retirement on hold. After all, he owed Elliott. But sitting in a lobby waiting for a client to agree to talk with him—on someone else's terms—was a first for him, too. Clients used to come to *his* office. If he hadn't owed Elliott so much, he'd be in his comfortable leather chair, in front of his big-screen TV, sipping a seltzer.

* * *

"Elliott, what is going on?" Jessie barked furiously. "You have no right—"

"Dr. Blake is a friend, Jess," Elliott cut in. "I trust him. I've asked him to spend some time with you, to help you deal with your childhood issues. Nothing else is to be on your agenda, with the possible exception of eating and sleeping."

"Are you crazy? You can't *force* someone into therapy. Besides, he isn't 'Dr. Blake' anymore, if my memory serves me right. I'm certainly not going anywhere with anybody! I can't afford to leave my clients for a week! Not to mention whatever *he's* charging. And besides, doesn't he have enough to handle with his harem of fifteen wives?" she spat angrily, pointing toward the door.

"Jess, Mormons don't do that anymore. You're intelligent enough to know that. And your clients will be fine. I'll have Tendra reschedule all your appointments."

Jessie was more than angry now. It wasn't unreasonable for Elliott to be concerned, but for Little Orphan Annie to be brought into the know—*that* was crossing the line.

"And since his license has expired, technically you're just going off with someone who can offer help. There isn't any fee. I've taken care of everything. And you *are* going through with this. I plan to see you in my office first thing in the morning, a week from Monday. That'll give you ten days to pull it together."

Jessie exploded, "Ten days! You and I both know that is totally unrealistic. We've been over this. I'm doing the best I can. You can't *tell* someone they have ten days to pull it together. He's a *man*, Elliott! What were you thinking when you called him? And what happens if I choose not to do this? Huh?" With each sentence, her hands flailed wildly through the air.

Elliott made no reply as he left the office. Jessie turned around and glared out the window, anger and frustration set firmly upon her face.

After several moments, she turned and found Ryan in her office, gazing at her. The look on her face could peel wallpaper. "This is still *my* office, *Mr.* Blake. It's obvious you're without manners or you would have knocked."

"It's Ryan. I did knock—three times. I figured you were a little preoccupied and didn't hear me," he replied casually.

Jessie regained her composure. After all, this man wasn't at fault, she told herself; it was Elliott. "I'm sorry, Mr. Blake. I'm a little on edge. Look, there's been a misunderstanding. Elliott hadn't cleared this with me before he sent for you. And, well, your services aren't needed. If you stop by Elliott's office on your way out, I'm sure you'll be well compensated for your trouble." Jessie motioned toward the door.

Responding to her dismissive gesture, Ryan threw the smile he was famous for. "Elliott said you usually leave around five-thirty on Fridays. I'll be back then to pick you up."

His grin gave Jessie the leverage she needed to be rude again. "I'm surprised you find this so amusing, Mr. Blake. Personally, I find this whole ordeal quite ludicrous. We shouldn't even be having this conversation. I won't be going anywhere with you at five-thirty."

Ryan's countenance withered as the door slammed in front of his 250-pound frame—again.

CHAPTER 2

Jessie paced rapidly. Her palms were sweating while thoughts sped through her mind. *Elliott's absurd. Why is he doing this? Not even the best therapist in the universe can get a client to open up and heal all wounds in ten days. Is he punishing me because I refused his help months ago? Is he trying to scare me into going back to him? Is he firing me?*

What if Mr. Blake does show up? Surely he's not that stupid. I need a plan of action. Okay, fine, Elliott wants me to get help. I'll get it. I'll convince him I'm ready. But it has to be with someone neither one of us knows. I'll just take the ten days as a personal vacation. Paris is beautiful this time of year. I can pull myself together there. Jessie slid into her chair, a feeling of nausea washing over her. *I should have taken care of myself months ago when my father died and the nightmares returned.*

* * *

The next few hours seemed an eternity as Jessie packed and tied up loose ends. She called as many clients as possible, fearing Tendra would say something to embarrass her. She was the sort to relish such an opportunity.

Everything would be in perfect order before Jessie left. If she *were* going to have a breakdown, it would at least be executed in an organized fashion. She explained to her clients that she was leaving due to a family emergency, and that Elliott Stone or Martha Welch would be taking over until further notice. Most were annoyed, but she could tell some savored the opportunity to pursue new insights into their old troubles. When would she be back? they asked. She didn't tell them that she may not return at all. Jessie wished she had someone intimate to contact, someone to offer *her* advice or encouragement. There was no one.

"Jessie! Dr. Blake is here," Tendra's voice shrilled over the intercom.

"What? It's only four-thirty. The moron wasn't even supposed to show up at all. Besides, it's *Mr.* Blake now!" she blurted to herself, hoping Tendra hadn't heard.

"Jessie, did you hear me? DR. BLAKE IS HERE."

"Thank you, Tendra. Could you say it a bit louder, perhaps? I don't believe the *entire* population of Denver heard you. And I realize it's a lot for you to remember, but could you work on the Dr. Winston thing we discussed?" It felt good to let off steam. "Mr. Blake will have to wait out there."

Now, Jessie thought, *I have to change course. Instead of leaving early, I'll just lose him on the road—even if it means breaking a few speed limits.*

She stood, breathed deeply, and tried to remain calm. As she looked around, she felt the same emptiness one feels after they've packed up their home to move on. The stabbing pain in her chest returned. *Who'll get my office? Where's Elliott? I've been paging him for over two hours! Tendra should've been able to locate him by now.* Jessie was too far buried in her thoughts to hear the knock or see the door open.

"Hello," was all Ryan said. It was enough. The nausea returned. *He is stupid.*

"Mr. Blake, you showed up after all. Not very good at telling time, though. I do believe you said five-thirty, not four-thirty."

"It's Ryan. Your receptionist announced me prematurely. I intended to wait outside until our arranged time," he replied in a perfectly controlled voice. "Technically, since you told me not to worry about returning at all—I'm not early, I'm just here."

"It wasn't *our* arranged time, it was yours. And, as I stated before, I have absolutely no intention of going with you. You're wasting your time and Elliott's money. So if you'll excuse me." Jessie's eyebrows crinkled so intensely it was difficult to tell she had two.

Once again, Ryan found himself being ushered out the door. Refusing to have this happen a third time, he stepped in quickly, catching Jessie off guard. Her pulse quickened, and her cheeks flushed.

Ryan had control of the door now. He flipped it shut with his foot and stood immovable. He stared into Jessie's large, watering green eyes. "Why don't we stay here for a few minutes and talk? I'm in no hurry, and we have no deadlines to meet."

"I have ten days, from what I was told. I'd consider that a deadline." Jessie spoke sharply while taking a few steps back in retreat. She returned to the window, no longer focusing her thoughts on what Ryan was saying. *Maybe Elliott hasn't given him the same time constraint. Where is Elliott!*

Ryan noticed Jessie's office had been packed neatly into ten boxes. Elliott hadn't mentioned she was leaving the firm. "Dr. Winston—I assume that's what you prefer I call you?" The question went unanswered, so Ryan continued. "Look, I know this isn't your choice. Obviously you can't be forced to do this. Why don't we just sit for a while and talk? If we don't accomplish anything by midnight, I'll accept defeat."

Jessie stared out the window, tears descending uncontrollably. She didn't dare move a hand to wipe them for fear he would notice. She silently vowed he would never see her cry. She cleared her throat. "I'd like a minute to myself, please."

"I'll go grab something to drink. Would you care for anything?" His voice took on a softer tone.

"No."

Ryan quietly shut the door behind him. Jessie wiped her face without delay. She reached for an old copy of *Huckleberry Finn* in one of the boxes, and pulled out an envelope tucked inside. She slipped the envelope into her briefcase, and, fumbling for her purse and the box with her personal items, headed toward the door.

A soft knock sounded before she could get away. At least Tendra wasn't crowing over the intercom. He couldn't have gotten a drink already!

Ryan entered holding a bottle of fruit juice. Jessie moved from the door and placed the box and purse back on her desk. Ryan sensed she was not in the mood for small talk and reached for the chair Elliott had used. Pulling it farther away from her desk, he sat, loosened his coat, and slowly crossed his legs. He opened the bottle and sipped as he looked through the office. Of the ten packed boxes, nine were filled with books and papers. Only one contained personal items. *Not typical for a woman,* he thought.

Jessie pretended to be on a quest, her nose buried inside a box. She was stalling. It was fast approaching five o'clock, and the office was shutting down. *What am I supposed to do now? I can't believe he was early. Why didn't I see that coming? I'll tell him I've changed my mind and want something to drink. I'll leave the second after he does. I can still get out of this.*

A knock at the door made them both jump. "Yes?" Jessie said. The door opened slowly. Elliott peeked around, then stepped in slowly.

"Jess, I wanted to make sure you were all right before I left."

"Uh-huh. That's why you considerately returned all my pages. And what, you're actually leaving the office before nine? Wow! What's the occasion? Do you have an important date? Or has the fact that you're screwing up my life been too much for you to handle today?" She was finally able to confront the person she was really furious with.

"I see things are going well," Elliott said coyly, winking at Ryan.

Ryan didn't dare respond. Jessie was his task at hand. He didn't want to alienate her further.

"Things are *not* going well. Why didn't you return my calls?"

"Well, I . . ." Elliott's eyes fell to the boxes on the floor. He turned toward Ryan and silently dismissed him. Jessie sat in the chair behind her desk. After shutting the door, Elliott leaned down onto her desk and began to explain how he felt.

"Jess, you understand this needs to happen. You've been struggling lately. Your clients are complaining. You're not yourself. You say you're fine, but it's clear you're not. You won't let me help you, and you've not sought assistance elsewhere. I told you awhile ago that if you refused to get yourself taken care of, I'd be forced to do so. Maybe you don't care what happens to you, but I do. I know Ryan can help if you let him. Leave the boxes. I'm not firing you. Don't let your pride get in the way of getting well. We say this to our clients all the time. Please, Jess, stop running. Just do this. Talk to him."

Jessie sat and listened, nodding every now and then. She then stood and walked to the window. "I did ask for your help once, remember?" Her anger now gone, a sadness trailed her words.

Elliott closed his eyes and winced. "That was a long time ago, and I was a fool. Will you let me help you now?" Everything was going as Elliott had planned. Surely she would drop Ryan and allow him to nurse her back to health.

"It *can't* be you. You know that," she retorted coldly. "Elliott, I promise, I *will* get help. But not from him, not Ryan Blake, or from you. I'll take the ten days and find *someone*. I'll keep you completely informed the whole time."

"If you won't let me work you through this, Jess, then I'm going to insist on Ryan. That way I can be sure you're on the up-and-up."

"Excuse me?" she fired back. "On the 'up-and-up?' Oh, that's completely ridiculous coming from you!"

Elliott had to remain calm. He just needed to be patient. She would seek his help in the end. "It's him or me, Jess."

Jessie picked up the box with her personal items, then grabbed her attaché and her coat. It was the middle of June, and her winter attire was still hanging on the rack, along with a backpack full of emergency items. She'd slept at the office on many stormy winter nights. The backpack held a couple of T-shirts, a pair of sweatpants and a shirt, a sweater, jeans, and a dress. She'd also thrown in a small hair dryer, some simple makeup, a curling iron, a couple old, well-read novels, and some granola mix. She opened her briefcase and shuffled its contents into the already overstuffed backpack. "I believe this belongs to you," she said, carelessly handing Elliott the briefcase.

"It was a gift."

"I don't want it anymore. I'll send someone for the rest of the boxes."

Elliott didn't reply. He stared long and hard into her eyes, yearning to say so much more than he had. He wanted to hold her . . . like before.

* * *

Ryan stared at the various pictures hanging on the hallway walls. All was quiet now. A few people were coming and going, but the twelve offices were mostly empty. He turned as he heard Jessie's door open. He headed toward her, but she pretended not to notice as she calmly walked through the building. Ryan buttoned his suit coat and followed.

Jessie quickened her step, hoping Ryan would fall farther behind. Once outside, she headed straight for her white Mercury sedan. Putting the box on the hood, she searched for her keys. *This is not aiding my quick getaway!*

Ryan stood back for a moment, then reached under the rear bumper and picked up the bright yellow, smiley-faced key chain.

Jessie hadn't even noticed them fall. *I'm an idiot.* She snatched the keys from his hand, opened the trunk, threw in her things, and slammed it shut. She slipped past Ryan, then slid into the driver's seat. Jessie started the engine and threw the transmission into reverse. Spotting Ryan in her rearview mirror, she toyed briefly with the idea of running him over. "Probably not a good strategy," she muttered irritably. Jessie took her foot off the brake, easing the car into motion, but he didn't budge. She stared into her rearview mirror.

A moment later, she opened the door, put one foot out, and placed her arm on the rim of the window. "I may be going out on a limb here, but would it be asking too much for you to move? I'm quite sure my insurance company won't cover me if I intentionally run you down. They frown on that sort of thing."

Ryan smiled slyly. "Elliott said you could leave your car here for as long as you needed. We can use mine."

She waved her hand in the air. "Hello? Which part of this is confusing to you? I'm getting into my car to go home. Alone! What I choose to do after that is none of your business."

"Well then, at least we're even."

"Even?" she questioned, confused.

"I lied about the time I'd arrive at your office. Well, actually, I didn't lie, but you're under the impression I did. And now you've lied about giving me until midnight."

"I never gave you till midnight."

"Yes, you did."

"Look, I don't know what you're on, but I never said YES. Now, you can move out of my way with or without my assistance. It's your choice."

Ryan remained quiet as she retreated back inside. Seconds later, she emerged slowly from the car and leaned against the open door. "Just out of curiosity, though, how could you have possibly assumed a yes?"

"I didn't hear a *no.*"

Jessie's thoughts shouted in her mind. *Ballots are in. I hate him. Not only is he arrogant, he's manipulative. I've had enough manipulative men in my life.* She set her hands firmly on her hips, curled her lips, and began tapping one high heel against the pavement. "You do this a lot? Follow clients out to parking lots and make them feel inferior?"

"It's not my intention to give you an inferiority complex. And you're not a client. I'm only hoping you'll give me till midnight to offer you some assistance on your road to mending."

Staring blankly, Jessie couldn't help but wonder if *she* sounded that nauseating when speaking to clients. She looked at her watch, then toward the window Elliott was watching from. *Elliott doesn't believe I'll actually leave with Blake. He thinks I'll crumble and go back to him. I'm sure I'm going to regret this, but if that's the way he wants to play it . . .* "Fine. I can do anything for six and a half hours. But I'm not staying here. Follow me to my apartment. You can stay there till midnight and have a nice, one-sided conversation. That is, if you can keep up. Sure would hate to lose you along the way," she said with biting contempt.

"I'll be around in a second, I'm on the other side."

Jessie ignored him as she slammed her door and turned on the radio. She leaned her head back so that she could watch him in the mirror again. *He probably drives a Jaguar or Porsche,* she thought critically.

To Jessie's surprise, a cherry-red truck pulled up. She almost smiled, but it faded when she spotted his grin. She backed out of the parking stall, accelerating quickly. Tires squealed as Helen Reddy began, *"I am woman, hear me roar . . ."*

CHAPTER 3

Elliott turned away from the window, baffled that Jessie had actually decided to meet with him. He wondered where Ryan would take her. Wherever it was, he knew that it wouldn't be more than an hour before his phone rang with Jessie begging him to give her another chance. He would then tell his wife he was working late and cancel their dinner reservations.

Three years earlier, Elliott and Jessie had attempted a romantic interlude. He had told her that Lydia and he had divorced and that she had moved out. It was a lie, though their marriage *was* struggling. When boredom set in, Lydia suggested counseling—a comment that evoked their first genuine laughter in years. It was out of the question, of course. Elliott couldn't admit failure in his twenty-year marriage, so he assured Lydia they would work through their problems without the aid of a mediator. When Lydia went home for a few months to take care of her dying mother, Elliott began seeing Jessie.

Once Jessie learned the truth, the relationship abruptly ended. His dishonesty had hurt her deeply. After that, she never returned his personal calls, repeatedly returned his gifts unopened, and all their conversation centered solely around work.

* * *

Jessie refused to look at the speedometer, but she figured she was driving at least twenty miles over the posted limit. This uncharacteristic rebellion was definitely having its effect on her heart rate. Ryan was glued to her bumper, apparently determined not to lose her. She laughed as she watched his expression through her rearview mirror. *He'll probably say that light was still yellow when he sailed through.* She smiled tightly.

Seventeen minutes later, both vehicles arrived at Jessie's apartment complex. Excellent. It usually took thirty minutes this time of night.

Ryan opened her car door, offering his hand. His demeanor was calm although he could feel small beads of sweat at the nape of his neck. He silently cursed himself for not researching Jessie's home address. If pressed, he would swear he never saw anything but green lights.

Jessie ignored him, instead reaching for her purse and stepping out of the car. She headed straight for the stairs of the building. Newly built and plain in its construction, the complex was separated from its closest edifice by a small, wooded area. All in all, it was quiet and peaceful.

Jessie had neglected to collect the rest of her belongings in the car, but Ryan decided it wasn't his place to remind her. He followed her up two sets of stairs and through two sets of locked doors. Jessie stalled momentarily at her door, fumbling with her keys. She was annoyed that she'd left dishes in the sink and clutter in the bathroom.

She sighed, pushed open the door, then headed down the hall to her bedroom. "Might as well make yourself comfortable since you're going to be here awhile," she said resignedly. After shutting the door, she collapsed onto her bed.

Ryan filled a glass with water and began his survey of the apartment. He could see only the living, dining, and kitchen areas, but quickly surmised that Jessie was extremely neat and organized. She had the latest in kitchen gadgetry, and everything was spotless.

The decor was modern and simple. Walls and tables were free of knickknacks, clutter, and even dust. Sipping his water, Ryan walked over to a painting of Christ, which hung above her blue leather couch. It was not the typical, somber-faced Jesus he remembered from all his Sunday School classes, but one rather spirited and smiling. It was quite unique. The portrait was centered between two mountain scenes with colors a bit brighter and more vivid than was common. He felt momentarily entranced, as if he were actually sitting at the base of the mountain, in the presence of the Master. He couldn't find an artist signature on any of the pieces. He made a mental note of her Christianity.

Pulling himself away, Ryan continued perusing the apartment. Bookshelves lined every wall of the living room, and each shelf was completely filled with literature ranging from psychology textbooks to espionage novels. John Grisham and Clive Cussler were in complete sets. Across from the couch, an entertainment center and an enormous collection of CDs and DVDs covered the wall. He wouldn't be surprised if her entire collection was alphabetized. He leaned forward to get a closer look. He was right. The collection was categorized into the appropriate genre and then alphabetized.

* * *

Jessie couldn't resist the urge to make her bed. She was in no hurry to get back to Dr. Doolittle. She put her bathroom in order from her morning's splash and dash. Opening a closet, she pulled out a pair of leggings and a long-sleeved knit top that fell to her knees. She wanted to be comfortable and unappealing.

Ryan didn't hear Jessie coming. She watched him while he stared out the kitchen window. *Most likely enjoying the view of the nearby pond,* she thought. *A possibility for me to open up* might *have existed if he were ugly.* "I see you found something to drink," she said, her tone flat.

"I did, thanks. Those paintings are interesting. Who's the artist?"

She stared at him for a few seconds, then slumped on the couch, picked up a pillow, and clutched it in her lap. She would remain silent. He was wise enough to know she wasn't going to discuss her life's trauma in six hours.

"Since I have you till midnight, I was hoping we could go to my cabin in the mountains."

"Excuse me?" She wanted to make sure she heard him correctly.

"I have a cabin in the mountains. It's about two hours north of here."

"You followed me all the way here—at top speed—just to turn around and head the other direction?"

"The cabin is a great place to relax and talk."

"I'm *not* talking. Besides, by the time we got there, we'd just have to turn around and head back."

"Not necessarily. It has five bedrooms, four bathrooms, a large kitchen, an office, a lounge, a library, and a solarium."

"A cabin with only five bedrooms? Gee, you got gypped. And when could you have possibly formed the opinion that I would stay with you in a cabin?" She was trying not to take her restlessness out on him, but he was the only one around.

"I have no intention of creating an inappropriate situation. As I said, I have an office there, and you would certainly have your privacy. Elliott left specific orders that you were not to be alone. Also, my grandfather—"

"I'm not to be alone?" she interrupted, condescendingly.

"Yes."

"Oh, you've got to be kidding! Look, if you want to use our time driving all the way up a mountain, then driving back down, that's fine with me, but I'm not staying."

"Great, let's go," he said.

Her sarcastic laughter stopped abruptly, and she felt her mouth drop open. She excused herself and returned to her room. She slammed the door and threw herself on the bed again. He was winning, and she was playing right into his hand. The backs of her eyes began to twitch. She needed to think this through. She was, after all, an adult. She didn't have to answer to anyone.

She lay there for what seemed an eternity, thoughts detached. *This is not happening to me. I should have just stayed at the office till midnight. Actually, if we drive to the cabin and back, there goes the time . . . separate cars, no talking . . . . What I really need is a good cry, an old black-and-white movie, and a half-gallon of something caramel and chocolate.*

Jessie emerged slowly from the safety of her room and silently headed toward the door.

Ryan extracted himself from the leather recliner, trying to conceal his shock. He hadn't figured on her actually going with him. He assumed she'd have a dozen reasons that going to a cabin with a stranger would be wrong. He'd been working on his next move— getting her to converse in a nondefensive tone.

They walked to the parking lot in complete silence. Ryan opened the door to his truck and again offered his hand. She chuckled as she climbed into her car. A second later, her passenger door was opened, and Ryan settled into the seat.

"Excuse me—what are you doing?" Jessie snapped.

"If you'd feel more comfortable driving, I understand," he said casually.

"I'd feel more comfortable if you just got out of my car."

"Then you'd rather I drive?"

"No. I wouldn't rather you drive." Jessie inhaled deeply. She was on the verge of exploding again. "Look, Mr. Blake, I realize you may find this hard to believe considering everything that's come out of my mouth so far, but I really am doing the best I can at maintaining my professionalism. I want to drive my car while you drive yours. Seems simple enough to me."

"Can't do that."

"Why?"

"Then you'd be alone."

"What do you think I'm going to do, drive frantically and try to lose you?"

"You did try that before. Our being together until midnight was in an effort to talk, not drive in separate cars."

Jessie stared out her window, took a deep breath, and turned the key. At least if she took her car she'd have some control. Instead of the gentle purr, the engine sputtered, then shut off. *This is not happening. I know I needed gas, but I've always managed at least twenty miles on empty. I don't need this.* She tried again. This time it started. *Yes!*

After she put the car in reverse, the engine sputtered again, then died. Ryan remained silent. Jessie took another deep breath. She threw the car into neutral, then climbed out to push it back into its parking spot. Ryan jumped out to help. Once it was parked, Jessie leaned against the trunk and folded her arms across her chest.

Ryan leaned in beside her. "Would—"

"Don't. Just don't say anything." She fought back the tears that were forming and closed her eyes. "This whole situation is taxing, Mr. Blake. You have no idea *how* taxing. I'm not sure I'm able to make reasonable decisions right now . . . Elliott could make things difficult for me—professionally—yet I don't think he really would . . . I could sue him . . . but, no, you're retired. Apparently if I want to keep my license to practice and Elliott off my back, I'm going to have to put up with this till midnight . . . as you proposed."

Jessie opened her trunk and grabbed the backpack before she slammed the door shut. She walked briskly toward his truck, taking in and letting out slow deep breaths. *Calm down. Don't hyperventilate. It'll be midnight soon enough. This will all be over in just a little while. Calm down, calm down . . . Go with him. Prove to Elliott that you can do this.*

Ryan stepped in front of her as they reached his truck and opened the front passenger door. Jessie ignored the gesture and opened the back door. She shuffled a few papers around and climbed in, keeping her eyes glued on the world outside the window as he started the engine.

"It's Ryan," he said gently as he eased out of the parking lot.

CHAPTER 4

Minutes of blissful silence passed before Jessie spoke. "So, where exactly is this place I'm being kidnapped to?"

Ryan stilled a smile that was playing on his lips. "You're not being kidnapped."

"Oh, right. I must be experiencing a momentary lapse of conscious memory. Do you plan on gagging or drugging me? Perhaps locking me in your torture chamber?"

Ryan knew the venting was healthy. "I'm not planning to keep you from leaving. Besides, the torture chamber wouldn't fit—too many bedrooms." Now the smile came.

"How professional, *Dr.* Blake. I feel like warming up to you already." She, too, often used humor to soften a client's mood. Another technique in the future may be more useful, she decided.

Ryan mentally committed to choose his words more carefully. "It's Ryan. Look, I'm—"

"No, don't," Jessie interrupted softly. "You're doing what Elliott's asked. I understand that. But let's set one thing straight. This whole thing is merely a ploy to get me to go back to him. He thinks I'm too afraid to talk to anyone else about my screwed-up life, and he's right about one thing—I have absolutely no intention of divulging my secrets to *you*. Ten days is a slap in the face. What a joke. But I'm here with you, so I've done what he's requested. During this time, I'll decide who I *can* talk to and where my life is headed. If I were you, I'd just think of this next week as a nice little vacation. Although you vacation all the time now, don't you? We'll get along just fine if you stay out of my way. The ball is in my court, Mr. Blake, and I intend to keep it there." She turned to look out the window. Sadness settled within her in place of the anger and frustration that had so completely dominated the last few hours.

Ryan didn't respond. She said she was going to stay longer than midnight, and she also mentioned something about there being more to her relationship with Elliott than a business partnership. He knew that pressing her in any direction would only alienate her further. The ball would eventually slip into his court.

He watched her through the rearview mirror. The mountain retreat offered an escape from the pressures of the city. Typically, within twenty-four hours, clients were relaxed enough to talk, and within a couple days, were ready to go back to work. A few regularly scheduled visits at his office in the city provided the necessary closure. All in all, it was a process that had helped save many careers. Would he add hers to the list?

He cringed at the thought of ten straight days with a messed-up female. At least his debt to Elliott would be paid. Jessie's perfume drifted his way on the breeze from the crack at the top of the slightly open window, and he cursed himself for the unwelcome thoughts and feelings invading his space.

* * *

Within an hour, Jessie awoke disoriented. It was unusual for her to have fallen asleep in a car. Dazed for a moment, she hoped her latest experience had been another nightmare. Spying Ryan yanked her back to reality. "Apparently the lull in conversation forced a long-needed rest. I hope I didn't say anything rude while I napped. How long was I out, anyway?" She began rubbing the kinks out of her neck.

Ryan smiled. Her voice had been gentle, and he found himself hoping the nap had softened her. "About an hour."

Jessie stared out the side window. Dusk was beginning to settle. The makings of a glorious sunset were visible.

Ryan finally broke the silence. "I use the cabin on weekends. It's quiet, serene, and comfortable. I think you'll like it."

"I'm more concerned with not getting lost. Who in their right mind would have four bathrooms in a cabin!" The nap had not softened her.

Thirty minutes later, they pulled into a rural grocery store and gas station. Ryan turned to her when they parked. "We're only a couple miles away. I need to fill up and grab a few groceries. Is there anything you want, or would you like to come in . . . ?" He felt somewhat awkward.

"I'm fine." Jessie had been devising a plan to steal his truck when he wasn't watching.

He met her gaze as he reached through the window and pulled out the keys. "Jerk," she muttered.

For an old, outdated station in the middle of nowhere, it was quite busy and very well kept. The pay phone, which read *ten cents,* was most likely of little use. "Surely this place has a movie theater or at least a K-Mart! What do people do here?" Jessie said out loud.

Inside the store, Ryan picked up his usual items: milk, bread, eggs, cereal, donuts, lettuce, fruit, vegetables, and toiletries. He also picked up yogurt, herbal tea, and ice cream, a few of the things he had snooped out at Jessie's apartment.

Jessie's thoughts of running away were interrupted as Ryan's voice approached the car. "Thanks, Gramps. See you later." She turned to see an older gentleman waving from inside the store.

"Great, there's more of them," she mumbled.

Ryan opened the back door and set down two bags of groceries and a gallon of milk on the seat. As he shut the door and started the engine, Jessie noticed a few cans of Alpo sticking out from the top of a sack. *Dogs. Where there's a dog, there's hair, and lots of it—everywhere. Wonderful, just wonderful.*

They drove about a mile before heading up a hill that seemed to go on for another mile. At the top they made a left turn at an enormous blue spruce, one that Jessie pictured at home on the lawn of the White House at Christmas. She held back a gasp as a view of the palatial cabin emerged before her. The front was lined with lilac trees, and although blooming season was well past, she could imagine how glorious spring would be. Lilacs evoked the few pleasant childhood memories she had. With the sun setting directly behind the cabin, the sky was an incredible sight. Streaks of red with bold swipes of maroon filtered through wisps of silver clouds. A cool breeze settled in from the mountains. Mesmerized by the awesome surroundings, she suddenly didn't mind being stuck here. It would be cheaper than Paris, she deduced. *With five bedrooms, a library and a solarium, he'd better have an HDTV and a wide selection of movies.*

Ryan pulled slowly into the driveway. He always enjoyed this time of night. "Well, this is it."

Jessie was silent. This was no ordinary cabin. It looked more like a miniature castle, albeit the modern version of one. The three-story edifice stood encompassed by the same bushes and trees that peppered the surrounding hills and valleys. A couple of dwarf trees and a soft-looking miniature hedge ran around most of the deck's perimeter. In the center of the porch sat an antique porch swing and matching chair.

Large, sweeping arcs graced the corners of the structure, and oval-shaped windows tastefully adorned the architecture. The third level had a sunburst pattern inlaid in the log structure that intensified at the roof's gables. All was capped off by a vaulted roof dotted with skylights.

"Jessie, I'll be inside if you need anything," Ryan tried again.

Suddenly regaining her focus, Jessie realized Ryan had completely unloaded the truck. Feeling trapped, she began twisting the gold band on her finger. "I'd like to walk for a while before we head back."

"Sure," Ryan answered gently, sensing her anxiety. "It'll be dark within the hour and it gets pitch-black out here, so I'll grab a flashlight."

"No, I'm fine. I won't be that long." Jessie stepped out of the truck and headed down the road quickly, not wanting to hear Ryan's opinion about her being alone. She looked around and picked a few points of reference, since getting lost wasn't part of her strategy. She glanced at the sky, searching for some recognizable beacon, but a fast-approaching cauldron of building clouds blocked any view of the stars.

Ryan watched until Jessie vanished from sight, hidden by the crest of the nearest hill. He returned inside, emptied the grocery sacks, and slid a pizza in the oven. He knew she wouldn't eat, but he had to offer. He then adjusted the jacuzzi from its vacation setting. It would take only thirty to forty minutes to heat fully, and he was really going to need it tonight.

A half hour later, the pizza was getting cold and the sky was getting darker. Ryan walked through the kitchen and across the three-story, vaulted family room to the wall of glass leading to the rear deck and checked for Jessie. A soft whispering voice could be heard outside.

"Easy boy, I'm nice . . . really I am! No threat to those hundred or so assorted teeth. Blake!"

Ryan knew immediately what was going on. Jessie had met Nelly. Nelly was a full-blooded eight-year-old Rottweiler who enjoyed scaring newcomers.

"Nelly! Here, girl. Jessie's our friend!" Running with all-out force, Nelly clambered up the deck's ramp and pounded into her master. Ryan stood grounded, welcoming her greeting. "I wondered where you were, girl," he said, scratching her behind the ears. "I should have warned you about her. Sorry." He was grinning in Jessie's direction.

Jessie's eyes were still fixed on Nelly's enormous mouth. "She kept staring at me as if I were a T-bone. At least I know who gets the Alpo."

"She'd most likely prefer the cold pizza." Hearing a noise in the distance, Nelly took off to find her next victim.

"Could I see the inside?" Jessie asked, relieved that all her body parts were still attached.

They entered the cabin through the sliding glass doors and crossed a large room on their way to the kitchen. "This is the family room," Ryan said. "Make yourself at home."

She slowed her pace to look around, taken aback by the immensity of the room. The entire back wall, nearly fifty feet across, was made of glass, as were portions of each wall on the sides. In the left corner of the room was a beautiful spiral staircase that lead presumably to the two floors above. To her right, a stone hearth anchored the room for which it had been designed. The floors were maple, polished to a high sheen and covered here and there by thick, beige pile rugs. Two couches matched two reclining chairs. The decor was simple—off-white leather with glass and chrome accents. The only real color came from a few items on the mantle and assorted throw pillows. Jessie estimated she could fit most of her apartment in this room.

When they arrived in the kitchen, the pizza was indeed cold and looked less appetizing than its box. Jessie declined the slice he offered her. "So, where's my cell?"

Ryan smiled. "Does this mean you're planning to stay longer than midnight?"

"Don't play ignorant, Mr. Blake. I'm tired. I'd like to sleep." She winced.

He gestured down a hall, concealing a sign of triumph in his smile. "It's Ryan. Your room is this way. Let me show you around."

"Tomorrow I'll find my way around. Right now just a shower and bed will be fine."

After a few steps, Ryan turned to face her. "I started to tell you earlier that my grandfather lives here too. He takes care of things for me when I'm in the city and works a few hours here and there down at the Gas 'N' Go when he's bored. When I'm here, he usually takes off and stays with my great-aunt. She's getting on in years, and he likes to spend as much time as he can with her." He continued his stride through the hallway. Jessie was quiet, not particularly interested in his family tree.

At the last door on the right, Ryan continued. "He'll be around while you're here, though. Thought you should know in case you bumped into a strange man in the middle of the night."

"I already bumped into a strange man. What's one more?"

"Yes, well, just thought it would be more comfortable having him around. Most clients stay at the local motel, but as I said before, Elliott's request was for me to be around at all times."

Jessie said nothing.

Ryan opened the door and stepped aside to let her through. As she walked in, a light breeze tickled her cheek. The room was large and spacious. A daybed, a nightstand, a dresser, and a small desk and chair were arranged neatly. Pictures of scenery adorned the walls, and miniblinds with white valances flapped over the open window. The bedspread was a white cotton with red highlights and matching pillow coverings. The decor was bright and cheerful, not one conducive to a pity party. Jessie laid her backpack on the bed.

"There's a jacuzzi in the solarium past the staircase. It's up to temperature now. You're more than welcome to get in. Suits and towels are in a closet next to the tub."

Jessie gave no reply. She moved toward the door, put her hand on the knob, and stood, waiting.

"Good night," Ryan said, staring into the depths of her bloodshot eyes. She blinked and took in a breath slowly. When he stepped out of the room, the door quickly closed behind him, and he was grateful that at least this time, he wasn't shoved out of the way.

CHAPTER 5

Jessie was glad her room had an attached bathroom. While the jacuzzi sounded inviting, she knew Ryan would try to strike up a conversation—something she had to avoid. Her plan was to get a hot shower, a good night's sleep, and then head back to her place in the morning. She felt little remorse knowing Ryan would be thoroughly frustrated. While she showered, she waited for the water to grow cool, but the warmth continued through the entire leg-shaving process. After she dressed for bed, temptation drew her toward the door. For a brief moment, she wondered what the good doctor was up to.

The guest room was about fifty feet off the kitchen. The large radial curve in the nook of her room seemed to match the ones she had noticed as they arrived, and she concluded she was in the corner of the house. She walked to the windows that started on the left and continued around the arched radial wall to the right. Leaning on the sill, she took in the beauty of the sky. The smothering clouds that covered the heavens earlier had dissipated. Mere wisps of white hung near the almost quartered moon. Countless glittering specks of bright light hovered, suspended in space by some unknown force. It was an awesome sight. Content with this glorious distraction, she lingered for a time before retreating to bed.

* * *

The moonlight streaking through the glass negated the desire for artificial light. The mixture of air and water being forced through the tub's jets bubbled like a subdued Niagara Falls, and the hot, soothing water lapped at Ryan's skin while the steam drifted to the surrounding spaces. On occasions such as this, time seemed to both stand still *and* flow forward. The blend of hot water, fresh air, and previous stresses and fatigues pulled him into a paralyzing vortex of thought that shifted in and out of reality's grip.

Slowly, Ryan's mind turned to Jessie. Jessica Nicole Winston was a strong name. His research indicated she was an accomplished therapist for thirty-two. Ryan's thoughts turned to Jessie's teal suit and long, flowing hair that occasionally graced her high cheekbones. Her perfume . . . He shook his head, chastising himself again for letting his thoughts wander.

Ryan spent over an hour in the tub before throwing on a bathrobe. He stopped and listened quietly at Jessie's door. Her breathing was barely audible. She had fallen asleep.

He threw on a T-shirt and shorts, then headed for the circular staircase that led to his favorite beanbag chair. The third floor loft overlooked the family room, and from there he could spot Jessie if she decided to roam the cabin. He picked up a novel and settled in to enjoy his preferred pastime.

A chapter or so later, the faint sound of whimpering raised his eyes from the page. He figured that Nelly was most likely dreaming of snacking on Aunt Ruth's cat. Stretching, he set out to find her and discovered her lying in front of Jessie's room. Leaning over, he patted her tenderly, "Hey, girl, catch that old pathetic kitty, huh?" Nelly's ears perked up, and it was then that Ryan heard the moaning. He tried Jessie's door. To his surprise it was unlocked. Moving gently, he eased it open about a foot and peered in. An intruder would have brought a different response from Nelly.

"No . . . please . . . The light, Daddy, don't forget the light . . . "

Jessie was tossing and turning. Then came the scream—it wasn't loud as much as it was horrifying. The hair on Ryan's arms stood straight and stiff as a tingle ran the length of his spine. He restrained himself from bursting in and shaking her. He quietly pulled the door closed and knocked softly. "Jessie, it's Ryan. Are you okay in there? Jessie, are you awake?" When no response came, he called her name with more intensity. "Jessie, it's Ryan. Are you all right?" Gramps rounded the corner and stopped.

"Yeah, I'm fine," Jessie responded hoarsely, sweat dripping from her nose.

"Can I get you anything?" Ryan asked calmly through the closed door.

"No, thank you."

"Are you sure you're all right?"

"I'm all right already!"

"Well, good night then." Ryan caught a glimpse of Gramps heading back to his room. He remained at Jessie's door for a few minutes, stroking Nelly and hoping Jessie would come out to talk. When she didn't, he returned upstairs to extinguish his reading light, then headed to his room. He flopped onto the bed and folded his arms behind his head, deep in thought. Her frightening words raced through his mind. Where was she when her dad forgot to turn the light on? How long was she in darkness? How old had she been? If darkness was still a fear of hers, the pain would resurface each time she tried to sleep. He decided she'd likely leave, too embarrassed to stay. He forced his eyes closed, determined to sleep.

* * *

Jessie turned on the lamp next to her bed, then wrestled back under her blanket. She wished she had her tea and files. There was nothing to keep her company except the sounds of the night. She began replaying the ghastly day. *Elliott's lost his mind. Bringing in a specialist to play with my head—what an idiot. Ten days won't even scratch the surface. Does he really believe I'll run back to him with open arms?*

What am I doing here? I've been uprooted from my home to a rural nightmare. I'm stuck in a cabin in the mountains with a Freudian wannabe, a dog the size of a pony, and an old man. I can't believe this is happening to me.

I should've resolved things with my father before he died. Is that why the nightmares are back?

Avoiding any further analysis of her situation, Jessie reached inside her backpack, retrieved the novel she'd thrown in earlier, and began to read.

* * *

The light of dawn began its assault a little earlier than Ryan had hoped. The thought of a morning run in the mountains, however, caused his feet to slide to the floor. It would prolong the inevitable. Jessie couldn't leave without him.

Ryan was an avid runner. Five miles a day kept him looking healthy and feeling good. He was consistent, rain or shine. Running in the city was hectic, but a run in the mountains was exhilarating. Today he would focus on Jessie—deciding how to keep her at the cabin, how to approach her, and how to keep the line drawn in his mind.

Nelly was at his side as he headed out the back door. He was surprised Gramps wasn't at the table reading. As a child, Ryan believed the roosters took their cue to rise from Gramps rather than the dawn.

He jogged down the path at a steady, even pace, warming up slowly, enjoying nature's splendor. The sky was a vibrant blue, the air fresh and crisp. The summer wildflowers were exploding into view, and shades of color carpeted the meadow before him. He was energized by the magnificence of it all.

Working out of the cabin full-time had once been his dream, but Ryan determined to leave the past behind for the time being. Focusing on matters at hand, he surmised that Jessie would do one of two things: be dressed and demand to leave as soon as he returned or stay in her room, refusing to come out even for food. He checked his watch. Gramps would surely complain about a cold breakfast.

* * *

The aroma of fresh coffee, toast, and bacon filtered into Jessie's room. She had planned on staying in her room, at least for the morning, but as she munched on the stale granola she'd stashed in her bag, the sensational odor was too much for her stomach to ignore. She slipped into a pair of jeans and another oversized shirt.

Mentally prepared to continue with her silent regime, Jessie entered the kitchen. She would quickly accept an offer of breakfast, grab it, and return to her room.

The kitchen seemed bigger than the night before. It was configured in a large U shape, with the bottom longer than the sides. Windows ran from the solid granite countertop almost to the ceiling, and off-white maple cabinetry lined the entire perimeter. A stainless steel fridge and freezer ran floor to ceiling on the right side while a freestanding range and cooktop were built into the island in the center.

"The smell got to ya, eh?" said Gramps happily as he flipped a pancake on the griddle.

Jessie glanced across the family room looking for Ryan. He was nowhere. "Got to my stomach, anyway." She smiled slightly. So much for remaining silent.

"Well, there's plenty, or there will be until my grandson and Nelly get back. So eat up."

"I wouldn't want to impose. If I'm eating someone else's portions, I'll just have some juice or something."

"Made enough for an army. The two of them eat like hogs, that's all. I appreciate you're bein' polite, but I'm not used to it, so just make yourself at home."

"Thank you. You must be Gramps."

"Yep. What would you prefer I called ya? Doc? Miss?"

"Jessie would be fine, thanks."

Gramps was a large man of rugged stature. His oversized hands were worn and toughened from years of doing literally everything himself, and most of it outdoors. Unlike most men at seventy-six, Gramps's limbs were caches of solid muscle. With his six-foot height and 205 pounds of total mass, Gramps cut an imposing figure of health.

"All right then, Jessie, this is ready. Sit on down over there." He gestured toward an informal dining area attached to the kitchen. "You sleep okay? City folk often have a difficult time with the quiet around here."

"I've had better nights, but it wasn't the lack of noise." *Did my screaming wake him too?* "This is a great cabin. It *is* awfully quiet, though. Do you ever get lonely?"

"Nope, not really. My sister doesn't live too far from here, and Nelly's great company."

"And of course you have that marvelous grandson of yours," she said smugly.

"Don't like him much, eh?"

"Actually, I've been unfair to him. It's not really him that I don't like. It's more the position he's in and how it affects me." She was curious as to how many others had met this doom. "How often does he get out here with clients, anyway?" She reached for the eggs and bacon Gramps set on the table and poured a small glass of juice.

"Now? Never. Before he retired though, I'd say it was at least once or twice a month on the weekends. Occasionally, it would be longer." Gramps sat across from her. Her probing would have to wait. She could hear Nelly romping up the path toward the cabin.

Jessie began to fidget, and she could feel her pulse quicken. She wanted to leap from the table and hide in the safety of her room.

"Smells great as usual Gramps," Ryan said, opening the screen door. Nelly galloped in after him. Upon seeing Jessie, Ryan instantly stopped. Although he mustered enough control to keep his jaw from dropping, the wide-eyed stare toward Jessie went unchecked. He took off his shoes, and casually said, "Hi."

"Hi? That's it?" Jessie challenged as she stroked Nelly.

"What would you prefer?" countered Ryan.

"How about, 'I didn't expect to see you so early, figured you'd stay in your room all day.'"

"Maybe I hadn't drawn that conclusion."

"Yeah, right," she said, chuckling.

"Boy, I'd really like to stick around and see how this turns out, but I've learned to know when three's a crowd." Gramps stood and placed his dishes in the sink. "I'll leave this mess for you two to clean up. But promise they'll get put away and not thrown 'round the cabin. Nice meetin' ya, Jessie. This kid's not half bad at what he does if ya give him a chance. Ryan, I'll just be outside tinkerin' around."

"Thanks for breakfast. It's delicious," Jessie said sweetly.

Gramps swiftly walked out the back door, and Jessie caught a wink meant for his grandson as he closed the door. Realizing Ryan was staring at her, she turned toward her food and sighed. She knew the time had come for him to share his wisdom, and while it couldn't possibly take too long, she just wasn't in the mood to listen.

"Look, Mr. Blake, I was hungry, and so I ate. There's no deeper meaning to analyze. Now I'll be returning to my room. No, I don't wish to leave today. In fact, I'll stay until a week from Sunday. That'll give me more than enough time to decide where I'm headed in life. I'll have an occasional meal now and then, but other than that, I'll be quiet as a mouse. So relax and enjoy your free time." She walked to the sink, her back toward him.

"It's Ryan. The jacuzzi and library are yours to use if you'd like. Also, under the TV you'll find a fair collection of DVDs. Help yourself."

Jessie stopped washing the dish she had in her hands. She lowered it gently in the warm rinse water as she gazed out the window over the sink. His reply had been simple, accepting, respectful, and nondefensive. *Not a bad card to play,* she thought. Moving slowly, she removed the grease-laden griddle from the stove. "I'll help clean this up, if you'd like."

"I'd be grateful. Gramps has a habit of creating a kitchen full of chaos when I'm here." He tried to sneak a look at her face, but she kept her back to him while she cleared the table.

Jessie found herself afraid to look at him, something she'd seldom felt. She had to figure out what to do next. *Finish the kitchen, head to my room, continue my book, take a nap, deal with reality . . .*

Ryan suddenly spoke, and since her response was not immediate, he could tell she had drifted somewhere. "Jessie?" he repeated.

"What?" Her back tensed.

"I was asking if you knew how to ride."

"Ride? Horses? Haven't been on one for a long time," she said, relaxing a bit as she finished wiping the table.

"Well, how 'bout it? It's a great day for riding. A storm may be headed in later, but not for quite a while. I could show you around the land."

"Sounds nice, but I don't think so."

"Have better plans?"

"Actually, John Grisham is waiting for me in my room."

"Lucky guy."

She smiled as she finished drying the griddle. Slowly laying the towel down on the counter, she turned to face him. "I was hoping I made myself clear last night and this morning, but obviously I didn't."

"On the contrary, you were quite clear. But I wouldn't be doing my duty if I didn't keep trying, now would I? We both know that a good therapist looks for any opportunity to get in, even when the client avoids a particular area of questioning. I'm trying to get in, Jessie, and I can't stop. As long as you're here, I'll try. But I can't force you to talk. Under the circumstances, I can understand why you wouldn't. This vacation was a command embarrassment. We usually deal with people who come to *us* seeking help. This is different . . . for both of us." He leaned back on the counter.

"I was under the impression that dealing with defiant behavior used to be your specialty."

"Well, in a manner of speaking." He chuckled as he laid down the dampened towel and jumped to sit on the counter. "The majority of my work dealt with therapists who'd reached their limits. As a professional, it's difficult to admit you've had enough or that you need an out. We're often under the misconception that because we help others work through their difficulties, we'll never have any—or that if we do, we always have to be in complete control. But hearing client after client talk about abuse, pain, or after repeated communication with a child who has been the victim of sexual assault, well, it can get to you. It doesn't mean you've failed and have to quit. It just means you need an out. Someone to unload on."

Jessie remained quiet as she leaned back on the opposite counter. A sense of peace was spreading within her, and she knew she needed to share her pent-up feelings. He was setting the bait, and she was nibbling at it. But today he wouldn't reel her in. She drew her eyes from the floor to meet his, staring for a moment before speaking. "Well, it must have been a sad day in the world of therapy when you left." She averted her eyes, knowing it was an unfair remark.

He wasn't at all sure he hadn't reached her. "Sarcasm . . ." he began in a textbook voice.

"—falls under repressed anger," Jessie interrupted. "Let's see, that would be Psychology 101. People paid you *how much* for your wisdom?"

"That's not all it means . . ." He slid off the counter and stood directly in front of her a moment before turning slowly and walking toward his room. Jessie stood quiet and still at the counter, until she was sure he was out of sight. Then she slumped to the floor in defeat. He was making headway, and she knew it. Even worse, *he* knew it.

CHAPTER 6

Jessie pulled herself off the floor and looked around. She would take the grand tour alone. Leaving the kitchen, she entered the family room where the spiral staircase led to the floors above. She climbed a few steps and stopped, her curiosity getting the better of her. She had an overwhelming desire to take a peek at Ryan's room. The trickling water and relentless humming told her he was in the shower. Snooping, of course, would be in an effort to gain any useful insights to his psyche that might give her the upper hand—or so she rationalized.

What exactly has Elliott told him? Has he mentioned our past?

Entering quietly, she surveyed the surroundings. The room invited comfortable relaxation. It was expansive, separated by areas of use and not by walls. His personal study, where she had entered, housed a contemporary oak desk and a massive, light-brown leather couch and matching chair clustered near one wall. French-style doors led toward the balcony.

The bathroom was off to her right and opened to the bedroom, which was kitty-corner from the room where she stood. As she started toward the bedroom, she noticed Ryan's attaché open on the desk. She controlled the urge to search through it, but a yellow, lined legal pad lying next to it offered too much temptation. Hastily she skimmed the first page. It was the beginning of a client profile, and at the bottom were scribbled notes: *Too early to know, making little progress, connecting is going to be hard. Clean, neat, too organized. Christian. Afraid of the dark. Whatever haunts her is deep, painful, and is causing fear. It's all in her eyes, exquisite eyes . . .*

Jessie suddenly realized the shower was no longer running. She put the pad back in its spot and, without the slightest hesitation, turned to leave the room. She knew she had to hurry, but her eyes suddenly found an object that did not conform to the decor. Hanging to the left of the door was a painting approximately eighteen inches wide and thirty-four inches high. The frame resembled heavy black glass but probably wasn't. The double mat was of a dark and then lighter grey. The simplicity and elegance of the painting within stirred her soul. It was a single, white, dew-moistened rose. A long, light green stem with its accompanying thorns contrasted its brilliance. If ever a flower could exhibit sadness, this was the one. This painting had a story.

The knob on the bathroom door squeaked, and Jessie fled to the relative safety of the hall. She slipped into her room and closed the door.

* * *

Ryan had finished dressing when it hit him. Perfume. He looked around and concluded Jessie had been there. He noticed his pen on the floor under the desk and remembered he'd left it on the legal pad. He sat on the edge of the desk, considering his next move. He would let it go. Bringing it up wouldn't aid him in any way. His curiosity as to her reason for coming in would have to remain, for the time being, just that. Snooping didn't seem to be an innate trait for Jessie, yet he reminded himself he didn't know much about her. He threw on a pair of jeans and a long-sleeved white shirt. He would go riding alone.

After grabbing a water bottle, he climbed the stairs to the second-floor landing and crossed the balcony to the double glass doors of the library. Slipping through, he entered his private office. He dialed Elliott's cell phone.

"Hello," Elliott's voice answered calmly.

"With a client?" Ryan asked.

"Not presently. How's it going?"

"I'm hopeful."

"She going to stay the full ten days, at your cabin?"

"Most likely, but ten days will barely scratch the surface. You already knew that, though. What's your game plan, Elliott?" Ryan noted Elliott's sly way of finding out where he had taken Jessie.

"I don't know what you mean," Elliott answered casually, although Ryan sensed his shock at Jessie's staying.

"Well, even after our many conversations, you really haven't given me much to go on, and instinct tells me there's more to this relationship than business."

"Professionally speaking, I can't give you any details. You know that. We went over this when you offered to help."

"Offered? When I *offered?*" Ryan stood, sending the high-back leather chair scooting behind him. "Wait a minute. This is payback, remember? This clears us. I'm not asking for any information that you hold confidential, but rather an insight or two. I was hoping that as her friend and employer, you would want to help her out as well."

"Can't," Elliott said. Ryan could hear the smugness in his voice.

"Fine." Ryan set the receiver back into its cradle. Surprised at his unprofessional outburst, he sat back in the soft leather and closed his eyes. Hearing movement in the library, he decided to postpone the venture into the cause of his behavior. He crossed the office to the library door and opened it quietly, catching Jessie's reflection in the glass door to the balcony.

* * *

Jessie was overwhelmed at the array of reading material on the bookshelves in the library. Every available wall was filled from top to bottom. A ladder of brass and maple allowed access to the sixteen feet of vertical knowledge. She picked up Volume One of *The Lincoln Papers* and retreated to a circular leather couch that sat squarely in the middle of the room. She was heavily engrossed in it when she sensed movement behind her and turned to see Ryan holding two glasses of iced orange juice.

"Didn't mean to startle you," he said.

Jessie shrugged impassively, ignoring the juice.

"I wasn't aware that Grisham wrote *The Lincoln Papers*," he said in a voice dripping with delight at his own wit.

"Yes, well, I decided that although John's book is still on my list of To Do's, Mr. Lincoln's prolific words would be more productive for me. By the way, how did you come with juice from that direction?"

"There's a minibar set up in there."

Jessie slowly closed the delicate book. "I was under the impression that Mormons didn't drink."

If Ryan was shocked at the mention of his past, he didn't show it. "None of my clients are Mormon," he answered matter-of-factly.

"I hope Elliott can afford your fees. Even though under the circumstances, if you're actually being paid, then I'm a client—and we shouldn't be here."

Ryan considered explaining his financial status and the indebtedness he felt toward Elliott, but Jessie left abruptly with Mr. Lincoln in hand.

* * *

Jessie lay on her bed, trying to clear her mind. She had to find some productive patch of grey matter if she was going to survive this. *Exquisite eyes? He's commenting on my features?*

Hearing noises, she rose to the window in time to see Ryan galloping off toward the lake. The stables looked inviting, but she was intent on making her way to the jacuzzi.

She found the laundry room across the hall, but the swimsuits and towels weren't there. "I'm losin' it," she said out loud. "Where did he say the suits were kept? I know he told me." As she walked out of the laundry room, she paused, her hand on the doorknob to his room. It was taking immense strength to suppress the urge to get a better look at that notepad.

A twinge of trepidation pulled at the edges of her consciousness. Both Gramps and Ryan were gone. She was used to being alone, but she was in the middle of nowhere, and this place was massive. While she knew she needed a good, hot soak, there would never be a better time to familiarize herself with the cabin's layout. And if she found a stray clue or perhaps a piece of ammunition here or there, so much the better. It wasn't snooping.

Reaching the base of the grand staircase, she was assaulted by a foul odor that caused her to cover her nose. It smelled of something dead. *What on earth?*

She climbed the staircase slowly, holding onto the banister with one hand, her eyes moving constantly. Something or someone was smelling up the place. At the landing, she heard groaning from the library's direction.

Has someone broken into the cabin? And how could they have gotten hurt? And where is Nelly? What's the use in having a watchdog if it doesn't watch?

She spotted a marble vase on the table just outside the library and picked it up gently, hoping it wasn't some priceless heirloom. She eased slowly toward the entrance.

In spite of not feeling particularly brave, she breached the threshold on all fours, half carrying and half dragging the vase behind her. She froze as she heard the sound again, slightly louder this time. It came from the partially open French door directly across the room. *Ryan's office.* Still on all fours, she inched her way across the white maple flooring and gently widened the opening between the two glass doors. She was definitely closer. Her nose told her so. Another leather couch blocked her view of the office to the right.

The faint moaning was definitely on the other side of this couch. Sweating, Jessie remained motionless on the hardwood floor. Peeking under the couch revealed nothing. The groaning grew louder, and she determined it was time to act. She held the vase before her in both hands, even though chances were whatever was moaning was not in a position to harm her. Jessie took one last glance around the room. No one. "What on earth am I doing?" she muttered tensely.

She crept out from behind the couch with the vase held high above her head.

The groaning became a growl. Nelly was slobbering over a dead heap of something indistinguishable. "Nelly? You have got to be kidding!"

The dog, obviously more concerned its treasure would be snatched than with the possibility of getting beaned on the head with a vase, leaped from the couch and headed downstairs, dragging her catch. Stunned and nauseous, Jessie sat on the floor, feeling like a moron. *Well, at least only Nelly knows how stupid I looked holding a vase over my head. I'll remember never to allow her to lick my face again!*

The air was already starting to clear, but it still needed ventilation. Jessie decided to open a door to allow Nelly the proper environment to toy with her latest kill.

Pulling herself off the floor, she started across Ryan's office to a set of doors identical to the ones from which she had emerged a few moments earlier. Plenty of light streamed through the glass panes in the library next door. Leafy green foliage greeted her eyes. She opened the doors and stepped out onto the balcony. The view surrounding her was breathtaking.

The back of the cabin had been enclosed in glass, creating a type of greenhouse. The palm trees and tropical vegetation, the smell, the moisture, the warmth—all of it was incredible. She wondered why she hadn't noticed this tropical Eden from inside the family room last night. It must have been too dark. She would quit calling this place a cabin, that was certain. The title had bothered her from the moment she'd arrived anyway.

Leaving the office and library behind, she crossed the hall and entered the next room. She cracked it open and peered inside. The room wasn't exactly dirty, but it was lived-in. A queen-sized bed with matching oak side tables, a small entertainment center, a fairly good-sized bookcase, and a well-broken-in recliner filled the large, rectangular room. It appeared, at least so far, that every room had its own private bath. The recliner bore a shirt she recognized as one that Gramps had worn the evening before, and she surmised that this was his room. She had no reason to look any further. She had taken an immediate liking to Gramps, despite his grandson. She saw in him an openness and honesty that were obviously genuine. She wouldn't betray his privacy.

Leaving the balcony, she entered a sitting area, her senses adapting to the fading stench. The sitting room was open entirely to the landing and balcony behind her. Sunlight filled the room with warmth. It had no doubt doubled as a waiting room when Ryan had been taking clients.

She opened a door to her right and found a spare bedroom. She continued down the hall as it took a short jog to the left. She then pushed open a thick glass door and stepped through onto another balcony similar to the one off the office and library.

She immediately noticed the similarities in the environments— the warm, moist air as well as the tropical vegetation.

Above her, the greenhouse glass ran in a gentle slope down to the back of the cabin, where it curved as before, continuing the three stories to ground level. There was a waterfall built up in the center with a stream running around its mountainous base. A path of stone and redwood bridges wound through the vegetation and around the waterfall. Jessie leaned as far out over the balcony as she could, looking for the hot tub that was supposed to be in there somewhere. Sure enough, almost directly beneath her in the corner was a redwood deck with a covered tub in its center.

She exited the balcony and continued down the hall. The last door opened to another bedroom, decorated similarly to the guest bedroom she had just seen next door. Its adjoining bathroom had an additional door leading to the hallway.

Retreating back to the landing, Jessie headed to the final floor, assuming there wouldn't be much up there beyond attic crawl space. She reached the top landing and found it lit by the sun's rays streaming through skylights that lined the ceiling. A banister ran the length of the opening on the landing where she stood, and the immediate area off the family room balcony was set up as a reading loft. A couch with its matching love seat and recliner created a corner arrangement.

Passing this, Jessie entered into a playroom. It consisted of a pool table, a ping-pong table, a cluster of commercial pinball machines, and an entertainment center.

She walked back through the reading loft and into an area whose use she was unsure of. It was a vast, almost empty space. Back-to-back folding chairs rested on the wall to her left. On the back wall were French doors she was sure opened to the same greenhouse she had seen earlier.

Her tour at an end, Jessie headed for the tub, hoping she would be able to find a suit and towel.

CHAPTER 7

Ruth McKnight was working in her garden when Gramps arrived. "Hey, Thomas, didn't 'spect I'd see you for a while," she said, walking toward the truck.

Gramps hopped out and gave his sister a giant bear hug. Standing five-foot-three inches tall and weighing a mere ninety-five pounds, Ruth completely disappeared in Gramps' embrace. Her silver-gray hair, wrapped neatly in a braided bun at the top of her head, had never been cut. Old-fashioned in looks and character, she had a heart of gold, and Gramps adored her. Five years his senior, Ruth was learning to live with increasingly failing health.

A sister and grandson were all the family Gramps had left. His only son was . . . somewhere.

"Thought I'd see if you needed anything done 'round here," Gramps replied.

"Things not goin' well with the girl? Did she leave?"

"Naw, she's still 'round. Ryan thinks I'm out back tinkerin'. Somethin' different 'bout this one. Feel it in my bones. She's sharp and gotta sense of humor. And I see the look."

"Who's givin' the look? Her or him?"

"Him."

Ruth remained silent. It had been a long time since Ryan had shown any real interest in a woman.

Gramps noticed the childlike expression of glee on her face. "Now don't go gittin' your hopes up. It's just a look, not a marriage proposal. Babies are a long way off."

* * *

The heat of the day was setting in as Ryan climbed off Steel, a magnificent, coal-black Morgan. Expressive eyes, short pricked ears, and a thick yet silky mane and tail set off Steel's muscular body. He was a good-natured, gentle horse who enjoyed being active. Ryan tied the reins to an old fence post outside the Gas 'N' Go.

"Hey, Cal, how's it goin'?" Ryan said, stepping into the musty atmosphere of the store.

"Hey to you, Ryan. Hear you got yourself quite a looker at your place."

Ryan picked up a granola bar and a small bottle of cold orange juice and walked back to the counter. "I forgot how fast things get around out here. Just put these on my account. I didn't bring any change."

Cal had been reading the town paper on a stool, but he now bent over and brought out a ledger from beneath the counter. Cal was in his midfifties, thin and always pale, as if he hadn't eaten in days. Flannel shirts were out of season, yet he was never seen without one. "Haven't seen Gramps today. Suppose he's keepin' an eye on you two."

Ryan ignored the tease as he signed his name and turned to leave.

"Ruth wants a little one around before she dies!" Cal yelled as Ryan pulled Steel's reins.

Ryan chuckled as he put the granola bar in his back pocket and opened the orange juice, gulping it down in a matter of seconds. Steel nudged the empty container, his dry nostrils flaring. "What's the matter, boy, a little thirsty? Well, you're not getting orange juice. We'll take a detour to the brook, then stop by and visit Aunt Ruth. We'll stall a bit, eh? I'm in no hurry to hear a lecture on having a 'little one.'" Steel neighed as if he understood.

They turned off the road and headed into the beauty of the summer valley. Spring had been particularly moist, resulting in a profusion of color that blanketed the valley with exquisite wildflowers and fruited bushes. The aroma was intoxicating.

Reaching the brook, Steel quenched his thirst while Ryan climbed off and settled into the grass, lying on his back. He stared at the popcorn clouds, his thoughts similarly adrift. He played back his conversations with Jessie, her nightmare, every facial expression and voice fluctuation, attempting to weave it all into one fabric that would give him some direction.

Ryan could sense in Jessie a strong independence, and for her to leave everything behind and stay in a stranger's cabin led him to believe she was seeking assistance. His thoughts turned to his conversation with Elliott.

Years before, under Elliott's tutelage, Ryan's doctoral thesis received a firm foundational start. He and Elliott had remained in contact after its completion. During that time, Elliott had become increasingly discontent with his professorship, so after consistent persuading from Ryan, he opened a private practice. Within five years it had grown to the current four partners and fifteen associates.

While Elliott maintained a standing invitation for Ryan to join him as partner, Ryan always politely declined. A move to the fast-lane simply was not his quest. A one-man operation carried enough abuse.

After his wife's death, Ryan had allowed his work to consume him. When he wasn't working, he was drinking. Life without Brecca had become a nightmare—he was lost without her. So at age thirty-eight, after hitting bottom, he decided it was time for a change. He stopped taking new clients, and within six months, the rest of his clientele had dissipated. He began dating casually and stayed at his condo during the week, keeping close to his new office and stock investments. The cabin was a weekend refuge. Life, for the most part, had become pleasant again. Then Elliott's phone calls began. Was the interruption the real reason for his anger toward Elliott? He wondered.

* * *

Gramps was kneeling to put the final touch of white paint on Ruth's aged rocker. It had been a gift from his father to his mother when Ruth was born. Ruth was sitting at his side, sipping lemonade.

"Why you don't just break down and buy yourself a new rocker I'll never understand," Gramps said, picking up the can of paint. He was proud of the new finish.

"Cuz I like this one. Besides, there ain't another'n like this in the whole world."

"That's for sure. People get fired these days for makin' junk like this!" Gramps wiped paint from his hands.

"Oh now, if it was junk, it would've fallen apart years ago. You're just jealous Mama gave it to me instead of you," she teased.

"Yeah, that must be it." She had unknowingly hit a nerve, and Gramps changed the subject. He rambled instead about the wild-flowers that had grown too close to the house for his liking, not listening to her subsequent reply. His mind had locked onto the fondest memory of his childhood—his mother. She had rocked him often in this rocker, even up until he was ten years old. She had died when he was fifteen, and he missed her.

Mischief had been a mainstay in Gramps's teenage life on the farm. He'd been a wild youth and had ignored her warnings more than once. When he returned after an evening of roguery, he would often find her sitting on the porch in the rocker, waiting. While she might gently reprove him for his misbehavior, other times they would just chat, and he would share his dreams with her. Yet he knew Ruth deserved the rocker.

Ruth offered Gramps more lemonade. They sat in quietude, wiping streaks of perspiration from their foreheads, enjoying the peaceful beauty around them.

The white, ranch-style home in which they both were raised and on which Ruth now lived was on fifty acres of land. It had everything a child could want: a wooded area, a babbling brook, and flat, open areas where the horses used to run. A storybook place, really. On several occasions, contractors had come trying to convince them to sell the property. They would simply laugh and offer them lemonade.

An old, battered barn once used for milking cows was nestled behind the house. Gramps complained about its condition every time he came, and this visit was no exception. "So, thinkin' it's time to tear down that barn yet?" he said, emerging from the reverie of his thoughts. "Lookin' pretty shabby next to the house."

Ruth's eyes twinkled. "Wondered when you'd bring that up."

"Well?" Gramps wasn't going to be brushed off as usual. Today he would push the point. With Jessie around, he'd have to stay at the cabin most of the time, but he would need an out once in a while. Tearing down an old barn would be just the thing to keep him busy.

"Why is it men always have to be buildin' somethin' up or tearin' somethin' down?"

"It's innate. I'll be by in the mornin' with Joe and get started." Gramps looked pleased.

"Whoa now, hold your horses. Why don't we just wait till next spring?"

"Cuz I'll be dead by then, and my dyin' wish is to tear down that hideous, mouse-infested . . ."

"All right, if it's gnawing at you that much, I guess I can grant an old man his dyin' wish. But tomorrow's the Sabbath, mind you, so you'll have to wait till Monday."

"Bible says you can yank your ox outta the mire on the Sabbath, ya know."

"Says it just like that, does it? Don't you go comparin' that barn to an ox in the mire now, Thomas."

"You Mormons—"

"Hush now, here comes the boy."

Ryan waved a hello, climbed off Steel, and led him through the rickety gate into the open pasture. Patting his companion, Ryan said under his breath as he approached, "Let's see how many seconds go by today before the usual marriage and baby issue, hmmm, boy?"

"It's good to see you, son. Thomas said you were here for a week or so." Ruth smiled, offering a glass of lemonade.

"It's been too long since I've been by. Sorry about that. Kids these days, eh?" He gave her a hug before taking the drink and sitting down in the porch swing, which also needed a paint job.

"Thought you were tinkering outside?" He directed this remark at Gramps.

"I'm outside, aren't I? So, how's the Doc?"

"It's a typical first day. Don't take off again. Need you around."

"Thomas tells me she's very striking." Ruth winked at Gramps.

"Is that so?" Ryan replied nonchalantly.

"Now that's not entirely correct. I never commented on her looks," Gramps said.

"She have serious problems, son?" Ruth asked.

"You know I can't tell you that."

"Are you tryin' that philosophy you and that other doctor was discussin' last time you were here?" Ruth asked attentively.

"What's that?"

"Being friends with your clients rather than strictly doctor-patient."

"Tried that once. Didn't work. Allan stayed three years, remember? Besides, she's not really a client. I just owe someone a favor, that's all."

"The prospect of having her around for three years doesn't sound all that miserable!" Gramps replied lightheartedly.

Ryan chuckled. "Therapists can't be friends with their clients. It doesn't work that way. If I became her friend, then I would no longer be open-minded. It would become too personal. Besides, her partner is her friend, and she's quite possibly plotting his murder. I'm safer as her therapist."

"How is Allan, anyway?" Gramps asked. Allan had been a young man of twenty when he first visited Ryan. Tossed around in foster homes most of his life, he began using drugs at age eleven. By nineteen, he had found himself married to a seventeen-year-old who had already miscarried two pregnancies. He was a steady heroin user, and if that weren't deadly enough, he'd added whiskey to the equation. Allan checked himself into rehab, then sought therapy to deal with his childhood and marriage issues.

"Last letter I got was about six months ago. He and Angie have been trying to have another child. His job is going well at the university. Angie is clerking at a local law firm, and they just bought a house. So I guess they couldn't be happier."

"So bein' his friend caused what problem there exactly?" Ruth asked timidly.

"The man stayed forever! Maybe it did help him, but it was a long time, and it turned into a major inconvenience."

"Well, son, it's after noon. Wanna head back?" Gramps smiled craftily. "She may want some company for lunch."

"I'm sure she'll manage just fine. But you go on ahead. I haven't had Steel out in a while. Think I'll take the scenic route back."

"Hang in there, young man," Ruth said. "Sounds like you're here for a few days, so come by again. I promise I won't harass you about babies."

* * *

Jessie located the solarium and eventually found a closet full of suits and towels near the tub. Her choices were limited, since most were too small or weathered. She entered a small sauna built into the wall behind the hot tub and changed. After opening the hot tub cover, Jessie climbed in the warm, heavenly water. There were several white buttons on a panel next to her, and she decided to explore those after the initial feeling of euphoria wore off.

Looking through the glass ceiling, she imagined what brilliance the night sky would bring. It would be an amazing sight. Jessie's senses took it all in, filling her with a peace she had not felt for quite some time. "If only life was always this quiet and serene," she murmured softly.

She lay back and closed her eyes. Letting out a sigh, Jessie resigned herself to the fact that the time had come to make some decisions. *It's taken quite a while to build up my practice. Quitting and starting over somewhere else would be an enormous undertaking. Taking an extended leave of absence would agitate a few clients, but the end result would be less taxing. Except then I'd have to return to Elliott.* "It's me or him," *he would say. What a moron. At least I've shocked him by actually staying with Ryan.*

* * *

Ryan arrived at the cabin to find Gramps puttering in the garden. "Thought you'd be inside drooling," he joked, climbing off Steel.

"They'd be puttin' me on medication if I drooled at my age. Didn't start any lunch cuz she's in the hot tub. By the way, before I went in, I spotted Nelly. She—and something dead hangin' from her mouth—went toward the pasture. Stinks in there."

"Skunk?"

"No, probably a squirrel or possum. Looks like the doc opened things up already, but it still reeks. Dog's gonna need a bath for sure."

"Due for one anyway."

Ryan opened a few more windows before entering his favorite room. Jessie had discovered how to work the jets. He returned to his room, slipped into his suit, then climbed in the tub.

Jessie's eyes were closed, but feeling movement by her right leg, she jumped. Opening her eyes, she found Ryan bending over her.

"What do you think you're doing?" she demanded.

"The tub won't get any hotter, so I was shutting down the heater pump. I didn't mean to scare you." He switched off the pump quickly and started to climb out.

"Don't leave on my account. I was getting out anyway." She abruptly moved past him and exited the tub, grabbing the nearest towel. "Your dog played with something dead today. I may not have opened enough windows. I got lost searching for all of them." She left before Ryan could comment.

Ryan cursed under his breath. He should have stayed clear of the tub.

* * *

Once in her room, Jessie threw on a pair of jeans and a T-shirt. She was grateful for the few minutes alone in the jacuzzi, and she resolved that at some point in life, she would own one.

Ryan could pop up anywhere she went, she deduced. Since she was safer alone in her room, she decided to grab a snack from the kitchen before locking herself in. After surveying the hall and finding it empty, she hurried toward the kitchen, snatching some fresh fruit, a glass of water, a few crackers, and some peanuts. Turning from the counter, she collided with Ryan. He was still in his swimsuit, drying his hair with a towel. Her treats had fallen to the floor, but she had managed to maintain her grip on the water.

"Seems I'm ruining your day," Ryan said, grinning. He bent over, picked up the fruit, and handed it to her.

"My day? No. My life, well . . ." Jessie took the fruit from him and knelt to gather the rest. He moved to help.

"Please, don't. I can manage," she said.

He watched as she finished scavenging for lost peanuts before walking silently to her room.

Spilling the food on her bed, Jessie sighed. *Ryan's frustrated, but it just doesn't matter. A week after this is over, he'll forget all about me and return to his safe little life.*

Reaching into her bag, Jessie pulled out the envelope and sat on the bed. The edges of the envelope were rough and weathered, and the coloring was now a dull yellow. Fighting the tears, she extracted a crumpled piece of note paper. After she read the hideous words, her tears flowed unabated. The paper and envelope slipped to the floor.

CHAPTER 8

It was past midnight when Jessie entered the kitchen. A light coming from the ice and water dispenser on the refrigerator illuminated the room enough for her to see. She had held out for a day and a half before her snacks were gone, and now her body craved real food. The wafting scent of Gramps's roast beef dinner had almost tempted her to the table a few hours earlier, but she had resisted. Quietly, she made a sandwich from the leftover roast, then found some fresh fruit and poured a glass of something purple.

All was silent as Jessie headed for the family room. The light from the refrigerator didn't begin to make its way to this room, but the moon reflected its light through the cabins southernly exposed glass.

Jessie sat cross-legged on the couch, setting the plate in her lap. She placed the purple juice on a large glass table in front of her. Momentarily, something sniffed at her knee. Apparently Nelly, too, thought a midnight snack was a good idea. Jessie gently patted her and whispered, "You won't get any of my dinner. Now go lie down." Defeated, Nelly went to the other side of the table and licked herself thoroughly before nestling her snout between her paws.

Jessie's thoughts ricocheted through her mind. *Why did Elliott have to turn out to be such a jerk? It took so long to find a man I thought I could trust. I should've known better.*

What's with that rose painting? And the furniture? There is no way the good doctor could afford all this even if he did make a bundle off his work. Stock market, maybe? Her noisy stomach forced her mind back to more urgent needs. She finished the sandwich and sipped at her drink.

"Was the roast good?" a voice asked from within the shadowy darkness beyond Nelly.

Jessie momentarily froze.

"I come out here sometimes at night when I can't sleep," Ryan said lightly.

Nelly's presence made sense to Jessie now. She remained still, probing the darkness for his silhouette. She wondered how long he'd been sitting there waiting for her. People often expressed feelings more freely late at night or after a few drinks. Since he hadn't seen her drink, a late-night conversation would have been a safe gamble.

"You've been cooped up for a while. You need anything else?" he attempted again.

"I'm not in the mood for conversation, Mr. Blake. Thank you for dinner." Jessie scooped up her dishes briskly and returned them to the kitchen before retreating down the hall. The sound of her door closing ended his hopes.

His mood was sullen as he made his way slowly to bed. He was determined to get through to her, not only because it was innate for him to want to help, but because he wanted his debt to Elliott paid.

* * *

Gramps was already at Jessie's door when Ryan finally heard and reacted. He'd only been asleep an hour when the screams echoed through the cabin. Gramps reached for the door handle.

Ryan grabbed his arm. "No, Gramps."

"Don't you think we should wake her?"

"Under normal circumstances, I would say yes, but I want to wait it out. I need her to talk. I know it sounds cruel, but it's my call."

"I guess you know what you're doin', son. Let me know if you need me."

"Okay. She'll be all right."

* * *

Jessie stared at the hands on the clock, her entire body covered in sweat. She got out of bed slowly and walked to the bathroom. After splashing cold water on her face, she stared into the mirror. The torment of the little girl within was etched on her features.

Wishing she had her robe and tea, Jessie slipped into a sweater and leggings and left her room. All was quiet, and she wasn't sure now if her screams had been real or imagined.

She ascended the staircase, finding her way to the loft. She gazed through the window at the star-filled sky before sinking down into the cool leather of the couch.

The scent finally reached Jessie. Cinnamon. She muttered under her breath. Someone else was there. While devising a getaway plan, she wondered if Ryan *ever* slept.

"I made some tea. It's orange spiced with cinnamon. There's also some sugar and honey. I wasn't sure which you preferred," he said calmly.

Her departure temporarily delayed by the tempting aroma of the spiced liquid, she looked around for its source. She could almost feel its soothing warmth spreading though her body. "Jerk," she mumbled. *How in the world could he possibly have known I would come to the loft? Or that I liked tea? One cup, then I'll be able to sleep.* Reaching for the mug and teapot directly in front of her, she filled the cup to the rim. Her hand was shaking as she set the teapot down. He had managed to raise her blood pressure yet again. His form was now visible in the recliner across from her.

"As I said earlier, I really don't want to talk, Mr. Blake, but I do appreciate the tea," she said uneasily.

He stayed quiet. He would let her relax. His patience would pay off eventually. At least she was being polite and staying put.

Knowing that she was tempting fate, she poured another cup. *I ought to take this one to my room. No! I'm comfortable, and I refuse to let him chase me away this time.*

"It's Ryan. Do you want to talk about the nightmares?"

"No."

"Would you like something to help you sleep?"

"No."

"What can I do for you, Jessie?"

"You could stop talking."

He chuckled and obeyed.

After a few minutes, she ventured, "Don't you sleep either? Or is staying up all hours of the night part of your head-cracking strategy?"

Ryan was thrilled that she had posed a question. It was a beginning. "I usually sleep okay. Gets harder when I hear screaming."

"Oh." There was a pause before she softly asked, "Did I wake Gramps, too?"

"Yeah, but he goes back to sleep quick. Probably won't even remember it in the morning."

"Sorry," she said honestly.

"It would probably help to talk about it."

"I would like to leave in the morning."

"No," he replied solemnly.

"Excuse me?"

"You need to stay."

"Oh, I see. I thought I wasn't a prisoner," she said, her words becoming icy as she banged the mug down on the glass table.

"You've been a prisoner for a long time, Jessie. It has nothing to do with location."

"Oh, don't get psychological with me. I know all that junk."

"Junk? Is that what you think about what we do, Jessie?"

"And quit using my name all the time. I hate it."

"You hate your name or the fact that I'm using it?"

"Okay, this conversation is over. I'm leaving in the morning with or without you." She ignored Nelly trotting up to her as she descended the stairs.

Ryan, still elated that it had been a two-sided conversation this time, sat back and breathed deeply. She would leave early, probably before sunup to avoid him and Gramps. He would sleep a couple hours, then get up. He had to get through to her.

* * *

True to Ryan's prediction, Jessie was packed and ready to leave at dawn. Etiquette required she leave a thank-you note to Gramps, so she laid the note on the bed, picked up her backpack, and left the room.

Ryan was sitting on the front porch steps sipping hot coffee. Nelly lay beside him, sniffing the air at nothing in particular. Ryan hadn't shaved since the day before, and a slight growth of stubble gave him a rugged look.

Jessie walked past the two of them in silence. Ryan finished his coffee and then told Nelly to stay. He walked briskly to catch up with Jessie.

"May I walk with you?" Ryan asked, avoiding the use of her name.

"Public road."

"It's a long way into town."

"I can use the exercise."

"I'll drive you home if you'd like."

Jessie stopped short. This she had not expected. "I've already arranged for a taxi from Summittville to pick me up at the gas station." She hadn't wanted anyone she knew to pick her up from "the cabin."

"I'll walk you to the store then."

"Suit yourself. Just no talking."

To her surprise, Ryan chose to remain silent for the first mile, though she knew it wouldn't last.

"Well, we are a little less than halfway to the store, so since you're stuck walking the next mile and a half either direction, I'll capitalize," Ryan said.

She wanted to hit him. Whatever he said would most likely make sense, and that would tick her off even more.

"I would guess that the reason you're struggling at work is because of your lack of sleep," he continued. "Lack of sleep due to the nightmares."

"Wow. You're good," she said flippantly.

"Sooner or later, you're going to need to talk to someone, Je—" He stopped before he said her name.

It's no use. He's going to talk all the way to the store.

Ryan waited a few minutes before speaking again. "How old were you when you were locked in the dark?"

"Okay, that's it!" She stopped, threw down her bag, and turned to look directly at him. "Look, *Doctor* Blake, none of this is any of your business. *I* didn't search you out. They are my dreams, so leave them alone! Go help someone else. I . . ." Light-headed, short-winded, and off balance, she stumbled forward.

"It's Ryan . . . Are you okay?" He reached to grab her and put one arm around her back, the other hand under her arm.

"I'm just a little dizzy . . . I'm fine now." She pushed herself free from his grip.

"My aunt's house is just down the hill. Let's get there and then I'll jog back for my truck."

"I'm fine," she reminded him sternly. Lifting her bag, she continued toward town. She hadn't fainted in weeks.

The scent of his cologne lingered in Jessie's head, and she began feeling dizzy again. Trees and flowers began to spin. This time she lunged forward. Ryan had been watching her closely, and his arms caught her before she tumbled to the ground. She was out cold, so Ryan gently laid her on a patch of grass. Patting her cheeks, he searched for any sign of movement. Her breathing was shallow and rapid, and after taking her pulse, he realized her heart was racing. For the next minute, he monitored her breathing and pulse, noting the slowing of both. He hoped she was just experiencing a panic attack. Putting one arm under her shoulders and his other arm under her knees, he lifted her and began walking.

CHAPTER 9

Ruth was arranging wildflowers in a brightly colored vase when she heard the slap of the screen door. Drying her hands quickly on a dish towel, she hurried out in time to see Ryan laying a woman on her front room couch. "What on earth . . . ?"

"She fainted. I need a cold cloth," Ryan said, slightly out of breath.

"Should I call 911?" she called over her shoulder.

"No. If we can't bring her around in a few minutes, I'll call Doc Brady. She's incensed enough as it is. She'll go ballistic if she wakes up with paramedics swarming over her." He elevated her feet and covered her with a blanket. A million questions raced through his mind.

"I found a bottle of smelling salts in the cupboard." Ruth handed them to him. He took the cold compress and laid it on Jessie's forehead, then slowly inched the salts under her nose. A few seconds passed before her nostrils curled and her head shifted right to left. With a slight cough, she opened her eyes and tried to sit up.

"Just relax and don't move around," Ryan said gently.

"What happened?" Jessie asked amidst her coughing.

"You fainted," he said, still kneeling at her side.

"May I have some water, please?"

"I've got some right handy," replied Ruth as she reached for a glass of water she had poured earlier.

"Thank you." After a few sips, she leaned back down. "I'm feeling better. Mr. Blake, I apologize for being rude. It's just that . . ." She closed her eyes and blacked out again. Ryan re-covered her with the knitted afghan, and he and Ruth went into the kitchen.

"Made French toast. It's still warm if you're hungry," she invited.

"No thanks, but I could use something to drink. Preferably something with a kick to it."

"How about my lemonade?" Ruth never added sugar, so it unquestionably had a kick.

"Not what I had in mind, but it'll do."

"Will she be all right?" Ruth asked Ryan as they walked into the kitchen.

"That depends on her." He sat at the kitchen table, holding his lemonade, then began shaking his head and repeating words like *stubborn, strong-willed, defiant,* and *unmanageable.*

"Now, now, son, calm down. I'm not supposed to be privy to any of that information, remember?"

"Get to know her, and it will become obvious to you, too."

"Ryan!" Ruth's face twisted slightly in gentle scorn.

"It's just that I'm not practicing anymore. I don't know . . . maybe I shouldn't have taken this case."

Ruth promptly changed the subject. She told Ryan of Gramps's desire to tear down the barn, and they chatted amiably about other household matters. An hour passed before they heard a cough from the living room.

Jessie struggled to a sitting position and attempted to gain her composure. She looked at Ruth as she and Ryan entered. "You must be Gramps's sister."

"Yes, dear, I'm Ruth. Thomas was right. You are very lovely, even with that pale complexion." Everyone smiled, and the tension eased.

"You're very kind. I'm sorry to have troubled you," Jessie replied.

"Do you have a history of these episodes?" Ryan asked. The tension rushed back.

"There he goes again. Just can't let anything go. Everything has to have a reason," Jessie said in slight annoyance.

"It's a valid question," Ryan countered. "If you can't offer an explanation, then the next time you pass out, I'm going to call 911."

"I'll be fine," she mumbled. "Don't call 911. I just need a few moments to think without you in my face. Can you do that?" She was trying hard to keep her composure in front of Ruth.

"Fine. I'll go for a short run, but I'll be back in a bit. Oh, Ruth, if she asks to borrow *any* means of transportation, the answer is no. Doctor's orders."

Ryan cleared his mind of Jessie as he turned down the path that had been his wife's favorite. The town had referred to his wife as Rebecca, and her family had chosen Becca. He had wanted to be different, so Brecca it was. This month would have marked their twelfth anniversary. He had spent the last eight alone. He would visit her grave tomorrow.

Let go. It came as a whisper, bringing Ryan out of his memories.

"What?" Ryan turned toward the voice. "Okay buddy, get ahold of yourself," he said aloud, taking a deep breath. The scent of lilacs suddenly surrounded him like a blanket. It was the scent of Brecca— she had always used lilac bath and shower gel, lilac lotion, she had lit lilac candles, and she had even found a lilac spray, which had intoxicated him. Where was the aroma coming from? He stood for several minutes breathing in the soft, sweet essence.

Let go.

Ryan jerked around. He knew that voice. It was Brecca's. *No, it can't be. That's ludicrous,* he told himself. "Guess Jessie's not the only one needing some shut-eye," he said as he quickened his pace.

* * *

"Are you hungry, child?" Ruth asked, a motherly tone in her voice.

"No, thank you. I should leave now." Jessie attempted to get on her feet.

"Now you just hold on there. You're not goin' anywhere. This is my house now, and you'll do as I say. So just lie back down there and I'll bring you some crackers and tea."

I see it runs in the family, Jessie thought, not wishing to insult Ruth. "Oh no, I've got to cancel a cab that's probably costing me a fortune by now."

"No need. Ryan already took care of that. Had Cal pay him." Ruth shuffled back to the kitchen before Jessie could respond.

Jessie surveyed her surroundings. The house was small but homey. The front room held a couch, a recliner, a coffee table, a bookshelf, and a fireplace. Down the hall, she could see what looked like a bathroom and two closed rooms opposite each other. On the other side of the house was the kitchen and possibly the utility or laundry room. She remembered the dirty underclothes she had on. She'd only packed enough for a day or two, so the use of a washing machine was becoming a definite must.

Jessie surmised that Ruth was a Christian as she noticed that a picture, a porcelain statue, or a book about Him was in every corner she looked.

Within minutes, Jessie was invited to sample an array of crackers, and after doing so, she decided she would have to broaden her shopping experience to incorporate something other than the frozen food, yogurt, and tea sections.

"You and your brother are so kind. Are you sure Ryan's related?" Jessie asked, picking up a wheat cracker.

"Thomas and I raised him ourselves. Quite sure he's related," Ruth said slyly.

"Oh." Jessie felt like an imbecile. She forced more crackers into her mouth to keep herself quiet.

Ryan was glad to enter a room where voices were attached to real people. He was certain that by now, Jessie would be ready to walk the next mile or so to the store. "You okay?" He smiled. She looked like a chipmunk stuffing acorns endlessly into its mouth.

"Uh-huh." She felt awkward as little specks of cracker flew through the sunlit air.

"Which way we walking?"

"Haven't decided yet. I'm still eating."

Ryan sat in the recliner across from her. "I can wait." He watched her manage a sip of lemonade in between a binge of crackers. The phone rang, and Ruth brought it to Ryan.

"Hello?" Ryan said into the receiver.

"Hey, kid, glad I caught you. Sure this is bad timing, but Joanie's having her foal. Could use your help."

"Now? You're right about the timing. Don't suppose nature could wait an hour?"

"No, son, it's happenin' now." Gramps voice was anxious.

"I'm on my way." Ryan handed the phone back to Ruth. "Jessie, I have to get back to the cabin."

"So go," she said sarcastically.

"You need to come with me."

"Nope."

"Jess—"

Ruth cut him off. "She can stay here while you take care of what needs done. Come back for her in a bit. Do her good to rest anyway." She walked him to the porch. "Everything okay with Thomas?"

"Yeah, Joanie's having her foal. Look, if Jessie faints again, call 911, then me," he said, climbing into his truck.

Jessie slumped back on the sofa and put the washcloth over her face. It had warmed, but she didn't care. "Thank you. I won't stay long," she said when Ruth returned.

"Don't be silly, child. You're going nowhere till he gets back. Now, can I get you anything else?"

"A new life, if you have one of those lying around."

"Can't be all that bad, child." Ruth sat in the old recliner and picked up a basketful of yarn.

"I didn't think so until now."

"What's changed?"

"Seems I can't sleep. Therefore, I can't function in society, and now I can't even remain upright on two feet."

"How come you can't sleep?"

"I'm amazed. Do you realize that your nephew, who made heaven knows how much money, asks the same questions as everyday people? Makes me wonder if we therapists really know anything at all."

Ruth's smile revealed straight but yellowed teeth. "Maybe you need a woman to talk to instead of a handsome, unattached man."

"Is he handsome? I hadn't noticed."

"Uh-huh. That's why your breath shortened and your eyes glazed over when he stood in the doorway just now."

"I'm not well, remember?"

"Is that why you can't talk to him?"

"Is *what* why?" Jessie was feeling almost normal now with two cups of tea and a year's supply of ingested carbohydrates.

"The fact that you're attracted to him."

"I'm not . . . that's not to say . . . I haven't really given it much thought."

"Mmm."

"Speaking of good-looking men, who's that?" Jessie pointed at a black-and-white portrait over the fireplace.

"That's my husband, Joseph."

"How long has he been gone?"

"About thirty years now. He died of cancer."

"I'm sorry. That must have been very difficult."

"It's never easy losing someone you love. He went quick, unlike most. He didn't suffer much. I wouldn't have had it any other way."

"And that woman in the picture next to him, is she your daughter?"

"No, Joe and I were never able to have kids of our own. That's Rebecca, Ryan's wife."

Jessie was glad she had slipped the one remaining cracker in her mouth, giving her time to digest what she had just heard. "I didn't realize he was married."

"Almost four years. She's been gone eight years now." Ruth let her knitting drop for a moment of reflection.

"She's very beautiful," Jessie said quietly.

"Yes, she was, inside and out. She was compassionate, genuine, and a bundle of energy! She was good for Ryan."

Jessie wanted to ask more about her, but the sound of a car was heard coming up the path.

"Oh dear, today's Tile Rummy. I nearly forgot. Milly's early, though." Ruth glanced at the grandfather clock. "I'll go cancel and be right back."

"Don't cancel on my account. Ryan will be back, and we'll be out of here. Besides, it will give you something fun to talk about to your friends, don't you think?"

"I don't talk about things that aren't my business, child," Ruth replied kindly.

"Oh." Jessie wished she'd learned better manners as a child.

"Maybe you'd like to join us?"

"Never played before, and I never was very good at games anyway. I'm content to just watch."

Milly entered without knocking. "Hey there. Didn't see you on the porch, so I wondered if you were taken ill. But I see you have company."

"Hello," said Jessie.

"This is a friend of Ryan's, came by for a visit," said Ruth.

"'Bout time that boy found a good woman. Come and let me have a look at ya, dearie."

Milly appeared to be in her late seventies, but only her wrinkles gave way to her age. She moved with the energy of a teenager. She was heavyset and short, and her silver hair was set in an old-fashioned bouffant style. She wore bright red eyeglasses and heavy makeup. She sat down at the table where Ruth was spreading out tiles used for the game.

"Come on, child. Get over here. Don't keep an old lady waiting," said Milly with a grin, patting the chair next to her at the card table.

"Um, well, you'd need to teach me. I'm not familiar with this game."

"We'll teach, you talk," replied Milly.

"There's not much to tell. I don't know Ryan, really. Only met him a few days ago."

"Love at first sight. How wonderful." Milly winked at Ruth.

Jessie was at a loss.

CHAPTER 10

Ryan left the stable after tending to the birth of Joanie's foal. Gramps would stay, keep watch, and clean up. Mia was an old pro. This was her third foal, and all had gone well. Watching the miracle of birth was always an incredible experience.

A shower and shave later, Ryan headed for his truck. This adventure with Jessie was a different experience. He'd make one last attempt to keep her there, but he was fast running out of options. When he arrived at Ruth's porch, faint sounds of laughter lilted through the whirl of a blustery breeze.

"Well, son, right on time, we're just starting a new round," said Ruth as Ryan stepped through the door.

"Yes, child, come, come!" Milly chimed.

Ryan placed his keys on the hall table and tried to read Jessie's face. She was still eating crackers and grinning like a Cheshire cat. He sat down in the empty chair at the card table and leaned toward her while Milly and Ruth were talking. "You're just full of surprises."

"She's quite good, son. Maybe even better than you are," Ruth commented wryly as the other two women laughed.

"I doubt that. I've held the record for a long time. I don't plan on losing, especially to her."

"Sounds like a challenge to me, dearie," giggled Milly.

"Care to make a wager, Mr. Blake?" Jessie was smiling broadly.

He couldn't believe this woman was the same one he had left only a couple hours before. "It's Ryan. What did you have in mind?"

"If I win, you take me home to my apartment today in complete silence."

"And if I win?" His eyebrows rose as he shuffled the tiles around on the table.

"I stay."

He looked at her playfully.

"What?" she asked smugly. "Isn't that what you want?"

"If I win, you stay here till Sunday *and* play a game of Truth or Dare with me, on my command." He sat back in his chair, folded his arms across his chest, and smiled.

Milly and Ruth kept very still, enjoying the exchange.

"Truth or Dare?" she said with sardonic contempt. "Grasping, aren't we?" The game was an obvious ploy to get her to break her silence.

"Well?" he snickered.

"Okay, you have yourself a bet."

"What if Milly or I win?" asked Ruth.

"Not a chance," said Jessie.

"Isn't gonna happen," agreed Ryan. "Oh, by the way, Gramps said he'd start tomorrow on the barn. He wants to stick by Mia and her foal today."

Then the game began. Jessie was beaming. She had a hot hand. She could "go down" or put down tiles totaling twenty-five points immediately, which would allow her to play other tiles in her hand. Milly and Ruth were also ready to go down. Ryan, on the other hand, had no play yet. Jessie was sure to win. Fifteen minutes later, she had only one tile left. Her face looked happier than Ryan had ever seen.

Ryan's turn was next. He was allowed three minutes to make as many moves as he could, and he played every tile, then turned over his empty board in triumph. Milly and Ruth smiled but remained quiet. Jessie was dumbfounded.

"In case you're confused, I won," Ryan said teasingly.

Jessie immediately apologized for the insults that spilled from her lips as the picture of Christ from the hallway stared directly at her. Pictures of Jesus hadn't kept her from speaking her mind before, but there was a peculiar air about this home. Her words were lost amidst the laughter.

Ruth nudged Milly. "Why don't you come help me in the kitchen for a few minutes? I'm putting on a pot of soup and could use help cutting up the vegetables."

"Sure, need a refill anyway," answered Milly, grabbing her empty glass of lemonade.

Both ladies casually walked out of the room, chatting and laughing.

Jessie sat still, watching Ryan put the game away. A few minutes passed.

"You okay?" he finally asked.

"Fabulous."

"Reneging on our bet?"

"The thought did cross my mind, yeah. How much do I owe you for the cab?"

"Not sure. We can take care of that later."

Jessie strolled into the kitchen. Ryan, apprehensive, took down the card table and shoved it into the corner where it had stood for the past thirty or forty years. The kitchen had a door to the outside, and for a brief moment he wondered if Jessie had left.

Ten minutes passed before she returned to the living room. She sat cross-legged on the couch, pushing her back as far into its corner as possible. "I'd like to stay here with your aunt. She said it wouldn't be any trouble. I'd stay in the guest room. Technically, in the bet you used the words 'stay *here*,' . . . I would just be more comfortable." *Comfortable? What am I saying? I'd be more comfortable alone. But if I have to choose between Ryan and a little old lady . . .* Jessie looked down into her lap and began fidgeting with the gold band on her finger.

Ryan sensed her vulnerability as she spoke. He found himself wanting to be near her. "So, you're avoiding me."

"I'd like to walk around without wondering which dark corner you're going to be in. Listen, Mr. Blake, I'm not naive to what's happening. I recognize that I need help; I'm just not sure I'm ready. I don't know if I'm even willing to *face* my issues, let alone take responsibility for them. For now, I feel safer blaming others for my problems." She was surprised at the disclosure.

"It's Ryan. While I respect your request, I'm not sure I'm comfortable with your not being under a doctor's care."

"The fainting seems to occur when I miss a lot of sleep and/or dwell on things I'm not at ease with."

"So your fainting today was because I asked at what age you were locked up?"

"I realize I've asked a few favors already, but I must insist on one more thing. Stop repeating everything I say. It's annoying and patronizing. I can't believe your intelligent clients allowed you to use that tactic."

"So if I understood you, you're saying . . ."

"Blake!"

He smiled coyly. "This is what we do, remember? And it's *Ryan*."

"It's what *you* did. I like to think I'm a little more practical and sensitive."

"Meaning?"

"After the first hour, I usually know how to talk to a client. I wouldn't use that tactic on someone like me."

"What would you use then? On someone like you, that is?"

"Smooth. Nice try."

He smiled, knowing she wouldn't fall for it, but it was worth the expression on her face. He was enjoying the conversation, even if it wasn't turning out in his favor.

"I think I fainted this time because I'm exhausted both physically and mentally. I don't believe it was the question you asked. Let's get back to the original topic. I wasn't 'requesting' to stay here, as you put it. I'm frankly informing you."

"So where do I fit into the picture?"

"Call. Make an appointment."

Milly and Ruth came out of the kitchen. Ryan and Jessie had nearly forgotten they were there.

"Well, you two, it's been fun. I enjoyed the game and the entertainment. Hope it all works out between you. Remember, communication and forgiveness go a long way in any relationship. Good to see you again, son," Milly said while gathering her things. She left before Ryan could stand up. Ruth followed her down the porch steps and to her car.

Neither Ryan nor Jessie commented on Milly's advice. Ryan stretched. "Well, I should get back to Gramps. I'll let him know he's off duty."

"You're not going to collect on our bet?"

"No."

"Not at all?" A curving of her lips showed a slight exhilaration.

"Don't get too excited. I said on my command, remember? Not yours."

"Call. Make an appointment," she said, edging toward the front door.

"I'll be by tomorrow. You *are* staying, right?" Ryan asked, still uncertain.

"I'll be here. But don't expect too much. Truth or Dare evokes simple truth, not lengthy explanations."

Ryan stepped onto the porch with Jessie at his side. The silence of dawn had vanished, a midday storm brewing in its place. Darkened clouds overhead bore the threat of thundershowers.

"Storms can be a bit fierce out here. If you need anything . . ."

"Thanks, I'm fine."

"Well, then, I'll see you tomorrow."

"Call . . . make an appointment."

* * *

It rained all afternoon while Ruth helped Jessie refine the art of Tile Rummy. Jessie was determined Ryan would not win their next game. The washing machine hummed busily in the background, her clothes grateful for a cleaning. Ruth mercifully allowed the conversation to revolve around idle nothingness.

"I want to thank you again for letting me stay here. I know it's an inconvenience," Jessie said as she placed the dinner dishes in the sink.

"Not at all, dear. If it were, I wouldn't have agreed."

"By the way, I should let you know that . . . I have bad dreams sometimes. You needn't do anything. It's just that if you hear, well, . . ." It was apparent to Ruth by the way Jessie was frantically splashing the water onto her dishes that this was difficult for her to get through.

"I appreciate you letting me know. But don't you worry none. I'm getting on in years. Hardly wake to my own snoring anymore." She patted Jessie on the arm as she reached for a towel.

* * *

Sunlight reflected on Jessie's fair complexion. Waking to a damp pillow, she wiped her eyes and checked her watch. It was seven-thirty. She had slept over eight hours!

All was silent in the house, and she figured Ruth must be on an outing or in the garden. She walked down the hall to the bathroom. It was time for a nice, hot bath.

The bathroom definitely aged the home. The walls were a pale pink, and one large window displayed a hot pink curtain with tiny embroidered butterflies. The tiles on the sink and floor were off-white with pink and black speckles. Towels were, of course, pink. Not much ambiance, but she assuredly felt feminine.

Jessie located purple bubble bath in a cabinet under the sink, and poured in more than the required amount. Water running, she went to her dresser and collected clean clothing. Taking a quick glance around and not seeing Ruth, she shut and locked the bathroom door in spite of knowing that if anyone had entered, the only image they would have been left with was an enormous bubble with a head.

After a twenty-minute soak, Jessie dressed in jeans and a T-shirt, left her hair down, and retreated to the kitchen in search of more crackers.

Spreading what she found before her, she vowed to leave money for Ruth. She hadn't used all the bubble bath, but she certainly owed for the pounds of crackers she'd consumed.

Suddenly, the aroma of aftershave floated through the air. Its fragrance was definite and indicated it wasn't from yesterday. It couldn't possibly be lingering from yesterday, she thought. "Hello?" she called curiously.

Ryan opened the door from the living room. "Good morning." He had smelled the lilacs when he opened the front door.

"What did you do, get here before dawn to see if I was leaving?" There was a trace of playfulness in her voice.

"No." Ryan came to the counter and pulled up a bar stool. The lilac scent was strong, but he shook it off and became serious. "Gramps was coming home around nine last night from town. Anyway, when he went past Milly's, he noticed it was dark. Milly keeps at least three rooms lit at night, even if she's gone. He thought it odd, so he went to check it out. He saw the stable gates open and the horses gone, and then he walked to the pasture and called out for her. He heard faint moans. When he found her, she was a mess. She had slipped in the rain and been down for quite a while."

"Oh, no," Jessie said, putting her hands to her face.

"Gramps took her to Doc Brady. He has her in the hospital in Summitville. Broken hip and pneumonia. Ruth went to be with her till Milly's daughter arrives from California tomorrow. Once she gets in, Ruth will come home."

"Ryan, I'm so sorry. Is there anything I can do?"

Ryan was noticeably stunned. Jessie had called him by his first name. "Ruth and Gramps have it taken care of. I didn't feel good about your being alone, so I told Ruth to tell you I was coming, but you were asleep. She opted not to wake you."

"I'm very sorry about Milly, but I'm glad you're here."

This was most certainly not the behavior Ryan had grown accustomed to. Jessie was using his first name *and* glad to see him. "You're glad I'm here? Ruth must be using something strong to sweeten her lemonade."

"I haven't been drinking. I actually need a favor, if you're up to it."

"Now I'm really worried."

"Can you take me out to the Miller home?"

"Sam Miller's old place?"

"Your aunt tells me he's trying to rent it."

"He's been trying for almost ten years. It needs to be condemned, not rented!"

"Ruth mentioned your dislike but reassured me it's not as bad as you say."

"Why?"

"Why is it not as bad as you say? Or why do I want to go?"

"The latter." He was enjoying this side of her.

"Well, I've decided I need time to . . . 'find myself' . . . if you'll forgive the cliché. I like it here. I want to stay for a while."

"Did you fall and hit your head on something? Spotted any unidentified objects in the sky?"

"I realize my past behavior hasn't been particularly amiable. I . . . Look, I just don't feel like getting into everything right now."

Ryan paused before speaking. This was the first nonthreatening conversation they'd had, and he wasn't sure he wanted to ruin it.

"Yesterday, you were taking a cab, then moving in with Ruth, and now today you're considering moving here permanently? I hadn't really considered split personality . . ."

"When you put it that way, it does sound a bit crazy. But I know *me*, and *me* needs a change."

"Change is when you take a break. What you're proposing sounds more like running away."

Jessie shifted her gaze to the kitchen window. "If you need some theory in order to make sense of all this, well, I haven't got one for you. If you want to call it running away—although I don't think that's what I'm doing—then fine. All I know is I want to see the Miller place. Do you want to take me or not?" Her eyes became impatient.

"I'm always up for a good adventure. Did you happen to bring some lilacs in here somewhere?" Ryan knew the lilac bushes were well past blooming, but he had to find the reason for the scent.

"Huh?"

"I'm smelling something that reminds me of lilacs."

"Lilacs, no, but I did use some purple bubble bath. It may have been lilac. Are you allergic to lilac?" she asked, sensing his discomfort.

"It's nothing." Ryan was relieved that there was a logical explanation this time.

CHAPTER 11

After pulling into Sam Miller's driveway, Jessie was at a loss for words. Her mouth hung open, and she pushed her sunglasses down the bridge of her nose.

Ryan chuckled. "Not as bad as I say, eh?"

"Well, okay, it's not exactly what I was imagining. Maybe the inside is better?"

Ryan broke into uncontrollable laughter.

The one-story cottage was in shambles. Shutters barely hung over cracked windows on each side of the front door, which was supported by only one hinge. A once-bright red brick covered the outside from the bottom of the windows to the roof line. From the windows down, white aluminum represented a half-finished siding job. Weeds, tall grass, and shrubs did a fair job of hiding the shack from the rest of the world.

To Ryan it resembled the gingerbread house from Hansel and Gretel—haphazardly put together with frosting. He was afraid to go near it, fearing it would collapse instantly, killing them both. "You really want to go in there?"

"Come on, Ryan, you said you liked an adventure." Jessie was practically skipping up the grass-covered walkway.

"A sense of adventure isn't the issue. Getting out alive is," he muttered. Although scared for his life, Ryan was intrigued by Jessie's behavior. She was like a child getting a new toy, albeit a toy that was broken and in shambles. Nevertheless, it was new for her. Delighted in her personality shift, he quickly realized he could become emotionally attracted to her if she were like this all the time.

Getting inside the home was easy, since after Ryan touched the front door, it was no longer on its last hinge.

Sam Miller was the town drunk, and it was evident inside. Broken beer bottles and wall-to-wall cobwebs had become part of the house decor, and the musty air picked up bits of dust in the light. Ryan pictured nights of drinking and gambling.

Jessie's face was glowing, and she was mumbling about a couch looking great on the east wall and her dining room set fitting perfectly in the kitchen.

"You're not really considering this place?" Ryan asked in shock.

"It needs me."

"It needs condemning." Ryan scraped what he hoped was only gum off the bottom of his shoe.

"Know much about plumbing or electrical wiring?"

"Okay, who are you, and what have you done with Dr. Winston?"

"Do you know plumbing or not?" Hands on hips, raised eyebrows, and pursed lips demonstrated she wasn't thrilled with the humor.

"If you're actually serious about this, you should talk to Gramps. His expertise is more toward the electrical, but he can certainly hold his own in the plumbing arena."

"Great, but I'd hate to bother him after Milly's incident."

"Ruth and Gramps will get back to normal as soon as Janet arrives. He'd love to help you out on this. He lives for this sort of challenge. Maybe Ruth will get to keep her barn for a little while longer."

"Look out back at that yard," she chimed, swiping away the spiderwebs and opening the back door.

A grassy field of wildflowers and weeds currently dominated the scenery, but Jessie imagined the beautiful flower and vegetable gardens that had undoubtedly adorned the yard in years past. The back porch would present a perfect view of the evening sunsets.

"So where can I find Sam Miller?"

"You *are* serious, aren't you?"

"Yes." Her excitement was unrestrained.

"Gramps may suggest you gut it and start over. And the outside, well, it speaks for itself. Do you have any idea what a project of this magnitude will cost?"

"I'm sure it will be tremendous."

Ryan searched for a safe spot to sit on the back steps. Finding one, he then leaned back against the only apparent secure post. "Jessie, all kidding aside, it's time to take a hard look at what you're proposing to undertake. It'll take at least a couple months, maybe more, to get this place even livable. And that's working twenty-four-seven. You certainly couldn't stay here during the renovation. What about work? Why not just stay with Aunt Ruth for a few weeks while you work things out before you change your entire lifestyle?"

"You think I'm cracking up, don't you?"

"You know that's not the most popular phrase in our profession, Jessie."

"Okay, how about saying I've lost touch with reality?"

"That works."

She laughed as she sat across from him. "Brace yourself, *Dr.* Blake. You're about to have your breakthrough. Just a little one, though. No pushing; just listen." She turned her face sideways, not looking directly at him. "I've known for quite some time that I'm not much use to my clients." Jessie's moistened eyes were evidence that this was a difficult admission for her. "When I was a little girl, I swore I would do whatever I could to keep other children from hurting the way I did. Social Services seemed to be the ideal setting for me, but it soon became emotionally and physically consuming. When Elliott made his offer, I jumped."

"How long have you known him?"

"We met four years ago at a fund-raiser for St. Michael's Children's Hospital. He'd been searching for a partner with expertise in child abuse issues, his specialty being marriage counseling." Jessie briefly considered the irony as Elliott's marriage had been on a downward spiral for several years. "A few weeks after our meeting, I found myself in association with one of Denver's finest psychologists. Becoming partners with Elliott meant choosing my own work load, my own clients, and, of course, earning a substantial raise. I assumed fewer hours meant less stress. It didn't take long for me to realize it wasn't the number of hours that caused my stress, but it was my desire to inflict pain on those who had harmed my clients. Every time I listened to a child or adult discuss what happened to them, I would see my father, and then my anger would boil up inside. My ability to assist in their healing was hindered." She paused, and her expression softened. "I suppose it would be like a drunk conducting an Alcoholic's Anonymous gathering. He can't possibly assist in the healing and recovery process while he is steadily drinking. It's only *after* he gets on the wagon and begins to heal that he can be of help to others. Likewise, I can't attempt to convince these kids that they can get past their nightmare while I'm still visiting mine."

Ryan remained quiet and motionless. He would wait until her thoughts were complete.

"I'm actually glad Elliott did this, although I'm still not convinced his motives were strictly for my emotional well-being. But that's for another time." She stood, moved from the shade, and glanced around. "It's enchanting and peaceful here. I've been wanting to leave the city for a long time, but I just couldn't bring myself to go through with it. Your aunt has offered to let me stay in her guest room. I could help her in the gardens and such. She won't let me pay her, but I will anyway. I'll buy groceries and anything else she needs. I won't be sponging off her generosity. And—" She stopped abruptly. Ryan looked up to search her face. She looked away for some time before she spoke. "I . . . well . . . I was also thinking that, maybe, I could, after all, use your help in working through some of my . . . I'm thinking Saturdays really would be best, but I do want it to be at your convenience, not mine. I'd pay, of course. If this doesn't work for you, I heard Dr. Milburn in town is good."

"Kyle's all right, but I'm better."

Jessie smirked at his arrogance as she resisted the tears. It had taken years to become independent. Asking for help was a very difficult thing.

"I realize this is none of my business, but can you afford to take time off work, rebuild this place, live here unemployed, and deal with your past?"

"So does that mean you'll have me as a client?" she asked, surprisingly relieved.

"I'm not taking clients, remember? But I will help the best I can."

"I've put away a little for a rainy day. Don't worry. I can take time off and still afford to pay you. Whether your license is expired or not, I would need to anyway. I have to look at you as a therapist and me as a client, or I'll never get through it." She wiped her eyes with the back of her hand.

Ryan watched her closely, confused by her sudden willingness to enter therapy. After all, just yesterday she was thumbing her way back to the city.

"Well, we'd better find Sam before the bar opens," Ryan said simply.

* * *

Clyde's Tavern opened at 11:00 A.M. sharp Monday through Saturday, and rarely closed before 3:00 A.M. *Are there really enough livers in this town to destroy in order to support this place?* Jessie wondered. "It's just now eleven. Are you sure he's here?"

"He's here before it opens, and he's usually the last to leave," Ryan said, turning off the engine.

"Every day?"

"Yep."

"And I thought my life was sad."

"It hasn't always been this way. Sam's been on and off the wagon for as long as I can remember, but ten years ago, getting wasted became a daily routine when the wagon went over the cliff."

"What happened ten years ago?"

"His wife left him for a younger, more handsome, wealthier nondrinker. She gave him ample warnings, but I guess he never thought she would actually go through with it."

"He must have loved her very much if he has to get plastered every day in an attempt to forget her."

"If he loved her, he would have given up the drinking."

"Hmmm. Maybe I *should* look up Dr. Milburn."

She didn't know the full story, Ryan reminded himself. "She wanted him to get help. He refused."

"But you said she left him for a younger, better-looking guy with money, right?"

"Yeah."

"Well, I would guess then that it wasn't just the drinking. Sounds like she may have entertained other motives for leaving. The drinking most likely just became the justification. Ever find out how long the relationship went on with the other guy before she gave her husband *ample* warning?"

This hadn't occurred to him. "Kyle's office isn't far from here."

Jessie smiled in triumph.

"There's Sam," Ryan said, pointing to a short, balding man of about sixty getting out of an old, beat-up Ford truck. The man looked as though he hadn't shaved in weeks, and his clothes looked as if they hadn't seen the inside of a washer for the same length of time. His gut was bulging to the point that the last couple buttons on his shirt were left unfastened.

"Hey, Mr. Miller," Ryan called, climbing out of his truck.

At first Sam didn't appear to recognize the young man coming toward him. Then it registered. "Hey there, kid, what you up to?"

"I'd like to introduce a friend of mine. Jessie Winston, this is Sam Miller."

"Hello," Jessie said sweetly as she put out her hand.

Sam quickly wiped his hand on his jeans before touching hers. "Well, hello, gorgeous."

"Jessie's interested in renting your old place," Ryan said.

"What? That disaster? Not for you, missy." Sam started toward the bar door. "Come in and join me for a drink, though. I'm buying."

"Don't worry. If you want it bad enough, he'll give in." Ryan whispered as Sam disappeared inside the bar. "Just needs a couple drinks in him." Ryan held the door for her.

"Great, now I'm contributing to his vice." It took a second or two for their eyes to adjust to the darker and already smoky atmosphere. "Isn't there any way we can persuade him to talk outside?"

"He'll drink anyway, with or without our company. If you want his place, you have to talk to him in his comfort zone."

Ryan and Jessie sandwiched Sam at the bar and both requested water. Sam glanced back and forth between them. "Not drinkers, eh?"

"A little too early in the day for me, Mr. Miller," said Ryan.

"Been there, done that, wasn't me," added Jessie.

Ryan looked up, surprised at the new piece of information.

"Mr. Miller, I really am interested in renting your place, but it needs a lot of repairs. It may even need to be completely gutted. I'd like to offer you a deal," Jessie began.

"Still thinkin' it ain't right, but willin' to listen."

"I'll agree to renovate it, inside and out, and you allow me to live in it rent free for one year after it's finished. I figure it will take at least two months to renovate, so a year from August, you can kick me out or offer to sell me the property. Either way, you have nothing to lose."

She was right. It was win-win for Sam. The three of them sat quietly for several minutes.

Sam spoke up. "Why?"

"Excuse me?" she asked.

"Why do you want that ugly heap?"

"It's not ugly, sir. It's just, well, depressed. It needs me. I need it. We would be good for each other." She felt slightly embarrassed at her sentiment. It seemed immature, but it was the truth.

Sam spun his stool completely around to face her, "Fine, shake on it."

"Really? Oh, thank you!" Her expression was one of elation. "We should sign some—"

Ryan nudged her roughly. She turned to look at him. Ryan shook his head back and forth quickly, and she shoved her hand out to meet Sam's.

"It's a deal, then," Ryan said as they were shaking. "Thanks, Mr. Miller. We'll have you out in a couple months to take a look at it."

"Don't bother. If I get out that way, I'll stop in. Otherwise, I'll see you, beautiful lady, in about a year or so." Sam ordered another drink, his third since they'd first joined him.

"Ryan, I have to sign something," Jessie said, inhaling a deep breath of the fresh outside air.

"Not in this town you don't. A handshake is law. You have to trust that, at least for now. If he decides to sell it to you in a year, then the paperwork can be processed. In his mind, you're freely renovating the place and occupying it for a year."

"What if he forgets or changes his mind . . . or dies?"

"He won't forget. And think about it—what does he have to lose? You're willing to do all that work for a rent-free year. Why in the world would he renege? I'm sure his liver has a couple of good years left."

"It just doesn't feel right. I'm not used to integrity without legal strings attached."

"That's the way it is around here. Better get used to it if you're planning on staying."

* * *

Driving to the hospital, Ryan mulled over what he'd learned about Jessie in the past few hours. "I'm curious," he said, grinning, "why the turnaround?"

"You mean how come I'm not a witch anymore?"

"Well, I wouldn't say witch *exactly*."

She grinned. "Nothing earth-shattering. A good night's sleep, I think. I woke up feeling, oh, I don't know, relaxed. I could think clearly. Don't get feeling too encouraged, though. I don't know how long it will take till I can talk about . . . well, things. I've spent my whole adult life disassociating from myself. I've told so many lies about my past that I'm sometimes confused about what is truth and what isn't. I really don't know how I'm going to open up, or if I ever really will. At any rate, I've got to get home and pack. I'll need to put a few things in storage, and I have a friend who's dying to rent my place for a while. Up for a visit to the city, or should I make other arrangements?" Jessie asked.

"Wouldn't pass up a drive with you for anything."

Jessie blushed. "I'll take that as a yes, then. Can we head out early tomorrow? We should wait until Milly is taken care of, don't you think?"

Ryan could only stare at the stranger sitting next to him.

CHAPTER 12

Jessie's eyes gazed dreamily out the passenger window as Ryan drove toward Ruth's. Their visit to Milly had been brief; Milly slept the entire time. Ruth was jubilant to learn that the Miller place would soon come back to life.

"Do you mind if we stop at the store? There are a few things I'd like to get," Jessie asked.

"No problem." Ryan slowed for a deer that sauntered across the road. "My stomach's reminding me that it hasn't had anything except a few crackers. Like to stop for a bite to eat?"

"Sure."

"Clyde at the bar makes great burgers."

"The hamburger sounds great, but isn't there anyplace around here that isn't attached to a bar?" *He'll be sure to ask about my drinking now,* she thought.

"There's a hamburger joint where kids hang out after school. Not sure what their menu is, though."

"That'll be fine."

"Were you a social drinker, or was it more?"

I knew it. "Neither."

"I thought you mentioned that you drank and gave it up."

"You're right. I did."

"You're not going to offer a whole lot here, are you?"

"Nope."

"Does it bother you if I drink?"

"It's your liver." Jessie wanted to ask him questions about his religion, but thought better of it. She was certain that Mormons avoided alcohol.

He smiled as he pulled into town and up to the local teenage hangout.

* * *

After the charbroiled burgers, Ryan and Jessie stopped at the country store to pick up a few healthier delicacies. Jessie tossed a load of crackers and some bubble bath into the small grocery cart, deciding on rose scent rather than lilac. She wasn't sure what Ryan's deal was earlier, but she hoped roses weren't a problem too. She found her favorite cookie-dough ice cream, tea, fresh fruit and vegetables, eggs, milk, bread, and hot cereal.

Cal stayed behind the counter, but he stood and grinned each time Jessie walked past him. The grin stayed as he rang up her items, and she smiled sweetly as she dished out the cash for the cab fare.

"Think you gave Cal a slight stroke," Ryan teased as they headed toward Ruth's.

"Why was that, anyway?"

"I'm not entirely sure, but I think it was just your presence."

"There *are* women in this town, right?"

"Yeah, but not as . . ." he stopped and thought for a moment, "educated."

"Ah." She turned to look out the window and smiled.

* * *

At Ruth's, Jessie put Barkley, the cat, outside. Although he meowed pitifully, she ignored him. Ryan helped put Ruth's groceries away and packed a sackful of snacks for the morning trip—Ruth always had better choices.

"Let me know when you're ready," Ryan said.

"Ready, for . . . what?" Jessie asked, confused.

"Well, since Ruth is staying at the hospital tonight, I just figured you'd . . . well, you know . . ."

"No, I don't know. What?" Her voice grew suspicious.

"Jessie, you can't stay here by yourself."

"Oh, come on, Ryan. We're headed into the city early enough."

"Yes, we are, so let me know when you're ready," he repeated as he folded his arms across his chest.

"This is ridiculous, Ryan."

"Your alone time begins Sunday, not before then."

Jessie let out a huge sigh and began to gather up her things. She knew it was useless to argue. She changed the kitty litter and left plenty of milk and food to last until Gramps or Ruth came back. After Barkley returned, she and Ryan headed to the cabin.

When they arrived, they emptied the sacks in the kitchen, and Jessie made an abrupt departure for the room she had used previously.

"Since I'm quite sure this will be the last I'll see of you today, is our seven o'clock departure still on?" Ryan asked.

Jessie didn't comment on his intuition. "Actually, could we leave at six-thirty? That way we can stop by Elliott's office and see him before his nine o'clock."

He left the kitchen in search of her and found her holding onto the doorknob to her room as if it were a lifeline. He leaned back casually against the wall.

"You want to see Elliott?"

"I have some things to discuss. I shouldn't have imposed, actually, so if you're not comfortable taking me to his office, then you can just take me home first and I'll grab my car."

"It's not that I mind. I'm just curious."

"So, you'll take me?"

"Of course."

"Thanks." She turned to enter her room.

"Jessie?"

Here it comes. Truth or Dare. "Yeah?"

"Should Gramps and I plan on you for dinner in a few hours? Say around six?"

She paused, grateful she was wrong. "No, I have some things to munch on. Thanks, though."

* * *

Dinner was a feast, since Gramps usually cooked enough food to feed the entire town's population.

"A lot has happened since I've been in town, so Ruth tells me," Gramps said.

"Yeah, the turn of events has astounded me," replied Ryan.

"Any theories?"

"As to her behavior?" Ryan leaned back in his chair and wiped a smudge of steak sauce from his chin. "I believe she's sincere in wanting to sort out her life. But I think she's running away from reality by buying Miller's place. I also think she plans on making this her permanent residence and ultimately quitting her job. And that's more information than I should have shared."

"A change of scenery never hurt anybody, son," Gramps commented as he placed his dishes in the sink. Besides, quittin' and runnin' away aren't necessarily synonymous. Gonna head upstairs and hit the sack early. I'm headed to the Miller place in the morning. Was kinda hopin' to talk with Jessie a bit tonight, but I suppose it can wait."

"Actually, Gramps, why not? I'm sure she'd like to talk about her plans, and it would get her out of that room."

"Ulterior motives, son?" Gramps winked.

"Of course."

"I don't suppose she'd yell at an old man."

The knock was soft. Jessie put down her novel and eased slowly to the door. "Oh, hi," she said merrily, relieved to see it was Gramps.

"I hope I'm not interruptin'. Ruth mentioned Miller's old place, and since you're headin' into the city, well, I was hopin' we could talk about what your plans were before you left. I'd like to head out that way in the mornin' and take a look around."

"Does this mean you're offering your services? I'll pay, of course." She opened the door enthusiastically.

"Money ain't important. We can discuss that later. But yeah, I'm yours for the takin'," replied Gramps.

"Then I would love to discuss my ideas. Shall we talk here or is Ryan striving to lure me out there?" she teased, pointing toward the family room.

"Well now, I'd be lyin' if I said it hadn't crossed his mind. But I'll respect your wishes."

"I'm sure I'll regret this, but we should go to the table. I've made some preliminary drawings that you can look at."

Gramps retreated to the family room while she gathered her sketches. Ryan watched him come out alone. "Not budging, eh?" he said dejectedly.

"I heard that. I budged," Jessie replied gamely. "But I have a date with Gramps tonight, not you. You have to make an appointment, remember?"

"Can I at least be a silent observer?"

"Didn't know that was a possibility."

"It's been known to happen," he countered.

"Are you two going to keep this up for long? Cuz if so, just hand over the drawings, and I'll muddle through 'em on my own." Gramps glanced at Ryan and then at Jessie.

"We're finished," Jessie said, handing Gramps her sketches of the renovation. She moved toward the cupboard. "Anyone want tea?" she asked.

Gramps and Ryan each declined, engrossed in her drawings.

"Jessie, this is incredible work," Ryan commented when she returned with her own cup. "Have you studied architecture?" he asked, leaning back in his chair. He watched as she cooled the tea with crushed ice.

"A little." Jessie's reply was short before she leaned over Gramps's shoulder. "So, what do you think?"

"Think you're onto some heavy work, missy," he replied, glancing up from the paper.

"Do you have resources for hire?" she asked.

"Sure. There's my buddy Joe, and a few guys in town are always looking for odd jobs. Can I take these with me tomorrow?"

"You bet," she said.

"Think I'll head to my room and look 'em over a bit more." Gramps removed his reading glasses and stuffed them in his shirt pocket. "I'll have tons of questions by tomorrow night. When did you think you'd wanna start this project?"

"Monday. Is that too soon?"

"Don't think so. We'll talk more when you get back if you're not too tired. That'll give us a few days to go into town and get what we need. Ruth don't like me workin' on the Sabbath, so Monday'll be fine."

"Great!" Jessie was thrilled to have someone else energetic about the undertaking.

"Well then, I'll leave you two. Good night."

Ryan stared at Jessie. She instantly looked away and placed her cup in the sink.

"Well, it's good night for me, too," she said.

"Jessie?"

She pretended not to hear.

"Jessie?"

She turned slowly and looked at him, knowing what was coming.

"Truth or dare?"

CHAPTER 13

Death is too merciful for him, Jessie thought. She had let her defenses down, and he'd capitalized. She remained motionless, although she did think about fainting again.

"Are you okay?" Ryan hesitated.

"Oh, sure." She leaned against the sink for security. "Just trying to purge my mind of all the awful, disgusting, nasty names floating about."

"You did walk right into it."

"Thank you. You don't know how much that helps." The sarcastic, frustrated woman resurfaced.

"Shall we head up to the loft?" he asked.

"I gotta go to the bathroom." She fled.

Ryan watched her disappear into her room, picturing her climbing out a window and running.

Fifteen minutes had passed before he heard the bedroom door open and saw Jessie ease her way into the kitchen.

"I'm up here. Got your tea," he said, leaning over the loft balcony.

Jessie sighed and ascended the staircase. Ryan was sitting in the recliner diagonal to the couch. A flannel blanket was on the floor next to him, and she reached for it. Slumping into the leather couch, she wrapped herself like a mummy for some semblance of security.

"Why now?" she asked. "Why not tomorrow on the way to the city?"

"Wanted you to be a little off guard."

"How long do we play?"

"One hour."

"Why do I not believe you?"

"One hour, that's it."

"What are the rules?"

"All questions must be able to be answered with a simple yes or no. Obviously, we tell the truth or go through with a dare. If we choose not to go through with a dare, we add an additional thirty minutes to the game."

"We?"

"Sure, we'll take turns."

This hadn't occurred to her. Maybe it wouldn't be so miserable after all. She would ask him uncomfortable questions, and maybe he would give up this cockamamy idea.

"Any other rules?" she asked.

"Answers must deal directly with the question. We're not politicians. Lastly, we are each allowed two questions that require more than a yes or no answer. The answer must satisfy the person asking but not require more than five minutes to answer." Ryan waited. The ball, once again, was in Jessie's court.

"Truth," she whispered.

Ryan let out a silent breath he was unaware he had been holding. "Are you a recovering alcoholic?"

"No. Is it my turn now?" she asked quickly.

"Yes."

"How many women have you lured up here?"

"Excuse me?" A slight chuckle edged his confused response.

"Problem with the question?"

"No problem. I'm just not sure I can remember *every* female who has ever been here."

"Oh, come on! What kind of answer is that?"

"The truth. Do you have family?"

"Dare," she sneered.

"I dare you to tell me about your family."

"Ah, so this is how it will work. A dare becomes an opportunity to pull out more information. You simply rephrase the question. Isn't that sort of cheating?" She walked to the window, afghan around her shoulders. The sun was beginning to set. It would be an awesome sight as usual—but she couldn't enjoy it.

"You didn't ask if there were boundaries for dares," he said matter-of-factly.

"And you said we weren't politicians. Fine. I have a sister, a half brother, a half sister, and four stepbrothers. My father is dead, and I don't know where my mother is."

"Are you—"

"It's my turn, and I get to ask two since you didn't really answer my first one. Why were you raised by Gramps and Ruth?"

"My mother died giving birth to me. My father never recovered from the shock. He stayed around till I was about five, then disappeared. He told Gramps he was sorry, but he just couldn't deal with life without my mother. I've seen him a few times through the years." This history had been delivered without the slightest hesitation or emotion, as if it had been read off a restaurant menu. "Do you have a relationship with any member of your family?"

"No." Jessie didn't elaborate as easily as he had. "Has Elliott told you the extent of our relationship?"

"No. Do you have a relationship with Elliott other than business?"

"Did. Are you intimately involved with anyone?" Jessie was hoping to throw his concentration. She walked back to the couch and sat cross-legged.

"No." Ryan paused for a brief moment. "How old were you when your father died?"

She was disappointed in his quick response. *How can he not be involved with someone?* "Thirty-two."

"So you lost your father this year." He waited for her reaction, but there was none. She didn't flinch, twirl her gold band, or even blink. "When was the last time you saw your mother?"

"I believe you're jumping the gun again. It's *my* turn. Are you lonely?"

Ryan's eyes narrowed, and a slight smile formed. "I'm not sure I understand the question."

"It's hardly confusing, Blake. I simply want to know if you're lonely."

"In what way?"

"Oh good heavens, if *you* can't be open, then how—"

"Yes," he interrupted. "And no."

"What does that mean exactly?"

"Are you taking your second liberty?"

Jessie sighed and rolled her eyes. This game was ridiculous. She'd save her second liberty for something else. "No."

"When was the last time you saw your mother?"

There it was again. Jessie tilted her head to one side and then the other. The gold band recommenced its twirl. Softly she said, "Ryan, I can't. Remember? I can't spill it all as easily as you'd like."

He pushed the stop button on his watch. "What are you afraid of?" he asked attentively.

"Why did you stop timing?" She fought back tears.

"We'll start back to the game when you answer the question you're avoiding." He was in control again.

"I don't want to play anymore."

"We can continue tomorrow, if you prefer."

"I *prefer* not to play at all." She walked to the balcony. "It's getting late. I want a good night's sleep before we head into the city."

Don't let her go. Ryan immediately dismissed the voice in his mind. He cleared his thoughts and swiftly blocked Jessie from touching the first step down. "It's not late, Jessie."

"This isn't fair Ryan. I'm . . . I'm not ready." She leaned on the railing, swallowing back the tears.

"When *will* you be ready? Tell me and I'll stop. Why are you renovating a fifty-year-old fire hazard if not to have space to heal? Why did you come up to this loft? Somewhere deep inside, you need, even want, to do this. Go there."

"I can't . . . I would have to relive the horror, something I have worked so incredibly hard to forget. And . . ." Her resolve not to cry broke.

"And?" He released his grip and handed her a tissue from the box on the table.

"Oh, what does it matter." Jessie reached up and wiped her checks frantically.

"It matters."

"This is just too fast for me. First you ask about my drinking habits, then my family, then Elliott, then my mother, all within five minutes . . . I just don't want to do this! I'm sorry. I'm reneging." She began descending the stairs.

"Would it be easier if I were a woman?"

"What?" She stopped midstep and turned toward him.

"Would you open up to a woman?" Ryan repeated.

Has he been talking with Ruth? "Look, I freely admit I'm not fond of men, but you're not a man, you're a therapist."

"Thanks—I think."

Jessie slumped down on the stair. "It's like I said before, it's too much at once. I can understand why you chose the game, but I can't do it this way. I'm not sure there is a way." She avoided his gaze. "I'm just uncomfortable."

"But you're still here."

She didn't respond.

"Will you give me . . . something, anything nonthreatening, to work with?"

Jessie spoke slowly and carefully. "I suppose I can talk about my drinking. But the game is over, okay?"

"All right," he said, glad he hadn't grabbed a beer from the fridge when he and Gramps were poring over Jessie's drawings.

She remained seated on the step. "I started drinking when I was around four. While most kids had milk or juice for breakfast, we had liquor. My father was the alcoholic, and he used to tell us that booze cured all hunger." She began sliding the ring up and down her finger. "I just got used to it. While my mother worked twelve-hour days to keep food on the table and a roof over our heads, my father ate, drank, became violent, and then slept it off.

"For enjoyment, he and I and . . . well, the three of us would play a lovely little game called target practice. He would draw a large circle on our bathroom door and then a smaller one in its center. From the couch, we would take turns to see who could shoot closest to the center using his Colt .45. Whoever won got a shot of Jack Daniels or whatever the drink of the day was. We did pretty good since he was plastered most of the time." She paused and stared off into space. "I can't even remember how many times our mother replaced that door, not to mention the disaster *behind* the door.

"As I got older, I used to watch my stepbrothers get drunk at parties. I would tag along, since there was nowhere else for me to go. I'd drink too, and I also got proficient at bartending. As time went on, I enjoyed starting and ending my day with a drink. While some may have called it an addiction, I rationalized it as a way of life—my life. It's just what I did."

She remained quiet for a few minutes before Ryan softly asked, "And now?"

"I stopped drinking completely six years ago. Nothing traumatic caused me to do it. I just decided it was a waste of money, a waste of mind, and a waste of a good liver. I get the urge on occasion for a drink—like now—but I've seen enough damage to lives because of alcohol that I'd just as soon not tempt fate."

Ryan didn't respond immediately, thinking about the detrimental role drinking had played in his life.

"I think I could become an alcoholic if I picked up drinking again," she said.

"Takes courage to admit that."

"It's not courage, just the truth. I need some fresh air. That lilac is quite potent. I thought you were allergic."

Ryan furrowed his brow. "You smell it, too?"

"Uh-huh. I'd like to go for a walk—alone."

"Take Nelly with you if you want. She won't need a leash. Just say 'come' and 'heel' when you want to walk, and 'sit' when you want to stop. She'll obey."

"Teach all your females that, do you?" Jessie sniffed and wiped her nose with the withered remains of the tissue.

Ryan heard Nelly's name being called and caught sight of them meandering down the path to the meadow as the sun began its descent behind the mountains.

Chapter 14

Ryan heard a noise in the kitchen. Gramps had left his room in search of food.

"Hey, heard Jessie leavin' with Nelly. Everything okay?" Gramps asked.

"Finally we were able to talk a bit. It was a little rough, but I have a place to start. She needed some air. Do you smell lilacs?"

"Huh? No, don't believe so. Why?"

"No reason. I did earlier, but it's gone now. Doesn't matter."

"Don't know what's happened to her, son, but she appears to be a good woman. Heads turn when she comes in a room, too. She's clever, with a sense of humor. What more could you want? Don't blow it."

"Blow what?"

"You know what I mean."

"Care to elaborate?" Ryan knew this conversation would not end in his favor.

"The good Lord blessed you with a gem once, son. And, well, if He's kind enough to do it again, consider yourself lucky, that's all."

"Gramps, you're way off about this whole thing. Jessie is a payback. I have no intention of making it something else. She certainly doesn't either." He leaned against the kitchen counter as Gramps finished making his sandwich.

"I've seen her lookin' at ya. I'm not so old that I don't recognize the meanin'."

"Not sure what looks *you're* catching! The only ones I see go right through me like an ice pick. Don't go matchmaking Gramps. It's not right and you know it."

"If you say so. But heed the advice anyway."

"By the way, don't you think it's about time you forgave me for Rebecca? You've carried that anger around long enough."

"It's not anger, son . . ." Gramps stopped. He picked up the plate of snacks he'd made, and headed back to his room.

Ryan retreated outdoors and surveyed the surroundings. There was no sign of Jessie. He knew she would be safe with Nelly at her side, but it would be dark within minutes, and he found himself anxious for her return. He sat in a chair on the porch and replayed Jessie's story of her drinking. There had been three shooting the .45, but she obviously didn't want him to know who the third person was. Ryan tried to speculate as to the rest of her childhood. He paused momentarily and gave thanks to God for Gramps and Ruth.

"Did you miss me?" Jessie came up the path with Nelly, bringing Ryan out of his trance. He was surprised and at a loss as to what response would be appropriate. He could see she enjoyed his uneasiness. "Can I ask you something?"

"Sure," he answered, looking up at her. The remaining ribbons of sunlight highlighted her auburn hair as it was tousled in the gentle breeze.

"When you talked of your mother's death and your father's leaving, you sounded at ease. Has it ever been difficult for you?" She pulled another chair out in front of him and settled into it. Nelly bounded off after an unsuspecting rodent that moved in the bushes. Luckily she hadn't had her bath yet.

"I consider myself very fortunate. Even with my father gone, I had two people who loved and sacrificed for me. Three actually, counting Uncle Joe. Their whole lives changed in that one day. They put up with a lot, since I was a rebellious teenager. For about three years, I don't think Aunt Ruth had a peaceful night's sleep. I realized that when I was seventeen and in jail. It was a long night for me, and very sobering."

"You were in jail?" she asked, shock in her voice.

"My friends and I were drunk and burned a house down. The kid living in it was dating a girl one of my friends was crazy about. We just wanted to scare him, but we got careless. We set fire to an old shed out back of the house. No big deal, we thought, but the breeze turned quickly to wind, and the blaze spread. The whole house was gone within minutes. My friends ran, but I stayed. I tried hopelessly to put it out, praying no one was inside. I spent the night in jail with some unusually ugly people. Scared me to death. Gramps came and bailed me out the next morning." Ryan felt oddly at peace talking with Jessie. He hoped she could feel the same soon.

"Gramps was silent the whole drive. I thought we were going home, but I was wrong. We drove to Timberline Lumber. Gramps gave me a list of materials to buy while he stayed in the truck. By then, I had a pretty good idea of what was going on. We were going to rebuild Mark's house, and we did. Well, *I* did. It took me five months. Gramps worked me to death. I missed three and a half months of school my senior year, so I had to work overtime to graduate. And I had to repay every penny of the rebuilding costs to Gramps. I'm not sure, but I think I might still owe him a few bucks." Ryan chuckled. It was a lesson he had never forgotten.

Jessie sat in silence, entranced by the story of his reckless youth, so seemingly at odds with what he had become. "Wow. And the other boys?" she asked hesitantly.

"They were each from religious families who never *made* mistakes." He spat out the words. "Anyway, doesn't matter anymore." Ryan shrugged indifferently.

Jessie was curious if any charges had been brought against him, but sensed this topic was finished for now. "I do appreciate you sharing, but you did manage to avoid answering the actual question. I asked if it had ever been emotionally difficult to deal with your mother dying and your father leaving," she said patiently.

"I guess I did slide right over that. There were times when it was hard. Kids teased me. Holidays were tough, especially Mother's and Father's Day. Sometimes I was angry, but with Gramps and Ruth in the picture, I never really thought of myself as alone."

The night was now emerging from the shadows. A pale wash of the moon cast itself on their faces as the crickets started their song. Jessie looked toward the star-filled night sky. "Do you believe in God?" she asked. With Ryan's earlier cutting remark regarding the "religious families," she wasn't sure how he would respond.

"Yes. And you?"

"Did once, but now, no," she murmured. "Why do you?"

"It's better than the alternatives, don't you think?"

"No. I like believing we've descended from apes."

"So why do you hate God?"

"I never used the word hate. Besides, you can't hate something that doesn't exist," she replied sadly.

"You despise your nightmares, but they aren't real."

"They may not be real, but they exist."

"You said you once believed and now don't. What made you change?"

Jessie pulled her knees close to her chest as her eyes again began to film over with tears. "He sits up there in heaven, picking and choosing who gets a miracle or even a fair shake and who doesn't. It's like we're puppets. He lets things happen as long as it's what *He* wants. He allows awful things to happen to little kids who can't possibly protect themselves. And the idiots who ruined their lives get away with it."

Ryan stared at Jessie. She had spoken with intense anger for a God she insisted she didn't believe in. Releasing the anger was good. Holding the vengeance inside would deprive her of years of peace.

"People have told me that we're all one big, happy family," she continued. "That we're all brothers and sisters, and He is our Father." Her hands waved toward heaven. "Well, He's a pretty lousy one, then. What father allows his children to suffer and hurt and die because of others' negligence or worse?"

"Who died?"

"What?" *What have I been saying? Why is he asking that?* "My father, remember?" Her whole frame began to quiver.

"I don't think this is a reaction to his death."

"You don't know anything. I'm sorry I brought up the stupid subject. Just let it go," she said pleadingly. Her body was still unsteady as she stood. "Well, unless you're interested in my favorite artist, movie, food, or book, we'd better call it a night. By the way, I wouldn't mind using the jacuzzi now and then. I don't suppose you have a suit that would actually cover my entire back end?" She tilted her head to one side in an attempt to catch his reaction.

Ryan chuckled. "I think I can find something more to your liking if you can give me a minute." Ryan was surprised to find that he *was* intensely interested in all her favorite things, but once again, he dismissed the thoughts.

Jessie remained on the steps, patting Nelly, who had recently returned from her adventure. She was panting and drooling, ready for water and sleep. At least nothing was hanging from her mouth, Jessie thought.

"Here, how about this?" Ryan returned holding a soft pink, one-piece bathing suit that could easily have passed for a bodysuit with a high neckline.

"Perfect. I didn't see this one the other day."

"It was in my room. It belonged to . . . my wife."

Jessie didn't have time to hide her shock. Her eyes opened wide as she stood, and her mouth slightly fell before she spoke. "Rebecca? Oh, maybe I shouldn't." She gently handed it back toward him.

"It would look much better on you than on that hook in the closet," he said, putting his hands in his pockets. Try as he might, he couldn't remember ever divulging his wife's name to her. Jessie still looked hesitant. "Really, it's all right," he reassured her.

"Well, okay, thanks," she said with reluctance.

* * *

Jessie waited for an hour before heading to the jacuzzi, allowing ample time for Ryan to fall asleep. She needed to relax tonight. The suit felt as if it had been made for her, but she still felt a bit uncomfortable wearing Rebecca's clothing. *Why has Ryan kept this?* Heading quickly for the tub, she dropped her towel on the floor and climbed in. The water once again brought a soothing warmth. All was quiet. The peace was refreshing. She couldn't believe she had talked about God. Where had that come from? Over the years, while she hadn't totally given up on the possibility of a Supreme Being, she certainly believed she wasn't on His list of concerns.

"Son? You in here? I'll never understand how you can sit there in the dark," muttered Gramps.

"I like the dark. What's up?"

Jessie froze. The moon had placed a small blanket of light down the center of the tub, but it wasn't enough to see Ryan on the other side. Then she remembered she hadn't lifted the lid before she got in. It was already up. Stupidity was becoming too close a friend.

"Number one priority when you get back tomorrow is washin' that mutt. Can't stand to be near her."

"Got it."

"Uh-huh. You think I'm gonna give in and do it, but I'm tellin' ya, it's your turn!"

"I'll take care of it."

Gramps mumbled a good night and left.

"You okay?" Ryan asked in a whisper.

Jessie was going to make a quick exit but gained composure. "I didn't know you were in here."

"It's been awhile since I gave you the suit, so I assumed you'd been in already. Would you like me to leave?"

"No, of course not. I'd love nothing more than to sit here and chitchat. You were here first. I can come back later." Jessie climbed out, careful to find a dark corner to dry off in. "Didn't you ever consider it unethical bringing clients here?" she blurted.

"I didn't get in the jacuzzi with clients, Jessie. The only time I had contact with them was in my office. Sometimes if the motel was full, which was a rare occasion, they would stay here. But Brecca was here, Gramps and Ruth were around, and horse shows were usually going on, which meant my wife had several people staying here also."

"Oh. So what made you decide to become a psychologist, anyway?" she asked, wondering where on earth that question had come from.

"Wanted to get out of the country and into the big city."

"Then how come you still live here?"

"Actually, I live both places. I have a condo in the city, and I come here mainly on the weekends. I keep this place because somewhere along the way, I grew up and realized what life was really about."

"And that would be . . . ?"

"Joy . . . peace . . . happiness."

"Except peace is a state of mind. Shouldn't be dependent on where one lives." She wished she would have grabbed two towels as her hair dripped continuously down her back to the floor.

"Actually, peace is a state of being. When possible, I chose to live and sleep in tranquility and just visit, for the sake of work, the fast lane of the city."

"But I thought you didn't work anymore."

"Not in the way I used to, no. But I do have some financial deal-ings there still."

Jessie was curious as to what they were, but was tired of talking. She wrapped the towel around her waist and reached for another one.

The stillness was suddenly shattered by the sharp crack of Nelly's bark.

"Ryan, are you back there?" A woman's voice traveled loudly throughout the solarium.

"Oh no, not now." Ryan stood instantly.

"Ryan! There you are," a female voice said as someone hit the light switch on the side of the wall. "What are you doing in there? It's almost eight-thirty! You've already made us late!" The woman finally noticed Jessie as she approached the tub. "Who are you?" Getting no immediate response from Jessie, she looked at Ryan, hands on her hips and eyes wide. "Ryan? What's going on?" She was tall and slender, and her haircut was short and blunt. Her dress was sleeveless and appeared to Jessie to be made of a black plastic wrap. It hugged her scanty waist.

Ryan fumbled with a towel. "Sandy, this is Jessie. She's moving into Sam Miller's old place."

Sandy continued her stare, hands on her hips. "And that's supposed to explain why she was in *your* tub? This takes being neighborly a stretch, don't you think?"

Jessie remained quiet, enjoying this side of Ryan. He was flustered and more than slightly out of control.

"It's a long story. Look, I forgot about tonight—"

"No, really? I thought you had one of those photo-whatever memories. How come you consistently forget me?"

"I didn't actually forget. I mean, I told you I didn't want to go. You said you'd get Monty to take you. What happened?" He was sitting on a bench now, frantically drying his hair.

"I called you Wednesday and told you he had strep throat, and you said you would take me. Remember?"

"What I remember is that I said I'd get back to you, not take you."

"Well, what do you expect me to do now? I can't show up without a date! This is so . . . so . . . so YOU! You'd think I'd learn, but no, I drive all the way out here, and you're *still* going to make me late! I just needed to make an appearance. Is that so much to ask?"

"Calm down. I'll take you. Just give me ten minutes, okay?" He turned to Jessie and said, "Well, looks like you can get back in now, and I'll see you at six-thirty?"

"Ryan, if you're already going to be in the city, it would be ridiculous for you to drive back and leave again in the morning. Why not stay there and I'll get a cab in town and just figure on meeting you at your office when I'm finished packing?"

"Ryan, kiss her good-bye already and lets get out of here!" Sandy's impatience was reaching a new level of intensity.

"Wait out front for me and I'll be there in a sec." Sandy made a slow exit as Ryan continued. "I don't mind the drive. I'd feel more comfortable if I were with you."

"I'm not going to ditch you, if that's what you're worried about."

"I'll be ready at six-thirty."

"It's your call. Frankly, I think you're insane, but then again, I'm certainly in no frame of mind to judge, now am I?"

Ryan smiled and left the room in search of something to wear for Sandy's event. He wanted to tell her to forget it, but she had been there for him at some awful times in his life. It was his turn, no matter the inconvenience.

Jessie indeed took the opportunity to return to the soothing heat of the tub. She was enjoying the quiet and reflecting on Ryan's facial expressions at Sandy's entrance.

"So, you're this week's dessert?" a voice cracked in the silence.

"Excuse me?" Jessie sputtered as she wiped her eyes.

"I said you're this week's dessert, right?" Sandy repeated.

"I suppose that would be your business because . . . why?"

"Oh, I'm not jealous or anything, just curious. You're not his usual type, that's all."

"He has a *usual* type?" Jessie had become quite intrigued now.

"Sure. Me. I used to go to him for help. Mental stuff, you know. He helped a lot. Wanted to die before he came along. Anyway, he and I hit it off, so we became an item."

"I didn't think he dated his clients." Jessie was pumping for more information.

"Nah, he wouldn't get serious till I was through. So I just found a new therapist. Problem solved."

"So, then, you're an item, so to speak?"

"NO!" Ryan said abruptly, adjusting his suspenders as he entered the room. "I mean, we're just friends now."

"Fine. Just finish up and get me to my party!" Her face turned red. She turned and dug her heels deeply into the wood floor, slamming the door as she left.

"I hope she didn't give you the wrong idea about me . . . her . . . us," Ryan said, buttoning his white dress shirt.

"Why would it matter?" Jessie asked, smiling. She had him now. She was in control.

Ryan stopped for an instant, then sat on a bench to slip on his socks and loafers. "It's just that she's not exactly the type of woman I usually . . . I just wouldn't want you to think . . . I'm making a fool of myself, aren't I?"

"Basically, yeah. Didn't think it possible."

"Well, now you've got one up on me. Must feel pretty good, eh?"

"I don't enjoy basking in someone else's misery, Ryan," she lied. She was basking in a most tremendous way.

"Uh-huh. Well, I think I'm all set," he said as he checked himself over. He picked up his keys. "Tomorrow, six-thirty, okay?"

"I'll be ready. Oh, and Ryan, you may want to comb your hair before you leave."

He touched his hair, muttered something inaudible, turned, and left.

Jessie relaxed and burst out laughing. It took her a while to remember how to shut the tub off.

CHAPTER 15

"Please don't die, Katie . . . breathe, Katie, breathe . . . Oh, please no . . . !"

"Jessie, wake up! Jessie, wake up. You're dreaming. Jessie! Jessie!" Ryan was sitting on the edge of the bed. He had both hands on her arms, shaking her gently. His voice was soft yet firm. He'd only been asleep an hour before the moaning began. Jessie's screams were too intense for her to hear Ryan's constant knocking. Gramps waited quietly in the hall.

Jessie suddenly awoke screaming, jerking her body up. She pushed him away, scared and confused.

The light from the hallway cast itself across the bed. Ryan walked over to her lamp and turned it on. Then, returning to her side, he knelt down, careful not to touch her.

"I'm sorry, Ryan, I . . . I didn't mean to . . ." She pulled a blanket up to her chest and leaned back on her pillows.

"Tell me about the nightmare." His voice was soothing.

"It was Katie. She was here, but, no, that couldn't be . . ." Tears now fell.

Ryan remained quiet, though questions swarmed his mind.

"Ryan?"

"Yeah?"

"Will the pain ever go away?"

He suppressed the urge to hold her in an attempt to calm her fears. "The pain you're feeling now? Yes. In time. Would you like something to drink? Tea, maybe?"

"No, I'm fine. I need to try and sleep." She wiped at her eyes. "I'm sorry about all this," she said, embarrassed. "Did I wake Gramps, too?"

"Don't worry about that. That's why we're here, remember?" He stood and walked over to shut the lamp off.

"No, don't! Please . . . leave it on." Her hand reached out to stop him.

He left the room. Jessie pulled the blanket tight around her in an effort to feel secure.

Ryan and Gramps headed to the kitchen.

"She okay?" Gramps asked, sitting down at the table and leaning back into his chair with his arms lying across his chest. He was in his jeans and suspenders, with an undershirt tucked in. This was his usual night attire.

"Yeah." Ryan took a beer from the fridge and sat down.

"Drinkin' at this hour, son?"

"What? Oh, thought it was soda. Don't suppose I need beer or sugar this early." He put the beer down and sighed.

"After Sunday, what happens?"

"She wants to see me on Saturdays," Ryan replied.

"You, or the therapist?" Gramps's eyebrows rose.

"You don't give up easily, do you?" Ryan cracked a smile before returning the beer to the fridge. He took a quick sip of water, then left the kitchen.

Returning to his bed, he tucked his hands behind his neck. Visions of Brecca filled his mind. Seeing Jessie in his late wife's bodysuit had brought back memories. He longed to hold her, to touch her, to converse with her. June and December were the roughest months. She had lived for Christmas. The festive music had permeated the atmosphere of their home on the first day of November each year without fail. The cabin was always decorated to the hilt, with mistletoe hanging everywhere. His heart ached as he drifted back to sleep.

* * *

Dawn's light crept through the room as Jessie stirred. She rolled from side to side, pulling the top sheet over her face to prolong the inevitable.

I wish I could forget Katie's face. Why do I have to see it every time I sleep? Why does her death still haunt me? I've done everything to get rid of this guilt. There has got to be a way to stop these nightmares. Is Ryan the key? He was right. I don't want to talk to a man. I hate men. I hate them all.

Remembering she had to be ready by six-thirty coaxed her to a sitting position. The clock read six-forty-five. After a quick shower, she threw her belongings into her duffel bag and headed for the kitchen.

"Good morning," Gramps said enthusiastically. "Now, I know you're in a rush, but ya gotta eat. I'm not lettin' you go anywhere till you have a couple of eggs and some toast in that belly!"

Well, I suppose I don't hate all *men.* She smiled as she looked around.

"He's outside doin' his usual routine, checkin' the oil, tires, etc. Forgot to do it before headin' in last night. He's already eaten, but I told him you were goin' nowhere till you've eaten too."

"Then I guess I better eat. It smells delicious. Thanks." She put her bag down by the door and sat at the table setting Gramps had laid out. He served a generous portion of sausage, eggs, applesauce, and toast onto her plate. "What can I get ya to drink?"

"I can get it. You've done plenty," she said, heading to the refrigerator. "By the way, how is Milly?"

"Seems to be recoverin' well. She'll want to get better fast. Can't stand to have her daughter hoverin' over her."

"Good morning," Ryan said, shutting the screen door, a wet but finally clean Nelly at his side.

"Sorry to make you wait," she said, returning to the table. "I woke up late, and Gramps says I have to eat." She didn't look directly at him. After last night, she wasn't sure she ever could.

"No problem. As I remember, you're not too squeamish when it comes to speeding through the city. With a bit of effort, I can probably rise to your level of expertise."

"Fine. As long as we reach Elliott before his nine o'clock, I don't care how you get me there." She began eating the feast in front of her, keeping her eyes focused on her plate.

"I'll be outside." Ryan picked up her bag on his way out. "Come on, Nelly, you've had your breakfast."

Gramps put down the tongs he used for the sausage and followed Ryan out. "Ruth ought to be back at home tonight."

"It may take a day or two to pack all her things and get them in storage. I'll call if we end up staying there tonight." Ryan leaned on the truck, waiting for Jessie's arrival.

"Son, I know you know what you're doin' and all . . . but . . ." Gramps stopped, looked down, and dug his boot tip into the dust.

"Go ahead. But?"

"Seems to me she's tryin'."

"And so . . . ?"

"So, I know you're going to try and talk on the road. I'd hate to see it backfire, that's all."

"Gramps, I did this for a living, remember?"

"Did I miss something?" Jessie asked, bounding down the steps with Nelly. She couldn't help but notice the concerned look on Gramps's face.

"Gramps is worried that I'm going to do something stupid that will make you change your mind. He is so looking forward to ripping apart Miller's place. He would kill me if I blew the opportunity for him." Ryan already had her door open, so she couldn't refuse the gesture.

She climbed in and leaned over the driver's seat, speaking through the open window. "Don't worry. Even if he does blow it, I'm still headed back here. If I can't find my way, I'll give *you* a call!"

"That a girl!" Gramps's face lit up. He was smitten. Ryan was glad he was far too old for her.

"So, what's on our agenda?" Ryan asked, pulling out of the driveway.

Keeping her eyes straight ahead, she answered, "Elliott's first, then the bank. After that I'll need about two hours at my place, one trip to the storage unit, then we can head back." She placed her legs Indian style on the seat, appearing to relax.

"That puts us leaving the city around two or three?"

"Yeah, is that a bad time?" She sensed a slight reservation in his voice.

"I have a hard time believing it will only take you three hours to pack your place. Are you planning to look at me at all today?"

"Three hours will do it. The furniture will stay for Linda to use until my place is ready. I've kept moving boxes from the last time, so it shouldn't take very long. It's only me, not like I'm packing a family of six."

"I can help."

"I appreciate the offer, but I would rather do it alone. I know what I have and where I want it to go, and it'll be faster if I do it by myself. Is there a way for you to kill a few hours in the city?" She remained focused on the road ahead.

"Always."

"If you need to stay longer, don't worry. I'm paying attention as to how to find my way back."

"Yeah, I've noticed your eyes haven't left the road. I won't need more time. Besides, I'm hooked to you till Sunday. This way I can be sure I have paid Elliott back in full." He winced slightly. He hadn't wanted to divulge the fact that his payment to Elliott was in the form of favors owed.

"Must have been a heck of a debt if it takes ten days of me to clear it!" The humor eased the tension, and a mutually beneficial silence ensued. Both were happy to enjoy the serene quiet of the road with its accompanying scenic splendor. The wildflowers were in full bloom, carpeting the valley floor with a lush mix of deep green and contrasting colors. Majestic mountains rose to grand heights, taking their positions to either side as sentry to the treasure within.

Jessie's thoughts ebbed and flowed with words and phrases that she might employ in her meeting with Elliott.

Ryan, noting the gradual spread of creases across her forehead, eventually responded. "You look deep in thought."

"I'm rehearsing my speech for Elliott."

"You need a rehearsed speech?"

"Yep."

"How come?"

"Elliott has a way of interrupting me when I'm talking and then changing the subject. I go in with a specific idea to express and leave never having actually stated it. That can't happen this time. That's all."

"Mmm."

"What's that supposed to mean?"

"All I said was, 'Mmm.'"

"Yeah, but it had a meaning."

"Want to talk about that relationship?"

"Nope."

"How about practicing your speech on me?"

"Why is it therapists can't take no for an answer? 'No' doesn't mean, 'let's find a way around that,' it means NO!" Her voice grew in volume with each word. "I don't want to talk about Elliott. Quite frankly, I don't want to talk about anything at all." Her hands began waving at nothing in particular.

He pulled to the side of the road and turned off the engine. "Jessie, look at me."

"No."

"You can't avoid me forever."

"I'm not planning to forever . . . just for a while. Look . . . last night was . . ." She began to squirm. "I'm sorry that I woke you and Gramps. That may be why you're there, but it was embarrassing. Just give me a little time, okay?"

He started the engine and turned back onto the road. "Would you like to listen to some music?" he said.

"Huh?" she asked, apparently lost in thought again.

"Music. It's sound that travels . . ."

"I know what music is. Fine, just none of that country-western lovesick, 'oh, woe is me' drivel."

CHAPTER 16

"Jessie? I mean, Dr. Winston," Tendra quickly corrected herself, "you're not due back till Monday! It's great to see you. Been hectic around here without you." She almost sounded sincere.

"We'd like to see Elliott as soon as possible. We'll wait out here. Oh, and here's a check for a kid who will be by later today to pick up the rest of the things in my office. And this one's to cover the cleaning service. Thanks." Smiling, Jessie turned and sat in the empty seat by Ryan.

Tendra, baffled, quickly paged Elliott and informed him of his visitors. He hung up before Tendra could elaborate.

Elliott entered the lobby. Spotting Jessie, he smiled broadly. His plan had worked. She was back! Before Tendra could get his attention, he approached them. "Hey there! What a surprise." Jessie and Ryan stood as Elliott put out his hand to Ryan.

"Don't want to intrude on a client, but I'd like to have a quick word with you. It's important," urged Jessie.

"Of course. Tendra, let my first appointment know I may be a few minutes," said Elliott. Tendra's third attempt at getting his attention went unnoticed as he, Jessie, and Ryan walked toward his office.

Elliott headed for the chair behind his desk, and Ryan shut the door. Jessie stood directly in front of the desk. Ryan remained a few feet to her side, close enough to see her expressions as well as Elliott's.

Jessie began, "Elliott, I want to thank you. I would never have agreed to talk to someone on my own. That must sound bizarre after my reaction Friday, but it's the truth."

Elliott appeared to be pleased with himself as he smiled slightly, attempting to maintain an air of humility.

"I'm also grateful for the opportunity you have afforded me here. I've learned from you tremendously."

"Jess, you're talking past tense." His smile quickly faded.

"Yes, well, that's because I'm giving you my notice. I'll arrange for someone to come today for my things so the office will be cleared out by closing time. I left a check with Tendra to cover any cleaning expenses you may incur. Also, I will call each of my clients personally and inform them of the change. I won't take any client with me, as per our contract. I'll let them know someone from here will be contacting them soon." She turned to leave. Ryan was shocked at her cold and callous treatment of Elliott. He had learned, however, that with Jessie, one never knew what was coming.

"Wait!" Elliott shouted. "Could we have a few minutes alone, please?" He lowered his voice and glanced at Ryan.

"No need for privacy, Elliott. I'm not out of line. My contract is up at the end of the month. I have vacation days coming." Jessie reached for the doorknob.

"Jessie, at least come back here and talk for a moment. Just the two of us," he pleaded.

She made it clear she had no intention of moving back toward the desk.

"I don't understand. What's happened? Ryan, what is going on?!"

Ryan hadn't seen this side of Elliott. He *always* remained calm.

"Elliott," Jessie interrupted, not wanting Ryan to answer. "I know you're upset, me leaving the clients and all, and I don't blame you. If I'm sounding rude, it's because I've allowed you to influence the path of my life for way too long. I'm simply not able to do that anymore."

Elliott, convinced she wouldn't budge, leaned over his desk and whispered in desperation, "I . . . I've left Lydia."

Jessie showed no sign of shock. "I've heard that before, remember? Besides, that has nothing to do with why I'm leaving."

Realizing he was not going to be able to freely say what he wanted, he asked, "Where can I reach you?"

"You can't. At least not for a while."

"Oh, come on, Jessie!" His calm demeanor had long since vanished.

Jessie glanced at Elliott's clock. "Well, I'd hate to keep a client waiting on my account."

"Ryan, stick around for a minute!" Elliott yelled in despair.

For the first time since the previous night, Jessie stared directly at Ryan before leaving the office.

Elliott walked out from behind his desk and angrily hurled his arms in the air. "What did you do?"

"I haven't done anything," Ryan said, trying mightily to keep his lips from curling upward.

"Then what is going on? Where is she going? How come she's so cold all of a sudden?"

"To use your words, I can't disclose anything. You know that."

"Oh, come on. I've just lost one of my best partners, not to mention the woman . . . Is she cracking up?"

"No, Elliott, she's not."

"It wasn't supposed to be this way." Elliott leaned into his desk, shaking his head.

"Enlighten me. How was it supposed to be?"

"Forget it."

"This may be poor timing, but remember that after Sunday, I'm out of the picture. And we're even."

"Even? You call this *even*? I saved your life, remember! I hoped you'd . . ."

"I'd what, Elliott? Look, you called in your marker. You could have let me in on what your motives were. You never said it had to end with you whisking her off into the sunset. I called you, remember? I asked for some insight, and you refused. I'm helping *her* now. It's too late for me to change sides." Curiosity got the best of him. "Incidentally, did you really leave Lydia?"

There was no reply.

* * *

"A little rough on him, don't you think? I've never seen Elliott so upset. Goes against his nature," Ryan said, turning onto the freeway toward Jessie's apartment. No response. Minutes passed before he tried again. "Want to talk about it?"

The brightness of the sky was fading as storm clouds moved in. It seemed the weather was intent on mimicking her mood.

"No."

"It may help."

"Probably."

Droplets of rain began attacking the asphalt. Within minutes, water was being tossed from the windshield in torrents as the wipers swished across its surface. Their view of the road disappeared.

"Which bank are we headed to?" Ryan asked.

Not wanting to bring attention to her fear, Jessie slowly dug her nails into the leather cushion. "Don't you think maybe we ought to pull off the road till this lets up?"

"I travel in storms all the time. But if it would make you feel better—"

"Just promise me one thing. When we go over a cliff or slam into a semi, make it quick and painless. If I'm left in a coma due, even in part, to what you do 'all the time,' I'd . . . well, I'd think of some revenge."

"I'm sure you would. I *am* being careful. So, what's the name of your bank?"

"Just get me to the Chevron closest to my apartment in one piece and I'll worry about the bank later. Need to get enough gas to get my car back on the road."

"Would music help?"

"No. My heartbeat will suffice for the moment, thank you."

"We could kill time with conversation," he coaxed.

"I would appreciate it if you could avoid using the word *kill.*" The rain was turning to a hail that thrashed wildly against the truck. "Why are you always so calm? It just isn't normal!" Her voice began to quiver.

"Getting upset about something I don't have any control over is useless."

"I suppose, but it's still not normal."

"Want to tell me about your family?"

"Nope."

"Want to tell me about Elliott?"

"Nope."

"Nightmares?"

"Nope."

"Want to tell me who the third person was that shot up bathroom doors with you and your father?"

A little surprised at the question, she tilted her head his direction but answered the same. "Nope."

"This isn't getting me anywhere, is it?"

"Nope."

"Well now, with that out of the way, what do you want to do?" Ryan grinned.

"How about you concentrate on getting me home in one piece, and I'll watch."

"Is Jessie your real name?"

"Excuse me?" Jessie's tone of voice assured him she was flustered.

He asked again. "Jessie—is it your real name?"

"Why would you ask a question like that? What could I possibly have done that would make you wonder if I've changed my name?" Jessie *wasn't* her real name. She'd changed her birth certificate, social security card, and everything else years ago. She'd wanted a new identity. There wasn't any way he could have found this out, though. Not even Elliott knew this piece of her puzzle.

Ryan had been working to take her attention off the storm. "You're avoiding answering the question, and so that says to me that Jessie isn't your real name."

"I'm avoiding the question because it was stupid."

"It's not important. I was only curious."

She began gnawing her bottom lip. "I didn't like my given name, all right?" she said, staring out the passenger-side window. The Chevron, her apartment, and tentative freedom were only minutes away. Ryan noticed she began rotating the gold band on her finger.

The hail was easing enough that further damage to his truck was unlikely. Then the storm was gone as quickly as it had come, leaving behind a soft drizzle that was almost soothing.

"So why the change?"

"Jessie is the name of an artist I admire. Her work is exquisite. Life dealt her a great deal of trauma, yet she endured it well."

"So what brought about the change, exactly?"

"Wow, what do you know, there's a Chevron, and you've kept your end of the bargain. We are still in one piece. Thanks for the lift, Mr. Blake." She was climbing out of the truck before he put it into park.

"I can help you get the gas and take you to your apartment, Jessie."

"No," Jessie blurted through the passenger window. "Look, I'm very capable of walking a half mile carrying a gas can. Shall I call you when I'm finished?"

"You can reach me on my cell phone, and it's Ryan." He jotted his number on the back of a business card. "Let me know when you're ready to head to the storage unit. Might as well make use of the truck."

"That would be great. I'll try and reach you around twelve-thirty or so," she said, glancing at her watch.

"You're not going to vanish to Mexico, are you?" Ryan asked with a grin.

"Mexico is too hot for my taste. Besides, I'm looking forward to having my own place up there." She pointed toward the mountains. "And, Ryan, if I come out of that gas station and find that you're trying to do the 'polite' thing by making sure I get home safely, it will really infuriate me."

Regretfully, Ryan only lingered until she disappeared into the gas station.

* * *

Linda was elated to have a new place. Her phone conversation with Jessie was quick, and it didn't take long for Jessie to pack. Her kitchen, bathroom, living room—including her entertainment center (except for the televison)—and bedroom items took all of two hours to box up. Furniture and TVs would wait until Miller's place was completely ready for living. She taped up everything that would be in storage. Several other boxes remained open for easy access, containing clothing and personal items she'd take with her.

Jessie reached into the almost-emptied coat closet and pulled one last box off the top shelf. She sighed, placed it on the floor, and knelt beside it. Pulling her knees to her chest, she just sat, staring at the box. Finally she lifted the lid and began sifting through its contents— a few photos, pictures painted at age five or six, a small toy, and a stuffed teddy bear. They were all that remained of her childhood. She picked up the bear and held it close. Its once-soft fur was matted beyond help, and the nose had been replaced several times by different buttons, no longer matching the eyes. Buddy had been her confidante on many sleepless nights. Ignoring the photos, she put Buddy back and gently replaced the lid. She placed the bear in one of the boxes that would go with her.

Finished with the apartment, Jessie headed to the bank and withdrew a sizable amount of cash. After she opened an account in Stone Ridge, she would transfer adequate funds. The male teller was overly friendly, and she hoped he hadn't written down her phone number for future use. Linda would answer the phone, and although she'd be flattered by his interest, he, on the other hand, would be baffled if they ever met.

Stopping to use the pay phone at an exit, Jessie dialed Ryan's cell phone. They arranged to meet at her apartment at one o'clock, giving her ample time to pick up a few novels at the bookstore. She would buy a dozen or so, just to keep her occupied for the next couple of weeks. The bookstore was quiet, which was odd for the lunch hour. She made use of the empty aisles, and collected a variety of readings. Susan Wittig Albert, Sue Grafton, and Tom Clancy each had a new novel. She also picked up the psychology text and meditation books she had put on order. The psychology text would only be opened in an extreme case of boredom. For the time being, she was receiving quite enough "personal" study.

Arriving at her apartment just before one, she kicked off her shoes and engrossed herself in the beginning of Clancy's novel. She was on the couch and to page twenty-seven when incessant knocking brought her back to reality.

"Come in," she called.

"I could've been a burglar or someone worse," said Ryan as he opened the door.

"Burglars or someone worse don't usually knock before they enter." Her hair fell to her waist when she stood, a wisp of bangs across her eyes.

"What?" she inquired.

"What, what?"

"You're staring," she replied.

"Am I?"

Nervously, Jessie looked away, reached for a box, and carried it awkwardly toward the door. Ryan reached for it and walked outside. Jessie followed with another box.

"Between my truck and your car, we could get all this up to the cabin. Would save on the cost of a storage unit."

"True. Too big an imposition, though," she said, setting the box down.

"I wouldn't have offered if it were. There's plenty of room in the shed behind Ruth's. We could also hook your car onto mine and pull it so that we could ride together."

"Yes to the storage shed, and no to the togetherness," she said very slowly. "Good try, though. I'm afraid any more questions will have to wait till our first session."

Within the hour, all boxes were secured in the cars, and a final inspection of the apartment was made. She gave a key to the manager along with a description the new resident, then paid for the next year's rent. She'd collect from Linda herself and keep the apartment in her name.

They walked together toward the vehicles. "When exactly *is* our first meeting?" Ryan asked.

"A week from Saturday, if that works for you. "

"What time?"

"You choose," she said, wiping the sweat from her forehead.

"Nine?"

"Nine it is."

"Okay, then. Are you hungry?"

"Actually, yes," she replied, realizing she hadn't eaten since Gramps's delicious breakfast.

"We could eat in the city. Or, if you'd rather, we can get an hour of driving under our belt."

"Let's drive a bit."

"There's a little place called Coal Miner's Inn about seventy miles from here."

"Sounds good." She allowed him to open and shut the door for her.

CHAPTER 17

The Coal Miner's Inn was a dump, but the aroma was a different matter. It was a mom-and-pop establishment *without* the comforts of home. Cleanliness wasn't a highly sought virtue, as was evident by the mound of dust on the fake plants. The booths were covered with red vinyl, worn from years of harboring guests.

Jessie was afraid to touch anything. Ryan shook his head as she took a napkin and strategically placed it where she would be sitting.

"Hey, this dress cost me sixty-five bucks!"

The menus sported nearly the same amount of dust and grime as the plants. Blowing lightly on the cover, Jessie couldn't help but wonder about the kitchen. No telling how much filth one would find in there! She ordered everything well done, including the lemonade. Minutes later, her overdone hamburger, charbroiled french fries, and a rust-colored lemonade were delivered. Ryan was brave and had ordered a rare steak, a baked potato, and a side of vegetables. He, too, ordered the lemonade. They both stared at its color.

"It isn't going to bother me if you get a beer. Don't go changing your preferences on my account. You should know by now that if it mattered, I'd have let you know," Jessie said.

"Yes, you would have." He decided to order a Coke, figuring at least it would be brown because it was supposed to be. Jessie opted to retrieve her water bottle from the car.

"You know, it's not too late to change your mind," Ryan said as she returned.

"I assume you're talking about my moving. What is it exactly you don't like about my decision?"

"I'm concerned."

"About?"

"About a year from now when you realize you belong in the city."

"Then I go back to the city. What's so wrong with that?"

"You're stalling."

"Stalling?"

"You're putting off dealing with whatever's in the city."

"If, hypothetically, you were correct, that would be my choice, now, wouldn't it? I'm certainly not hurting anyone by renovating Miller's old place and beautifying its landscape. I'm taking time for myself and getting the help I need. If it *is* running away, what's the harm? Change is good for the soul anyway." Her words surprised herself as much as they did Ryan.

"Change can be good when it's for the right reasons. You yourself said that peace is a state of mind and shouldn't be dependent on where one lives," he reminded her.

"That memory of yours is a curse, if you ask me. Sometimes it's not a choice between right or wrong. It's a choice between two rights." Her face had a faraway look for a brief moment.

"How long were you and Elliott together?" Ryan asked with what appeared to be oversteamed broccoli stuck to his bottom lip.

"This isn't a week from Saturday. But since you're intent on knowing about this issue, I might as well get it over with." She wiped her mouth and took a couple swallows from her water bottle before she began. "When I started working with Elliott, there was an immediate attraction on both our parts—which surprised me, considering the fact that I hated men. He was subtle with his attention at first, and then he started leaving little gifts on my desk. I didn't feel comfortable accepting them until I'd learned that he and Lydia had split up. Then one night after working late, we got a bit physical. Nothing serious, but enough to make me nervous. I wanted to be positive his divorce was final before I could get intimately involved." Ryan's eyebrows raised slightly.

"Yeah, yeah, yeah, I know, *old-fashioned* is outdated, but there *are* a few rare believers still breathing." Ryan chuckled as she continued. "Elliott assured me that the papers had been signed by the courts and that he was merely waiting for them to be delivered. He made it clear it was over."

Ryan was listening intently, momentarily forgetting the sizzling steak before him.

"We began going out after work and on weekends. While he was in a hurry for a more physical relationship, I still wanted to take things slow. Hasn't Elliott told you this already?" She wiped a dab of ketchup from her chin.

"No. If he had, we most likely wouldn't be here."

"Well, when his birthday came around, I decided to decorate his place and make a romantic dinner. He told me Lydia was living at her mother's, so I knew his place would be free. I took the spare key he had in his office and went there while he thought I was out on business. When I got there, I realized it didn't have the air of just being a man's place. I became curious and checked the bedroom and bath. Feminine articles were everywhere. I had sat down in the kitchen to think things over when the phone rang. Scared me to death. The machine picked up, and it was Lydia. She said his cell battery must be dead because she couldn't reach him." Her voice grew cynical. "And she said since her mom was recovering better than expected, she would be home in plenty of time to have a birthday dinner."

"Ouch."

"I think what hurt the most was that I allowed myself to flirt with a married man."

"He lied."

"That's no excuse for *my* behavior. The papers hadn't come. I had only his word to go on."

"Why do you feel it necessary to take all the blame?"

"Because it was my fault. Somewhere inside I knew—I knew—he wasn't telling the truth. I just for once wanted . . . to be wrong. There isn't anyone else *to* blame."

"Did you confront him?"

"I stayed that night at a motel, not wanting to face him. The next day at work, he was hurt because I had 'forgotten' his birthday. I told him I was sure Lydia hadn't, since she had flown back early from her mom's just in time for the birthday boy. That pretty much said it all."

"How long ago was that?

"Almost three years now."

"And he's still after you?" He shook his head in disbelief.

"I'm sure it's just his male ego. He'll never let go of Lydia."

"What if he truly is leaving her now, for good?"

"I figure, if he leaves her for me, then sooner or later he'll leave me for someone else. He's more unhappy with himself than Lydia. Another woman won't solve that."

"Are you still in love with him?"

"Excuse me?" she asked, stunned.

"I felt the urge to ask."

"Well, keep your urges to yourself! You're good, I'll give you that."

"Meaning?"

"You managed to get me to talk about something that should have waited till our session."

"It makes it difficult if you think everything I bring up is in an effort to probe your mind for some benefit of my own. You freely gave up that information."

It's not his job I hate. It's the fact that he's right all the time, Jessie thought to herself.

"Got another question for you, but this time it concerns me," he said.

Jessie was relieved. "Okay, I'll bite. What is it?"

"Why haven't you asked about Sandy?"

"Unlike you, I know when something is none of my business. Anyway, why do you care what I think about Sandy?"

"Women are usually curious about things of that nature, that's all."

"Hmm. Well, I hate to have disappointed you. Shall we go?" she asked, already standing. She *had* been incredibly curious about Sandy.

During the drive home, Ryan's thoughts drifted to his many unanswered questions and a myriad of conjectures. He considered the voices and the scent. It was, after all, his and Brecca's anniversary month. Surely his subconscious was just working overtime. He'd wanted to visit Brecca's grave today, but it would have to wait till morning.

Jessie's mind was unfolding the previous week's events. How on earth did her life get so complicated? Obviously all the self-help books and psychology texts she'd invested time and money into were failing miserably. They had served their purpose when she'd counseled others, so why was it that none of it seemed to help her? The countless articles she had read on meditation, finding the peace within, and all the others meant nothing at this point in life.

They arrived at Ruth's long before nightfall. Gramps and Ryan unloaded the truck. The day's excursions had taken their toll, and Jessie soon excused herself to unpack and catch some shut-eye. She headed to the kitchen in search of her tea bags.

Ryan followed. "I still have a couple days on Elliott's tab. Wondered if you'd care to join me for a ride and picnic tomorrow."

She looked over her shoulder as she searched through the cabinet. "Ride? As in, on a horse?"

"Yeah, unless you can figure out a way to ride Nelly."

"It's just been a while since I've been riding, that's all. And if we're doing this on Elliott's tab, that means you'll undoubtedly be pickin' at my grey matter."

"Maybe I just want to spend some time with you and show you around your new home."

"Ah, but that sounds more like a date."

"Nope. I merely thought you would enjoy a ride."

"Uh-huh. You said on 'Elliott's tab,' so if it's not a date, then your asking me out is just an attempt to psychoanalyze me before Saturday, is it not?" *Where has Ruth put my tea?!* Frustration was setting in. Cupboard doors began slamming.

"Will you go if I try not to delve into any uncomfortable topics?"

"Good try. You don't know what I'm not comfortable with."

"I have a pretty good idea."

"My tea! Yes!" Ruth had put it behind baking items. Elated, she felt her mood alter. "Ain't gonna happen." She waved the peppermint tea bag around by its string.

He stayed quiet while she used the microwave. At the beep, she politely excused herself but stopped just shy of the door. She turned slowly back toward him. "Oh, um, thanks for your help today. I really do appreciate it."

"No problem."

* * *

After a brief visit to Milly's, Jessie spent the rest of Friday and all of Saturday in her room. She unpacked all her items, placing them in the spaces Ruth had cleaned out for her earlier. Sunday morning started with an early knock at her door.

"Just a second." Jessie threw a robe over her nightshirt and opened the door.

"Sorry to disturb you, dear, but I wanted you to know I was headed to church, in case you needed anything," Ruth said politely.

"I'm sorry I haven't been very good company the last couple days. I've been selfish."

"Happens to all of us from time to time. But if I have to tell Ryan one more time that you're not taking his calls, I'm afraid he'll just end up campin' out here." Her voice was kind but firm.

"I understand. I shouldn't have placed you in the middle. I'll take care of it."

"Thank you. I'll be home in a few hours. It would be nice to see you for lunch today."

"I'd like that. Anything I can do to get it started?"

"No, I'll be back in plenty of time." She hesitated before leaving. "You know, child, it might do you a little good to go to church."

"Not sure I would be bringing the proper spirit."

"Important thing is you *leave* with the proper spirit."

"Maybe another time." Jessie quickly shut the door.

She threw on a pair of jeans and a T-shirt and went outside to the garden. She would pick a bouquet of flowers for the dining room table. That would surely brighten the aura she'd left in the house.

The flower garden behind Ruth's house was magnificent. Rows of pansies, petunias, baby's breath, and various wildflowers lined the patch. Lilac bushes off in the distance brought the only pleasant memories of Jessie's childhood back to mind. She reminisced of playing in the bushes that surrounded her father's home. When she was six or so, she recalled playing Cinderella after school and late into the evening. She'd neglect her household tasks like any normal kid and hide in the lilacs when her father came looking. She'd get quite a beating when she was found, and after the physical pain was inflicted she'd be sent to bed hungry. Nothing could have kept her from those bushes, though. In them, she was free—free to mourn Katie's death, free to imagine a glorious, peaceful world. When she was ten, her father chopped them down to mere sticks just to spite her. It was odd, but Jessie could smell the lilacs even though they weren't in bloom.

She knelt and began clipping roses. *Ruth's been kind. She's let me have my space. Truthfully, I don't know what I'm doing. I should be back in the city. There isn't any way I'm going to be able to tell Ryan about my nightmares. I haven't been able to tell anyone. What good is it going to do me, anyway? What does calling up the past and reliving it do for you? Becoming a therapist was a poor attempt to overcome my issues. I'm not so sure I believe anything I tell my clients anymore.* A shadow surrounded her.

"Need some help?" Ryan asked, bending down.

For a fraction of a second, Jessie's hands froze. "Sure. Thought I'd fill this vase for Ruth. I noticed it was empty and figured it was time for some fresh flowers inside."

Ryan began to pick from the various assortment. "Relieved it's Sunday?" He noticed the all-too-familiar fragrance in the air and looked around quickly before returning his gaze to Jessie.

"I suppose." She sat in the dirt and put the vase down. She brushed her hands clean on her jeans and continued, "I've been avoiding you. I shouldn't have inconvenienced Ruth by putting her in the middle." She glanced at him quickly, and he busied himself in the dirt while she continued. "I was hoping to avoid you for a week or so. Until next Saturday at least."

"Sorry to have spoiled your plans."

"Well, you're off the hook from Elliott anyway. And it's up to me now."

"So it is."

She sat back and nestled herself into the dirt. "I'd like to ask you something."

"Sure."

"Why do you care, anyway? I mean, if a client comes to you once, then doesn't return, is it normal procedure to track them down and ask them why?"

"Not usually, no."

"Then why do you care?"

Ryan had been drawing in the dirt with a stick, hoping this conversation wouldn't come about. He chose his words carefully. "I like you."

"Generally speaking, you don't usually *like* your clients?" she queried, shaking more dirt from her hands.

"It's different." He chuckled.

Her heart beat suddenly faster, spurred on by adrenaline to her bloodstream. "You care to elaborate, or should I just let my imagination run wild here?" She avoided his eyes and continued to shake dirt off that was no longer there.

"First and foremost, I owed Elliott. I had to feel I made the best possible attempts. Besides, you and I both know good therapists are hard to come by. You're needed in this profession. I can help you utilize your own knowledge to help you deal with your past and to get you through this pain. I want to see you get past these nightmares, or at least understand them, and," he paused, surprised at how easily the words flowed, "you remind me of someone I once cared for. I made some mistakes then, and I'm determined not to make them again." He became instantly uncomfortable, fidgeting in the dirt and bending his neck from one side to the other. He had said too much.

"Okay, okay. Don't strain yourself. I get the picture." His attraction hadn't been imagined after all. "Is it Sandy I remind you of?"

"What? No, no, no, no, not in the least." He picked up a blade of grass and placed it between two bottom teeth.

"I'm not sure if that was a compliment or an insult," she said, glaring at him.

"Neither. It's a long story for another time. Are you having reservations regarding my ability to help?"

"Nope. Just wanted to make sure we both had the same agenda. I believe it's unethical being friends or romantically involved during therapy."

"I agree with romantic involvement being unethical, but I wouldn't say being friends is." He instantly remembered his previous conversation with Gramps and Ruth. "I wouldn't even say romance is unethical. Rather, difficult."

"It's unethical for me," she stated firmly. "Look, it's practically impossible for me to trust anyone, most of all men. I've only made one attempt at trusting a man since my childhood, and we both know how that turned out. You *have* managed to get me to talk about him, so from that I conclude that somewhere deep down, I want, need, or at least have decided it's okay to talk to you. But that's all I can concentrate on right now. I don't have the energy for anything else. Being friends would just make it harder for me to open up. If you can be my therapist, then I'm willing to keep going. I know you're not practicing anymore, but that's how it needs to be. If you have ulterior motives, I'll need to seek help elsewhere."

"Understood," he replied gently. "Saturday, nine o'clock, at my office?"

"Thank you." Carrying the flowers in her hands, she headed for the house. "I swear I can almost smell those lilac bushes over there. When do you leave for the city?"

"In the morning." Ryan turned to look in the direction Jessie was gesturing as she walked. It was one thing for him to be smelling Brecca, but why was Jessie able to? "Ruth at church?"

"Yes, I believe so."

"Did she say how long till she returned?"

"I'm sure she said a few hours. Why?"

"Just wondering." Ryan had hoped that with Jessie here, for time's sake, Ruth would go to the Methodist sermon. Obviously she'd chosen to attend the Mormon meetings.

CHAPTER 18

"Jessie? Is that you?" Gramps called from the crawl space under the floor.

"Yep, I've got everything on the list," she answered, dropping the sacks from the hardware store onto the kitchen floor.

"Good. Bring me that torch, will ya? It's by the back door."

"Torch! It's a little late to just burn the place down and start over, don't ya think?"

"I'm just trying to get this water main replaced. This old pipe is almost rotted through. That's why the water in the bathroom was lookin' like weak coffee."

"Ah, have you worked up an appetite yet?"

"I can always eat. Whatcha got?"

"Ruth sent over some of her fried chicken, potato salad, and chocolate pecan pie." Jessie pulled up the old stool and handed Gramps the torch through the hole in the floor.

"That sounds great. Enough for me?" Ryan entered from the hall bathroom wearing denim overalls.

"Hey, what are you doing here? I didn't see your truck. Thought you weren't going to be here till later this afternoon?" she said, pleasantly surprised to see him.

"I jogged over from my place. Decided to cut the week short," he said. Paint was dripping from his T-shirt.

Jessie began dividing up the lunch and handed him a thigh.

"Come look what I've been doing to the bathroom," Ryan said.

Jessie was surprised at his excitement. His calm, in-control demeanor had vanished. She hopped off the stool and followed him.

She and Gramps's crew had spent the entire week cleaning out all the debris and working to get the bathroom done so the rest of the job could be done more comfortably. They'd hung new exterior doors, front and rear, and replaced a couple of rotted sill plates before they had started on the bathroom. With its newly cleaned and polished tile floor, new tub, vanity, and sink, it was ready for paint, and Ryan had apparently taken it upon himself to do this.

Jessie had chosen a soft, off-white color to match the tub. Her childlike glee had been a source of great amusement to Gramps when they had lucked out and found her a free-standing antique tub complete with polished brass feet and matching hardware. Her colors of choice for the room had been mostly white with black and gray accents. She would add red and black curtains, red towels, and black washcloths.

"Well, what do you think?" Ryan asked, standing behind her as she inspected his work. There was no immediate answer. Instead, she continued her inspection, her nose gliding along mere inches from the layer of fresh paint.

"There's a run above the towel rack, but other than that, it looks great."

"What? Not on your life!" He looked past her, and sure enough, there was a slight run of about half an inch. "That? *That* bothers you in this house?"

"Hmm."

"It adds character. It's staying!" His voice rose and he looked at her wryly.

"Okay, okay! I was merely pointing out a slight error," she laughed.

"You two gonna chat all day or can we finish eatin' this here food?" Gramps yelled after his second piece of chicken.

"I ate with Ruth, so you two can have what's there," Jessie yelled back. "Go ahead and eat," she said, prodding Ryan out the door. "I'd like to try out the facilities here."

Gramps was talking when she entered the kitchen a minute later. "Crew got finished late last night, so I told them to take tomorrow off. They'll be back bright and early Monday. We're a bit ahead of schedule. I've been working them like Clydesdales." It had only been five days since the start of the renovation, and if they remained on schedule, it would be at least livable by the middle of September, which was only eight weeks away.

Jessie watched the two men eat while she poured lemonade. She had become quite close to both Gramps and Ruth in a very short time. Tonight Gramps had planned to serve his famous spaghetti dinner, and although she'd already decided to decline an invitation extended earlier, she knew Ryan would most likely try to drag something out of her before tomorrow's session. He would simply have to stick to their agreement.

"Hey, Gramps, I need to cancel tonight's dinner date," she said.

"What? And miss my spaghetti?" Potato salad was smudged on his chin.

"Sorry. There are a couple projects I'd like to finish while I'm already dirty."

"Come now, you're not going to work an old man to death for days and then turn down a dinner, which, by the way, has been simmering since six-thirty this morning, are you?"

"Well . . ."

"Great, see ya at seven then. Whatever you needed to do can wait. We're ahead of schedule anyhow."

* * *

Dinner was delicious. Leftovers would be nonexistent. The men cleared the table while Ruth and Jessie washed and dried dishes. Nelly licked the floor spotless, changing course now and then to be sure not to miss any snacks by the sink. Jessie had to lean over her to finish rinsing out the sink. Experience had taught that if Nelly was in your path, it was best just to accommodate her.

"How 'bout we all play some euchre?" Gramps asked, toying with his suspenders.

"Let's you and I go chat. Haven't had you to myself this whole week," said Ruth, shoving him not so gently out of the kitchen and toward the solarium.

Jessie and Ryan stood alone, listening to Nelly scour every last inch of the floor.

"I'm impressed with how much has been done at your place this week," said Ryan.

"Well, it's not my doing. Gramps has been incredible. By the way, thanks for pitching in today."

"Glad to help, even if I did err."

"So, how come your week was cut short?"

Ryan cast his eyes to the floor. "One of my previous clients was arrested for distributing crack to junior high kids. His lawyers subpoenaed me to testify in his behalf."

"I've never testified in court."

"Believe me, you don't want to. And when I wasn't in court, I was baby-sitting Elliott. He wore me out."

"Elliott?"

"How about if you join me in the loft to unwind and I'll tell you all about it?" Ryan grabbed a beer from the fridge, then left the kitchen.

Jessie picked up Ruth's teapot and a mug and walked slowly to the staircase. *He's up to something. The loft creates the perfect opportunity for him to corner me. Why are my feet still moving?* She tried to relax on the couch, pulling the nearest flannel blanket around her legs. She wasn't particularly cold, but she required the security.

It was early in the evening. The sun hadn't yet begun to set. The light coming into the loft was refreshing. Ryan entered, removed his shoes, and pushed up his sleeves before sitting in the recliner across from her.

"So," she said, bringing the tea to her lips for a swallow, "what's his problem?"

"You."

"He'll get over it. Did you tell him where I'm at?"

"No, of course not. Besides being unethical, the last thing I need is him hanging around."

Jessie laughed softly and listened attentively as he spoke. "Did he leave Lydia?" she inquired.

"I don't know. I'm positive he would, though, if he knew you'd be there with open arms." He was pressing.

Ignoring the invitation, she asked, "So what happened to your client?"

"The verdict came back guilty. He's awaiting sentencing."

"What were you testifying to exactly?"

He cleared his throat, and his answer came out in a professional tone. "'Mr. Albert is unable to control his actions in the same way as you or me. I have no doubt he suffers from multiple personality disorder.' There were a myriad of physicians and psychiatrists present to back up my diagnosis."

"Ah."

"I haven't seen him in over a year. He moved out of the city and found a doctor closer to his residence. I'm still not sure why I was subpoenaed. M.P.D. wasn't particularly my specialty."

The sky had taken on a cast of blue-grey, and a soft spatter of rain could be heard against the drain pipe.

"Looks like it'll turn out to be a cool evening after all. We could use that," Ryan said, closing the window. He settled onto the opposite end of the couch Jessie was occupying. She became instantly squeamish and began twirling the gold band.

"I notice you never take that off," Ryan said conversationally.

"Nope."

"It holds a special meaning?"

She stopped and placed her hands under the blanket, pulling it up around her shoulders. Her heart was speeding. He had invaded her space. Sensing her uneasiness, he crossed to the balcony.

She sighed softly before speaking. "I should be getting Ruth back. I'm sure she's ready to go by now."

"I mentioned to Gramps that we might visit here awhile. He has probably already taken her home, and is on his way back."

She tried not to show her anger as she spoke. "Why would you do that?"

"He mentioned he could use my help tomorrow at your place. He begins bright and early. I thought it would be convenient to have our session now, since we're here."

"Convenient for you, maybe. Don't do that."

"Do what?"

"Presume."

"Figured I could give Gramps an extra hand and work straight through the day."

"You figured at my expense."

"Would you be any more prepared tomorrow than you are now?"

"That's not the point!" She was beyond agitated.

"Jessie, tell me you would be and I'll let Gramps know to expect me later in the day."

She sipped her tea, listening to the rain. She *wouldn't* be any more prepared tomorrow. It was the fact that he knew this that was annoying. He was altering her schedule. *The only positive aspect of talking tonight is that it will give me the opportunity to avoid him clear through next weekend. And sleeping may come easier, since the need to stress about a morning session would be null and void.* Barely audible, she replied, "Fine."

"Did you repaint that spot in the bathroom?"

"What?" This was not the question she anticipated.

"Did you?" His voice soft.

"Did I fix your mistake?" she corrected callously. "Yes, I did."

"Why?"

"Why?! Because it was there. Why does it bother you that I fixed your error?"

"It was an eighth-of-an-inch run, which would be hidden by a hanging towel."

"Yes, I know. I fixed it, remember?" She glared at him. "I know where this is going, and you are way off the mark."

"Am I?"

"I'm not a perfectionist. I just knew it was there."

"Actually, I wasn't alluding to perfectionism."

"What then?"

"Your need to fix things."

"Well, duh! The house is a disaster." *Did I just say "duh"?*

"That's not what I mean."

"My need to fix things is wrapped up in other issues, and you know it. Got another question up your sleeve?"

"The third person involved with shooting bathroom doors, was . . . a friend of your father's?"

"No. My younger sister, Katherine." *How come I offered that so easily?*

"When was the last time you saw your mother?"

"Now you're raising my blood pressure."

"Where would you start if you were me? Tell me where to start, Jessie."

She sighed, eyes wandering for a minute, then yielded. "When I was four, my mother took my sister and me to see a movie."

"When you were four?" he interrupted. "You have vivid memories of being four?"

"No, I'm lying." She rolled her eyes. "Do you want to hear this or not? I can't believe you interrupted me. Do you have any idea how hard this is?"

"Sorry."

"I was almost five, okay? I don't remember what the movie was. That should make you feel better."

Ryan cursed himself mentally for opening his mouth.

"Some kind of cartoon or something, I don't know. I remember being thrilled at the little box of popcorn, drink, and candy surprise that my sister and I got to share." She sipped the tea again slowly. "My mother said she was going to the bathroom and for Katie and me to wait where we were. So, we waited. As people were clearing out, a man in a red vest came over to us. I remember him asking who we were with. I told him our mother had gone to the bathroom. The next thing I remember was sitting out in the front by the candy stand and everyone staring at us. I kept looking at the glass doors, knowing that any second my mother would walk through them. The man in the red vest kept giving Katie and me popcorn, which kept Katie occupied. Then, after a while, a woman appeared. She was very tall. She told me that my sister and I needed to go with her while they looked for our mom." She paused to fight back the tears. "I didn't want to go at first, but the woman was very nice and said she was going to stay with us until our mom came. Typical lie to appease a child. Anyway, I held my sister's hand so tight she began to cry. I couldn't loosen my grip. The woman kept trying to pry our hands apart, but that just made it worse. That was the last time I saw my mother." Jessie sat very still. She hadn't relayed this story in many years.

"What happened next?"

Jessie remained motionless.

"Did your sister stop crying?"

"What?"

"Katie, did she stop crying?" Ryan's voice filled with concern.

She quickly wiped her moistened eyes. "Yeah, after we got in the car, I loosened my grip a little. Her fingers were discolored. I sang her a couple songs my mom used to sing." She stood and walked to the window, quivering slightly.

Ryan leaned into the recliner and watched her. He realized that Katie was most likely a nickname for Katherine. He wondered how the younger sister had died and what Jessie's role had been in the whole ordeal. Why would their mother abandon them at a theater?

"May I ask *you* a question?" Jessie asked, her back still toward him.

"Sure," he replied casually.

"You were right last week. I am curious about Sandy. You've stated that you don't date your clients. She mentioned that you and she were close, and well, you *were* taking her out that night. Obviously, this is none of my business."

Ryan changed positions and began rocking the recliner. It was time to let her in, increase her trust in him. "Initially she was Elliott's client. He sent her my way because he had bit off more than he could chew. His calendar was full, and he couldn't fit her in."

"Elliott didn't have room for a client who looked like that?"

"That's the story he's sticking to, anyway. She came into my practice during an unstable time in my life. It was shortly after Brecca's death. We met weekly at first, then twice a week. I was a safe refuge for her. After a short time, she began showing her appreciation in inappropriate ways. I chose to respond improperly, and we became intimate. I knew it was unethical and morally wrong, but I wasn't much in the mood to analyze the situation. I was angry with having lost Brecca, and well . . ." He paused for reflection, then continued. "I pulled it together enough to suggest she find another therapist. Our personal relationship lasted for several months before we ended it as good friends. We don't have anything in common, really. I just haven't been able to drop it completely. Apparently I look good on her arm when she needs an escort to some flashy club. She brags about having a doctor friend, and it at least gets me out once in a while. She's been kind, considering my foolishness."

"My curiosity was a poor attempt to shift gears," Jessie said, blowing her nose.

"I don't mind addressing your curiosities. I will always be honest."

"Honesty," she muttered under her breath.

"Something against honesty?"

"Highly overrated."

"How do you mean?"

"If you were to look in a thesaurus under *honesty* you would find, among other related words, *fidelity, truth, conscience, moral sense, character, candor, frankness,* and *integrity.*"

"Okay."

"It's been my experience that people throw the word *honesty* around loosely, that's all. Even you have."

"Go on."

"You said you would always be honest, but already in our short time together, you haven't." She walked back toward the couch.

"When haven't I?"

"You lied about the time you'd come back to my office that Friday." She flopped on the couch, folded her legs beneath her, and wrapped herself completely in the blanket.

"No, I didn't. I said I would *see* you at five-thirty. That's what I planned. I did arrive earlier, but I had no intention of seeing you until five-thirty. I merely sat in the lobby. That was your receptionist's error in judgement."

"During truth or dare, I asked you if you were seeing anyone. You answered no. Enter Sandy."

"I'm not seeing Sandy in the way you were suggesting. We're friends. I've explained that. This discussion of honesty is a cover-up for something else. Ready to explore the real issue?"

Jessie didn't want to explore anything. What she wanted to do was flee, but something inside forced her to stay. She cleared her mind and tried to decide what her beef with honesty *was* covering up. Minutes of silence passed before she spoke. "When I asked you the other day if you were lonely, you answered, 'yes and no.' What did you mean by that?"

Ryan took a deep breath before he spoke. "I answered no because, like I said before, I have Gramps and Aunt Ruth, and I'm content in my retirement."

"And the yes?"

"I'm lonely because I miss being with Brecca."

She closed her eyes briefly, accepting his openness. "Trust," she offered. "Trust is my issue of anger."

"Define trust," he said, sitting forward again.

"It means inevitably you'll be hurt. Depend on someone, and sooner or later you'll be let down. I don't want that pain, so . . ."

". . . you don't trust anyone."

"Yeah. I've dealt with my solitary life. I like it. No husband, no kids, no friendships."

"No God."

"Back to that, are we? There isn't a God, so I can hardly be without Him."

"Then why the picture of Christ in your apartment?"

"I thought you were trying to help me find peace."

"I am." He paused. "The reality is, Jessie, if you didn't believe in God on some level, you wouldn't have that painting. Can true happiness exist for you without people and God in your life?"

"True happiness," she scoffed. "I know many people who *have* all those things in their life, and they aren't any happier than I am. I'm not ignorant, Ryan. I understand that a 'full life' means experiencing both joy and pain. You're right. As I said before, I believed in God once, but . . . well, I just don't know anymore. He's never answered my prayers. My life was obviously meant to be filled with pain, not joy. I've grown comfortable with it, and I can deal with it. It's my choice to live life this way, and who does it hurt anyway?"

"You. It hurts you." His voice was tender. "Why are you here with me if not to find happiness?"

"I'm not searching for *happiness*, just peace." Her fingers began massaging the gold band.

"Is one truly possible without the other? Tell me about the ring."

"What ring?" she asked, quickly letting go of it.

"The one on your finger."

"It's a gold band."

"I know that," he chuckled. "What special meaning does it have?"

"Why do you insist that it has a special meaning?"

"Because you twirl it quite often."

"I'm a woman. I have a ring. I twirl it because it's there."

"You're angry."

"I'm not angry," she said, lying. "This isn't working, Ryan. I don't know how to do this." She got up and walked to the window once again. The rain had ceased its rhythmic beat. Opening the window, she took a deep breath of the moistened air.

He chose his next words with care. "To what end do you want to find peace?"

"Oh, no, not that question. I hate that question. That prefaces 'What are you willing to go through to find peace?' Have you ever been asked that? Do you have *any* idea as to the depth of that question?"

"Yes I have, and yes I do." In the momentary silence, he deliberated on his selfish behavior after his wife died.

Jessie turned to face him. "Am I willing to suffer the pain that comes with letting go of self-defeating behaviors?"

"Are you?"

"I've grown quite attached to my behaviors. It's a safer path."

"Safer than . . ."

"The unknown, you idiot. Where on earth did you get your degrees?" She turned her face back to the incoming breeze.

Ryan rose and leaned against the wall next to the window. "Your conscious mind may want to cling to its old and comfortable patterns, but obviously your unconscious is yearning for something else. It's yearning to find some happiness—or peace, if you prefer to call it that. You wouldn't be here otherwise." Taking his gaze off the wet landscape below, he looked directly at her. Her eyes were still fixed on some unseen object in the distance, but she felt his probing stare. He continued. "There's no right way to do this. You know that. I'm not here to pass judgement. I am simply a place for you to express your feelings, air your problems, and lighten your burdens. You'll experience pain either way—the pain you're now in or the pain of letting go. One pain will last until you accept the other. It's up to you to decide how long you want to be a prisoner. I'm offering you freedom."

The words were all too familiar. How many times had she used similar phrases? She was beginning to sense how each of her clients must have felt when presented with these expressions. She pulled away, folded the blanket, laid it on the floor next to the love seat, and picked up the teapot and cup. "It's a misnomer that you or I can offer someone freedom. The choice lies within them, not us. I'd like to go now. A week from tomorrow around nine at your place, okay?"

"Okay," he said, pleased with her apparent agreement to continue. She had offered more than he'd thought she would for their first real session.

CHAPTER 19

Jessie awoke with a jolt. She stayed in bed, leaning her back against the headboard. A new nightmare had surfaced. For Ruth's sake, she hoped she hadn't screamed. Luckily, the clock announced that dawn was just a breath away. She put on her usual morning attire—jeans, a T-shirt, and a sweatshirt.

After steeping blackberry tea, she stepped onto the porch. It had sprinkled again sometime during the night. She enjoyed the crisp air of morning here as opposed to the sticky warmth of the city.

As she sat in the rocker, her thoughts strayed to her new home and its renovation. In a short time, she would have a place of her own. These thoughts filled her with a comfortable satisfaction. Eventually she rested her head back against the rocker, closed her eyes, and drifted into a light sleep, wishing time could stop in this peaceful atmosphere and all her problems would fade away.

The warmth of the sunrise crept slowly up her face, forcing her eyes to open. The brilliance of the emerging day displaced her previous thoughts as its magnificence burned itself forever on her memory.

Momentarily, a distant movement captured Jessie's attention. Peering through the light wisps of steam rising off the moist grasses, she discerned a figure bending over something in a nearby copse of trees. She set off to find her shoes, assuming maybe Ruth needed some help.

* * *

A towel lay by Ryan's side, soiled with the night's rain and muddy leaves that had come to rest on the engraved stone. His eyes were closed as he replayed the graveside prayer through the silence of his mind. That had been a dark day in his life. Brecca had meant everything to him. Would he truly meet her in the heavens, and would she forgive him? He could only wonder. The nearly silent footstep on the crushed stone path invaded the serenity of his thoughts. He looked toward the sound to see Jessie's image slowly backing away.

"Ryan, I'm sorry. I thought you were Ruth. I was trying to leave quietly."

"It's okay. I'm finished." He remained on one knee, picked up the towel, and wiped it one last time over the names imprinted on the highly polished granite surface. "Today would have been our twelfth anniversary. Our son would be almost eight," he said, trying to control his voice.

"You must miss them tremendously," she said, inching next to him. She hadn't known of a son.

"You can have the ultimate life, and then, in an instant, have nothing." He gazed toward the sunrise. Tears swelled in his eyes. He fought the urge to let them fall then quickly stood.

"I should go," Jessie said respectfully.

"No. Please, stay."

She silently read the names on the tombstone: *Rebecca Lynn Blake* and *Joshua Thomas Blake*. She desperately wanted to ask about Joshua but suppressed the impulse. Her instincts were to reach out and comfort Ryan, but that, too, she suppressed.

"Brecca was an incredible woman." The tears now fell in earnest. Jessie related to the pain of losing a loved one. "How come you're up so early?" he asked, briskly wiping the tears that had reached his chin.

"Bad dream." A change in subject would help him, Jessie decided.

"Usual one?"

"Actually, no. This one was incredibly worse than that. Didn't think it possible."

"Got any tea steeping?"

"Of course. Just working on my first cup."

"How about I join you? I could use a cup of coffee."

"And analyze my nightmare?" Jessie asked, sighing.

"You brought it up." He was standing close to her. The scent of perfume was faint, lingering from yesterday, but it was enough to entice him. Silently cursing himself for having such feelings at the side of Brecca's grave, he took a couple steps backward. Here, of all places, it should be lilacs he was smelling.

"I think I've pretty much figured out the dreams. It's just that I can't keep them from coming."

"You're not letting go of something."

"Yeah, I know."

"Want to start there?"

"We have an appointment next week, remember? Besides, last night's session was so you could get an early start with Gramps."

"Don't have to if you're wanting to talk." He half smiled.

"Nope." She was on the verge of anger again. After all, he had begun a day early with last night's session. There was no way she would allow another to follow today. But considering the moment and his sadness, she would bite her tongue. Her face lit up instantly when she turned to look out in the nearby pasture. "Hey, that's an Oldenburg!"

In an instant, she was gone. Shocked that she could recognize any breed of horse, and, in particular, that one, Ryan jogged after her.

Jessie reached the horse and began talking to her. "Hey, girl, aren't you a beauty! How on earth did you come by an Oldenburg?" she asked as Ryan approached.

"She was Brecca's favorite. We got her just before she . . ." Ryan's voice cracked. "How did you know she was an Oldenburg?"

"What's your name, huh, girl?" Jessie was rubbing the horse down from head to tail. She was a brilliant brown with a hint of white on her rear ankles. She stood sixteen hands high, her eyes mirroring kindness and gentleness.

"She's Joan of Arc," said Ryan. "Joanie for short. Good-natured but stubborn. Brecca named her." Joanie neighed at this, perhaps in agreement.

"Where did you find her?"

"Right out of Germany. She was just a foal then."

"So are you the equestrian, or was Rebecca?"

"It was Brecca. And you haven't answered my question yet. Do you show or compete?" He began patting Joanie.

"Me? Not on your life! Never had the courage to compete. Some people I used to live with had stock horses. Once in a while they brought others in to sell, but usually they dealt with quarters and paints. Anyway, I developed an interest. I read everything I could get my hands on. Let's see, so far I've seen a Morgan, an Oldenburg, a few paints, a Walker, and a couple Holsteiners. Now what's that all about?" She pulled gently on Joanie's reins and began walking toward the house.

Ryan walked on the opposite side of Joanie and Jessie. He picked a long blade of grass and began chewing, pleasantly surprised with her interest in horses. He rarely had a conversation with a woman who knew anything about horses. He considered himself fortunate if they knew pony wasn't a synonym for foal.

"Brecca came from a long line of horse breeders and equestrians. Her grandparents lived near Vienna, and they owned a horse enterprise worth millions. Brecca followed family tradition by attending the Vienna School of Riding. She was extremely brilliant in dressage. It was where she belonged."

"So, how did you two meet, if you don't mind my asking," she said, continuing their stride toward Ruth's.

"When Brecca turned twenty-one, she inherited her share of her grandparents' fortune. She moved to the States and opened her own enterprise. A friend of mine was looking to buy a thoroughbred, so . . ."

". . . you landed at Brecca's?" *Of course! Her money must have been left entirely to him.*

"Yeah. For me, well, one look at her and I was hopeless. I opened my mouth on several occasions, but nothing intelligent came out."

It felt good to laugh. Jessie tied Joanie's reins to a post, and she and Ryan took up a perch on the porch.

"I kept finding excuses to visit her. One day, she just up and asked me out. I think she figured I would never get around to it on my own. A few months later, we were married." He paused, picked up a rock, and tossed it several yards away. "And we didn't live happily ever after."

"How about that coffee? If you're hungry, there are some leftover blueberry muffins from dinner." Jessie held the screen door open, awaiting his response.

"Sounds good. You know, though, if you decide to join me here, I'm going to try and pry that nightmare out of you."

"Yeah, I know. It's what you do." She disappeared into the kitchen. Ryan sat alone with his memories of Brecca. He thought of their wedding. He had managed to talk her out of wearing her favorite riding outfit, though he knew they would have been married in the stables if she'd had it her way. Instead, she played the elegant bride at the town's Methodist church. Her family had come from France to attend the small ceremony. They hadn't been pleased at her decision to leave home and set up shop in the U.S. and were equally unexcited with her marriage to a foreigner. Her family stayed two weeks, enough time for them to be convinced of her genuine happiness. In the end, they left satisfied.

"Here you go," Jessie said, handing him two muffins and a warmed cup of coffee.

"Thanks. Come, sit, tell all."

"Well, that's a horrid technique to get me talking," she said as she sat down next to him with her tea-filled mug.

"This isn't a session. Merely two friends talking."

"Oh, here we go with the friend thing again." She bit into a muffin.

"Hey, how come you two are up already?" Ruth stepped out onto the porch.

"Saved!" Jessie sneered at Ryan before looking up at Ruth. "Good morning. I hope we didn't wake you."

"Nope. But I'm a little surprised to see you both out and about." Ruth sat in the rocker and adjusted her robe to protect her knees from the nippy air.

"Jessie found me at Brecca's grave."

"You doin' all right, son?" Ruth asked gently.

"Yeah. In fact, I was just about to delve into Jessie's nightmare before you came along." Ryan winked at Jessie.

"We were not going to delve into my nightmare. Not until next week as scheduled."

Chapter 20

Hail thrashed against Ryan's office window. The city had been drenched with rain for hours.

"Mr. Blake? A Dr. Stone is here to see you. I mentioned you were leaving, but he is being persistent. What would you like me to do, sir?" Unlike Jessie's receptionist, Ryan's assistant was polite and respectful. At nineteen, she had gained his admiration immediately during her interview. Three years later, she still held that respect.

He looked once again at the pouring rain, deciding it would be just as well to stick around the office awhile and give it a chance to let up. "It's all right, Jill. I'll see him." He finished shoving papers into his briefcase and quickly closed it.

After Brecca's death, Ryan had invested her fortune into various areas. He regularly spent time at his city office watching over his assets. His successes helped lessen depression's hold on him. Brecca's horse-breeding organization had brought several interested buyers, but Ryan had refused to sell. After the excitement of the stock market wore off, he had decided to put more effort into restoring Brecca's business. After a couple years, his efforts paid off, and he had become absorbed in the industry. Buying and selling horses became his passion.

Elliott entered, his calm demeanor true to form. "Hello, Ryan. I figured you'd leave early today. I wanted to talk a few minutes." Elliott sat in a chair, unbuttoned his suit coat, and crossed his legs, a sign that he intended on staying a while.

"What's up?" Ryan inquired from behind his desk.

"I would like to know how to contact Jessie." Elliott appeared relaxed, yet his fingers were nervously tapping at his legs.

Ryan answered with a smile. "C'mon, Elliott, we've been over this. I can't tell you anything." He picked up his briefcase and headed toward the door. "You've wasted your time and mine if that's all you came for."

"I figure she's probably at your cabin. It won't take me long to find out for sure. I was just hoping you'd make it easier. I'm beginning to wonder about your motives." Ryan knew Elliott was purposely trying to discomfit him.

"Motives?" Ryan let go of the door handle and turned to face Elliott.

"She's incredibly beautiful," Elliott said coyly. "You two alone at that cabin of yours. And if my memory serves me, it's been quite some time since you've been with a woman. Things happen. It's easy to fall under her spell. So, naturally I question your motives. It's not like it hasn't happened before."

Ryan felt himself pushed toward confrontation's precipice. "In an ugly mood, are we? You didn't question my motives a few weeks ago when you called in your marker. You invited me into this part of your life. I didn't volunteer." Ryan slammed his office door.

"Jill, lock my office on your way out. Call the police to remove Dr. Stone if he's still there in five minutes!" His anger needed to be vented.

Fifteen minutes later, Ryan checked his rearview mirror. He was certain Elliott wasn't following, but he wanted to be safe. He dialed his office on his cell phone.

"Dr. Blake's office, this is Jill. How may I help you?"

"Hi, Jill. Is Dr. Stone still sitting in the recliner, or has he left?"

"He left immediately after you did, sir."

"How immediately?" He checked his mirror again.

"He waited for about one minute, then bolted out the door."

"You didn't give him directions to my cabin or its whereabouts, did you?"

"Of course not, sir." She sounded slightly insulted.

"Any messages I didn't pick up?"

"Yes, two. Sara Matthews needs to reschedule Monday's appointment concerning the buyer from Paris. And Sandy called."

"Did she say what she wanted?"

"She was a bit intoxicated, sir, and I would rather not repeat the dialogue. But paraphrasing, she said she would never forgive you for standing her up at Club Fortune last night."

"Was that last night? I thought that was *next* Thursday!"

"Sorry, sir. The usual flowers and toffee?"

"No. Stopped that a long time ago. Did you remind me about last night, Jill?" he said anxiously.

"I remind you of your professional appointments, sir. You haven't requested that I get involved with your personal ones . . . well, except when I'm sending flowers and toffee . . ."

"Oh, all right! Have a good weekend. One of us ought to." Ryan threw the phone into the passenger's seat. The interstate was packed. Ryan decided a law should be enacted that said no one could leave work early on Fridays. Was Elliott following him? What was he driving? Reaching for his phone again, he dialed Sandy. Her machine picked up and he waited for the beep. "Hey, Sandy, I can't believe I missed last night. I swear I thought it was next Thursday. Look, I'm close to your place, so I'm headed over. I know you're there. Most likely premeditating my murder. Let me in when I arrive."

He took the next exit, watching closely in his rearview mirror. Two cars exited behind him. One was an elderly woman driving rather fast for Ryan's comfort; the other was a man. He was too far back for Ryan to get a good look at him, but the car wasn't Elliott's Mercedes.

After a few turns, the old lady disappeared but the beige sedan stayed with him. Ryan pulled in front of Sandy's condo. He usually parked in the attached garage, but today he would leave his car where Elliott could see it.

Entering the complex, he took the elevator to the twelfth floor then knocked on apartment 12D.

"Go away!" an irate voice from within shouted.

"Please, Sandy, I can explain," Ryan said emphatically.

"Sure you can. You always can! I don't want to hear it. Just go away. Go back to your redhead!"

Down the hall, an old woman wearing curlers peered through her slightly opened door, no doubt in an effort to garner some gossip to share at that evening's bingo game.

He flashed a smile and spoke more softly. "Sandy, I was at the condo last night. Why didn't you call and remind me? I would have come right away. I know it was a big night for you."

"I didn't want to have to remind you again. Just go away."

He turned and, lacking patience, gave the busybody woman a dirty look. She quickly shut her door. He walked to the corner of the hall, lifted up a leaf on a fake tree, and uncovered a key with which he unlocked Sandy's door and slipped inside.

"Forgot about that!" Sandy yanked the key out of his hand. Her robe was striped like a beach ball and her hair was wrapped in a towel. Her makeup wasn't layered on yet. It was refreshing for Ryan to see her normal flesh color.

"You interrupted my bath, so make it quick." Sandy slumped into the nearest chair at the dining room table. "Well?"

"I honestly thought it was next Thursday."

"Uh-huh. Well, one thing's for sure—you've never rushed right over here to apologize. So what's up?"

"I could just be here to beg your forgiveness, you know."

"Right."

"How did last night go, anyway?" He was being sincere.

"It went fine. I felt stupid showing up without a date, but most of my crowd is used to it." She shot him a painful look of disapproval. "Monty said I was the most glamorous woman there and that Ash would outsell Promise." Both were perfumes that Ryan didn't care for. Of the two, Ash was the one whose name and scent seemed, to him, synonymous. But she was making a lucrative living doing what she loved, and she was apparently happy—even if Monty, her agent, *was* taking far too big a cut in profits.

"That's great, Sandy. Are you already working on your next scent? Or are you going to end on this one?"

"What do you think?" She smiled, her anger gone.

"Think maybe I could help pick out the next name?"

"No! That's the best part!"

"I need a favor," he asked quickly.

"No kidding."

"Go over to your blinds and open them. Then make a phone call and pace around so you can tell me if you see a beige, four-door sedan lurking around. If so, describe who's driving it. Don't tell me till you're off the phone and sitting back here."

"Great, now what've you done? I have enough strange people after me without you bringing them around."

"This one's after the redhead, okay?"

"Delightful." She got up and did as he asked. Blinds open, she picked up the phone and called Monty. Pacing and checking out the window casually, she giggled and chatted with him like a teenager.

Ryan, growing impatient, waved his arms to get her attention. Sandy ended her conversation by saying someone annoying was in need of her attention.

"So?" Ryan asked as she hung up and came back to the table.

"Yep. It's parked at the end of the block by the liquor store. There's a man at the wheel, but I can't make out any features or clothing. I think he was alone. Are you going to tell me what's going on?"

"Probably, but not now. Do you mind if I borrow one of your cars for the weekend?"

"Would it matter? You're in luck. Ted took the Jeep to wash it for me. His place is about a block from here. You can go out the back way." Sandy wrote the address on a yellow Post-it note and called Ted to inform him a friend would be by. After she finished, she gently kissed Ryan's cheek and whispered, "It's the redhead that has you all flustered, eh?"

"Her name is Jessie, and I'm not flustered." He took a step back, determined not to allow her to tempt him.

Sandy walked in closer and began to play with the buttons on his shirtsleeve. "I don't have to be anywhere for the rest of the day." She walked her fingers softly up his arm and began stroking his cheek.

Ryan reached over and gently took her hand in his. "Sandy, I don't mean to hurt you . . . It's just, well, I can't. We can't. We both made this decision months ago."

She moved away from Ryan and walked to the window. "Actually, *you* made that decision for both of us."

"I was under the impression it was mutual." Ryan sat down behind the curtain, careful not to reveal his whereabouts in case Elliott was lurking around.

"I just miss you sometimes, you know? Does she know you're Mormon?"

"I'm not a Mormon anymore, you know that. Besides, Jessie is not the reason that I can't stay." Ryan was a bit on edge at the mention of his past. "We don't have anything in common anymore, Sandy. We never really did. I took advantage of you at a time when I was a wreck."

"Ah, so you're all better now, and I'm not good enough." Sandy headed for her purse that was hanging over the arm of a dining room chair. She reached in and pulled out a cigarette, then began muttering under her breath and tossing items in search of her lighter.

Ryan pulled the cigarette out from between her trembling lips. "Don't smoke, Sandy."

"Oh, don't start with that now, Ryan! It's against your religion, not mine!"

"Please, sit down and let's talk a minute."

"Don't want to!" She'd found another cigarette, but her quivering hands couldn't get the lighter to flicker.

Ryan walked over and took the lighter out of her hands. He then escorted her gently to the couch, where they both sat. "Sandy, if I stayed, it would be for the wrong reason. I can't do that to you anymore. It's more than Jessie, and it's not just that we have nothing in common. I've stayed in this relationship because I didn't want to be alone. I'm not afraid to be alone anymore. In fact, it's time I was. And you, well, there's a myriad of men just dying to have you on their arm."

"It's just that I always got the idiots until I met you. No one has ever broken up with me before." Sandy paused and looked into his face. Ryan simply stared back. "I guess from that look I'd better accept that it's time I found someone else. I'm going to miss you." Her bright, piercing blue eyes looked up to study his response.

"You don't give yourself enough credit, Sandy. I've always told you that. Are you still seeing Laura?"

"Yeah. But she's not you."

"No. But her motives are clearly professional. She's good, Sandy. I know she's trying to help you gain confidence. Heed her advice and stop settling for the first jerk that comes along. You deserve a good, healthy relationship. But first, you have to *believe* you deserve it."

"Am I paying for this hour, Doc?" For the first time that morning, Sandy's smile was sincere.

"All right, I'll stop. Thanks for being there and . . . for letting go."

"Well, if it's over for sure, I guess I better get ahold of myself." She stood and brushed her tears away then went to the window again. "Hey, he's standing outside the car now. He's wearing a suit and has a goatee. Looks like that Dr. Stone fella that I went to before you."

"I can't figure him. This is totally out of character. I'll bring the Jeep back sometime Monday. I'll stick the key outside if you're not around. And with all the vehicles you have, you don't have to drive my truck at all, okay? I'm sure he wouldn't bother you, but then I was sure he wouldn't follow me, and I was wrong." She was a lousy driver.

"Worried, are we? I'll try to remember it's not mine and keep it in one piece."

After Ryan left, Sandy returned to her cigarettes and glass of wine and then let the tears fall.

Chapter 21

The envelope and note lay on the bed next to Jessie. She sighed as she turned over. *I can't possibly meet officially with Ryan tomorrow. God, you could show me a sign of Your existence by causing a natural disaster or something. Wasting my breath, aren't I? I suppose confronting issues, crying, and inevitable good-byes can no longer wait.*

"Jessie?" Ruth called as she knocked lightly on the door.

"It's open. I'm just being lazy." She shoved the papers into a book and sat upright as Ruth entered.

"Don't mean to pry, dear, but I haven't seen you all day. I wondered if you needed anything?"

"I'm fine. Just thinking about tomorrow with Ryan." She motioned for Ruth to sit in the chair by the bed. Ruth hesitated, having been crawling through the garden dirt all morning. A few weeks earlier Jessie would have cringed at the thought of anyone dirty sitting in her chair, but farm life had a way of relaxing her neurotic tendencies. "It's okay. As you've said to me time after time, 'Dirt's good for the soul.'"

The week had proven to be quite therapeutic for both of them. Ruth enjoyed the company and the help, and Jessie was enjoying, for the first time, the security and love of one who was, in her opinion, the epitome of motherhood.

"If you want my opinion, and even if you don't, it seems to me that you and my boy have more than the typical doctor-patient relationship. I imagine it would be difficult to speak to him now in a purely professional manner."

"But I thought all this was standard procedure for him. I mean, he brings clients here, they stay in town for a few days, he helps them deal with their fears, and they go on their merry way. So how is this any different?"

"First of all, they don't come against their will. Second, they don't move in with his family. Third, they don't renovate old homes and relocate here. And fourth, none have caught his fancy like you have."

"Oh," she replied awkwardly. "So, what would you suggest?" she asked, turning her red face away from Ruth's fixed look.

"Quit the professional road and admit to being friends. He'll give you the best advice he can free of charge. I'm sure of it. He can't help himself. Why, just last week he was advising me about Gramps's inane behavior of tearing things apart and putting them together again. Luckily, thanks to you, I still have a barn. It's what he does, Jessie. He can't *not* help."

"This I've noticed. I'll give it some thought. It's more my idea to go the professional route anyway. I'm not sure what I need now is a friend."

"We all need friends, dear."

"I suppose, but . . ."

"What are you afraid of, honey?"

"Friends tend to come and go, and well, truthfully, he and I wouldn't be friends if we hadn't been thrown into this."

"Keeping him at a professional distance is most likely safer, I suppose, but I still feel it's too late for that, and that's why you're uncomfortable. Say what you will, but I've seen the way you look at him, and I've seen the way he looks at you. Bottom line is, you're both smitten."

"I don't know about that, really." Jessie sighed. "I almost feel like running away again." She flopped back into the bed.

"How long you gonna keep runnin' till you let someone keep you?"

"That's just it, I don't want to be *kept*. Why is it that everyone believes you can't be happy alone?" Jessie's voice grew tense.

"Are you?"

"Alone? Yeah."

"I meant happy, dear. Are you happy?"

"You're sounding like Ryan now." She smiled, stood, and changed the subject. "May I ask you something?"

"Sure, dear."

"How come no one ever mentions Rebecca?"

A frown creased Ruth's forehead. Jessie immediately felt a twinge of regret for asking. "I shouldn't have asked. Curiosity gets the best of me from time to time."

"It's a long story. And I suppose that I feel it isn't my place to talk about her with you, at least not until Ryan has. Have you asked him about her?"

"No. I almost asked Gramps once, but it didn't feel right."

"Good instincts. Gramps has some things to work out with Ryan concerning Rebecca. It's taken a long time for him to find it within himself to forgive Ryan. Anyway, I would be more than happy to discuss Rebecca after you've spoken with Ryan, okay?"

"Fair enough. Oh, by the way, I found this in a drawer. I didn't know if I should give it to you or Ryan, but since this is your home . . . well, anyway, here." She handed Ruth a lavender-colored leather-bound Book of Mormon. The pages were well used, and many scriptures were marked with various colors of pens and markers. The front was engraved with Rebecca's name in antique-gold lettering. Rebecca had evidently paid a small fortune to have the book rebound in her favorite hue of purple.

Ruth massaged the book gently. "So that's where this went. Thank you, my dear."

"Oh, wait, that's mine," Jessie called in a panic before Ruth left the room. She leaned forward and pulled out the yellowed envelope from the inside cover. "I was using this for a bookmark. Not that I was reading it. I mean, I wasn't being nosy or anything."

"Have you read some, dear?" Ruth's voice was kind, not at all resentful.

"Well, I've just been kind of flipping through it. I'm assuming this is the Mormon Bible? I'm more familiar with the King James Version."

"That's a popular misconception, I'm afraid—that Mormons have their own Bible. They actually use the King James Version. This book is an added testimony of Jesus' existence in the Americas. If you've been reading a little, why not hang on to it for a while? Rebecca certainly doesn't need it, and I don't mind. Just take your time with it. I'd be happy to answer any questions you may have."

"Well, I'm not much into reading about God right now. No offense. It just isn't the right time, I guess."

"No rush, dear. Never know when the right time will come, now, do you?"

* * *

The beef stew was simmering and the pies were cooling when Ryan and Gramps entered Ruth's kitchen. Dinner was only minutes away, and both men were starved.

"Smells mighty good in here," Gramps exclaimed, pinching at the raspberry pie crust.

"Get your fingers out of that till it's time!" Ruth slapped his arm and shooed him into the living room. "Come help me hang some curtains to keep your hands busy elsewhere!" Gramps uttered a quick hello to Jessie over his shoulder as he left the kitchen.

She giggled, turning toward Ryan. "Hey, how's it goin'?" she asked, suddenly feeling her knees weaken. Ryan was wearing a navy blue T-shirt, jeans, and just the right amount of his cologne. She rummaged through the silverware drawer, pretending to look for something. The table had already been set. She felt like a moron—again.

"The week seemed like it would never end." He hopped on the counter and sat above the silverware drawer, where Jessie was still actively searching for nothing. "How about you?"

It had only been a few days since he had last seen Jessie, and only hours since she had filled his dreams. Ryan was looking forward to their time alone tomorrow—certainly for professional reasons. Would he learn what had happened in her childhood? Would he find out how Katie died? What was the attachment to the ring? What were her nightmares about? Did she still care for Elliott? He wondered how many of his questions would actually get answered and how many would be avoided. Ryan tuned into Jessie's voice.

"I helped Ruth weed in the garden, and I learned how to make pie. That raspberry one there is all my doing," Jessie said triumphantly, pointing to the pie in the windowsill.

"Guess I'd better have the lemon then." He was enjoying her nervousness. "By the way, what are you looking for so intently?" He leaned toward the drawer, inches away from her face.

"Nothing we can't do without." She slammed the drawer shut, sauntered to the sink, and washed her hands, mistaking the hand cream dispenser for the liquid soap.

"You okay?" His voice changed to a softer, concerned tone.

"I'm fine. Just like to wash and moisturize at the same time. Anything wrong with that?" She frantically wiped her hands on a towel, avoided his stare, then left the kitchen abruptly.

Ryan quickly assumed that she had decided to cancel the morning session.

Jessie worked herself into helping Gramps and Ruth hang the freshly cleaned, white-laced curtains. Ryan followed suit, and after a few moments work, the project was finished.

"Well, now that that's done, I say let's eat!" Gramps said, rubbing his stomach.

"I'm for that," agreed Ryan.

"Table's all set, Ruth. I'll bring out the salad and stew," Jessie said as she set off toward the kitchen.

"Wanna tell me what's up?" Ryan questioned Ruth as he slid her chair into the table.

"What do you mean, son?"

"She's not herself."

"You still tryin' to figure these women out?" Gramps laughed while seating himself across from Ruth. "Might as well give it up. Ain't gonna happen."

"Well . . ." Ryan's words were interrupted by a clamorous crash from the kitchen. He was the first to reach the scene. Jessie and the stew were sprawled out on the floor. It would have been a moment of laughter if the stew hadn't been so hot.

"Jessie, you okay?" Ryan stepped around the stew and reached to pull her up. Her sun-dress was little protection against the scalding gravy.

"Land sakes, child!" Ruth put both hands to her mouth in panic. "Thomas, get a cool bath started!" Gramps was headed for the bathroom even before Ruth spoke. "Grab a towel, too! Gotta get this dress off. Ryan, get out of here!"

He hesitated, evidently wanting to help.

"Out now, scoot," Ruth yelled. Ryan hastily exited.

"I'm fine, really," Jessie said as Ruth pulled her dress down around her knees.

"I'm sorry about dinner. It's been cooking for hours. I am so sorry." Tears welled up in her eyes. Gramps dangled the towel through the slightly opened kitchen door. Ruth yanked it from him and wrapped Jessie's trembling form. "Dinner is the last of my worries, dear. I'm afraid your skin is awfully pink, and you need that bath whether you want it or not. Now let's go." Ruth put her arm around Jessie's waist and guided her to the bathroom.

Ryan and Gramps waited until they heard talking in the bathroom before they began cleaning up the mess in the kitchen. Minutes later, Ruth appeared and gave her approval of the cleanup then joined them at the table.

"How is she?" Ryan asked.

"She's fine. Wasn't as bad as I feared. She's more embarrassed than hurt." Ruth placed a napkin on her lap. "I see you found the leftovers from last night. Good, there's plenty. She'll come out when she's ready."

"Did she black out?" asked Ryan.

"Not for me to say."

"That was a yes."

"Don't go puttin' words in my mouth now, boy."

* * *

Jessie lay on her bed with a towel draped around her, not wanting to go to dinner. She was still trying to figure out what had happened. *What must they be thinking out there? This was not the evening I'd imagined. I've been sleeping fine, no intrusive questioning, what happened?* Glimpses of her childhood flooded her mind. She remembered having spilt milk one day when she was trying to pour some for Katie. She was spanked with a flyswatter by her father on her naked bottom. It had stung for days afterward. Spilling was not allowed in her home. It was classified as wasting—and wasting resulted in beatings.

* * *

Gramps fell asleep on the couch while Ruth and Ryan finished washing and drying the dishes. "Go on, son, I can finish up here. When Gramps wakes, I'll tell him you're gonna stay here for the night," Ruth said after she'd noticed Ryan looking toward Jessie's door for the third time.

"There's no need for that. I can call in the morning."

"At least say good night to her then."

The knocking was soft, barely audible to Jessie's ears in her half-asleep state. She was just about to say come in when she realized she was still wearing only a towel. The knocking continued.

"Yes?" Jessie answered.

"It's Ryan. I just wanted to make sure you were all right."

"I fell asleep. Sorry I missed dinner. It wasn't my intention to be rude."

"Can we talk a minute? I've made some apple-cinnamon tea. Was hoping you would join me for a cup."

"You're drinking tea?"

"What I meant to say was that I made some tea for you if you're in the mood."

"Ah. Um, okay. I'm a little hungry, too. I'll just need a couple minutes to change."

Ryan retreated to the kitchen to pour some tea and heat a plate of chicken and rice in the microwave.

Emerging from her room, Jessie heard the sounds of a stampede rampaging through the living room. Sure enough, Gramps was snoring on the couch while Ruth read by a lamp next to him. Glancing out the door, she spotted Ryan in the porch swing.

Ryan looked up to see Jessie standing in the doorway. She had put on an off-white, short-sleeved gunnysack dress that fell to her ankles.

"How on earth can she read in the same room with that?" Jessie chuckled as she sat down on the other end of the porch swing.

"Used to it, I suppose." Ryan gently handed her the tea and dinner plate.

"Thank you," she said.

The sun had set hours before, and the crickets were singing as they took in the evening sounds. He picked up a lemonade he'd set on the ground.

"It is so incredibly calming here," Jessie said, oddly feeling at peace.

"It is a relief after a day in the city, that's for sure. What happened tonight?"

So much for the peace, Jessie thought. "Jump right to it, why don't you!"

"I'm concerned."

"I'm not sure what happened. Could make a few educated guesses, I suppose."

"I'm all ears." Ryan turned to face her, pulled one knee up, and rested an arm on the back of the swing. He was prepared for a speech regarding rescheduling.

"Maybe nerves due to tomorrow's session or a conversation Ruth and I had earlier." Jessie closed her eyes, hoping he wouldn't seek for more information.

"Want to tell me about it?"

"Of course not." She began swinging faster.

"You've considered not showing tomorrow?"

"Uh-huh."

"Why?"

She remained silent for a few moments, then decided she might as well get it over with.

"Ruth also mentioned, like you did, that maybe I shouldn't see you professionally. I mean . . . maybe we *could* be friends, and she said that naturally you would help me because you can't not help. But on the other hand, I'm just not sure I can do the friend thing. We've been through this, and the idea itself, well, it scares me . . . and . . ." She was gesturing nervously, her voice quivered, and the plate on her knees began to jiggle. "It's what you do, right? I mean . . ."

"Whoa, slow down." Ryan took the plate from her lap and gently slowed the frantic movement of her hands. Letting go slowly, he said, "Let's start over, slower this time."

"I just can't do it, Ryan. I can't sit on a couch and be probed! My father used to lecture me like that, and . . ." She couldn't finish the sentence. "I know I said I had to be a client, but it makes me too uncomfortable, that's all. So now I'm at a loss as to what to do." Tears began to form. Her trembling hand placed a rice-filled fork into her mouth from the plate beside her. Ryan knew this conversation was draining every ounce of courage she had.

"What can I do to make it a comfortable situation?"

"Turn into the hunchback of Notre Dame, for starters," she replied, food still in her mouth. *Please tell me that I didn't just say that.*

He smiled. "How about we try again to deal with the issue of our mutual attraction and get it out of the way."

Jessie was glad she was still chewing. This made the choking more believable. She gasped for air.

"I've handled being attracted to clients before. It happens. But I seem to be attracted to you on a different level. I haven't come across *that* in a long time," Ryan said.

"Since Sandy?" Jessie sipped at her tea, washing down the half-chewed chicken.

"This isn't even remotely close to what I felt for her. If Sandy had come along when I was sober and in control of my life, a relationship would never have happened. That relationship was wrong. I was weak and foolish, but I learned a great deal from that experience, Jessie. I'd like to believe I would handle a similar temptation a bit better."

"You don't know me, really. Men are always lured by mysterious women. We haven't had a real talk, and we don't have anything in common. Besides—nothing personal—I hate men, remember? If we become friends or more, when this is all over, I'll be hurt again."

"We're both therapists, we enjoy reading, the country, and horses. I think that's quite a bit in common. And you're intelligent. I believe your hatred for men will lessen as you heal. When this is all over, as you put it, you may be possibly sad, but not hurt. I know you've been hurt many times over, and for that I'm truly sorry. But I have absolutely no intention of hurting you, and someday when you're in a different place of understanding, this will make sense to you. For now, you're going to have to trust me. This is where it begins, Jessie. You have to trust me. I won't make any advances. If we don't ride off into the sunset, it will be a mutual choice, not mine alone."

"What if I hurt you?"

"It's my choice to care for you, and I'm not naive, Jessie. I know that when you heal—and you will—that you may need to leave. You'll have to find where you fit, and it may not be here or with me. But knowing that doesn't change my attraction."

"Maybe I *should* make an appointment with Kyle." Sadness filled her voice.

"To achieve what end?"

"I'm not attracted to him."

"If you believe, deep inside, that you can and will open up to him, then I'll respect your decision. My foremost concern is for your well-being. My attraction is entirely secondary. But I believe that if we mutually agree to put our romantic feelings aside, I can help you."

She rearranged herself on the swing. Her feet were now tucked under her, and she was sitting sideways, facing him. "I'm not sure how I'm feeling right now. Having to tell you all the facts I know I'll ultimately have to tell you, well, that creates a whole new terror."

"Why are you attracted to me exactly?"

"What? Your ego need a boost or something?"

"No," he laughed, "I'd just like to hear why."

"You're trying to find out if I'm attracted to you because you listen to me, you're there for me, and you accept me for who I am, or if I'm looking at our relationship as a replacement for the father I never had. Essentially, you're curious to see if my feelings for you are because of your role in my life."

"You'll make a great therapist."

"Well now, I have no idea. I don't know you personally, really, any more than you know me. Right now, you annoy me. You're arrogant, wealthy, and way too calm about everything. I don't know how to have you help me as a 'friend.' I have come to the conclusion, though, that sessions in an office won't work. I'll never open up that way. On the other hand, maybe that's ultimately the best route to take."

"Is that what you're choosing, then?"

"I don't know." She stretched and began pacing.

"What did your father lecture about?"

"Huh?"

"You said your father lectured you. Can you tell me what about?"

"Life," she sighed. "Different topics arose each week. Why do *you* think I blacked out?"

"Could be from lack of sleep, but most likely it was a form of avoidance. When it happens, you're probably thinking of something traumatic and can't deal with it on a conscious level, so as a form of survival, your mind shuts down. Or you have a brain tumor and only have a few days left to live."

"Thanks." She smiled faintly then sat next to him again and picked up her tea. "I'd like to take a ride tomorrow. Would it be all right with you if I borrowed one of your horses?"

"Of course. Would you like some company?"

"Depends. Are you going to talk?"

"It's what I do best."

"I'll make a decision tonight about where all of this is headed and let you know tomorrow. I'll be ready by ten."

CHAPTER 22

Midmorning, Ruth found Jessie at the kitchen table partaking of her ritual tea and crackers. Jessie's fingernails tapped rapidly to some unfamiliar tune. A picnic basket was packed by the door.

"Good morning! You're feeling better, I take it," Ruth greeted.

Jessie's cup shook with the startling noise, sending minuscule rivulets of warm tea through her fingers.

"Sorry about that, dear. Didn't mean to startle you." Ruth selected an apple from the bowl of fruit on the table and settled heavily into the chair across from Jessie.

"That's all right. I didn't hear you come in."

"That's because you're concentrating so intently on something else. What's up?"

"Last night, when I kind of liked Ryan, I sort of agreed to let him join me in a ride this morning."

"Wow!" Ruth's shock was apparent.

"Yeah, of course, now I'm regretting it. By the way, do you know what's happened to his truck? He drove a Jeep here last night."

"A Jeep? Hadn't noticed. Maybe it's getting worked on. It will be a splendid day for a ride. Miller Falls is spectacular, especially this time of year. Wish I were up for a ride," Ruth said quietly.

"You're welcome to join us. I don't mind. In fact, it would be great." Jessie rose swiftly and headed for the refrigerator. "How about I get some more food, and . . ."

"No, no, dear, I'm stayin' put. Just said I wanted to go. Ain't plannin' to put these old bones through that! Come, child, don't be so nervous. Everything will be just fine."

Disappointed, Jessie returned to her tea. "After our conversation last night, I'm not sure if I'm a friend or a client. I don't think I'm ready for all this."

"Yes, you are, dear, you just need to be patient. Be yourself and don't tell him what you think he wants to hear."

"I know. I tell that to my clients regularly. Everyone tends to think therapists are looking for something in particular, but really, *their* reality or truth is the only thing that is therapeutic. In the beginning, it's often hard to get at. I've always asked my clients to do one of two things: to start at what they perceive as the beginning or to tell me what's going through their mind at that exact moment." Ruth listened intently. "If Ryan would ask me to do either one of those, I would be forced to fabricate something. The beginning of what, exactly? And what on earth would it matter what I was thinking at some exact moment? I could be thinking about the marvelous fragrance of the wildflowers, or if I had packed enough food, or how my new place is coming along. I may be wondering if Miller Falls was named after Sam Miller, or if Ryan is allergic to lilacs. See? What possible conclusion can one draw because I am thinking of wildflowers? I've built a practice using questions like that, and now I'm beginning to wonder just how many people I've really helped." She let out a sigh, then froze as she smelled the slight scent of Polo on the breeze. "He's standing behind me, isn't he?" she whispered. Her face a flushed red. Ruth smiled, nodding gently.

"I'm amazed you can speak so intensely without breathing," Ryan said, leaning over to snatch a bagel from another bowl on the table. He chose a seat next to Jessie.

"Well, if you two will excuse me, I think it's time for my morning bath. Will you be back for dinner, or should I just mind my own business?"

Jessie dealt with her embarrassment by shutting her eyes and wishing the world away.

Ryan spoke up. "Don't worry about us. Not positive when we'll be heading back. But from the look of that basket, I'm sure we'll have plenty to eat." He'd been surprised to see a picnic packed, but pleased nonetheless.

"Shall we go?" he asked, picking up the oversized basket of goodies.

Jessie pushed her chair into the table and picked up her sweatshirt. Tying it around her waist, she walked out the door without looking at him.

"Hey, those are riding boots," Ryan said as they reached the pasture.

"You're a bright boy."

"Uh-huh," he said as he guided a colorful paint toward her. "Jessie, this is Tawny. She's very gentle."

Jessie took the reins and strolled with her for a few moments. She was a brilliant horse, all white except for a coal-black head accentuated with a white face. Black, oval spots also extended down her neck and chest, giving the appearance of a shield.

Jessie took to her immediately. "Hey, girl, you're quite the horse. Let's see what you can do." She checked the cinch for proper tension. Holding the reins and facing the rear of the horse, she twisted the stirrup and put in her left foot. Placing her hand on the cantle, she lifted her right leg high enough to clear the rear end of Tawny and sat deep in the western saddle. Tawny stood still. Jessie held her shoulders back and her elbows comfortably at her side. She pulled lightly on the reins and waved good-bye to Ruth before prompting Tawny to trot off.

Ryan was still on the ground, speechless as he watched her.

"Ryan, may I ask you something before you go?" Ruth asked timidly.

"Sure, but make it quick. The way Jessie's riding, I may be alone after all," he said in shock.

"It's just that Jessie mentioned lilacs."

"Yeah. Well, it's nothing. There've been a couple times when I've sworn I could smell Brecca's lilac and heard her voice. But since it's this time of year and I've been a little stressed because of Jessie's employer—and obviously this thing with Jessie—added to the fact that I've not been sleeping . . . it's only logical that something like this would happen eventually."

"Hmm." Ruth watched him.

"Ruth, you know I love you, but don't be getting that look in your eyes. This isn't one of those churchy spiritual things. I'm tired. That's it."

"If you say so," Ruth said patiently.

"Brecca is not trying to reach me from the other side. If she truly were, she'd be choking the life out of me."

"It's just that—"

"I can barely see Jessie. We'll discuss it later, okay?" Ryan quickly mounted Steel and prompted him in Jessie's direction.

"Hey!" he called, finally pulling in beside her. "Thought you said you hadn't been riding before!"

"No, that's not what I said. I said I hadn't been riding in a long time. If your photographic memory is that bad at remembering nonessential items, I'd hate to see what it does with pertinent information."

He was captivated, falling deeper and deeper. Confusion was mounting, and he wished Ruth hadn't brought up Brecca. Riding had been his favorite pastime with her. "There's a valley just below Sam's place—correction, *your* place. Good area to picnic."

"Sounds great." Jessie dreamed of riding Joanie and decided that someday she would find the courage to ask. *A bodysuit is one thing, but riding her horse . . . Well, that could definitely bother him.*

"Miller Falls ahead." Ryan pointed to their left. Without thinking about it, he dismounted and began a slow walk into the narrowing canyon. He had always done it this way, ever since his first visit here with Gramps in his youth. It was like slowly unwrapping a present, savoring the moment of unveiling. The valley faded away as the great, mountainous walls embraced their arrival. The fragrance of moist pine air rose on a cool breeze.

They walked the horses in silence as the scene before them unfolded. The narrowed canyon walls opened abruptly to a small valley of green splendor. Miller's waterfall made its three-hundred-foot trip to a small mountain of naturally polished rock where it cascaded into an expanding pool of glass. There was no apparent river flowing from the pool and down the valley, indicating an underground escape of some sort. Jessie noticed a plateau cut into the side of the hill in front of them.

Ryan led them up the path to the plateau, and as they reached it, they stood silently for several moments. The oasis of peace and splendor washed over them, awakening a warmth and inner joy that neither had felt for some time.

Finally, Ryan took both sets of reins and led the horses to a nearby tree, where he loosely tied them to a limb. He returned to find Jessie sitting contentedly, gazing at nothing in particular.

Sitting next to her, he watched as she wiped her forehead and then her neck with a bandana. "I'm assuming the beginning was your experience at the movie theater. The wildflowers *are* quite fragrant. We have plenty of food. Your place is coming along fine—ahead of schedule actually. Miller Falls *was* named after Sam's great-great-grandfather who, incidently, came from Illinois by wagon train, and no, I'm not allergic to lilacs."

She was briefly immobilized, shocked that he remembered with such exactness the order and questions she had thrown around at Ruth's house.

"I really can retain *pertinent* information. So, what *are* you thinking right now, anyway?"

"I'm thinking what an arrogant . . ."

"Hold on now." He picked up a blade of grass and placed it between two teeth. "Ruth mentioned how great it's been having you around this week."

"I've enjoyed her company. She has a way of making me feel at home. She's easy to talk to—not at all like you."

"Thanks. Made an appointment with Kyle?"

"There's not a subtle bone in your body, is there?" She leaned back on her arms and played with the grass, twirling it between her fingers. "A little early to be phoning his office. Besides, I doubt he works on Saturday."

Ryan lay down on his side, facing her, searching for a new bit of foliage to toy with. "I'm sure he'd make an exception for you."

Jessie drew in a deep breath. She'd already decided Kyle wasn't a good idea. She would have to start over, and she wasn't much in the mood for that. "I'm not planning on calling him."

Ryan didn't move an inch. He was pleased but careful not to show it.

She continued, "While I'm flattered that you're attracted to me, I'm not convinced that you will be when we're finished with all this. And whatever I feel toward you right now isn't really legitimate because I'm not particularly fond of myself. I have come to another conclusion, too."

"That being?"

"We've become friends."

"Yes, we have."

"So, with that in mind, I don't think I can do the hourly session. I think I need to work through what I can on my own, with an occasional discussion now and then. However, if at any time you make inappropriate advances, I will stop utilizing your expertise. I need to believe you will tell me the truth at all times and not with-hold certain views because you're worried about how it will affect my feelings toward you. Understand?"

"Yes."

"Can you do that, Ryan?"

"Yes."

"You answered that too quickly." Ryan's blue eyes twinkled. "I'm serious here, Ryan. I need to know if you can do this."

"I felt you were uncomfortable with our relationship. That's why I put it all on the table last night. If the time ever comes that you allow me to pursue those feelings, I will. If not, then, I won't. Therefore, the answer is yes, I can do that. Can we begin with the nightmare or will you tell me where you went when you left the theater with your sister?"

"Excuse me?" The tension in her body intensified as she straightened up.

"Since we're here and it's quiet, I thought it would be a good atmosphere to delve into the nightmare," he coaxed.

Jessie shivered slightly. "Which part of 'work things out on my own, with an occasional discussion,' was confusing?"

Ryan shrugged and smiled.

"You are something. Has Elliott asked about me this week?" She was carefully going in a direction she was comfortable with.

"Yes."

"Was he a pest, or has he come to terms with things?"

Ryan had already made the decision not to discuss Elliott's bizarre behavior. "I'm not sure he's capable of coming to terms with anything yet, but I can handle him."

"Social Services," she blurted. Ryan noticed the shaking of her shoulders again.

"You were placed in a home?"

"Yes. Katherine and I were put together in an emergency placement home for a short while. Then a foster home." Her voice cracked. She was massaging the gold band again. Ryan remained quiet as she turned away. Jessie focused on the tranquility of the sun's warmth and breathed in the scent of the towering pines. She felt the peace of control finding its way back to her and retreated to the safety of silence.

Ryan watched her intently out of the corner of his eye. Waiting for her to confide her deepest wounds to another would take patience. After a few minutes, he said, "I'm getting a little hungry. Want to start on the picnic basket?"

"I could be persuaded to munch." They arranged the food on a blanket. The basket held leftovers—fried chicken, potato salad, a marshmallow pistachio salad, the traditional selection of raw veggies, homemade oatmeal raisin cookies, and, of course, crackers.

"Getting me to talk is like pulling teeth, I know. I'm lousy at this. We're getting nowhere. Somewhere inside I know I want to get through all this, but each time I begin, anxiety takes over. I swear I don't know how I managed to get anywhere with my clients." Jessie took a carrot stick and bit off the end.

"You're doing fine," Ryan said softly, spreading mayonnaise and mustard on a slice of bread for a chicken sandwich. "Fear of what?"

"Huh?" she said, her mouth still full of carrot.

"When you start relating the past, what exactly is the fear that creates the anxiety?" He leaned on his side and watched her closely.

"I suppose it would be the fear one experiences retelling the event."

"Hmm."

"Hmm, what?"

"That's a great textbook answer. Not you, though."

"You tell me then. What am I afraid of?"

"I think you're afraid to accept that you're unhappy, sad, and lonely. In order to share your fears, you're admitting that you need help and that eventually you'll need to change something about yourself."

"Pride? You think this is a pride issue or a fear of change?" Her tone became defensive.

"Only a suggestion."

"Well, it's a lousy one. Just be quiet and eat."

"Okay."

After a few moments, she asked, "What happened to your truck?"

"Want to go for a swim?" he abruptly changed the subject.

"What?"

"In that pool of water down there. You know, you jump in, splash around, that sort of thing."

"We haven't anything to change into." Pretending not to notice Ryan's smirk, Jessie pointed toward the sky. "I'm no meteorologist, but it looks to me like we might be in for a storm. Besides, that water looks a bit cold for my taste, and I'm not getting these clothes wet."

"It's a long time before that hits. You'd never know it to look at it, but there's actually a hot spring that opens into the pool over on the far side." He pointed past the waterfall. "It's invigorating to swim back and forth between the hot and cold."

"Well, swimming is the last place I want to be when that storm does hit." *He avoided my question about his truck.*

"Where's your sense of adventure?"

"It's stuck somewhere alongside my pride."

CHAPTER 23

Ruth awoke disoriented and confused. *Why can't I move? Why won't my eyes open? Where am I? What happened? Where is Thomas?* She had lain there, scared and baffled, for more than an hour. Her aged, wrinkled lips attempted speech, but nothing came out. *Open! Come on, open!* Only the sounds of muffled voices encircled her in the room. She tried to turn toward the sounds, but the movement would not come. A shadow loomed above her paralyzed body.

"Oh, Ruth, I'm sorry I got so involved in this project. I've been selfish. I was just excited to be working again . . . I've neglected you. Please forgive me." Gramps had raised her hand to his wet cheek.

I forgive you! I forgive you! Just get me out of here! Take me home. I don't like it here. Please, Thomas . . . please . . . somebody please hear me . . .

* * *

It was fast approaching two o'clock when a torrential downpour hit. Ryan and Jessie packed up their lunch and headed to the cabin.

"I'll get the horses to the stable, and you head for the house!" Ryan shouted above the din of rolling thunder.

"Fine by me!" Jessie's response was lost as as a fiery crack split through the darkened sky.

Ryan finished with the horses and headed for the closest door to the dryness of inside.

"I borrowed a pair of sweats," Jessie said to a dripping Ryan. "I should have asked, but I was soaking your floor with buckets of water." She grabbed an extra towel from the back of the couch and handed it to Ryan. "Here. Give me your wet things after you've changed, and I'll throw them in the dryer with mine."

"My clothes? Now?"

"No, you go right ahead and keep standing there. I'll be happy to clean up the puddle once you've moved." She folded her arms across her chest.

A look of stupidity raced across his face. "Oh, yeah, of course. I'll be right back."

* * *

"I've put my things in the dryer already," Ryan said, entering the kitchen in shorts and a jersey. Jessie was making her usual tea.

"Great, thanks. I wonder if Gramps is working over at my place in this rain. I swear he's there twenty hours a day." Her shirt was baggy and the sweatpants, folded three times, were still dragging slightly on the floor.

"I enjoy being around when he's in the middle of a project," Ryan said. "I plan on staying in the city for an entire month when he's finished. He'll mope for weeks."

Jessie poured her tea and sat at the table. The ride home was exhausting, and she needed to relax.

"I want to hear the nightmare, Jessie." Ryan slid off the counter and sat in the chair across from her.

Jessie closed her eyes and drew her cup to her lips slowly. *So much for relaxing.* Her fingertips moved around the cup, feeling its surface as if reading a compelling Braille text. "Didn't I say no to this earlier?"

"Yeah."

"I thought so."

Ryan continued his stare.

"Oh all right, but not here," she said.

Ryan stood and politely pulled her chair out. Jessie's heart pounded rapidly as she approached the loft. She sunk into the safety of the recliner's depth, precluding any possibility of Ryan sitting next to her on the couch. Once Ryan was settled, she quickly grabbed the afghan, folded her legs under her, and wrapped the blanket around her already warm body. She sat motionless for minutes, wishing she could just disappear.

Ryan remained quiet while Jessie's shaking hands reached for the tea. He watched as she began to unconsciously massage the gold band on her finger. Her breaths were short and quick, and her eyes were blinking rapidly. He wondered if she would summon the courage to begin before she hyperventilated.

Jessie tried twice to open her mouth but ended up only gnawing on the inside bottom of her lip instead. Out of nowhere, a story from the Book of Mormon flashed through her mind. While she wasn't highly impressed with her reading so far, there was something about the book that kept her drawn to it. And on a professional level, it never hurt to gain knowledge of various religions. This was, at least, a logical explanation for her continued reading.

She had admired Nephi's courage when he went back alone to collect the brass plates his father wanted from the wicked king who tried to kill him. He must have loved his father deeply, to want so desperately to obey. She wondered what that kind of love would feel like.

After a long, deep breath, words finally spilled from Jessie. "The nightmare begins with me in a kitchen. I'm stirring something on the stove. Then I'm screaming because there's a rat running around my feet. Somehow it gets into a brown paper lunch sack, so I grab the sack and hold it tight." She stopped and raised her face toward the ceiling, fighting back tears.

"Go on," he said softly.

"Then I find myself in my garage. I go through a door from the kitchen and enter the garage, holding the bag." Her arms and hands were stretched out in front of her as if she was acting out a part in a play. "But the bag is bigger now, grocery-store size. It's heavy, so I drop it. I slowly bend over to look inside, and . . ." Her breathing became more rapid. She blinked frantically to control her tears.

"What did you see?"

"I . . . I saw . . . I can't, Ryan."

"Take a slow, deep breath."

Jessie laughed crazily as she quickly wiped the tears with her quivering hands. "A slow, deep breath. Do you know how many times I've said that in my life? What exactly is a slow, deep breath going to really accomplish at a time like this? By the time I'm done breathing, I've had more time to think about the horrific thing I'm trying to forget. Who made up all that nonsense about breathing anyway?" She jumped out of the recliner and began pacing.

Ryan decided now wasn't the time to debate psychology techniques, so he let her pace for a minute.

"What did you see, Jessie?"

She sat back in the recliner slowly and, unconsciously, took a deep breath. "When I open the bag, it isn't a rat. It's . . ." Her head dropped again, and she whimpered. Ryan reached for the footstool and scooted to her side. She buried her face in her hands and sobbed. "I'm awful, I'm so awful."

Ryan put his hand on her shoulder. "You're not awful, Jessie."

"Only an awful person could have such a dream." Each word came out slow and harsh.

"I hope you don't say that to your clients." The humor didn't work. "Sorry. You're not awful; the nightmare was awful. That's why they call them nightmares."

"It was my little sister Katherine in the bag!" she yelled suddenly. "Okay? Happy now? Katherine was in the bag—and she was dead. I gotta get out of here!" Jessie had reached the top of the stairs when Ryan grasped her from behind. She turned to face him as he held her wrists firmly.

"Jessie, it's okay. It was just a nightmare. Let's try and figure it out together, all right? Don't run off."

"Ryan! Did you hear me? I'm crazy!" Bending her arms to his chest, she began pounding on him. "Let me go! NOW!"

"How did Katherine really die?"

"Wh . . . wh . . .what?"

"How did Katherine really die?"

"Are you insane? What gives you the right to . . . NO! Let go of me!" Her head was down and she began to quiver.

"No," he said calmly, still holding firmly to her wrists.

Fear swelled in Jessie's eyes. "Please, Ryan, I don't want to do this anymore. I think I'm going to throw up."

"You're in no state to be running off yet. If you leave now, you probably won't be able to do this again."

Her once-tight fists went limp. "At least let me go to the bathroom. I need a few minutes. Don't make me beg."

Ryan let go gently. She descended the staircase to the first floor and sequestered herself in the bathroom.

Ryan took up station in the kitchen. He phoned Ruth's, hoping to catch Gramps on his usual stopover so he could ask him to return quietly. He wasn't sure how long Jessie would keep talking, but he hoped it would be long enough to deal with the issue at hand. He hated the thought of sending her away with the wound ripped open anew, no real healing done. He hung up when no one answered. Fifteen minutes passed before Ryan heard the bathroom door open.

"You okay?" he asked as Jessie entered the kitchen.

"Oh sure, it felt just great to get that off my chest. I can't tell you how elated I am." Her eyes were bloodshot and her cheeks were flushed. She was back to her original, sarcastic self.

"I'd like to know how Katherine really died."

"I'm sure you would." Jessie leaned on the back of a chair. "Not today. Tell me what you think about the nightmare."

"Now? It would only be a guess without knowing how she really died or about the rest of your past and how it relates. It'd be a pure textbook analogy."

"Ryan, I just relayed my nightmare from the netherworld. Just textbook it for all I care." She sat on the counter.

"Maybe you had some part in your sister's death or think you could have prevented it. In any case, you feel responsible. There is also the possibility that since you've decided to deal with your issues, you're killing off the old self, and the nightmare is a representation of that. Katherine exists as a substitute for you. The old self took on the appearance of someone you loved, and it's fighting to stay alive."

"Do you think I did it?" Jessie asked, looking away.

"Did what?"

"Do you think I killed her? You must be wondering."

"Did you?"

"Can't you just answer me without asking another question?"

"No," he replied softly.

"No, you can't answer me without asking a question or—"

"No, I don't think you killed her. Explain to me what the garage looked or felt like."

"What? I don't know. What good will that do?"

"You said *a* kitchen, but then you said *my* garage. Was the garage one you were familiar with? Think. Close your eyes and remember."

"I don't want to close my eyes." Her voice instantly grew angry.

"Okay. Pace and try to remember."

"I still can't believe you earned the income you did." She climbed off the counter. A few minutes after she began pacing, a list of descriptive adjectives began popping out. "Dark, musty, old, creepy, dripping. Something was dripping—rain, or maybe water. I never saw it, just heard it."

"What gave you the impression it was old?"

She stopped pacing for a brief moment and looked at him curiously. Straining to remember, she pulled her arms across her chest and held her shoulders tight. "The walls were all cement and cracking. The lighting was dim, with only one small window up high. There were lots of cobwebs, and the stairs were rotting."

"How many stairs were there?"

"I don't know. There was a railing to hold on to. A lot, I guess."

"Could it have been a basement rather than a garage?"

Jessie's head quivered. "What?"

"It seems a great deal of stairs for a kitchen leading into a garage. Cement doesn't rot, but wood does. Stairs into a garage are typically cement. Basement stairs are usually made of wood."

"Basement?" Her eyes instantly moistened as she made her way to the bathroom.

Sounds of vomiting could be heard as Ryan called Ruth again. Still no answer. He then checked his messages. He had turned off the ringer before Jessie began talking. Gramps's frantic voice filled the air. Ryan collected his wallet and keys and waited for Jessie to finish. He was at the bathroom door when it opened. "Gramps called while we were talking. Ruth fell and is at the hospital. It's serious. Do you want to come with me or stay here?" Ryan began walking toward the front door.

"I'll come. Give me thirty seconds to grab my clothes." She pulled on her still-damp jeans then tied her sneakers in the Jeep as Ryan sped out of the driveway.

CHAPTER 24

Gramps was holding Ruth's hand when Ryan and Jessie entered the room. "Hey there, son. Jessie, nice of you to come."

"What happened?" Ryan asked. He pulled a chair closer to Ruth and picked up her other hand, placing it gently between his palms. Jessie stood by Gramps's side.

"I came down to her place from workin' on Jessie's to see what time she was expectin' you two home. Needed your help on somethin'. She was lyin' on the kitchen floor. Doc says it was another stroke, serious one this time. She hasn't come out of it yet, and he says she may not. Have to wait and see." His voice cracked and a tear fell from his cheek. "My fault. I've been consumed with the house and haven't paid any attention to her. No offense, Jessie. If only I could have gotten to her sooner."

Offense or not, Jessie felt horrid.

"She's come through before, and this isn't your fault. She was exhilarated when you took this job. Meant she could keep that old barn a while longer!" Ryan said.

Gramps smiled as he wiped his eyes, then solemnly said, "I don't think she'll pull through this time, son. There was a moment of brain activity, but now . . . I just wish I could talk with her one last time. There's not much you can do here, but I'd appreciate a change of clothes. Can't go home tonight. Ain't leavin' for nothin', but I'm pretty sure these nurses would be mighty grateful if I didn't stink up the place."

Ryan didn't want to leave. He hadn't seen Gramps look so old before. Ruth had dodged death several times. Surely she would pull through again. She had to. Gramps would be lost without her. "Sure, and we'll bring you something to eat, too. Know you're probably not hungry, but you need to eat."

"They're feedin' me fine here, son. Don't bother with that. Just the clothes." Gramps never took his eyes off Ruth, determined not to miss it when she woke up—*if* she woke up.

"We'll be back soon," Ryan said.

"Jessie, I'd like you to stay," Gramps requested.

Jessie glanced at Ryan with a questioning look. Ryan shrugged his shoulders as he walked out the door. She sat down. *He's going to tell me he's finished working on my place. Does he really think I would expect him to work now, anyway? Certainly he could tell me this with Ryan here. Does he just want some company?*

* * *

Ryan pulled up in front of the cabin to find Elliott standing on the front porch drinking a beer. "This is all I need," he muttered irritably. "Help yourself," he continued, staring at the beer as he walked passed Elliott and slammed the screen.

"Don't mind if I do," Elliott retorted, following Ryan. "Nice Jeep, and quite a place you have here. Surprised you never told me of its whereabouts."

"I come here to get away from annoying people. So how much does my privacy go for these days?"

"Didn't cost a dime. Not wise to keep your truck doors unlocked."

"What are you doing here, Elliott?" Having seen Ruth with tubes all through her body gave him little patience for Elliott's demented problems.

"You know why." Elliott followed Ryan into Gramps's room and sat in the recliner, watching him.

Ryan began packing a duffel bag. "I've known you for years, and I don't ever remember you behaving this way. Have you always been this way, or have you just suddenly snapped? Jessie's not in love with you. The last thing she needs is you here. Go home, Elliott." Ryan threw in a change of clothing, a toothbrush, toothpaste, shampoo, and deodorant, then zipped the bag and headed downstairs.

At the outside entrance, Ryan continued, "I would never have taken this challenge if I knew what was going on. It would've been in your best interest to tell me of your involvement with her. Now my concern is for her. She won't see you."

"Don't you think that should be for her to decide?"

"Fine. I'll ask her. Where are you staying?" Ryan turned to face Elliott before exiting the front door.

"I can wait here."

"Ah, no."

"I'm at the Sunnyside Motel in town."

"Fine." Ryan slammed the door, climbed in the Jeep and sped out of the driveway—a habit he seemed to be forming of late. He pulled off the side of the road where Elliott wouldn't see him but where the cabin remained in view. Elliott stayed for a few minutes then left. Ryan followed him to the motel and watched him enter room forty-three.

* * *

"About a week ago I heard you singin' in the garden. It was a song about a miracle. I was hopin' you could sing it for me."

Jessie wanted to leave. She was embarrassed at the thought that Gramps had heard her singing. It had been a private moment. The song was one her mother often sang. Jessie had come across the music one day while she was snooping through an old chest in her father's attic. Although as a child she hadn't fully understood the meaning, she had sensed it was a prayer of sorts—one that God had ignored.

She searched frantically for reasons not to sing but knew there were no adequate ones. After pulling the door closed, she began.

"I'm looking for a miracle
coming down to me,
looking for that miracle,
God has promised me . . .

I know it's out there somewhere
I'm waiting patiently,
God promised me He'd send it
upon my humility . . ."

Jessie watched as Gramps held tighter the hand of his sister. She fought back the tears that wanted desperately to emerge.

"Miracles are out there
given to those in need,
Jesus broke the bread,
five thousand did He feed.

Peter walked on water
till doubt and fear set in,
crying for his Savior
Christ reached and pulled him in."

Jessie's mind wandered to the place in her mother's lap. Her mother's arms were wrapped tightly around the little girl as the soft, gentle words of the song flowed. Jessie had felt safe in those arms. *Mom, I miss you. Why did you leave?* She cleared her throat slightly as she continued.

"So, I've put my faith and trust in Him,
who suffered, bled, and died,
whose tender mercy's given
after that faith is tried.

I'm not asking to walk on water
or feed a hungry crowd,
I just need to feel some peace
in a soul that's filled with doubt.

But I fear my knees are tremblin', Lord
My flesh is becomin' weak,
The walls are closin' in on me,
I'm pleading to hear You speak."

Unrestrained, the tears flowed freely from both Gramps and Jessie. She didn't want to continue. God had never answered *her* prayers. Would His tender mercies recognize Gramps's plea?

"Whisper words of hope and love
tell me what more to do,
to realize that miracle
promised me from You.

I'm looking for a miracle
coming down to me,
looking for that miracle,
Thou has promised me.

I know it's out there somewhere
I'm waiting patiently."

Gramps released Ruth's limp hand and wiped his tears. He slowly walked to the open window, where the scent of rain had a distinct calming effect.

Jessie remained in her chair, her frame trembling. Would her mother ever know what that song had meant to her?

"You believe in miracles?" Gramps asked.

No! Please don't make me answer this right now. Get a grip, Jessie. He needs to be comforted. This is his time of sorrow. "I believe that miracles happen all around us, often going unnoticed. Usually we rationalize these as being merely the result of good luck. As far as the bigger miracles, well, I believe those come, too, but not always the way we want. And typically, the miracle we're searching for isn't what was in God's plan." *Where did all that come from?*

"Then what's the use of hopin' for a miracle when what comes is just what was gonna happen anyway?"

"I'm probably not the best person to ask. I'm afraid I've lost that hope myself. I know for many people, though, miracles do happen. There's no reason to believe you won't get one."

"If you've lost hope, why sing the song?"

Jessie tried hard to maintain her composure. She didn't want this conversation to continue. "I've been singing it since I was a small child. I think it's as much a part of me as *Twinkle, Twinkle Little Star* is to other children. My mother wrote the song. I wish I could offer more

comfort than that." She turned back to face Ruth, desperately wanting
to speak to her, to tell her of her admiration and beg her to come back.

Nearly an hour passed before Ryan entered the room. "Any
change?"

His question was directed at Jessie, but it was Gramps who
replied, "No."

"Here are the things you asked for. Jessie and I can stay as long as
you'd like."

"No need. I'll call you as soon as I know anything."

"Gramps, I'd like to stay." Ryan was drained and wanted to be
near Ruth.

"I know you do, son, but no sense all of us sittin' here feelin' sorry
for ourselves. Besides, I'd like a little time alone."

Ryan conceded. "Do you know my cell phone number, or should
I write it down?"

"Headed somewhere other than home?" Gramps raised his
eyebrows.

"It's a long story, but I may need to take Jessie away from the
cabin and Ruth's. We won't go far. We'll get here quick if there's a
change."

Jessie gave Ryan an inquisitive look.

"I have the number." Gramps's words were monotone. Any
concern for Jessie was secondary at the moment.

Jessie said good-bye to Ruth then rested her hand on Gramps's
arm. "You have every reason to expect a miracle. Don't stop asking."

Once outside, Ryan began, "We had a visitor at the cabin."

"A visitor?"

"Elliott."

"Elliott! I thought your cabin address was confidential."

"I forgot to write *confidential* on my truck registration."

"So is he still there?"

"No, he's at a motel in town."

"Oh, brother." She couldn't believe the last few hours' chain of events.

"If he found the cabin, he'll find Ruth's place too, and possibly
yours. I figure we go where he is and stay right under his nose."

She climbed into the Jeep. "This is ridiculous. Take me to him."
Her eyes narrowed.

"I'm not so sure that's a good idea."

"You're probably right, but you know what? This is about *me*, and *I* want to see him. I can walk."

Knowing she would, Ryan conceded. "I'll want to stay with you the whole time."

"Whatever." When her temper calmed, she asked, "Does this have anything to do with why you have this Jeep?"

"Yes."

* * *

At the motel, Ryan parked in the stall adjacent to Elliott's car. He had barely shut off the engine before Jessie was pounding on door forty-three.

The door opened slowly. Jessie pushed her way through and yelled, "Are you insane? What are you doing here?"

"Very subtle," muttered Ryan.

"Jessie, I . . ."

"And you're worried about *my* ability to practice psychology? What are you thinking by showing up here? Do you not have enough in your life to keep you busy that you have to leave your clients to chase after me? I told you it was over. What do you not understand about *over*?" She was in his face now, hands on hips, reddened cheeks, her lips pinched off in a tight line.

"Are you quite finished?" Elliott said, remaining composed.

"I suppose that depends entirely on what comes out of your mouth next."

"Can we speak privately?"

"We are."

"I mean without him." He pointed toward Ryan, who had taken his post in the open doorway.

"Him who?" She remained in his face.

"Fine, if that's the way you want it. I've left Lydia." Reaching inside his suit pocket, he pulled out a bundle of papers.

"You drove all the way out here to replay that sad tale?"

"I admit my motives in calling in the cavalry—" he again pointed at Ryan, "may have appeared selfish, but my intentions were to help you. Just look at these, Jessie. They're real!" He shoved the papers directly in front of her face.

She ignored them. "You should feel fine then. Your 'intentions' worked."

"I'm ready to take over now." He looked at Ryan and dropped the papers onto the bed.

"Don't look at him. This is between you and me. I've *tried* talking to you, remember? You were preoccupied with other things."

"I'd like another chance."

She began to pace. "You *lied* about your marriage, Elliott. And when I did come to you for help, you turned me away. You said it was a conflict of interest. That, too, was a lie. I'd refused to engage in an affair with you, and you were hurt, so you declined to help me." She stopped, refusing to cry. She took a safer route—anger. "It had taken me *years* to trust men again, and when I finally did, unfortunately I picked a married one. Look, the best thing you could have ever done was call him." It was her turn to point at Ryan. "Elliott, I'm getting better. I'm sleeping more, and I'm slowly working through things. If those papers are real, it just doesn't matter." The strain in her face intensified as she forced herself to keep her voice low. "If I had wanted you to find me, I would have told you where I was. How dare you invade my privacy." She continued, "You and I are through, Elliott. You and Lydia are good together. You're just bored. She may have issues, but who doesn't? It isn't simply her that's wrong with your marriage."

"I'd really like some time, just the two of us," Elliott softly requested to Ryan. Ryan glanced in Jessie's direction. She nodded a frustrated yes.

"I'll wait outside."

"It's been a long time since that lie about Lydia," Elliott said when the door closed. "I've apologized over and over for that. Since then, I've tried to be honest."

"No, you haven't," Jessie said bluntly. "This little episode with Ryan was not honest. I know it was an attempt to scare me into running back to you. You figured because of my fear of men, I wouldn't be able to handle being alone with him. You thought I would get scared and flee back to a more comfortable atmosphere. Look at me and tell me I'm wrong."

Elliott slumped onto the bed. "I tried to get you to open up, but you wouldn't. I made one lousy error, and you shut me out. I just wanted you back."

"One lousy error? You lied about being divorced, Elliott. I accept that I may not have seemed very forgiving, but, Elliott, you knew enough of my past." She sat down on a chair at a nearby table. "You knew that trusting was difficult for me. "

"I wanted to be sure I had you first. I'm not a gambling man."

"Sure you are. You gambled with my trust, and now with my future."

"Your future at work is stable. Come back and this whole thing can just go away." He looked directly at her.

"That would be easy for you, but not so easy for me. The time I've spent here has opened my eyes. I can't offer myself to others till I'm whole. When or if I do go back to work, it can't be with you." She stood and walked toward a window, pulling open the blinds to let some light in. "I will always be grateful for the time I worked at your practice. However, even if you had left Lydia when you said, we wouldn't have lasted. There were strikes against us from the beginning—our age difference, for one. I want children someday; you don't. I could go on, but . . ." She inhaled deeply and then exhaled. "I know this isn't the ending you hoped for, but I am a better person now. That will have to be enough."

Elliott gave her a steady look then gathered his few belongings and walked toward the door. "I'll leave for now, Jessie. But I'm not going to give up. Take the time you need to work things through. If you don't come back, I will."

She was dumbfounded. "Elliott . . ."

Elliott walked outside. "Your payback hasn't turned out the way I intended," he said to Ryan.

"Noticed that."

"This is far from over, Ryan."

CHAPTER 25

Barkley pounced in Jessie's lap as she lazily awoke. Surprised she had fallen asleep at all after the day's traumas, she swung her feet heavily to the floor and threw aside the crumpled sheets. She headed to the kitchen holding the little ball of fur, smothering him with affection. She walked quietly by Ryan, careful not to wake him from his slumber on the couch.

Their late afternoon visit at the hospital had not been what they had hoped. Ruth's diagnosis hadn't changed, and Gramps was no longer even trying to put up a good front. Everyone felt hopeless.

Ryan had accompanied Jessie home. While she steeped her tea, he'd fallen asleep, and she'd left him there. She hadn't had any urgent desire to be left alone, especially with Elliott nosing around.

Tea and crackers in hand, she maneuvered her way back to the living room and sat in the semi-darkened room, across from Ryan. As she watched him sleep, a surge of remorse washed over her. His surrogate mother, the only one he'd ever known, was at death's door. And she had forced him to take her to see Elliott.

Leaning up on one arm, Ryan quietly spoke, "Hey, partying without me?"

"I'd hardly call tea and crackers partying," she replied. She laid the tea-filled saucer carefully on the coaster. "I didn't mean to wake you."

"You didn't. Besides, a few hours of shut-eye is all I'm used to, anyway."

"Want to join me in my binge?"

"No . . ." he trailed off. He placed both hands over his face momentarily, scratching at the forty-eight-hour growth. "Although I think I'll grab some coffee."

"Barkley's hiding in there somewhere, so be careful not to step on him."

The silhouette of a cup could be seen in Ryan's hand as he returned.

"I'm truly sorry about Ruth. I woke up a few minutes ago wishing it was all another bad dream," Jessie said as Ryan settled back into the comfort of the couch.

"Thanks," he whispered. Clearing his throat, he added, "Another Grisham novel?" He pointed toward the book at her side.

Jessie was stunned. *Rebecca's Book of Mormon. In the dark, he won't be able to tell, will he?* "No, uh-uh. It's something different."

"Is it taking your mind off things like those dreams we haven't finished discussing?"

For the first time in her life, she almost wanted to discuss her dreams rather than explain why she was reading his late wife's book of scripture. Jessie wasn't even sure why she was still reading it. There was just something about it that kept her drawn to it. "The dreams should probably wait, don't you think? I mean, considering everything that's going on. Besides, I took enough of your time running Elliott down."

"There's not anything I can do for Ruth. Gramps is with her. If I were to go and stand around, it would make him crazy. Until he calls, talking with you may be my only distraction. By the way, what would you like me to do with the papers Elliott left on the bed at the motel?"

"It wouldn't be ladylike to tell you what I'm really thinking, so just throw them away. I really don't want to deal with that right now."

"Okay then." Ryan's smile went unnoticed in the dark.

"I have a question," Jessie said, glad for the opportunity to change the subject.

"Go ahead." Ryan leaned back in the couch, clasped his hands together, and rested them behind his neck.

"I haven't ever heard about your grandmother. I'm assuming she existed because you had a father. It's just that I've never seen any photos of her—not here or at the cabin."

"She died of complications with lupus when I was around seven. I have vague memories of her. She was pretty sick when my dad left. The disease attacked her organs, and eventually everything shut down. My only memories of her were here, sick on the couch, in this very room. In fact, this is the same spot the other couch was in." He dropped his head momentarily and looked at the couch. "Gramps was a mess for a while. It was a rough couple years. Between her illness and me, I'm surprised he made it through. Ruth was an angel. Don't know what will happen to Gramps if she dies." His voice lowered, then he switched gears. "He has pictures of Ellen in his room. You would've seen them if you would've examined his room as throughly as you did mine."

She froze. *How could he have possibly known?* "I'm sorry about that. I was curious. It was wrong."

"Did you read your profile?" he asked, suddenly remembering his comment about her eyes.

"Not in its entirety." She stayed very still. The music of sleepless crickets seemed to grow in intensity.

Ryan interrupted the symphony. "I understand Elliott isn't your choice of topics, but I noticed he didn't seem to take no for an answer."

"I realize he came here after me, but I don't think he really knows *what* he wants, other than being in control. Sooner or later, he'll have to accept that my feelings aren't romantic, but more of gratitude and father-figure stuff, and no, I don't wish to elaborate—in case you were going ask, that is. Have I put a strain on your friendship?"

A surge of joy swept through Ryan as he calmly responded. "No. Our path divided long before you. Now that my debt is paid, I'm not sure how much contact the future will hold." He took a sip of his coffee, straining for a better view of Jessie's face. "Incidentally, why did Gramps ask you to stay at the hospital?"

"Wanted to talk about miracles, with *me* of all people."

"Ah, would've liked to been a fly on the wall for that conversation. Will you talk about what happened at your first foster home?"

"Don't you think we ought to call Gramps?"

"Now?"

Jessie looked at the clock on the wall. "I suppose not, huh? Fine, okay, I can do this." She pulled her legs in underneath her and searched for a blanket. Ryan reached beside the couch, found an afghan, and handed it to her.

"As I said before, Katie and I went to a crisis intervention home for about two weeks till they placed us in a foster home while they looked for . . ." She hesitated, not wanting to continue. Ryan waited patiently. "Our father."

"They found him?"

"Yeah."

"And?"

"Thought we were talking about the foster home."

"Of course. Go on."

"We were only there for a couple months. It was probably the happiest time of my entire childhood. All the kids there were in foster care. Eight total. We were the youngest, and so we got spoiled. It was an easy transition for Katie, since I was with her. We had food, clothes, toys, and a puppy. What more could a five-year-old want?"

"Love?"

"We were loved. At least I felt loved. They were good to us. The system stinks. They find one living relative, and everyone thinks you're better off with them." Ryan couldn't see the resentment in her eyes, but he heard it in her voice. "Should've stayed in the social system."

"You two went to live with your dad then?"

"Father. He was never a dad," she corrected.

"Why did it take so long to find him?"

"Well, for one thing, he lived in Denver, and we were in Montana."

"Montana?"

"Yeah."

"Your mother left you in a theater in Montana?" Ryan was failing miserably at hiding his shock. "Have you ever tried to find out why she left you so far away?"

Jessie's agitation was mounting. "Gee, Ryan, no, it never occurred to me to *research* it. Wow, what a fabulous idea." She needed to end this discussion soon.

"Yeah, that was a stupid question on my part. Sorry."

"My father told me it was because she was insane and wanted us to be abducted."

"Is that what you think?"

"I don't know why she chose to leave us there, but I don't believe she wanted to bring harm to us."

"Tell me about your da . . . father."

"He was an angry person. He drank all the time. Beat our mother and hated us. Why he remarried I'll never understand. My stepmother brought four sons with her. She and my father had one together, and she was pregnant when I left. If you ask me, I think my mom was trying to just get away. But why she left us—that I don't know."

"Not a great bonding experience with your father, I take it."

"No. Their hands were full, and we weren't wanted." The tears came again. She remained motionless, yearning to break free of her insecurities, but guilt and anxiety were crippling her efforts. Before Ryan could speak, she changed the subject. "There's something else I'm curious about." She wiped her eyes quickly.

"Okay."

"Why does there seem to be a mystery surrounding Rebecca?" There wasn't an immediate response. Had she gone too far?

Ryan was silent. He wasn't prepared for this, but it was plain that the time had arrived to extend himself. Sharing struggles, showing his trust—this was the way in. It had worked before. "I haven't talked about this in a long time." His voice was quiet.

"I shouldn't have asked. I haven't any right, really. I can't tell you things I need to. I certainly can't expect . . ."

"Everyone adored Brecca, especially Gramps," he quickly began, not allowing time for thought. "She was an incredible woman. I, on the other hand, was a fool."

He took his arms out from behind his neck, leaned forward, and placed his elbows on his thighs. "Gramps blames me for her death. At some point early in our marriage, I became selfish and arrogant." A cynical smile formed on his lips. "Hard to believe, I know. I was good at my work, and I knew it. Brecca and I had more money than we knew what to do with. I began spoiling myself but soon became tired of it. Ran out of things I wanted to buy. So, I started drinking more and more, and more. I stayed in the city for days at a time, drinking with guys I called my friends, though I barely knew their first names. Brecca was forgiving. Too forgiving. Most women would have packed my bags and sent me on my way, but not her. No, not her." He stopped for a moment to gain composure. "I was at a bar the night she went into labor. She called me several times on my cell phone. It was turned off for obvious reasons. Gramps and Ruth were in the city, so she tried to drive herself into town. It was dark and stormy. She drove off the road, the car rolled, and . . ." He paused. "Before driving herself in, she left a message on Gramps's answering machine. When the hospital said she hadn't been admitted, he went looking for her." Ryan rose and walked over to the screen door. He gazed out into the starlit sky.

A single tear rolled down Jessie's cheek.

"She was still alive when he got there, but he couldn't get her out of the car. She was pinned in. By the time helped arrived, both she and the baby were gone." Ryan's words were barely audible now as his voice quivered. "The last thing she said to Gramps was, 'Please forgive him. Just love him.'" His emotions were on the edge of his control. He blamed her religious beliefs for his nightmare. When her church taught forgiveness seventy times seven, she took it literally. If she had left him, she would be alive, and he would have a son.

Jessie wept openly now, unable to put her feelings into words. She hadn't known Rebecca personally, but she still felt sympathy for the pain the woman must have endured. She slipped Rebecca's Book of Mormon under the recliner before walking outside. Ryan joined her on the porch steps. The dawn was upon them, and as usual, the experience was inspiring.

"It's been years since I've cried this hard while someone watched," Jessie admitted. "I guess it's the combination of everything that's happened. When we first met, I despised you and what you were about, although your reputation as a therapist was envious. You struck me as one of those wealthy, pretentious womanizers whom I swore I would have nothing to do with."

"Well, most people place me in that category, and while I wasn't a womanizer, I was a drunk. Once you have that reputation, it sticks to you forever. Even if you do change, people have a difficult time allowing you to do so."

"I just assumed that you lived the carefree life of a spoiled child."

"I have been spoiled. That's what created the problems. I didn't know how to handle responsibility, money, and the power that came with it. I blew it, Jessie, but luckily I learned from it, late as it was. I went into a pretty severe depression for a while. It was my own nightmare. It took a while for Gramps to even acknowledge my presence. We've never talked about it. Eventually we'll have to."

"Ryan?"

"Hmm?"

"This being Sunday and all, I wondered if you could tell me where the nearest church is?"

Ryan squinted his eyes, attempting to conceal his surprise at her request. "Sure. I suppose the closest is the Methodist one, although the Catholic church isn't much farther."

"Not sure God really cares at this point which one I choose. I'm sure He's stunned I've even considered going."

"Want some company? I mean, if we're going to surprise God, we might as well do it right and include the whole town as well."

"It's not my place to keep a man from worshiping, but are you sure? I mean, I sense that church is not something that . . . I just mean that I can handle it alone. I . . ."

"I'm fine, Jessie."

"Okay." Jessie's response came with a sigh of relief. "Are those the only churches in town?"

"Pretty much, yeah." He lied. There was one more, but nothing, not even Jessie, would get him there. He instantly resented having promised that he'd always be honest.

"All right then, how about we just head in the general direction and see where we end up?" she said.

"If my memory serves me, they both begin around nine," Ryan said.

"Then I think I'll take a long bath and grab a bite to eat. I'll be ready by eight-thirty."

"Kickin' me out, are you?"

"Call it what you like." She stood and stretched. "Let me know if anything changes with Ruth."

CHAPTER 26

The hot, rose-scented bubble bath felt almost sinful to Jessie as she slid underneath the water. What right had she to feel so good? Ruth was in a coma, Gramps's heart was broken, and Ryan had been forced to reminisce about the loss of his wife and son. There was little consolation in knowing there wasn't anything she could do to change those situations. But why had she chosen *now* to ask about Rebecca, when he could be losing Ruth, too?

She closed her eyes and thought about the morning's revelations. She decided Ryan must be just as curious about her as she was about him. In fact, after only a couple weeks, there were still more questions than answers.

What will his next move be? If I were him, I would pursue the nightmares. That's the most obvious manifestation—which means he'll take a different road. Katie's death? My father? If there wasn't a Mormon church around, where had Rebecca and Ruth worshiped?

"Jessie?" The voice came from outside the door.

She sputtered a startled, "Yeah?"

"I just wanted you to know I was out here. I'm getting some fresh things for Ruth," Gramps said.

"Oh. I'll be right out." She jumped up and dressed hurriedly, grateful she had brought her clothes into the bathroom. She had chosen a simple dress to wear for church. It was short sleeved with a curved neck and fell to just above her ankles. She then put on a simple strand of pearls with matching earrings. She would wait on the hair and makeup.

Gramps was sitting in the kitchen, sipping at the cup of coffee Ryan had made earlier. There was a small suitcase at his side.

"Hey," Jessie said sympathetically as she tenderly patted him on the back. "Any change?"

"No. Just decided she needed her own nightgown, instead of that ugly hospital thing."

"She'll like that. I thought I'd make up a bouquet of flowers from the garden. I was going to bring them by later, but you could take them now if you'd like."

"You bring them by. It would do her good to know you came. I know she can hear us. I'm not sure if she wants us to keep fightin' or let her go. Reckon I'd better take a quick shower before I head back. Leave me any hot water?" He forced a feeble smile.

"Of course I did." She smiled back, not at all sure she had.

"By the way, where you headed all gussied up?"

"Oh. Well, . . . I . . . ," she fumbled.

"Sorry. None of my business. You're dressier than usual, that's all."

"I'm headed to church with Ryan," Jessie blurted out before Gramps closed the bathroom door.

"Maybe you need a little more time in here?" He pointed to her hair still in need of a comb.

Jessie stifled the urge to respond humorously. "No thanks. I have everything I need in my room. Take your time." She was grateful he hadn't made a big deal out of her going to church. Although he didn't know of her expressed hatred toward God, he was probably wise enough to have discerned in her at least a slight antipathy. She'd decided he was probably more amazed that Ryan was going. Was it because of Rebecca that the town would be surprised to see Ryan at church? Did *everyone* blame him? Certainly God-fearing people should be forgiving and nonjudgmental.

Jessie pulled her hair back in a pearl barrette, allowing it all to fall on her back. The sun had been kind to her since her arrival, blessing her skin with just a slight tan. A touch of rouge and mascara, a splash of lipstick, a little powder to shadow her nose, and she was ready.

She was completing her bouquet of flowers when she heard the screen door's latch slip its catch.

"Over here, Gramps." She waved.

"Mighty nice of you, Jessie." He breathed in the fragrance of the roses, daffodils, and violets bound with a vine of honeysuckle woven through the stems. "She'll be able to smell these for sure. I should get goin'. I've been gone too long as it is. Ruth will be happy knowin' you kids went to worship. You know, she could use another song if you don't mind."

"Another song?" Ryan quizzed as he approached. He wore navy blue pin-striped slacks, a white shirt, and a navy blue necktie. Jessie felt hot and cold at the same time.

"Sure sings nice, son. Surprised you haven't heard her."

"Me too," he added, enjoying Jessie's discomfort at the latest revelation.

"You're early, as usual!" she greeted with slight sarcasm.

Gramps turned to leave. "See you kids later. Oh, and son, when you walk in and the entire congregation stops dead, that's your opportunity to sneak up to the front pew. It's easier to hear from there, and you avoid all those nasty stares."

"Any change?" Ryan ignored his incorrigible sarcasm.

"No change, son. Doubt there will be. Put in a few prayers while you're in God's house and come on by after. Got to make some decisions. Can't avoid 'em much longer." His shoulders dropped slowly with his reply.

"I know. I have my cell. Church or no church, call if anything changes."

"Will do." Gramps walked slowly from the garden.

"So what's this about singing?" Ryan asked.

"No big deal. I need to get some water in this vase." She brushed past him.

"You're avoiding the question." His grin was proof that he was enjoying the situation.

"No, I'm not. I said, 'No big deal.' That's a reply."

The walk to church was peaceful. A soft breeze had survived the daybreak's birth to join the sun's increasing heat and the vibrant, ocean-blue of the morning sky. Somehow both Ryan and Jessie understood it was a perfect time for silence. They walked awhile enjoying the time alone, without the loneliness.

"I'm sorry I dug up memories of Rebecca at a time like this. It was insensitive." Jessie's voice was a whisper.

"It's not like I don't think about her all the time, anyway. It felt good to talk. I haven't been able to talk to Gramps much. Ruth tries, but I know it hurts her. She was so excited about the baby and then she lost him, too. Decided which building we're headed to yet?"

"Nope. What do you think Gramps will do if Ruth . . ."

"I don't even want to think about it. I suppose he'd stay with me still," Ryan said.

"At least working on my place will occupy his time for a while."

"It'll certainly help. I can't believe you're still serious about living there." He bent down and picked up a large stick, pushing it in and out of the dirt as they walked.

"You thought I would change my mind?"

"Wasn't sure, really."

"Does it bother you, my living here?"

"No, not at all. Someone ought to give Kyle a run for his money. A female competitor would send him through the roof!" Ryan's glee manifested itself in his flushed cheeks.

"He needn't feel threatened. At this point I'm not planning on opening a practice here. I have other options. I don't have to be a therapist."

"Other options like . . . ?" Noticing the sudden trepidation that came across her face, Ryan stopped. The Methodist church had come into view. "You okay?"

"Yeah." Her response may have been in the affirmative, but her face was draining of color, and he was convinced she was going to faint.

"Why don't we sit here on the grass for a few minutes? We made good time." Ryan pointed to an old, hand-carved bench shaded by a towering oak just across the street from the church.

"I'm okay. Clyde's open today?" she asked, spying the bar.

"Ah, no. He conceded to close on Sunday after constant bombardment by both churches' ministers. What do you want to do?"

"Doesn't matter what I want. Clyde's is closed, remember?" she snapped.

"We don't have to do this today. We can try next week."

"There you go, giving up already!" She paced in circles.

"You're a confusing woman."

"Met one who isn't?"

"Actually, no."

"Okay, I think I can do this." She walked slowly up the path to the church.

"We can just stay here, Jessie. I'm not too eager to have you fainting in the pew."

"Man . . . look at all those people!" Jessie pointed at several groups of people entering the church.

"That's usually what one sees at a church on Sunday."

"Yeah, yeah, yeah . . . but look at that man there." She pointed to a tall, thin man, in a black suit. "Wasn't he at Clyde's? He was sloshed, if I remember right. Why does he go to church? Most likely a hypocrite. That's all I ever see at churches—hypocrites!"

"I don't believe it's for us to judge him, Jessie."

Her facial expression showed her disapproval of his comment.

"I'm getting the feeling this wasn't such a grand idea," he muttered to himself. "Let's, um, sit here for a few minutes. We could try the Catholic church, but I'm afraid we'd actually find people there, too." He led her back a few steps to the old oak and helped her sit down in the long grass.

"Look, I didn't mean what I said about that man or anyone else," Jessie apologized.

"Yes, you did. Somewhere inside, you definitely meant it. You're apologizing for the wrong thing."

"Fine. I'm sorry I made a fool out of myself, okay!" she said louder than necessary.

"That's not what I . . ."

"Oh, just forget it."

"I thought I was seeing a ghost! Ryan Blake! Long time, son." Ryan turned around in time to find a short, gray-haired man extending his hand. The pastor pulled him into a back-slapping hug. "And who's this lovely young woman?" he asked.

"Pastor James, may I introduce you to the soon-to-be resident of Sam Miller's old place, Jessie Winston." Ryan feigned pleasantness, hoping Jessie would follow suit. Snapping at the minister wouldn't accomplish anything. Each knew that unless Pastor James was deaf, he'd heard at least the last minute of their disagreement.

"Nice to meet you. Sam Miller's old place, did you say? That's great to hear. It needs some tender loving care. Now tell me, son, how is Ruth?"

"She's still in a coma."

"Well, our prayers will be in her behalf today. Now, if you're worried about what folks are gonna think when you stroll in there, you just put that right out of your mind. Only thing that matters is that you're here to worship. They aren't any more perfect than you are. They have lessons to learn too. So how about it? Shall we go in together?"

"Jessie?" Ryan asked softly.

"I may not be able to stay long. I have to be somewhere soon." She directed this at the minister.

"Oh, that's all right. Just glad you're both here." He patted each of them on the back and gently nudged them toward the entrance. Pausing to shake the hands of others, the pastor motioned for them to go ahead without him.

"You ready?" Ryan asked, extending his elbow like a proper gentleman.

"No," she replied as she placed her hand inside his arm. "But, this isn't for me, it's for Ruth."

Ryan wondered if this was *entirely* for Ruth. There had to be some silent part of her that wanted to be here too, he thought.

* * *

Gramps read the paper quietly, listening to the monitors. Every now and then, he would look up to see if there was any change. It had been over twenty-four hours. This was the longest Ruth had ever been unconscious. He glanced toward the door, sure he had heard the doctor's voice at the nurses' station. Gramps stood to meet him as he entered the room.

"Mr. Blake, the nurses tell me you've been here pretty much the whole time," the young man said with genuine compassion. He was thin and clean shaven, with coal-black hair.

"It's Thomas. And where else would I be?"

"Of course. As I've said before, Thomas, it's not looking good. We can keep her hooked up to this machine for as long as you like, but there's no apparent brain activity at this point. This is all that's keeping her body alive." He pointed toward the respirator with his pen. Gramps roughly wiped tears from his cheeks. This was the announcement he'd been fearing.

"Maybe she would be better in Denver."

"Certainly you are free to do whatever you feel is right. If you'd like, I can call the chief resident neurologist at Denver Regional. You could speak with him and get a second opinion. I can fax him the relevant charts and test results."

"I'll let you know," Gramps said softly. The doctor quietly left the room.

"I wish all this folderol had never been invented in the first place. Should be God's decision, not mine."

* * *

"Take a deep breath and calm down," Ryan said, watching Jessie grind her teeth and fidget with the ring on her finger.

"Oh, stick a sock in it!"

Amused, Ryan smiled and crossed his legs, trying to find a comfortable position in the wooden pew.

The choir had finished singing their second hymn, and Pastor James stood to offer the invocation, a beautiful prayer including a plea for Ruth's well-being. When it ended, he immediately began his sermon. "Brothers and sisters, it is wonderful to look out on this congregation and see all of God's children here where they ought to be on the Lord's Sabbath. It's easy in this day and age to get caught up in what the world offers instead of what God has to offer."

"That would be because it's easier to get what you want from the world. God just gives to who He wants and not to those who deserve it." Jessie whispered this to no one in particular. Ryan kept silent but made a mental note of her comment.

"Being consumed with material things can often bring sadness," the pastor continued. "Being consumed by physical ailments that cannot be changed often brings sadness. Being consumed with spiritual questions that cannot or probably will not be answered in this lifetime may also bring sadness. But what I would like to touch on today is our tendency to be consumed with the judgement of others."

A few heads turned and looked at Ryan with a hint of disdain. Obviously Pastor James's sermon had been modified upon the arrival of Dr. Blake and his companion.

"Uh-oh." Ryan's head ducked.

"Gee, aren't you glad we came now?" Jessie smirked.

"It's your turn to stick a sock in it!" Ryan whispered back.

Pastor James continued, "Let us open to St. Matthew's words from the New Testament." An old, heavy Bible found its way out from underneath the pulpit. The cover, most likely a shiny black at one time, had faded over its years of use. Pastor James slammed it down on the top of the pulpit, spreading a cloud of dust over the first few pews.

"Get the feeling he doesn't pull that one out very often?" Jessie grinned deviously.

Ryan was tugging at his tie, which had suddenly turned to a noose.

The pastor began reading, "Judge not, that ye be not judged. For with what judgement ye judge, ye shall be judged: and with what measure ye mete, it shall be measured to you again. And why beholdest thou the mote that is in thy brother's eye, but considerest not the beam that is in thine own eye? Or how wilt thou say to thy brother, Let me pull out the mote out of thine eye; and, behold, a beam is in thine own eye? Thou hypocrite, first cast out the beam out of thine own eye; and then shalt thou see clearly to cast out the mote out of thy brother's eye."

"Is *everyone* staring at me?" asked Ryan.

"Not everyone. The children can't get a good look over the pews."

"Great."

These people can't possibly hold Ryan responsible for his wife's death . . . can they? I've seen the clientele at Clyde's, so I know Ryan isn't the only man who drinks in this town. They must have been hideously rude to him . . .

" . . . Now let's translate that into our own modern tongue so there can be no misunderstanding as to its meaning. Friends, whatever judgements you make about one another will be returned to you by our good Lord. Now, we all make mistakes. That's why we're here—to learn. Judging is an action that's as destructive to the soul doing the pointing as much as the one being pointed at. There is not one of you in this congregation who has not sinned. It just simply isn't so. Some of you have been lucky, however, and your sins have been ones not up for review on the stage of public opinion. But God in heaven knows. There *will be* equity *and* justice.

"Which of you will say that you are greater than your God? I daresay none. Then why is it so many of you choose to take upon yourself the task that He has, by divine decree, kept only for Himself? He and only He has the right and wisdom to judge us. Who here would wish their own judgement to be by one who judges as harshly as we?" His eyes burned ahead unblinking, and his tone was deadly serious.

"We must leave Him to His work. We must love, support, and forgive. We must act as Jesus did when He was here. Even as He was the only One who could justly pass judgement, He instead was the exemplar of compassion and forgiveness. We must love as He loved. Love, brothers and sisters, *love and forgive*. Amen."

Ryan let out a huge sigh of relief at the amen. The choir and congregation sang the closing hymn together, and Pastor James again offered a prayer. The meeting was adjourned.

Ryan quickly grabbed Jessie's arm and bolted for the door. After she had hurried with him for a few blocks, Jessie pulled her arm from his viselike grip. "Whoa there, Trigger, I need a breath or two."

"Anxious to get to Ruth's and call Gramps," Ryan said, his breaths coming as rapidly as Jessie's.

"Yeah, right. You have your cell, remember? You just wanted to avoid all those people back there."

"I can't believe he gave that sermon!"

"Well, the bright side is, he already has one prepared for next week. Besides, it was actually quite good. Rather short, I thought. We were only there thirty minutes. I remember church being much longer."

"It seemed an eternity to me." Ryan's cell phone let out a quiet hum. "Hello?" Ryan answered. "Yeah . . . Okay, be there within a half hour. We're on the road to Ruth's . . . No, we walked. . . . Okay."

"May I come?" Jessie asked.

"Of course."

"I'd like to stop and get the flowers."

CHAPTER 27

Jessie and Ryan entered the solemn hospital room. Gramps was staring out the window. Jessie placed the arrangement of flowers on the table adjacent to the bed. She stood next to Ryan and waited in silence.

There was a soft tap at the door. All eyes looked up to see an elderly gentleman. Jessie guessed him to be around seventy years old. He was shorter than her and thin. He wore a dark suit and was clean shaven.

"Brother Blake, I am deeply sorry about your aunt."

"We don't need you here. Please leave. And I'm not 'Brother Blake' anymore." A hardness accompanied Ryan's words.

Jessie was shocked. She took a step back.

The man glanced toward the window. "Thomas, I saw your truck outside as I was driving by." Gramps turned and walked toward the man. He shook his hand, ignoring Ryan's request. It became Ryan's turn to gravitate toward the window.

"What have the doctors told you?"

"Another stroke, and this time it's mighty serious," replied Gramps solemnly.

"If there's anything you need—"

"Done enough, don't you think?" Ryan interrupted the gentleman sharply, his back toward everyone.

"Ryan, this is not your affair," Gramps replied.

"Not my affair? NOT MY AFFAIR!" Ryan snapped.

"Let it go, son." Gramps kept his eyes focused on Ruth, avoiding Ryan and the other man. "Could you offer a blessing while you're here, Bishop? I know she would want one. And I could use a little help myself."

Jessie watched as the man took out a small vial of yellowish liquid from his inside suit pocket. He poured a drop of what looked to Jessie like oil on the top of Ruth's head. He then laid his hands on her head and bowed his head. Gramps also bowed his head, and Jessie followed suit. Ryan continued to look out the window.

If asked, Jessie could not have repeated exactly what was said, but the words evoked a sense of peace in the room that she had never before experienced—in spite of the rebellious Ryan at her side.

After the blessing, Gramps whispered his thanks and escorted the bishop from the room.

When he returned, he announced quietly, "I've made the decision to take her off the respirator, and I don't want an argument." He turned slightly toward Ryan, but not enough to look directly at him. "She's lived a good life, and this is what I believe she would want. I thought you might want to say somethin' to her. I'll be outside."

If Ryan was surprised at all, he showed no sign. Jessie silently headed toward the door.

"Would you like a minute with her?" Ryan said.

"Yes, but I can wait."

"No, go ahead." He stepped back and shut the door.

Jessie reluctantly approached the chair next to the bed. "Hey, Ruth." She gently clasped Ruth's hand, "I wish Ryan and I hadn't gone on that stupid picnic." Her tears now fell freely. "You should have come. I invited you. Oh, why didn't you come? We could have gotten you help sooner." She rested her forehead on Ruth's arm and sobbed. Between her halting breaths, she muttered, "I am so sorry, Ruth. I am so sorry." She softly caressed Ruth's cheek. "That bishop was from your church, wasn't he? From our conversation, I figured you were Mormon. I should have talked more with you about it. Oh, Ruth, why do you have to go? I don't understand your God. I wish you could stay and help me. Thank you for taking me in. You didn't even know me." She wiped her tears from Ruth's arm, giving her frail body one last embrace. She tenderly plucked a rose from the flower arrangement and placed it on the bed at Ruth's side.

Ryan seemed to barely notice Jessie as he walked intently across the hospital's linoleum. But as she sat next to Gramps, the direction of his thoughtful pace slowly altered. He pulled the door to Ruth's room closed behind him.

Seeing the rose, his eyes became immediately moist. The deepness and vibrance of the bouquet struck him as he stared at her garden flowers. The garden would miss its creator. Fighting to hold back the tears, he knelt down on the floor opposite of where Gramps and Jessie had sat and clasped her lifeless hand. Stroking it against his cheek, he began, "What can I possibly say? I remember as a child peeking into your room and listening to your prayers. You always asked that you pass away quietly in your sleep. Hopefully God has answered and you haven't felt pain.

"Your life changed the day my dad left. You never once considered me an inconvenience, but I know I was. I caused you a great deal of grief. There was Brecca's death, for one. And the baby's. I was hoping you could put that rocker to use one more time, but I guess it wasn't in the cards." He stopped to wipe his face with the back of his hand. "Thank you for your patience and love. I wish I could have seen it all sooner. God willing, I'll see you and Brecca again someday, and maybe my son, and beg you all for forgiveness. Thank you, *Mother*, for everything." His fight to maintain emotional control now failed. He let go of her hand and kissed her softly on the cheek. "I love you." He pulled a second stem from the arrangement and laid it next to Jessie's.

Ryan joined Gramps and Jessie in the hall. Gramps stood slowly and walked through the open door. He whispered something inaudible and put his big arms around Ruth's still and quiet form. A third rose soon lay next to the others.

After he left his sister's side, Gramps joined Ryan and Jessie. "You know 'Amazin' Grace'?" He cocked his head toward Jessie.

For a moment Jessie wanted to lie. Then she cursed herself for the selfish thought. "Yes. Would you like me to sing it for you?"

"Not for me, for her. It's one of her favorites, and I believe it would be comfortin' for her to hear it as she . . ." He didn't finish as he made his way somberly toward the nurses' station.

The doctor with nurse in tow approached the machine and switched off its assist function. All was quiet. Gramps nodded toward Jessie, and softly she began. By the last verse, her voice had taken on a power no one had expected. The hospital staff, previously maneuvering to leave them alone, now stood entranced as the last notes hung with fervor in the air. No one moved. God had called Ruth home.

* * *

The day of the funeral was tranquil. Ryan insisted it take place at
the graveside, claiming that if the Mormons were going to be in
charge, at least he wouldn't have to walk into the ward building. It
had been two days since Ruth's passing. Wisps of grey-white clouds
lay scattered across a brilliant blue sky, faintly filtering the sun's heat.
The entire town and many from the surrounding area turned out for
the funeral, which was recorded as having the largest attendance since
the town's birth in 1925.

Ryan was the last to leave. He stared across the open grave to
Brecca's headstone, mourning the June loss of both his life's loves. It
was faint, but the scent of lilac was there. "You've taken her too,"
Ryan solemnly called out. "First my mother, then Uncle Joe and
Grandma, then Brecca and my son, and now Aunt Ruth. Why not
just take me and spare them?"

You're needed. It came as a whisper again.

"And they weren't?" Ryan asked indignantly.

A wind carried the fragrance away. Ryan subdued the urge to
chase after it.

* * *

Gramps had invited everyone to a luncheon at Ruth's. Jessie had
spent hours getting things ready the day before. She cut practically
every flower from the garden to decorate the house, creating an
atmosphere full of life and memories of Ruth.

Ryan stood at the kitchen door and watched Jessie busy herself for
the crowds to come. Gramps had asked her to sing "How Great Thou
Art" at the funeral. The performance and reaction had paralleled that
of a couple days prior.

Milly came up behind Ryan in her semireclined wheel chair, her
legs braced in front of her. "Hey there, son. You okay?"

"I'm okay," Ryan answered. "Just wishing I'd have spent more
time here lately, you know?"

"Now don't go feelin' guilty. She wouldn't want that. Not her way.
You did what you were capable of, as all of us do. She knew that.

Loved you like her own, she did. Now let it go, or it will eat you up. But you know all this already." Milly reached up for his face and kissed him on the cheek.

"And how are you, Janet?" Ryan asked the wheelchair's chauffeur, a Milly look-alike, thirty years younger, wearing the same heavy makeup.

"I'm fine. We'll all miss her, Ryan. She was an angel. She helped everyone in this town at one time or another."

Ryan nodded his appreciation, his eyes dropping once again to Milly. "You've been a good friend these many years, Milly. I appreciate it. By the way, how are *you* feeling?"

"I'd be better if my daughter would get out of my house and back to her family!" Milly looked around to gauge her daughter's response but couldn't twist far enough. She softened to a whisper and leaned forward. "Between you and me, she's driving me crazy." Milly patted him on the arm and motioned for Janet to drive her in the direction of Gramps.

Pretending not to see the bishop talking with Gramps, Ryan returned his attention to Jessie. He decided the conversation between her and Kyle had gone on long enough. "So, Kyle, lowered yourself to soliciting business at a funeral luncheon?" he said as he briskly entered the kitchen.

"Ryan!" Jessie exclaimed in shock.

"Just having a polite conversation with the lovely lady," Kyle replied, poised. He was in his late forties with a head of thick brown hair and a mustache that almost buried his lips. He had a muscular frame that he'd acquired the hard way—two hours a day at the gym.

"Isn't it customary to be giving condolences to the *family* instead of hitting on the 'lovely ladies'?"

"I've already spoken to Gramps. I was actually looking for you, but I noticed you were busy talking to Milly. So I came in here to see if I could offer any help."

"Uh-huh," Ryan said, picking up a carrot to dip in the vegetable spread Pastor James's wife had brought.

"Oh, no, you don't." Jessie grabbed the carrot before he dipped it. "Get a plate like everyone else."

"If I want to dip, I'll dip!" He gave her a dirty look, shoved the carrot back into the bowl, and glared at Kyle before walking out the back door.

"Ah, Kyle, since you offered, would you take these napkins and extra casseroles out to the buffet table? Thanks."

Taking off the apron she had been wearing, Jessie walked out in search of Ryan. She spotted him at the rosebushes. "You doing okay?"

"Other than the fact that I'm hearing voices and smelling the scent my wife used to wear, I'm doing just fine." It came out more sarcastically than he intended. He leaned down to pick a rose, and a thorn sliced his finger. He winced.

Jessie pulled a handkerchief from her dress pocket, reached for his hand, and said, "Here, let me." Obviously Ruth's death and the houseful of Mormons had his nerves on edge.

He softened his demeanor and smiled at her concentration. "Am I going to live, Doctor?"

"I just want to make sure part of the thorn isn't still in there."

"I thought maybe you were just looking for an opportunity to hold my hand."

"Oh fine, bleed to death." She dropped his hand. "At least you're not yelling anymore."

"Sorry about the scene in there with Kyle. I can't blame him for being male. I guess I just needed someone other than Bishop Grant and his faithful followers to blow some steam at."

She desperately wanted to talk about his anger toward the Mormons but resisted. "How about when this is over you and I go somewhere?"

"You mean . . . out?" His eyebrows rose.

"Well, out like as in a walk, or a ride . . ." Her palms started to sweat.

"Okay, it's a date."

The word *date* instantly turned her stomach. *What on earth am I doing?* "I'd better get back and see what needs to be done. Is Kyle safe or do I need to call for backup?"

"I'll leave him alone." He smiled ruefully.

"Good."

Ryan lingered in the garden, fighting to regain control of his emotions. He wanted to get drunk and bawl like a baby, but those days were over. He tarried for an hour, thinking of Ruth and Brecca. He longed to hear Brecca's voice again. This time he would listen.

* * *

"Hey, Milly, how are you doing?" Jessie asked as she picked up her apron.

"I'm just fine, dear. I've asked Janet to wait outside so we could have a minute alone."

"Sure, did you need something?"

"Not a thing. Ruth mentioned you were reading the Book of Mormon. I'm not sure how far you are, but I wanted you to know that I would be happy to spend time explaining anything you may be confused about."

"You're Mormon?"

"You sound shocked!" Milly laughed.

"Sorry. I just thought Mormons were more . . . oh, I don't know . . ."

"Reserved?"

"I guess so."

"Like any religion, Jessie, we all have different personalities."

"Of course."

"I'm here if you need me," Milly said quickly as Janet returned.

"It's getting late, Mom, and you've had a big day. I think it's time to tuck you in," Janet said in a lullaby voice.

Milly rolled her eyes. "Do I get a bedtime story, too?" She winked at Jessie.

* * *

The grandfather clock in the hall chimed eight times. Gramps was sitting in his usual spot on the couch reading sympathy cards. Jessie and Ryan had long since dressed down to jeans and T-shirts. Jessie had finished in the kitchen and was putting away the linens. A sharp pain of memory raced through her as she placed the card table in its long-standing spot.

Ryan finished stacking the last of the folding chairs after reading the sympathy card Sandy had sent along with three dozen roses. The house had been put back in order. All that was missing was Ruth.

"You ready?" Ryan said.

"Think he'll be all right alone?" Jessie looked toward Gramps.

"One thing I know about Gramps—if we stay, it won't be helpful to talk about any of it. And if we try to cheer him up, he's likely to tell us where to go."

"I know you're talkin' 'bout me. I'm fine. It's plain to see you two have somethin' to do." Gramps never once looked up from the cards.

"See?" Ryan whispered.

"I thought he was hard of hearing," she whispered back.

"Hearing's fine. Now go! Let an old man be."

She gave it one last attempt. "Are you sure?"

"Seems to me you're the one with the hearing problem," he said, peering above his glasses, which had slid down on his nose.

"Okay, okay. I got it." She carried the stool to its usual place in the corner of the kitchen. "We're just going for a walk. Ryan's got his phone if you need *anything*." She reached down and kissed Gramps in the middle of his bald head. This was completely out of her character, and it surprised Gramps. He stared at her blankly then mumbled something under his breath and waved them off.

The sun was making its descent for the evening. The color of the sky was brilliant as it met with the mountain peaks. Jessie and Ryan headed toward the pasture.

"Jessie?"

"Yeah?"

"I found something interesting in the trash tonight."

"Ah. Yeah, well, the trash is where it belongs." Jessie had opened an envelope addressed to her. She figured it was something from Linda, but it had been another copy of Elliott's divorce papers. No note attached, just the papers.

"Elliott's not going to give up without a fight," Ryan said.

"It takes two to fight. For now, there's only one. You think Gramps is okay?" She didn't wish to dwell on Elliott's stupidity.

"I'm sure along with Ruth's death, he's thinking about my grandmother, Brecca, and possibly my dad. Sad. All he has left now is me."

"And how are you?"

"Nothing downing ten beers couldn't take care of."

"You mentioned something earlier about voices." It came as a statement rather than a question.

"It was nothing. I'm just exhausted. I'm still relatively sane."

Jessie didn't comment. What could she say? He *had* lost a great deal, and he probably felt responsible—and maybe he even *was* responsible in some way—for his wife's and unborn child's death. And now he'd lost the woman who had raised him.

* * *

Gramps stared at the rocker on the porch. As he caressed the well-worn ridges, his focus began to fade. The pain heated up inside him like a forest fire, consuming his thoughts and numbing his senses. In that moment, there was no one. There was nothing. There was only the burning anguish and desolation of loss.

Chapter 28

It was early in the morning when Ryan found Gramps tending the garden. As he glanced around, he realized that it was as if the garden knew its caregiver had died. Bermuda grass seeds were producing far too rapidly. Soon the grass would release chemicals into the soil, impeding the growth of the plants.

Ryan knelt to aid in the fight against the surmounting weeds. It had only been a few days since Jessie had removed the unwanted greenery. But this time of year, the beds needed weeding almost on a daily basis.

"Jessie and I were thinking we'd like to spend the day with you," said Ryan.

"Doin' what?"

"Thought maybe we could take some plants and put them around the grave. And that blue spruce over there is still young enough to replant," he said, pointing toward the patch of yard at the end of the road.

"Hmm. She'd probably like that. Okay by me. But, son, don't be makin' this a habit. I'll be fine. It was God's will. I may be a little lonely now and then, but in time, I'll adjust." It had been a well-rehearsed speech.

"Understood."

They fell silent. Ryan's mind cursed the weeds. He picked up the spade and began working at the roots.

"You okay, son?"

"Not sure yet. I've been avoiding the reality of it, I suppose. I'm driving to the city tonight to pick up my truck. It'll probably hit while I'm alone."

"I've been meaning to ask where the Jeep come from."

"Remember that therapist friend of mine, Elliott Stone?"

"Sure. Helped you out on your thesis, right?"

"Yeah. Well, he has a thing for Jessie."

"I thought he was married."

"That doesn't stop people anymore, Gramps. Besides, apparently he's divorced now. Anyway, he tried to follow me here to see her. I caught wind of it and stopped at Sandy's. She was kind enough to make a trade for the weekend."

"You still seeing her, son?"

"No, that's been over for a long while."

"What do you think of Jessie?"

Momentarily dodging the obvious meaning of his question, Ryan answered, "I think she'll be fine in time. We haven't had much chance to work out her problems yet."

"Well, best be gettin' at it, don't ya think?"

"Can't rush healing, Gramps."

"I just like her, that's all."

Ryan stopped working and sat cross-legged in the dirt. He set the trowel and spade at his side. "We've been through this once before, only you weren't in the mood to discuss what was really on your mind. Are you now?" Ryan wondered if the climactic explosion he'd been waiting for was about to surface. He knew that eventually Gramps had to release his anger concerning Brecca. With Ruth's sudden passing, his emotions would be sensitive.

"There's a substance to her. And I think you two are good together. No big deal."

"No big deal? You are so stubborn. Why can't you just admit this is about Brecca?"

"Rebecca?" Gramps stopped his digging, leaned back, and stared at Ryan.

"Yeah, that's what this is about, isn't it? You like Jessie. You want her and me to get together. I blew it with Brecca, so I'd better make sure I don't mess up and lose the only other good woman the Lord has sent my way."

"How long you been holding that in?"

"What?" Ryan looked confused.

"Is that what you think I've been feelin' all these years?"

"Well, isn't it? You brought it up just the other night."

Just then, Jessie emerged from the kitchen to take breakfast orders. She was wearing a pink taffeta summer dress that swayed as she walked. Both men stared at her awkwardly. Even as she was unaware of the conversation, the unnatural lines of their faces told her that the moment was not right for her presence. She intuitively decided that perhaps a retreat to the house would be in order.

"You know what?" she said uncomfortably as she approached, "I think I forgot something in the . . . I left the tea . . . I'll just go now." She disappeared into the safety of the house.

Gramps joined Ryan in the dirt, massaging the pain from his aging knees. "I suppose a part of me feels that way. I was angry with you for being so stupid. But then Ruth laid into me pretty good one night. She reminded me that it wasn't my place to judge you or to hold your mistakes against you. I guess I figured it was. I mean, after all, I raised you. I must have done something wrong to raise such an irresponsible . . ." He stopped himself. "I blamed myself next. If only I'd been stricter."

Ryan reflected on how strict he'd been and couldn't imagine him having been any more severe.

"I know you loved her, son. I know you had things to overcome. You lost your mother, father, and watched your grandmother die. And then there was Rebecca's money. I just expected with all my great training that you'd handle it okay. I figured you'd work through it with her, though, not in spite of her." He sensed the pain in Ryan's face. "In time, I realized that you were okay. It just took Rebecca dyin' to make it that way. We don't always understand the Good Lord's plan. It certainly ain't up to me to go tellin' Him what to do. I was lookin' forward to that great-grandson too. Selfish, I know. I resented you, I guess, for havin' taken that away from us. As far as the young lady inside goes, well, I think you'd be a fool not to let her know how you're feelin', ethics or not. Life's short, boy. You and I both can attest to that. Tell her, son. Help her through her problems, and have the life you want."

Ryan sat motionless. This was not what he had expected. He'd been pumped for a good fight. He also didn't think now was the time to share his feelings about Jessie. He wasn't sure how it was all going to turn out. Gramps had experienced enough pain.

"Wonder how come God keeps *us* around?" Ryan said.

"Suppose we're still good for somethin'."

"Or not good enough."

"Either way, isn't our time. Best make use of what's left us, eh, son?" Back on both knees, Gramps continued with the weeds.

"You know I couldn't be more sorry about Brecca, don't you, Gramps?"

"I know."

Quiet set in for a moment before Ryan spoke. "Up for planting those flowers after we're done here? Or do you have something else you need to do?" he asked.

"Sounds fine. I gotta decide what to do with the place. Suppose I should move in and let you have yours to yourself."

"No need to leave. I've gotten used to you."

"I belong here, son. Let Jessie know she's still welcome till her place is finished. Also, let her know I'll be startin' back on her place in the mornin'."

"I know she'll understand if you want to take more time."

"And do what? Putter around here feelin' sorry for myself? No, I need to get workin'."

* * *

Jessie was putting away the dried dishes from the night before when Ryan entered. "I am so sorry about that." She pointed toward the garden.

"It's fine."

"You'd think I would have heard something to give me a clue. Everything was so quiet when I went out there. I guess *that* should have been my clue, huh?"

"It's okay, really. Gramps wanted me to let you know he'll be staying here permanently now." He poured a glass of water. "He also said that you're still welcome here until your place is finished."

"You think I should stay?" she asked sincerely, not wanting to be a burden.

"You could stay with me." He grinned.

"It would probably be best if Gramps wasn't alone, huh?"

"What about my being alone?"

"You have a dog, remember?" She removed the meat from the griddle while he walked over to her.

"Is that bacon?" His stomach turned.

"Senses aren't fully working yet, hmm?"

"What do you mean?"

"Ryan, I'm not stupid. I smelled the beer on your breath."

"I stopped at four."

"Uh-huh."

"Gramps will get back to work on your place tomorrow." He needed to change the subject.

"Tomorrow! He should take some time off. It will take him a couple days to move his things, won't it? And what about all of Ruth's things? He'll need help going through all of them. He can't be thinking I expect him to get back to work! Should I talk to him?"

"I had the same reaction, but he's determined. And I think he's right. It'll be good for him. Sulking has never been his way. He'll heal best if he's working."

Jessie brought the bacon, scrambled eggs, and hash-browned potatoes to the table. "Help yourself. I want to make some juice. I'll go get Gramps."

"He wants to be alone a while. We had quite the discussion. Got the Brecca issue worked through." He stared at the food before him, and the nausea returned.

"Are you okay?"

"The smell's getting to me. Not sure I'm ready for food yet." The color drained from his face.

"I was talking about your conversation with Gramps, not your stomach."

"Oh. It wasn't the fight I had planned for all these years. In a way, I guess I wanted him to be angry. I could have used that against him to justify my position. I could have walked away knowing I was right and he was wrong. Truth is, neither one of us came out ahead. I hurt him. I hurt everyone involved. No way around that. Maybe I can let go now."

"Let go?"

"Brecca. It's time to let go."

Jessie sat next to him, placing the juice on the table. "Would you like some company into the city?"

"You afraid I won't make it in one piece?" He smiled, sensing her awkwardness.

"It's not that. I just thought you might like some company." She began drinking the juice in front of her.

"I'd feel better if you were around here. I know Gramps is okay, but I'm not sure he's ready for another quiet night alone."

"Okay. By the way, if you continue to use drinking as an escape, I'll be looking for a new friend. You got away from that years ago, and so did I. I won't be going there again."

"Understood."

The screen door opened and Gramps entered. "Smellin' mighty good in here."

"Plenty of food if you're hungry," Jessie said.

"Don't mind if I do." He pulled off his garden gloves and washed his hands. "You heading into the city with Ryan tonight?"

Since Ryan had already told him that he was going alone, Jessie spoke up. "I'd like to do a few things around here."

"Nothin' round here needs to be done, and I don't need a baby-sitter." Gramps looked them both in the eye. "It'd do you two good to spend some time together. Things to resolve, if I remember right." He was at the table, scooping hash browns onto his plate.

"Gramps . . ." began Ryan.

"Course that memory of yours doesn't work quite as well when it's bogged down with alcohol, now does it?"

Jessie and Ryan remained silent.

"I wasn't born yesterday, son. Smelled ya in the garden, and you haven't even touched what is a feast for the pallet. You know how I feel about your drinkin'."

"I only had four."

CHAPTER 29

"Thank you, young lady," Gramps said to Jessie as she carried the last suitcase of clothing to his truck. "That spaghetti sauce ought to be ready for eatin'. You two head down in about twenty minutes, and I'll have the pasta close to done and ready." His old truck creaked as he closed the tailgate.

"Thinking we ought to just head to the city now, Gramps. A storm's coming this way tonight," Ryan said.

Jessie shot an angry look in Ryan's direction. "Storm or not, I'm not missing spaghetti, especially yours, Gramps. We'll be there."

Gramps's pride manifested itself as he strutted to the front of his truck.

"What?" Ryan looked quizzically at Jessie.

"I can't believe you told him no to dinner! What were you thinking?"

"Storm. I was thinking storm," he replied, following Jessie to the porch.

"You were the one saying he shouldn't be alone and that you would feel safer if I were with him. And you say NO to dinner?! Why don't you just leave me here, go off to Sandy's, and return the Jeep by yourself!"

He stood, bewildered, as his front door slammed before he got through. He rubbed his hands over his face. After some thought, he concluded that he had absolutely no idea what had just happened. Or what he'd done wrong.

* * *

Dinner was delicious. "You're right, son, there is a storm due here late tonight," Gramps said, listening to the weather station.

Ryan was finishing with the disaster Gramps had left in the kitchen while Jessie headed to the bathroom. "We're just going straight there and back," said Ryan. "Should return by ten or so. We'll dodge the worst of it." Ryan snickered as he stared at the counters. Dinner consisted of sauce and pasta, but Gramps had managed to dirty no less than three pots and two pans.

"By the way, son, a letter came for Jessie today. Forgot to give it to her. Do ya mind?" Gramps pulled the letter from a stack of sympathy cards.

"No problem." Ryan recognized the writing. Walking toward the front porch, he opened it quickly. He slipped the divorce decree into his pants pocket. "Hey, Gramps, don't mention that letter to Jessie, okay?"

"Ah . . ."

"She doesn't need this right now, trust me."

"Okay."

In the bathroom, Jessie began opening and shutting cupboards and drawers loudly while muttering to herself. It was inaudible, but he was sure he heard, "Stupid idiot."

"Don't suppose you know what that's about in there, do you?" Ryan asked Gramps, leaning on the arm of the recliner.

"Nope. But it's been my experience, son, that when a woman starts slammin' and mutterin', it ain't good." Gramps looked over his shoulder in the direction of the bathroom then resumed his television viewing.

"Are we going or not?" Jessie was at the bathroom entry with both hands on her waist.

"Going, definitely going." Ryan sprang from the recliner and grabbed his coat and keys. "Bye, Gramps. See you in a bit."

Jessie waited for him to leave then leaned over and kissed Gramps on the cheek. "I got him a wee bit flustered, hmm?" She winked.

"Just a *wee* bit," he replied, smiling.

* * *

"Ryan, would you pull over please?" Jessie looked out the passenger window, avoiding his look of surprise. After pulling into a quiet wooded area, he turned off the ignition and waited, watching while she fidgeted with the gold band on her finger. He sensed something interesting was about to surface. Minutes passed.

Quietly she spoke, eyes focusing outside her window on nothing in particular. "I . . . I . . . would? . . ." She scratched her head, twirled the band again, and then blurted out, "Do you have to go into town tonight? I mean, does she need her Jeep now? Or did you need to see her, or . . ."

"Slow down." He placed his hand on hers. "What's this about, Jessie?" His voice was low and soothing. She stared at his hand. He removed it.

"I despise the fact that you handle everything so well." Her utter frustration was apparent in the harshness of her voice.

"Somehow, that didn't make things clearer for me." His eyes narrowed.

"Are you going to see her for . . . for what?"

"Huh?"

"Of course, *I* can't run away, but when *you* do, it's okay?!"

"Jessie, I can't even begin to read between the lines here. Can you give me something I'll understand?"

She turned her body toward him, her hands gesturing in frustrated motions. "The only sign you've given that you even realize your aunt, who was like a mother to you, has died, is that you get drunk the night of the funeral. Today you plant flowers around her grave while humming 'The Hills are Alive,' and now you're driving off to play with Candy!"

"Sandy."

"Whatever!" she shouted.

"I didn't get drunk, Jessie, and I have no intention of *playing* with Sandy." Ryan tried to keep a straight face. She was most assuredly upset, and possibly a bit jealous. Not taking her seriously could jeopardize everything. "She's had my truck for five days now. That's five days too long. She's good at many things, but driving is not one of them. The police have ticket books printed with her name and information already filled in." He shook his head and shivered. "She shouldn't even have a license."

"Oh." Jessie folded her arms in her lap, looking like a scolded puppy.

"As far as my grieving process is concerned, I'm not sure what you believe I should have done, but Ruth raised me to accept life and all that comes with it. Death in Ruth's case was a natural process. She was old, she had lived a good life, and she would not have wanted to suffer—or put those she loved through the pain of *watching* her suffer. She died in peace, Jessie. I can't mourn that. I am sad, intensely so, that she isn't here anymore and that she won't get to use that old rocker again. I will miss her. But I'm alive, and my life has to continue.

"When Brecca died, I grieved a long time. Her death was not natural. It was robbery. I felt that I should have been the one God took, not her and our son. When she died, I drank heavily, smoked two packs of cigarettes a day, and played around a great deal with 'Candy.' None of that helped at all. It kept me feeling like the scum I was, and it postponed my dealing with the issues at hand. I learned from that experience and handled this one better—well, except for the four beers. And if you remember, I said I was hearing voices and smelling my dead wife's perfume. I'm not exactly a poster child for sanity."

"We can go now." She wiped the tears off her cheeks.

"I'd rather talk."

"We just did that."

"It seemed to be going rather well," he jested.

"For you, maybe. I, on the other hand, am cold, and I have to use the bathroom."

"You do that a lot," he said, starting the engine.

"Yeah, well, I have a bladder the size of an ant," she replied, rubbing her hands up and down her arms.

"I think it's all that tea you drink." He turned the truck around and headed in the direction from which they came.

"Hey, where you going?"

"Home."

"Oh, no! I'm fine, really. I don't need to go home," she said apologetically.

"I'd like to go home."

Dropping her chin, sadly she replied, "I didn't mean to ruin your evening."

"You're way too hard on yourself, Jessie. I'd like to go to the cabin and talk. I think you would too. That doesn't spoil the evening; it enhances it."

"What about your truck?"

"It'd be a miracle if it's still in one piece anyway. Another day won't make any difference."

When they arrived, Jessie quickly ran inside while Ryan called Gramps to let him know of the change in plans.

When she came out, Jessie found Ryan bent over, searching the refrigerator with Nelly pushing her nose past him. "Looking for a beer?"

"Actually, no. I was looking for that apple pie I brought home from the funeral."

"You can't possibly be hungry after that dinner."

"Nope. Not hungry one bit. But I still want the pie." He held the dessert in one hand, and reached for a soda. Nelly stuck her inquiring nostrils in the air and gave a requesting whine.

"Down girl, it's all mine."

"Pie and pop. Hmmm, going for a sugar high? I should call Gramps and let him know we're here."

"Already did that. He's headed over, just because . . ."

"I understand." She walked over to the stove to begin steeping tea.

"Do you ever drink anything else?"

"Nope."

"Why not?"

"Some things are simple, Ryan. I like tea."

He took a sip of his soda then wiped his mouth. "Kind of boring, don't you think?"

"You're saying I'm boring?" She stirred a teaspoon of honey in the tea.

"Not you. Tea."

"Ever tried it?"

"It's hardly a manly food product."

"That was definitely a sexist remark. I'm glad we decided to come back and talk. So far, it's been enlightening." She sat at the table.

Ryan joined her. "Seriously, now. Your singing is unbelievable. You've obviously had professional training. Why not the stage instead of counseling?"

She laughed. "I haven't had any voice training."

"What? You've got to be kidding."

"First I'm boring, now I'm a liar?"

"TEA is boring! And you're not a liar. Typically a voice like yours is a product of years of professional training and practice."

"Ryan, my voice is okay for lullabies, but it certainly isn't star quality. When I was singing at the hospital and at the funeral, it wasn't me. I mean, my body was there, but something took over my voice. I felt the words coming out, but I have never sounded like that before. I felt, I don't know, strange."

The room fell silent. Ryan knew that he, too, had felt something. It had been a long time since he'd felt the Spirit. He knew he wasn't capable of articulating this to Jessie.

"Ryan? Remember when we were outside the church, you told me I was apologizing for the wrong thing?"

"Yes."

"What did you mean by that?"

"You tell me."

"I want to hear your version first." She smiled and folded her arms.

"Okay. You said you didn't really mean to call Ken, the tall man, a hypocrite. I think you did."

"I don't even know him."

"No, but maybe you believe if he's a drunk, he shouldn't be worshiping in church."

"It's not the worshiping part that bothers me. It's more that he tries to pretend to be something he really isn't."

"But you don't even know him, remember? So the person you're really talking about is your father."

She lowered her head, narrowed her eyes, and changed the subject. "What's the history behind the rose painting in your bedroom?"

Ryan stared at her for a while. "Why do you think it has a history?"

"To use your own words, 'It isn't a manly thing.'"

"I take that all back. In England and Ireland, men love tea."

"Uh-huh. Who's avoiding the question now? Seems to me you once said, 'Anything you ever want to know, just ask.'"

"I painted it for Brecca. White roses were her favorite." Ryan lowered his head slowly, slightly embarrased.

"You painted that?"

"Yeah."

"I'm impressed. Why such a rose, though? From all I've heard about Brecca, it seems to me that the picture should appear joyous and full of color. Instead it seems depressed and lonely."

"Don't you want to know where or when I learned to paint?"

"Not really," she said, gazing directly at him.

"Well, I'll tell you anyway. One day when I was about ten, I found an old box in the shed. Inside were art how-to books. The paints with them had long since dried up, but the brushes were still in relatively good shape. I haven't painted in years. That was the last piece I did."

She stared back.

"Okay, I painted over the original. If you would have looked closer—which you couldn't have because you were too involved with snooping—you would've noticed. The original had two white roses, symbolizing her and me." He paused before continuing. "When she died, I removed one."

"Hers," Jessie said with a trace of sadness.

"No, mine." A tone of bitterness lingered in his voice. "I took out my rose and left hers. That's what I felt God should have done."

"Since you don't feel that way anymore, why not put it back?"

"I'll do it when it's right. Satisfied?"

Jessie nodded. "How long has it been since Nelly's been fed?"

Ryan turned and spied Nelly chewing on a new pair of loafers. "Hey! Stop it, Nelly! That's my best pair!" He leaped from the table and grabbed at his shoes. Nelly was up for a challenging game of tug-o-war.

Jessie filled the dog dish and sweetly called, "Here, girl, something better awaits you." Nelly let go of the shoe and raced toward the bowl.

Ryan fell back against the wall holding the loafer. "This isn't my day."

"Good save there, son," Gramps said as he walked in.

"Yeah, right."

"Well, I'm tired. Gonna do a little readin' before I hit the sack."

"Can we get you anything?" Jessie asked.

"Nope. I'm just fine."

"Thanks, Gramps," said Ryan as he eased his way up from the floor and dumped his shoes in a pile. Washing his hands, he said, "How about we venture upstairs to the loft?"

"You're assuming I'm still in the mood to talk."

"Yep."

She took her teapot and mug, kicked off her shoes, and led the way.

CHAPTER 30

The loft felt warm and cozy. There was no need for an afghan, but Jessie looked around for one anyway. Ryan set about opening the windows.

"Could we keep them closed for a while?" Jessie asked.

"Sure." He noticed from the corner of his eye that she had already positioned herself in the recliner and wrapped herself in the afghan. He, on the other hand, was feeling a bit on the cooked side after spending the majority of the day out in the heat. But if it meant that Jessie might actually talk and put some issues behind her, he could endure his shorts shrink-wrapped to his skin. He settled into the love seat, enabling him to watch her from an angle.

After a moment of silence, Jessie began. "When my sister and I went to live with our father, we would get locked in the basement for long periods of time. The only thing that would calm her was my singing."

"And you were five?"

"Almost."

"She was two?"

"She wasn't quite two yet. Usually we were locked in for hours, but once in a while it would be longer. When he'd forget to turn on the light, it would be . . . well, frightening."

"You couldn't reach the light switch?"

"Sure I could. I just enjoyed being in the dark," she said testily. "What kind of question is that? If I could have reached the light, we wouldn't have been in the dark. I can't understand why people paid you so much." She threw off the afghan and began pacing. "The light was a bulb, and the only way to turn it on was to reach the little silver chain that hung from the socket." She stood in the center of the room, imitating the scene, one hand on her hip.

"I'll try not to be so stupid," Ryan said apologetically.

She turned toward the window and exhaled. "I tried stacking everything that wasn't nailed down to climb on, but I was still too short. We played in the dark for hours on end." She dropped back into the recliner, snuggling into the afghan.

Ryan suddenly realized something. The past couple of weeks at Ruth's, he had walked around shutting lights off constantly—or so it seemed. However, if Jessie needed the lights on to feel some level of security, then that would certainly take priority over saving a few bucks on electricity. "What did you play?" he asked.

"Huh?" She had been deep in thought, recalling the times she tried to pull a chair down the steep steps. Often her stepbrothers would taunt her by tripping her and keeping the chair. They'd never once offered to help.

"You said you played for hours. What did you play?"

"I don't know. Make-believe, I suppose. I don't really remember that. I'm surprised I remember as much as I do. I guess I remember feelings mostly. We were hungry, cold, miserable, and scared. Katie's diaper would be a mess. I'd take it off, and she'd mess on the floor. Then she'd cry. Man, she could cry. That's when I would sing." She continued playing with the gold band on her finger. "The woman who lived next door used to sunbathe. She'd leave her radio on, and I'd listen. I learned a lot of melodies and many of the lyrics that went with them, but after a while I'd just make them up as I went along."

Jessie's body shivered. Ryan remained quiet. Was she finished? The fact that she was still firmly sitting in the recliner indicated that she probably intended to continue.

"I find it difficult to sing just for the sake of singing anymore. When I sing out loud, it brings back memories that I'd just as soon forget."

"Can we go back, for a moment, to the basement?" Ryan inquired in a serious tone.

"Why?"

"I'm curious about something."

"What exactly?"

"The lady next door."

"Why her?"

"How did you know she was sunbathing?"

"I just knew."

"You were under five. At that age, it's unusual for a child to make that connection."

"At that age it's unusual to be locked in a basement for days on end!"

"Just think for a minute. Close your eyes . . ."

"No!" Jessie retorted gruffly.

"Pace then."

"You're convinced I think better when I do that, aren't you?"

"I'm not sure I'd say *think*, but it appears to help you cope with your frustration. It's more an observation than anything."

"You know, I just don't want to go there right now." Jessie's face held a pleading expression.

"I believe you do," Ryan said with a calmness and surety. "I think that's why we didn't go to the city. How did you know she was sunbathing?"

"I just did! Let it go!" Her face was flushed, and her voice sounded desperate.

"Okay. You lived in a motel when you were sixteen?"

Jessie turned her face away from Ryan's view and swiftly wiped away the tear that had formed. "Yes."

"Were you with your father till then?"

"More or less. I lived in the motel on my own for a little over a year. When I was seventeen, the owners of the motel took me in. They had grown fond of me and didn't consider it proper—my being alone. They had assumed me to be at least nineteen or twenty. When they found out I was only seventeen, they were appalled." Her eyes were distant.

"Can you be more specific regarding the 'more or less'?"

"No."

"What do you mean, they took you in?"

"They hired me to keep their books and help clean the rooms. It became full-time work, so I gave up my previous career as a waitress and embarked on the glorious life of a cleaning woman."

"Were they good to you?"

"Yeah. I earned enough to go to night school at the local college. I began work around six o'clock each morning, finished at two in the afternoon, studied, then went to class."

"No time for fun."

"Considering what I'd left behind, that *was* fun."

"You want to tell me about the ring?"

"I have already. It's a ring. R-I-N-G."

Ryan remained silent. Jessie crossed her legs and straightened her back, rubbing her tired eyes. "Ring, ring, ring, okay. My mother gave it to me before she went to the bathroom at the movie theater. She had been crying. I remember her wiping her eyes, taking the ring off her finger, and giving it to me. Then she told me she had to go 'potty' and for me to stay with Katie. She said 'I love you' to us, kissed us, and was gone." Jessie remained quiet for a moment. "I wore it on a string around my neck for years. When it fit, I placed it on my finger. I guess I rub it when I need her. Somehow it makes me feel safer. Silly, I suppose."

"You don't have any idea where she is?"

"No."

"Where were you living at the time you lived with her?"

Jessie sipped at her tea, trying desperately to regain control of herself. "In an apartment."

"I'd like to hear more about your father."

"Not giving up on that one, are you? I've told you, he was cruel." She swiped away a falling tear.

"Will you be more specific?"

"Which one of thousands of times, in particular, should I refer to?" Her voice was trembling.

"How about starting with the earliest memory you have of his cruelty."

"He used to come around a lot when he was drunk, after the divorce. Don't know why, really. Maybe he was angry with his new wife so he took it out on our mother. I remember at the apartment, before we left, I heard him picking up the chairs to the kitchen table and throwing them at her. What did Elliott do, exactly, that got you stuck with me?"

Ryan wasn't prepared for the abrupt change. "It's a long story."

"Planning on going somewhere?" She put her knees up and wrapped her arms around them.

He attempted to conceal his discomfort by rubbing Nelly's back. She had taken up residence at his feet before the discussion began. Now savoring the sudden attention, she rolled over.

"Difficult, isn't it?" Jessie commented.

"Difficult?"

"Coming up with answers on the spot."

"Yeah, I guess it is."

"So?"

He gave Nelly one last pat, leaned back, and folded his arms across his chest. "Weeks after Brecca's death, I still wasn't eating or sleeping. I was useless at work, so I took a leave of absence. I stayed in the city, not wanting to be around here. I spent most of my days wandering and my nights drinking. One particular evening, I graced the same establishment as Elliott. He was there on business, helping some client who had declared an emergency. Anyway, after he was finished with his client, he came to my table. I was beyond help, incredibly sloshed. When I was ready to go, he reached for my keys. I insisted I was fine. After all, I'd grown accustomed to driving drunk. He followed me to my car and got in the passenger side to give it one more attempt. I started the engine and endeavored to prove I was fine. I peeled out of the parking lot and raced up the street. The next thing I knew, he had grabbed the steering wheel and jerked hard to the left. He yelled for me to slam on the brakes, which I did. Seconds later, my eyes focused on a woman crossing the street, cradling an infant. If Elliott hadn't been there, I could have killed them. Another woman and child dead because of my selfishness." He shook his head. "I was going fifty in a twenty-five, and I was drunk. I still can't fathom what she was doing on that street at two in the morning."

"Maybe she was an angel on a mission to save you." *Huh?*

He remained quiet for a minute then said, "I thought you didn't believe in miracles."

"I believe in them, just not for me. I'm glad Elliott was there."

"Yeah."

"Is that what woke you up, helped you get back to living life?"

"It jerked me back to reality, that's for sure. I haven't been drunk since—well, not counting those four beers, of course. I don't know if the woman was an angel or not. But I do believe it was God who helped me back and gave me a sense of peace." Ryan couldn't believe he had just said that.

"Well, I'm glad He helped someone who deserved it."

"He's helped you, Jessie," Ryan's voice was soft.

"No! No, He hasn't," she snapped. "But save the speech. I'm not in the mood to be spiritually enlightened. I think it's about time to call it a night anyway." She wrapped the afghan around her and started for the stairs.

"I'll grab my keys."

"Don't bother. I feel like walking." She continued her descent.

"It's raining."

"I don't mind." She folded the afghan and placed it on a corner table in the foyer.

"Jes—"

"I'm a big girl, Ryan. If I want to walk home in the rain and risk catching some respiratory disorder, that would be my choice now, wouldn't it?"

"I don't think you really want to leave."

"Yes, Ryan, I do." Tears were forming.

"It's time to stop allowing your past to control you. I can't make things all better, and you know that. But I can help. I believe you want me to."

"I just can't figure out what has brought this whole ordeal about. These issues go way back, and I've managed to keep things well under control until recently. The only thing that has changed is the death of my father. But I hated him, so I can't see why that would have thrown me into my current quandary."

Ryan remained quiet for a minute, making sure her thought was finished. Then he said, "Losing someone will often bring out all of the symptoms you've experienced."

"But that's losing someone you care about. I didn't care about him, Ryan. That's what I don't understand."

"But you have unresolved feelings toward him. He was integral to your life in one way or another. He obviously caused you a great deal of pain. You've known all along that until you resolved those feelings, you couldn't be in complete control. While he was alive, there was still a conflict. And as long as the conflict existed, there was still a relationship, no matter how awful it may have been. The knowledge that someday you would have to deal with it, talk to him, and perhaps resolve it, was a subconscious constant. Then he died. The relationship was gone, and any hope of understanding his viewpoint went with him. You're left to resolve it alone."

"Hmm. Okay, so how do I do it? Forgive him, I mean. Obviously I have to or I'll never have any peace."

"Is it the forgiving or having the sense of peace that makes you uncomfortable?"

"Huh?"

"You're appearing angry."

"Is there any way you can do this without doing that?" she hissed.

"I'm trying. It's kind of hard to avoid using the skill for which I was trained."

"It's just that every time you say something clinical, I remember myself using the same phrases. I don't like it."

"Are we finished avoiding the question at hand?" Ryan asked.

"I forgot what it was."

"I asked you whether it was the fact that you had to forgive your father or gaining a sense of peace that makes you feel uncomfortable."

"Oh, yeah. Good memory, Dr. Blake."

"Thanks."

"Both, I suppose," Jessie replied dryly.

"The act of forgiving someone that hurt you is difficult at best. But why do you think the idea of being at peace makes you uncomfortable?"

"You already know the answer to this, as do I. Must I really say it?"

"Yes." Ryan closed his eyes for a brief moment then slowly opened them.

"Okay, fine. If I feel a sense of peace, then I'd have to venture into an avenue I'm not comfortable with. I'd have to let go of my anger and hatred after they've been my constant companions for so long. And eventually, I'd need to involve God somehow."

"Yes, you would."

"And that means forgiving Him, too."

"Yes, it does."

"I have no desires in that area at this point in the process."

"Okay. I'm not a preacher, and I certainly don't tell all my clients to find God in their lives, but *you've* looked to Him. You've needed Him. And you also blame Him. Where there is blame there must be forgiveness, or complete healing is impossible. So for you, it's necessary."

"And for you it wasn't?" Jessie wished she could take that back.

"Excuse me?"

"Never mind. It's nothing."

"No, it was something."

"You blame God for Rebecca's death, don't you?"

"No. I blame myself, and I was angry that God allowed my stupidity to kill her." The verbalization of this hit hard. This was truth, and he knew it.

"I'm sorry. I shouldn't bring your issues into this. It's just that this whole thing is arduous. I thought in a couple hours I would tell you everything, I'd have a good cry, and we'd be done."

"You must not have a great return base if all your clients solve their problems in two hours."

"Where do I go from here?" Jessie asked after her chuckle.

"Your name change. Was that because you disliked your father?"

"Yes. As soon as I was eighteen, I had it legally changed."

"Last name too?"

"Yep."

"Can I know your full, given name?"

"Why?"

"No psychological reason, just personal curiosity."

"Oh. Samantha LeAnn Borne."

"I know how you came up with Jessie, but what about Nicole and Winston?"

"Nicole was . . . Katherine's middle name, and Winston was my mother's maiden name."

"It's a nice name."

"Which?"

"The one you're using now."

"I didn't really mind Samantha, but my father was drunk so much that he couldn't remember it. He called me Sam most all of the time. When I learned my father had picked out my name anyway, I didn't feel bad when I changed it."

"Stella brought four boys to the marriage and they had another boy together, is that right?"

"Yep."

"The name Sam made you one of the boys then."

"I suppose. But he knew I was a girl when . . ." She stopped, picked up a cracker, and began chewing.

"Wanna go there?"

"I've dealt with all that."

"Are you sure?"

Seconds turned into minutes before she was able to respond. She hadn't dealt with any of it, but the thought of bringing it out in the open with Ryan terrified her.

"No," she said quietly, lowering her head. "This is where it gets more difficult, Ryan." She pulled herself out of her comfort zone, picked up the afghan, and walked toward the window. Keeping her face from seeing his, she began. "I have vivid memories of my father and mother yelling. I often hear their voices in my nightmares. My mother would put us in our room when he came by drunk. Katie would usually end up in my bed, but I suppose I climbed in with her as well. She was too young to know what was happening. I knew yelling and hitting wasn't a happy thing, but not knowing anything different, I just assumed everyone was treated that way." Tears were forming. "I would hear the slaps then the sobs from my mother in the corner of the kitchen after he'd leave. I hated him. So when I was told by my foster parents that we were being sent to him, I got scared. Scared for myself, but mostly for Katie. She was so little.

"No one paid much attention to her, though, after we got there. I changed her, fed her, and clothed her. The boys teased us and locked us up so they could . . . be alone with us."

Ryan bowed his head and closed his eyes. This part of his profession was the worst. It was why he had switched to aiding therapists only. He'd heard enough horror stories of women and children being brutalized. It turned his stomach.

"Sorry," he muttered.

Jessie closed her eyes and continued. "Our father didn't want us at all. We often overheard Stella, our stepmother, say that we were his responsibility and that he didn't have any choice. She was kind to us for the most part, but she was a busy woman. My father chose not to work. He had a room in the house that he said was his locksmith business, although I don't ever recall seeing a customer there or him ever working in it. He had all the equipment, though, so who knows? Anyway, Stella was a hard worker. We hardly ever saw her. If she made the mistake of leaving any cash around, my father would take and spend it on alcohol. You know, I don't really know what her profession was. I think she was a waitress or a cook or something. Funny that I wouldn't know that. I guess I spent too much time trying to keep away from . . ."

Ryan closed his eyes. She was headed into scary territory again, and this was when the conversation usually ended.

"You asked me how I knew about the lady next door?" Jessie's frame, held tight within the yarn of the afghan, began to shake.

"Yes."

"Well, our bathroom had a window. That's where our stepbrothers usually took us. I could see her reflection in the mirror. I wondered what it would be like to be her. She lay on a long lounge chair and had her music blaring while she tanned. Our window was always closed, but I could still hear the music. They didn't bother Katie if I didn't cry."

Ryan concealed his pain. "This continued till Katie died?"

She nodded.

"Did you ever tell anyone?"

"Sure, like anyone would believe a five-year-old. I didn't know any of the right words. I didn't know anyone to tell that I thought would care. I was ignored anyway. I think on some level Stella knew, but she didn't want to. Or she didn't know how to deal with it. My father was cruel to her too, and the boys learned how to treat women through his wonderful example. It was a lost cause all the way around." The sun was beginning to set. "It's beautiful here in the evening."

"Yes, it is."

"I remember that when school started, everyone went except Katie and me. I turned five in time for school, but if my father had sent me, he would've had to be the one to watch Katie, since she was only two then. That wasn't going to happen. It would have interfered with his drinking. After the boys and Stella left, he locked us in the basement. As long as he returned home from the bar before three-thirty, who would know? It wasn't difficult to keep us silent."

"So you spent every day from morning till late afternoon in the basement?"

"Yes. Sometimes when he would remember to turn on the light, it didn't seem so creepy. I had hidden some blankets and toys in a corner. I don't think he knew those existed, or if he did, he didn't care. After a while, I kept a supply of diapers hidden, too. Food was the hardest thing to acquire. I was too short to reach anything. I tried canned foods, but I couldn't quite handle the can opener. I could usually reach the bread, so we had a lot of that."

"Jessie, I am so sorry."

"Yeah, well, some people have it worse."

Ryan didn't comment. He had grown very fond of her, and he was having a difficult time maintaining his impassive role.

"I tried hard one day to get something tall down the steps so that when my father would forget to turn on the light, I could do it. But it was too difficult. We didn't have little stools, just chairs, and I couldn't get a chair down there. There weren't any boxes or anything. I should have tried harder." She began to sob. A few minutes passed before she could continue. "The only thing that maintained my sanity was the woman next door. She could never see us because of the way the light hit the window, but I could see her and hear her music. It would get us through the late mornings. I knew it was time to eat lunch when she would come out. And when she went in, I knew that we only had an hour or so till our father came home. The days she wouldn't come out were miserable." She returned to the couch for her tea. Ryan picked up his water and swallowed hard. On some level, he wished he didn't have to hear all this.

"I wrote her a letter one day, years ago, after I had moved out. I learned her name was Loretta Pine. I didn't even know if she still lived there, but I wrote her anyway. She must have thought it was the most bizarre letter if she read it. I told her what a great help she had been to me for that year or so. Strange, huh?"

"No."

"Yes, it is."

"Jessie, you thanked the one person who gave you a sense of sanity. How is that strange?"

"I don't know . . ." She poured the last of the tea. Her hands hadn't stopped trembling since she'd first entered the room. "Figures. Tea's all gone. Ten years ago I would've reached for something stronger to get me through this."

"I'll be right back," said Ryan.

CHAPTER 31

Ryan returned from the kitchen holding a mug of hot chocolate with marshmallows. "Will this work?" he said.

"Thanks, Doc." She nodded as she took her first swallow. A few minutes passed before she continued. "The recurring nightmare I have . . ." Her eyes narrowed momentarily at the sweet taste of the smooth liquid. ". . . is of me being locked in the basement."

"What happened in the basement?"

Gently, Ryan.

"I've told you. Katie and I were locked in!" she yelled.

Ryan breathed in the delicate fragrance surrounding him and responded softly. "Okay. Do you want to tell me what happened to Katie?"

"No."

"What happens in the nightmare?"

"It's just Katie's face, that's all!"

"What happened to her, Jessie?"

"I can't do this . . ."

"Take your time."

"Yeah, yeah, yeah. That's easy for you to say. I'll tell you what—you tell me about your father, and I'll tell you about mine."

"We were talking about the nightmare and the basement."

"The basement is about my father, you moron!" Her voice quickly softened. "I . . . I didn't mean that, it's just . . ."

"It's all right. My father, let's see. I got off the bus from kindergarten and ran up the steps to see Aunt Ruth, like always."

"So, you and your dad lived at Ruth's?"

"Yeah, he had a place in town, but when my mother died, we moved in with Ruth. She and Gramps took care of me while my dad was at work. That particular day, Ruth wasn't in the rocker as usual. I found her on the couch, holding a piece of paper. I learned later it was a letter from my dad saying he just couldn't take it anymore, so he had left. She was crying, and when I asked what was wrong, she told me my dad was going away for a while. I instantly hated him for making her cry. I sat by her and told her I'd take care of her."

"That sounds like you."

"Well, turns out they took care of me."

"But you've heard from him over the years?"

"Yeah, every now and then. Last I heard, he was living in Texas. Has a wife and two girls."

"Do you still hate him?"

"No. I called one day and asked him why he left."

"You asked that over the phone, just out of the blue?"

"Yep."

"What did he say?"

"Said what I already knew. He missed my mother and couldn't stand looking at me because I reminded him of her. He told me that he loved me and that I had been better off with Ruth and Gramps. He had another family now, and that's where he needed to be."

"And after that conversation, does it still hurt?"

"Sure it does. But he was a kid when he married my mother. How many eighteen-year-olds are ready to be a dad? I'm curious about his wife and my half-sisters, but I'm betting they don't know of my existence." Ryan let the silence linger after he spoke.

Minutes passed before Jessie took her turn. She wished her father had shown even the slightest concern, as Ryan's had. "One day, our father was in a hurry to get down to the bar. He practically threw us down the stairs, and of course, neglected the light. It was storming, and the sky was black, so the basement was much darker than usual. I knew it'd be a long, gloomy day because Loretta wouldn't be tanning. No one had changed Katie's diaper, so I took one from my stash. After I changed her, she began to cry. I figured she was probably hungry. Stella had made hot dogs the night before, and I had snatched a couple whole ones and hid them in my shirtsleeves before we'd gone to bed. Looking back, it's a miracle we never got food poisoning." Jessie took a deep breath. "Anyway, I remembered seeing Stella cut the hot dog into little pieces before giving them to Katie. Since I didn't have a knife, I broke them into what I thought were small enough pieces." She stopped talking. Tears were surfacing again. Her whole frame began to tremble. "I tried to help her, but I couldn't." A river of tears ran freely down her cheeks. Ryan was immobilized. An icy surge of revulsion tore at his throat.

"In most of my nightmares, all I see is her pale skin and gray lips, and those eyes . . ." The room went silent for a few seconds before she broke completely and cried uncontrollably. "I tried . . . She couldn't breathe . . . I shook her, but she just stared at me. If I'd had a chair to reach the lock, I could have gotten help." She downed the rest of her drink in one swallow. Wiping her mouth and gasping for breath, she said, "I was holding her when my father returned. He shook me really hard, repeating over and over, 'What have you done, you stupid brat?! What have you done?!' His face was . . . horrible. I don't remember much after that. They took her away and there was a funeral, I think. Kind of blocked all that out. I've thought of undergoing hypnosis, but in the end, I guess I don't really care to remember. I've enough of what I do remember to deal with." She wiped her eyes and blew her nose with the tissue Ryan had handed her earlier.

Ryan tried not to show his shock at what she had just revealed. She needed his strength.

"Well, say something," she said through the tissue.

"You've never told anyone about Katie? Not even Elliott?"

"No, it's not the sort of thing I've ever felt like sharing. When I lived with the Ericksons—the people at the motel—I began studying self-help books. I thought I did a pretty good job at fixing myself, so I plunged into a life of helping others. I needed to put myself into something. Do you have any old black-and-white, unrealistic love stories hanging around here?"

"I have *Casablanca.*"

"That will do. How are you in the ice cream area?"

"Depends on the flavor in question, but I have an assortment."

"Great. Then I'm headin' to the kitchen." She avoided looking at her reflection in the wall's mirror.

"Jessie?"

"Yeah?" She turned to look at him, afghan wrapped around her quivering form.

"I'm sorry."

* * *

Ryan spent a few minutes showing Jessie how the DVD player worked, although it was obvious that she wasn't concentrating. She stayed wrapped in the afghan and sat on the floor in front of the wide-screen TV, looking as though she had just been hypnotized. Ryan turned everything on and watched her slowly lose herself in a concoction of chocolate, marshmallows, cashews, and ice cream. Once the movie was started, he turned to leave.

"You don't like *Casablanca?*" Jessie looked in his direction, careful not to reveal her red, swollen eyes.

"I do."

"Well, this is an awfully big room for only one person." The sound of her voice was barely audible as the metallic spoon clanked against the rim of the porcelain bowl.

"Is that your way of inviting me to join you?"

"It's the best you're gonna get tonight."

"I'll be back in a sec." After he filled a small bowl of the dessert, he headed to the family room.

Jessie didn't pay much attention to the beginning of the movie. She had finished off her entire bowl of ice cream while he'd been gone. She noticed the smirk on his face as he caught sight of her empty bowl. "Well, you know, I'm a little hungry, and it tasted good. Besides, I don't think I have to justify my eating habits."

Ryan sat a few feet from her on the floor and leaned back on the couch. "I wasn't going to say a word." He waited a few seconds before he continued speaking. "I noticed something tonight."

"Oh, please don't analyze me right now. I've just relived the epitome of horror, and I'm absolutely exhausted."

"Just one thing, all right?"

She began scraping her spoon around the sides of the bowl, hoping to find one last spoonful of the ice cream. *I swear, if he keeps talking, I'm going to rip that bowl right out of his hands.*

"You didn't twirl your ring."

"What?"

"Not once did you play with that ring," he said, pointing at the gold band.

"I'm not sure I'm following."

"I've noticed that when you're talking about something difficult or painful, you mess with that ring incessantly. Tonight you didn't."

"So, what are you saying, exactly? That my sister's death wasn't painful?!" Her voice grew more tense with each syllable. *Why is he doing this now?*

"No, that's not what I'm saying. Do you blame anyone else for your sister's death or just yourself?"

"Obviously I blamed my father and God. Look, I just want to watch this movie and have another bowl of ice cream. Please drop it, Ryan." She glared at him.

"Okay." He returned his attention to the movie.

"And so what exactly does *not* twirling my ring have to do with my placing blame on my father and God?" she asked anxiously seconds later.

"It has to do with your mother."

"Huh? She wasn't even there!"

"Yes, I know." Ryan focused on her eyes. She was struggling to find the link.

"Oh, I get it. You think on some level I blame her because she wasn't there?"

"Yes."

"Just watch the stupid movie. You think you know everything." She jumped up to get more chocolate, grumbling something rude under her breath.

"And another thing," she said, returning with the entire carton in hand. "I remember saying I was done for the evening. Why would you still push me?" She sat behind him on the couch.

Ryan had attempted to fill her mind with something other than the vivid image of her sister's death. "Because I wanted to raise your blood pressure." His face was serious, and the tone of his voice paralleled his concern.

"Well, it worked." She stared blankly at the screen.

* * *

Casabanca ended, and Ryan covered Jessie with an afghan. She was resting peacefully, so he decided to leave her there for the night. He retreated to his room for a looser-fitting T-shirt and cotton pajama pants.

Ryan reclined in the couch in the family room below the loft. He could reach her quickly, if necessary. He lay awake for a while, replaying in his mind the evening's conversation. What a horrible, traumatic ordeal. No child should ever have had to experience anything even remotely similar to that. She had been physically and mentally abused, humiliated, and degraded. She had experienced severe psychological trauma. No wonder she had neurotic tendencies—keeping a spic-and-span house, repainting his tiny error in her new bathroom, and not maintaining any ongoing relationships. These were all areas she could control. Having no relationships meant no one could hurt her again. It was the "I'll desert you before you desert me" syndrome. He realized that the very fact that she had committed to therapy was a miracle in itself.

Sometime later, Ryan awoke, startled, jumping to his feet far too fast. Jessie was sitting and shivering on the couch. "Jessie? It's okay," he said, staggering up the stairs.

"I . . . I . . . I can't get her face out of my mind, Ryan! This isn't fair. My mother and father should have been responsible. Not me! It just isn't fair . . ." The tears streamed freely down her checks. He leaned in next to her, took her by the shoulders, and pulled her close.

Ryan held Jessie as she shed her pain and grief. Finally she pulled away gently. "Thank you. I'm fine now. I'm sorry. I'd like to be alone."

"Of course."

Ryan returned to his spot and watched as she tossed and turned. Eventually her breathing slowed, and he closed his eyes.

Chapter 32

Gramps was standing on the porch of his new home in his usual morning attire when Ryan arrived. It was a little after dawn. The rooster had long since finished his predawn routine, and the birds were well into their carols. "Now, son, I think she's needin' some space."

"You two could have left a note. I searched the entire cabin and the stables. Why didn't you at least call?" Ryan's sweatshirt had been thrown on inside out, and his hair was matted.

"You okay, son?" Gramps voice bordered on laughter. "Wouldn't want ya goin' and gettin' all 'emotionally involved' now." He held his coffee as he sat in the well-used rocker.

Ryan sighed as he reached over and snatched the warm liquid out of Gramps' hands and leaned against a post. "Thanks. Is she inside?"

"She's gone for a walk."

"Alone?"

"No, I sent the Fourth Cavalry with her. All on horseback. What a crowd! Of course she's alone, son. She'll be fine. Ain't nothin' up at this hour 'cept the birds anyway."

"Hey, Gramps, sorry I missed breakfast. I was just . . ." Jessie stopped speaking as she rounded the outside corner of the house. She was gripping a cluster of roses.

"Hey there," said Ryan.

"Hey," she echoed. A quiet, awkward moment ensued.

"Yeah, well, okay," Gramps said as he rose from the rocker. "Won't take long to reheat breakfast, young lady, so come on in." Ryan followed the older man inside to the kitchen, with Jessie behind him.

Jessie stepped past Ryan in search of a vase for the flowers. After a few minutes of stalling, she settled down at the table across from him and reached for a slice of toast.

Ryan noticed her tendency to look everywhere but his general direction. "You planning on looking at me today?"

"Already have."

"I caught you off guard outside. You had no choice."

Gramps brought the rest of the warmed platter of food to the table.

"I'm eating toast. There's no reason to look at anything other than my food," Jessie retorted.

"Nobody stares at their food during an entire meal."

"I do. At least I can dress myself."

"I was in a hurry."

"You two are doing real great for a couple of so-called communication experts," Gramps said, picking up his newspaper.

Ryan threw Gramps a scornful plea for silence. Any silence, however, ended with Barkley's entrance. Chaos struck. Nelly scrambled from underneath the table, no longer tempted by the ham. Her sudden rampage took her between Ryan's legs and his chair. The coffee mug he had just been drinking from flew from his hand as he grabbed for the table. Barkley leapt to the windowsill above the sink, every hair on his back pointed straight up. Ryan was still choking on the coffee when Nelly broke into an enraged howl that was no doubt intended to hail the successful treeing of her intended prey.

Nelly had just clawed her way to the bottom of the windowsill when Jessie finally stood and yelled, "NELLY, NO! YOU GET DOWN THIS INSTANT, OR NO FOOD FOR YOU EVER AGAIN!" Nelly gave one final growl toward the trembling cat and slowly returned to her place under the table. Jessie opened the window. Barkley slithered under the glass and was gone before she could finish opening it.

"A lot of help you two were!" Jessie said, turning to the table. "You probably would have enjoyed watching her tear Barkley to shreds!" This was directed at Ryan.

Ryan laughed. "No, I'm sure we wouldn't." He looked toward Gramps, who simply sat, staring in disbelief.

"You hate that cat, admit it!" Jessie said.

"I don't hate the cat. I just think that on the Sabbath when God rested, one of his angels didn't. When nobody was looking, she created the little, hairy, uncontrollable beasts."

Jessie's eyes narrowed. She grabbed his plate of food and walked toward the sink.

"Hey, I wasn't finished!"

"Well, you are now!"

Ryan couldn't tell if he had seriously angered her or if she was just teasing.

"You guys just put the food away and leave everything in the sink. I'll get to it tonight. I'm anxious to get working on my place," Jessie said, having taken several deep breaths in an effort to calm down.

"Hang on and I'll drive you," Ryan said.

"No. It's a great morning. I'd rather walk."

"I'll walk with you then."

"NO!" she shouted louder than she had intended.

Gramps raised the local paper up a bit higher, disappearing behind the front-page excitement of the Johnsons' prize-winning calf.

"Jessie . . ."

"No, Ryan. Now stop." She turned toward him, avoiding his eyes. She held tightly to the dish towel. "You've been anxious to get to the city. I think now would be a great time to go. Last night was horrifying for me. I'm not ready to forge ahead yet. Look, I know I'm hard to figure out. One day I want you here, the next I don't . . . I don't know what to tell you except that today I don't. Okay?"

Ryan watched her face turn pale. He looked at Gramps. "You need anything from the city while I'm there?"

"Me? Ahhh . . . nope. I don't think so," Gramps said.

"You?" He lifted his eyes to meet Jessie's.

She gave her head a quick shake.

"Well, then, I'm off. I may stay through Monday to catch up on a few things."

"Be back for the town picnic and fireworks?" Gramps had set his paper and reading glasses down on the table.

"Wouldn't miss it. You'll have time to look after the horses and Nelly, Gramps? I don't know how that's going to work out now that you're living here. I hope it won't be too big a burden."

"Not a problem, son."

Ryan took a few steps closer to Jessie. "You're welcome to ride anytime. Use the cabin if you'd like."

"Thanks," she managed to say.

"Okay, well then, I'm off." Ryan hesitated to see if Jessie would look up. She didn't.

CHAPTER 33

Ryan's truck was not where he had parked it. He hoped Sandy had moved it to the garage and that it wasn't sitting in the nearest scrap yard. He rapped softly on her door and waited. When no response came, he searched for the hidden key.

Sandy's soft snoring filtered through the room. She was napping. The scent, most likely her latest discovery, was enticing as he entered her bedroom in search of his keys. He considered waking her, but something inside told him it was best to leave. He picked up Sandy's purse from the floor and located his keys. He scribbled a short note on the pad by the phone and left before the scent of lilac reached him.

Ryan wondered if his conscience would forever take on the voice of Brecca. And why was he *now* hearing voices? Why not when Brecca's life was on the line or when he was setting fire to Mark's house? Why hadn't it told him to run away like the bishop's son had?

* * *

Jessie was exhausted. Her emotional disclosures were taking their toll. She lay in bed, the Book of Mormon at her side. *Why did God have to be the answer to Ryan's quest for peace? And if he was at peace, then why didn't he forgive the Mormons and the townspeople for their behavior, whatever it was?*

Jessie reached for her box and pulled out the worn envelope she'd stolen out of her case folder at Social Services. She was fifteen and had run away again. During her reprimand, an emergency had surfaced and the worker had left the office. Jessie swiped the envelope marked

Samantha and stuck it in her pocket. She remembered returning home and wanting to read it, but there wasn't any privacy there, so she hid the envelope inside a shoe box to be read later. She should have read it then because shortly thereafter, her father had replaced whatever was inside the envelope with a hideous note. Had it been a letter from her mother? Had she pled for her to take good care of Katie? Maybe it had been a picture.

Her father, in a drunken frenzy, had taunted her that he hadn't destroyed it, but had rather hid it. Jessie remembered searching everywhere for it—but it had been in vain.

Jessie slipped the envelope back into the box and took out her worn and frazzled teddy bear. "Hey, Buddy, it's been a while, eh? I'm surprised you're still in one piece. I can't count how many times you listened to me cry. God may not have cared, but you did."

She closed the box and leaned back against the headboard, reflecting on her limited amount of religious study. She had vague memories of her mother reading to her and Katie from the Bible. There was a particular place she would frequently turn to in that old black book with the red-trimmed pages. When Jessie asked her about it once, her mother snuggled her in her lap and read to her the story of Job. As Jessie grew older, she never quite understood what it was her mother liked so much about the story. In a conversation with God, Satan proclaimed that Job's righteousness and obedience were due merely to His sheltering him from life's difficulties and blessing him with a life of prosperity and ease. In response, God gave Satan power over all that Job had.

Job received boils covering his entire body. He lost every earthly possession. Job's wife, his friends, and everyone he knew turned against him, saying he had done something to bring this great evil upon himself. But Job continued in his love for God, saying "The Lord gave, and the Lord hath taken away; blessed be the name of the Lord." Granted, in the end, Job was given more than he had to begin with, but Jessie wondered what kind of parent tested a child to that degree? Why was Job so content with what God allotted him, however terrible or traumatic?

Although not sure where she stood in her religious beliefs, Jessie had made it part of her practice to find out each of her client's. She noticed that those who were atheists often healed quicker, yet an emptiness encompassed them. Those who believed in God may have healed a little slower, but they eventually found the peace and wholeness they needed.

Memories continued to invade her mind. Children lying in bed, the older one holding the young Katie close. Katie's tiny, hungry body shivered against her own, causing her sister's eyes to fill with tears and her soul to be torn with grief. They would hear the yelling of their father and the slapping and the struggle. He would get so angry when her mother's tips from the restaurant weren't enough to pay the bills and keep him supplied with liquor, too. More often than not, the bills went unpaid. And then she saw Katie's lifeless face . . . *Where were you then, God? How could you let two innocent children suffer like that? How could you allow Katie to die? Why not take me, too?* Jessie gripped the pillow tensely as her body curled into the fetal position.

* * *

The muffled sound of Gramps's snoring could be heard on the porch, where Jessie was sitting with a phone book in hand. It was a small town, and the book was a mere pamphlet. She had already looked up Milly's number and called it, but Milly had been resting. *Now what do I do?* Instantly, an idea came. Finding nothing under *Mormon,* she looked up *Grant.* There was only one listing. She dialed the number.

"Hello?" came the pleasant voice on the other end.

"Ah, hello . . . I, uh . . . I'm sorry, I think I have the wrong number." Jessie was hoping to leave a message on a machine, not actually talk to someone.

"This is Robert Grant. Whom were you looking for?"

"Well, actually, I was looking for Bishop Grant of the Mormon Church."

"You've found him."

"Oh, well, um, this is Jessie Winston, a friend of Ryan Blake's. I realize it's awfully late. If you've retired for the evening, I can call back."

"It's never to late to speak with you, Miss Winston. What can I do for you?"

"Well, I'm not sure. I just had a few questions for you, if that's okay."

"That's just fine. Would you like to discuss them now? Or maybe we could meet at the church in the morning."

"Oh, well, could I just ask you something now?"

"Absolutely."

"How long was Ruth a member of your church?"

"Ruth joined the Church shortly after she and Joe married. She's been active ever since."

"And Ryan?"

"Well now, he's the one you'd need to discuss his beliefs with, but I suppose I can give you the very basics, as they are a matter of record. You know, I'd not typically know much at all about Ryan, since most of his history precedes my calling as bishop, but I've been good friends with Ruth for years, and she'd brought it up numerous times. He was baptized when he was eight. It was difficult because they needed his father's consent, and it took a while to get, as I was told. I believe he was almost nine by the time he was baptized. Anyway, he stayed pretty active until he reached about sixteen or seventeen."

"Was it the house-burning escapade that made him turn away?"

If the bishop was surprised, his voice didn't reflect it. "That would be for Ryan to answer. When Rebecca joined the Church, for the most part, he supported her. By that I mean he didn't do anything to keep her from participating in whatever she wanted. But he personally didn't want anything to do with it. He was coming around a little there for a while until . . ."

" . . . she died," Jessie responded softly.

"Yes. But I have a feeling that this isn't all you have on your mind."

"Why doesn't God intercede on the behalf of little children who are being harmed when they obviously can't protect themselves?" There, she'd asked it!

"That's a loaded question, my dear."

"I know, and no one seems to be able to answer it for me. I guess I was hoping you might."

"I could. But it would be best if you found it out for yourself."

"Now you sound like Ryan," she said sarcastically.

"Then he's giving you sound council. Ruth mentioned before her passing that you were reading the Book of Mormon. Is this correct?"

"I do have a copy, and yes, I guess I'm reading it some."

"There's an event in a section called Alma that addresses the essence of your question. You could just read that section, but I think the answer would be more clear if you started from the beginning. If you want to find and understand your answer, then I would council you to do just that."

"Actually, I have read from the beginning. I'm in the section called Mosiah. What if I don't like the answer?"

"Well now, you may not like the answer, but I believe we can fix that too. I'll be waiting to hear from you."

* * *

Sunday afternoon Jessie mentioned she was in the mood to cook, so Gramps relinquished command of the kitchen. He sat at the table doing his daily crossword puzzle from the newspaper while she worked up a plate of broiled pork chops with mashed potatoes, coleslaw, and a fruit plate. She would have been satisfied with just the coleslaw and fruit plate, but she knew Gramps needed his meat and potatoes.

"Smells great!" Gramps commented. "Hey, here's one up your alley. What's a six-letter word for therapist?"

"Cretin," she retorted sarcastically.

"It starts with an H."

"Oh, sorry. This is just about ready. Try *helper*," she said.

Gramps had just busied himself with his puzzle again when he was interrupted by an all-too-familiar crash. He turned with a jerk, afraid to find Jessie sprawled out on the floor. Her subsequent yell told him that she had definitely not passed out.

"Now you just get out of here! You've caused enough trouble. NOW, OUT!"

Nelly scooted dejectedly away from the spilt pork chops.

"You okay?" Gramps asked, trying not to laugh at the expression of disgust.

"Oh, I'm just peachy. But dinner is ruined, thanks to that . . ." Her lips pursed and her face tightened as she tried to form the appropriate phrase. "Jolly brown giant there!"

"Well, could be worse," Gramps said as he scrounged up a couple rags and went to work beside her.

"You thought I blacked out again, eh?"

"Well, no . . . not exactly," he stuttered.

"Uh-huh. You're a lousy liar." She turned and shouted at Nelly, who was slowly bellying her way back to the mess. "GO!" She turned back to Gramps.

"What would you like as your main dish?" She held a plate of soiled pork chops.

"These will do just fine. You been keepin' this floor just as clean as the table, so what difference does it make? If you must scrape, then scrape. But I sure wouldn't bother."

Jessie tried to control her expression so Gramps wouldn't be offended at the absolute horror she felt at his mere suggestion. *Barkley licks himself on this floor, and Nelly slides across it when she has an itch she can't quite get to.* Even though Jessie did wipe the floor nearly every day, the thought of what may have taken place since its last sterilization mortified her. She would have a *very small* portion of pork chops.

Jessie's eyes fell to a piece of paper on Gramps's stack of mail behind him. "Hey, Gramps, is that for me?"

Gramps quickly turned to see the letters he thought he'd hid well enough. "Um, well . . ."

"Gramps?"

"Yes, Jessie, they're for you. Two of 'em. They look the same as the one that came the other day. Ryan was concerned it might upset you. Sorry."

"Not a problem." *Okay, Elliott, this has got to stop.*

"Supposin' I better get to the stables."

"I'll clean up in here then come give you a hand."

Jessie waited until she was sure Gramps was busy with the horses before she gave the bishop a call. "Hello, Bishop Grant?"

"Hello, Miss Winston," the cordial voice came back. "I trust you've finished your reading already?"

"Please, call me Jessie. Yes, actually I did. Am I calling at a bad time?"

"Of course not. I was hoping to hear from you today."

"May I run something by you?"

"Certainly."

"I believe the point you were hoping I'd get is that in order for justice to be carried out in full, those women and children had to die. God couldn't intervene, even with Amulek's pleading. I'm not really in the mood for a lecture, but is that the gist of it?"

"Lecture aside, yes."

"If there truly is a God—and you need to know I'm still not convinced there is—" she lied, "I think it stinks."

"Yes, I suppose in a way, it does."

"Since God supposedly knows *everything*, then couldn't He judge people on the intent of their hearts? He knew they were going to burn them. Why isn't knowing that enough?"

"If He did that, Jessie, there would be no need for the test."

"The test?"

"May I ask *you* a question now?"

Jessie hesitated. "I suppose."

"Do you know why you're here?"

"Well . . . I'm struggling with my work, and . . ."

"No, no, *here* on earth?"

"It's the only planet that has both oxygen and water?" It was silent for a moment before she continued. "You're asking if I understand my purpose in life?"

"In a way, yes."

"I didn't want a lecture."

"Yes, I know. However, the questions you ask require answers based on a knowledge you currently lack."

"I stopped at a Ph.D. How silly of me."

"Why don't we stop there for now and you ask the other question that's on your mind."

Sigh. "Okay. I sorta had a prayer. Not that I thought it would do any good or anything, but I just thought I'd give it a try." It was the first prayer Jessie had attempted since she was a teenager. Alma's words concerning faith had touched her. She decided she did indeed have a 'particle of faith.' But a particle was about it.

"Okay."

"Well, something odd came into my mind during it."

"May I ask what it was?"

"Lilacs."

"Lilacs?"

"Doesn't make much sense to me either. I played in them a lot as a child, but I can't see what they have to do with anything."

"Well, I would have to say that it's an answer or a clue as to what you're searching for."

"But it's like me asking you what day it is and you answering *spaghetti*. It doesn't make any sense."

"It makes sense to your Father in Heaven. Maybe to Him, it's Spaghetti Day."

"And I thought I was confused before."

"When you're ready to accept the answer, it will make sense. Until then, keep praying to understand. Anything else I can do for you?"

She wanted to blurt out that he hadn't done much for her up to this point. "No. Thank you for your time."

CHAPTER 34

The Fourth of July town picnic was its typical annual success. Every family took part. There were games for the kids, a dunking booth for those with pent-up aggression, and the music and food were a given constant.

Jessie had entered the pie-baking contest. She used Ruth's recipe and stood in anticipation as the judges delved into her Raspberry-Lemon Swirl. At least they were smiling! She would have to wait for the results, though, as all contest winners were to be announced later that evening.

Jessie also took her turn in the dunk tank. She wore knee-length jean shorts and a heavyweight shirt. She'd drawn quite a crowd and hadn't been dropped into the chilly liquid for quite some time when Ryan offered three bucks for three tries.

"You're lookin' awfully dry there," he said, sporting a wide grin.

"Kinda figuring to stay that way, too. There's only ten more minutes on my shift," she teased. "And it seems that few in this town are much into baseball." It had only been a couple days, but he hadn't even called. She realized, as thoughts raced through her mind, that she had missed him.

"Ten minutes, hmm? Well, I guess I should have stopped and had something to eat first. But since I'm here, it'd be a shame not to at least give it a try."

"You know, if you get me soaked, I'll have to leave, and then maybe I won't come back."

"Uh-huh. Good try. Knowing you, you've brought an extra change of clothes. Maybe even two." He winked as he cocked his arm back, ready to throw.

That part of him she *didn't* miss. The first ball left his hand like a bullet from a gun, but curved to the right and into the net. She let out a loud sigh of relief. Still, somehow she knew she was in trouble.

"Don't you worry none. I did that on purpose. At least now you're looking at me. I just wanted to get your attention," he chuckled.

"Yeah, right, you couldn't hit the broad side of a—" The next word was lost in the sound of the ball hitting metal followed immediately by the splash of cold water. She floundered to her feet, sucking in large gasps of air. As her foot hit the ladder to climb out, Gramps gently reminded her that she still had seven minutes left. She was the only one failing to find the humor in the situation. She straightened her shirt and tugged at her shorts. Scooting herself back onto the spot that had been marked with an X, she looked up to find Ryan massaging the last ball in his hands.

"Oh, you can't be serious . . ." The now-familiar sound rang though the air. This time she came out of the water a bit slower.

"Wipe that smirk off your face, Blake!" she yelled with less energy than before.

"It's Ryan," he said as he contemplated the entertainment value of another turn.

"Hey, only three tries every ten minutes. Read the sign. That's the rule!" She was squeezing the excess water from her hair. Ryan glanced at the sign. She was right, but there was no one present other than Jessie who would have stepped up to reinforce it. Finally he conceded the mound, figuring that it might be best to give it a rest.

After sequestering herself in the bathroom of the church across the street, Jessie emerged a new woman. She had changed into the white gunnysack summer dress she had worn the evening after the kitchen mishap at Ruth's.

Kyle was standing on the steps waiting. She had promised to have dinner with him, and as they approached the food tent, she caught sight of Ryan talking with Milly. He met her gaze with a smile and continued his conversation. He would let Kyle have her for the time being.

Dinner consisted of small talk, barbecued chicken tenders, a potato salad, a garden salad, and a fruity sherbet of some sort. Jessie declined Kyle's invitation to join him on his blanket for the fireworks, saying she'd made previous plans. She hadn't, but after one hour of listening to

Kyle's stories of great success, she'd had enough. She went off in search of Ryan, hoping she wouldn't be too obvious. She found him sitting underneath a shade tree with a novel, the latest horror by Stephen King.

Jessie leaned over his shoulder and then shivered. "How can you read that?"

Ryan didn't respond immediately. The smell of her perfumed skin and the sight of her tanned face completely fogged his mental processes. "It's not so bad, really. It makes reality more hopeful."

"If you say so. They're about ready to announce the winners of the pie-baking contest. Want to come with me?"

"You entered a pie?" he said, dumbfounded.

"No, a pizza. Yes, I entered a pie. It's the Raspberry-Lemon Swirl. You've had it before and liked it, remember?"

He began to chuckle, first to himself and then out loud. It really wasn't that amusing at all, but he just couldn't stop.

By the time they reached their seats, she'd had about enough. "Oh, quit it already. I have a chance. It was Ruth's recipe."

"Milly's pies have won every year for as long as I can remember. It's the only time I ever saw Ruth scowl at her. I guess that's your job now," he added.

"Well if you would have called like you said you would, I'd have told you about the contest and you could have warned me then," she said in a whisper as the announcer walked toward the microphone.

As the winners were announced, Ryan tried hard to refrain from laughter. Jessie's earlier enthusiasm had vanished. Her narrowing glare found Milly, blue ribbon in hand, being congratulated by the judges.

"Look on the bright side, Jessie. For your first year, you didn't do too bad. You earned third place," Ryan said, acknowledging the ribbon placed by her pie.

"I didn't want third place!" she said in disappointment.

"No, but I think *she* did." Ryan pointed to the old spinster who had always taken third place. She was looking in Jessie's direction and whispering something to her neighbor. Jessie eventually realized the humor the situation held and laughed lightheartedly.

Ryan and Jessie walked together to the food tent and each selected a can of soda. Pastor James announced that the fireworks would begin in ten minutes.

"I have a blanket, if you want to . . . I mean, unless you have somewhere else you'd rather—"

"I would love to," he interrupted quickly, relieving her from further discomfort.

"Okay." She took a deep breath to slow her racing heart. *What am I doing?*

They staked their claim on a piece of grass far enough away to dim the noise of onlookers but close enough to provide an awesome view of the sky. He helped her spread out the king-size blanket she'd found in the back of a closet at Ruth's. It was old and weathered and had probably seen many a picnic in its day.

The trees above them shook with the shock of the first firework's explosion. In turn, the sky came alive with the exploding brilliance of sparkling glitter, streaking the blackened canvas with a rainbow of pulsating color. They lay on their backs, enveloped in this grand display of power and beauty.

"Heard you've received some interesting mail," Ryan said softly.

"Yeah. But I figured out a way to stop that."

"Oh yeah?"

"Yep. Went to the post office and filled out a change-of-address form. I'm not expecting any other mail for a while, so I put Elliott's office address down."

"That'll do it."

* * *

The finale's fire and thunderous roar gave way at last to a smoke-filled sky and appreciative applause. "Who pays for all this?" Jessie asked.

"Well, most of the people in town chip in here and there. Some of the wealthier ones put in more."

"Like you?" Embarrassed at having said that, she immediately added, "Sorry. I don't know what's come over me tonight."

"I didn't pay for the whole thing, if that's what you're curious about," he offered, taking a swig from his can of soda.

"I really am sorry. I've often wondered what it must feel like to be rich. I think it would be difficult if everyone knew about the money.

Eventually people would ask for some, and when do you help versus not? I don't know. Better you than me, I suppose."

"A few people in town have asked for help, but usually with the intent to repay whatever I loan them. Most have, and the ones who haven't . . . well, I knew at the onset that they wouldn't be able to, so I made it clear that I considered it a gift and expected nothing in return. It's difficult at best for people around here to ask anyone for anything. Most are older and it hurts their pride. I offered to get Miller's place cleaned up on several occasions, but he refused. Now I'm glad he did." He smiled, hoping to ease the friction he'd caused. "It's only money. Those who don't have it dream of the freedom it offers. Those who do have it and aren't wise with it are imprisoned by it. It doesn't buy happiness, just a few luxuries that no truly happy person needs anyway."

"I wouldn't mind a few luxuries."

"What would you do if you had millions of your own?" He rolled to his side, propping himself up on his elbow so he could study her face as she searched for the answer to his question.

"Hmm. Well, I would open my own home for kids, to start with. I would work to get rid of the foster program as it exists in the states and go to a system of privately funded orphanages. Only I wouldn't call them that. The foster program needs to go back to where it came from. Too many problems. Of course, any system would have to be administered properly and overseen by caring people who are in it for more than the money. And it should be totally nonprofit."

"Who would continue to fund your homes if not the government?"

"There are enough tycoons searching for charities."

"Tell the government they can't take care of their own, and they'll shut you right down."

"*They* don't take care of them now. They merely administer and fund the system that does. What are you trying to do anyway, ruin my aspirations?" she asked, shifting her position to mirror his.

"No. I'm just trying to sprinkle a little reality on it."

"See—that's the thing most *rich* people lose."

"What's that?"

"Humanitarian dreams."

He returned to his back, gazing into the thick field of stars that spread across the night sky. She had struck a chord. It was true. He'd had many dreams of what he would do if he got rich, and here he was, a millionaire many times over, but what did he have to show for it? What had he done with Brecca's gift?

"You know, Jessie, I've been going over and over the last conversation we had before I left for the city, and I don't remember telling you I'd call. Did you want me to call?"

How on earth do I answer that? He's not a total idiot. He has to know I'm attracted. Have I been that cold?

"Jessie?"

"Hmm?"

"Did you want me to call?" Ryan repeated.

Jessie's cheeks flushed. "Well, no, not exactly. I mean, that's not to say . . . it's just that I thought . . . Well, I mean, if you had called, I could have thanked you for your help the other day." *Phew, that's over.*

"Then I should have called." Ryan didn't tell her that an hour hadn't gone by that he hadn't reached for the phone. But he had decided to give her the space she insisted she needed. His smile produced goose bumps on Jessie's arms.

"You know, your cabin is large enough—not to mention all the land around it—that you could start a summer getaway program, maybe for troubled kids and/or adults. You have a lot to offer here. You'd have to renew that license of yours. Although, retirement has treated you well."

"I may give that some thought." Years ago, Brecca and he had discussed the same idea. He had forgotten all that until now.

"Hey, you two, thought you might have already left and missed all this," Gramps commented as he approached. "Well now, I see you've dried off there, little lady." Gramps winked at Ryan.

"Yeah, well, I had intended to stay in my shorts tonight, but he sorta ruined my plans," Jessie retorted, pointing at Ryan.

"So, son, can I still plan on your help at Jessie's tomorrow?" Gramps asked.

"Absolutely. I'll be by after I've tended the horses. You also figuring to get the rest of your things out of my place?"

"Doin' that on Saturday. Wanna use the boys as much as possible at Jessie's during the week. Well, I'm headin' home. Need a lift, little lady?"

"I promised Milly I'd help clean up. Most of the tents will be taken down tomorrow, but I offered to help wipe tables and whatnot. I may be an hour or so."

"I'm sticking around a while. I can take her, Gramps," Ryan said.

* * *

An hour and a half later, Jessie was hunting for her ride. She had washed every table and folded over a hundred chairs. She finally found Ryan lifting the card tables into a rental truck.

"I'm about finished here. What about you?" he called as he saw her walking toward him.

"All done."

"Hi there, Jessie," Bishop Grant said. "Thanks for your help tonight."

"Anytime." She shook his extended hand with a strong grip.

"Good to see you again, Brother Blake."

"I would prefer Ryan," Ryan said. While he ignored the offered handshake, he *had* actually spoken to the bishop.

Jessie's eyebrow's rose slightly, and even Bishop Grant was momentarily at a loss for words. "Well, I best be getting on over there and seeing what's left," Bishop Grant finally said.

Ryan and Jessie walked to Ryan's truck in silence. "You're unusually quiet. Is there something wrong?" she asked.

"No. Just thinking about the bishop. Letting go of Brecca logically means letting go of some other issues. You want to come by early tomorrow and help with the horses? I can always use an extra hand. We could go for a short ride afterward. Gramps isn't in any hurry for me to show up."

"Could I ride Joanie?" Jessie blurted out.

Ryan nearly tripped but recovered gracefully. "I'll give it some thought and come by around seven."

CHAPTER 35

"It's a little late to be prowling around the stables," Ryan said as he walked up. He had seen the lights after he raided the refrigerator at midnight. "And you've done more than just *read* about horses," he said, noticing the rhythm of the brush stroke Jessie was using on Joanie.

"I couldn't sleep. Is it all right that I'm brushing her?" Jessie asked hesitantly.

"Sure, although I'm amazed she's letting you do it. Usually only Gramps can work with her. She won't have a thing to do with me."

"Smart girl," Jessie said, patting Joanie's side. "I didn't mean to just make myself at home here, but I didn't want to wake you."

"I wasn't sleeping either. So, want to let me in on where you acquired your depth of horse knowledge?"

"I helped with the horses on the property when I lived with the older couple, remember?"

"There's more to it," he prodded.

"Why does there always have to be more to what I say? I worked with their horses, that's it. I watched and learned. I rode a great deal when I had free time." A faint neigh caught her attention. Joanie's new foal was doing her best to remain hidden behind its mother. "You have a new one, I see."

"She came along the day you passed out on the way to town. Her arrival was a shock. We weren't expecting her for another week or so."

"Well, it didn't do her any harm from what I can see." She was a beautiful paint with a coat of chocolate brown and a few dim white spots that would brighten with age. Her eyes were blue, and she had a mane of both brown and white. "What have you named her?"

"Haven't yet. You got any ideas?"

"Would have to be around her a while. That sort of thing takes time."

"Jessie, I've been thinking about something you said."

"Ryan, I'm enjoying this peaceful moment."

"Just hear me out," he said as he handed Jessie a smaller brush. She began brushing the foal gently. "Fine."

"When you mentioned that the man from the theater came to you and your sister, it was *before* the theater cleared, right?"

"Yeah."

"How did he know at that time that you weren't with someone?"

"Hmm."

Ryan stood quietly while Jessie thought.

"What is it about horses that you find so fascinating?" Ryan asked, feeling the need to change the topic.

"Let's see. They're strange creatures, really," she said, breathing deeply. "Each one is an individual in the sense that they are unpredictable, powerful, proud, and that they command respect. It takes time to get close to horses, to get to know them. But when you do and you've built up a trust, they'll do anything for you. I've seen horses heal sadness. But then, you know all that. Why are you asking *me* about horses, anyway?"

"I wasn't asking you about horses per se. I was asking why you took to them so readily."

"Oh." Now it made sense. She knew that oftentimes, a person's personality modeled the kind of animal they were drawn to. Her next statement would prove that. "Horses have allowed me to gain their trust. And when that's established, they've always been loyal."

"You've had your own horse, then?"

"No. Not really. I was never in one place long enough to invest in one."

"You've been in the same place the past few years."

"Yeah, but change is inevitable. I'm not one for staying put too long."

"I'd like you to have her."

"What?"

"She's yours, if you want her."

"Ryan, you can't be serious."

"Sure I can. She needs to stay here for a while, but it won't be too long till you can take her up to your place."

"You are serious! I don't know what to say." She walked in front of Joanie and stroked her mane. "I'll take good care of her, I promise."

Joanie neighed sedately.

* * *

Jessie lay awake thinking of her new foal. Sleep wouldn't come. She began repeating the word *lilacs*. It had to mean something, since those lilacs had been her only sanctuary as a child. She picked up the book of scripture by her side. She flipped through the book called Mosiah, remembering what she had read earlier about King Benjamin. *Repent of my sins? What have I done? After all, I'm nothing, right? I am an 'unworthy creature.' So, why repent? Call on the Lord daily, and He will deliver me out of bondage. Oh, please. I've done that. I'm still in bondage.* She returned to her reading of Helaman and his people. They were going to battle against a group that highly outnumbered them. *One thing is for sure—this book has a lot of bloodshed.* Helaman's army was suffering because they hadn't received the reinforcements they had hoped for. She read aloud from Alma 58.

> *Therefore we did pour out our souls in prayer to God, that he would strengthen us and deliver us out of the hands of our enemies, yea, and also give us strength that we might retain our cities, and our lands, and our possessions, for the support of our people.*
>
> *Yea, and it came to pass that the Lord our God did visit us with assurances that he would deliver us; yea, insomuch that he did speak peace to our souls, and did grant unto us great faith, and did cause us that we should hope for our deliverance in him.*
>
> *And we did take courage with our small force which we had received, and were fixed with a determination to conquer our enemies . . .*

"Why is it that some people can pour out their soul and those prayers are answered and others aren't?" she spoke out loud. "What makes the difference? Why were they able to conquer their enemies while I simply want to know what lilacs mean?" Images of lilacs again filled her mind. As a child, she'd had to bend every now and then to avoid being tormented by the overgrown bushes as she entered the back yard.

She jerked up. "That's it!"

* * *

"Ryan! Ryan! Get up!" Jessie yelled as she pounded vigorously on the door. Nelly's fierce barking could be heard loud and clear.

"Whoa, Nelly, knock it off! Jessie, is that you?" Ryan called through the door.

"Yeah, yeah, open up!"

"What? What's the matter? What's happened?" Ryan's eyes were trying to focus in the light Jessie turned on as she swept by him.

"I need to go home. Would you go with me, please?"

"It's three-thirty in the morning, Jessie."

"I'm well aware of that, Ryan."

"Home as in where, exactly?"

"Where I grew up. It's a little town about an hour from the city."

"And you need to go now?"

"I'll give you all the details as soon as we're driving. Now get dressed already!"

"Can I ask what brought this about?"

"Lilacs."

"Lilacs?"

"Yes. Now hurry up, please. It'll be light soon."

"And this would be a bad thing because . . . ?"

Jessie had barely allowed Ryan time to put on his tennis shoes before she jumped in the driver's side of his truck.

"Why don't you just go ahead and drive," he said.

"Thanks."

Ryan rubbed his entire face with his hands. "Are you going to elaborate on the lilacs or leave me to flounder in my confusion?"

"After my father died, I drove past the house we lived in, the one where he had chopped down all the lilacs. The bushes had grown back and were blooming again. They were large and lopsided. They hadn't been tended to, but they were blooming, even thriving." Her face lit up. "I smiled to myself, glad they had survived. Staring at the bushes out back today, I started thinking about those lilacs." She wanted to tell him about her prayer and that God had actually listened, but she still felt it wasn't right yet. "I realized they had survived because my father didn't kill the source—the roots. He merely chopped them down to the ground, probably because it had been easier and took less time and effort.

"All these years, I've only chopped at the issues. I ignored them, hoping that they would simply go away. Now, years later, the pain is in full bloom. Chopping at it will only prolong the inevitable. Present circumstances have forced me to deal with a real solution at the root. The lilacs didn't go away any more than my problems have. I need to deal with *root* issues. It's the only way I can ever hope for a lasting solution. I also noticed that even though the lilacs needed a trim, they had become even stronger—matured, if you will. 'Death of the old is birth of the new.'" It was a quote she remembered from a text, years ago. "See? Simple."

"Right. Simple."

"I've done a great deal of soul-searching these past few days. Before that night, I'd never told the events of Katherine's death to anyone. I guess I figured if I didn't talk about it, it would simply go away. I wasn't going after the roots. Are you following me?"

"I need some caffeine."

Anticipating this, Jessie handed him a thermos.

"Thanks." Ryan took a few sips.

"For years I resented, even hated, my brothers and father. They had tortured me physically and emotionally. I realize I told you I had worked through that, but obviously I haven't. But I'm confident I will.

"My father was always drunk and spiteful. There were times when he would call all of us kids into his 'office' at home for those lectures I mentioned earlier. We were required to be properly dressed, the boys in nice slacks and white shirts and I in a dress. He never acknowledged the existence of Katie. I don't know what he did with her during his little sermons, but she was never around. She was probably alone in the basement.

"He would lecture on random topics. If I hadn't been so terrified of him, I'm sure I would have been bored. We didn't dare move or squirm. We all had to be very still or he'd take his belt to us. I learned to nod at strategic moments in agreement with whatever it was he was saying, just like the boys did. I remember urinating where I sat during one lecture and being beaten for it. I'd told him several times I had to go, but he'd scolded me for interrupting and told me to shut up until he was finished. Being unable to take care of my physical needs and then being belittled and beaten over the inevitable outcome is probably the cause of half my issues. Do I need to slow down?"

It was too early for any traffic, but a heavy fog was plastering the view before them. "If you're worried I'm not getting everything you're saying, there's no need to slow down. I'm following just fine. In reference to your driving, the speed limit here is only sixty-five, not eighty, and usually you slow down when you can't see two feet in front of you."

"Oh." She eased her foot off the accelerator and started speaking again. "As I grew older and went out on my own, I understood intellectually that virtue could not be taken from me, but only given voluntarily. In spite of that knowledge, I felt robbed. It was mine to give, and no one had the right to take it from me. I've allowed that loss to affect almost every area of my life. My father should have protected me, not been a party to my pain. Clearly I can't talk to him, but during these past few days, I have found a place where I can *begin* to forgive him. Knowing what I do about alcohol, I realize that he was a sick man and, to some extent at least, a servant to the drug. He couldn't handle being a parent, and he shouldn't have been one. But I can break that cycle in my own life."

Why didn't I get all this before?

"After I shared what happened to Katie the other night, you alluded to the possibility that my anger could be toward my mother. I had never before considered such a possibility, so I found it immediately absurd. But it stuck in my head. I've come to the realization that you were right. Where was she? Where was my mother when everyone blamed me for feeding Katie those hot dogs? Where was she when I was holding my dead sister? Where was she when I was repeatedly abused? Where was she that night I tried to end it all? Why did she leave?" Jessie pulled off the side of the road before her eyes filled with tears completely. They sat quietly for a few minutes.

"Let me drive awhile," Ryan said.

She was in no mood to argue, so she slid to the passenger's side. It took a few minutes of deep breathing before she could go on. "Becoming angry was the only way I could survive. But I've realized I don't have to survive anymore. No one is abusing me now. Problem is, I know how to live a life of fear and how to endure the resulting pain, but a life of peace is truly foreign to me. It will take some time. But it's all clear now."

"And God?"

"Yes, well, I'm not sure yet. What I thought God was as a child I'm not convinced was the truth. I wanted someone to give me comfort and peace. I didn't have parents for that, so I expected God to do it. But I didn't feel it. I felt I wasn't one of those people He deemed worthy enough to help, or someone who was worthy of His love. And if a child isn't worthy enough, then who is? I gave up on Him a long time ago, and I've managed just fine on my own. But somewhere deep down, I guess I've always believed in His existence, I just haven't understood why He deserted me. Until recently, that is."

"What's happened recently?"

She reflected on her reading. She wanted desperately to tell Ryan about what she learned from Alma and Amulek and King Benjamin. "I've had an experience, which I'm not feeling ready to share, that has helped me understand—sort of—why I think God did what He did. But while I understand in part, I'm still hesitant to give in fully. I'm struggling with this being humble thing and acknowledging Him for all the good things in my life."

"Jessie, I'm amazed at all your growth, but can you tell me again why we're headed to your old home?"

"It's the lilacs!" Jessie's words drew him from his thoughts.

"Okay."

Jessie pulled out the worn envelope. Ryan glanced over to see the name *Samantha* written in cursive. "Here, read this."

Ryan read the small note as she held it up. *You'll never know about your mother, you ugly little brat. Ha ha ha.*

"That beautiful prose is from my father," Jessie spat out.

"I still don't understand."

"Don't you see? This is a legal-size envelope. That's a two-by-two piece of paper. Obviously there was something else in here. My name is written in my mother's handwriting. This must have been something from her, and he took it."

"I'm really trying to follow here, Jessie."

"When I first got this, it was heavier, like it held a letter or pictures or something. I couldn't read it right away, so I hid it. My father found it and removed whatever was in it. He used to tease me by saying he'd hid it somewhere, but I always figured he had destroyed it and was just being mean."

"Okay . . . "

"Just get me to my old house."

CHAPTER 36

Dawn was fast approaching as they pulled in silently to the old, weathered, brick home. Jessie hopped out and opened the back of the truck. She pulled out two shovels and handed one to Ryan.

"I'm not sure I even want to ask," he said, taking the shovel.

"Come on," she whispered. "Over here."

She walked up the grassy hill to the side of the home where the lilac bushes were still growing out of control.

"I'm sure if we just asked, Jessie," Ryan said, jumping up and down on the shovel, breaking the dirt.

"Oh sure. Excuse me, we realize it's five-thirty in the morning, but do you mind if we dig up your lilacs? If it's too early, we could come back later . . . Yeah, there's an idea."

"Jessie, there are at least ten trees here."

"It'll be under one of these three. This is where I always played."

Ryan's eyes darted around nervously.

"Just get as close to the roots as possible. If you don't see anything, fill it back up," Jessie said.

"Uh-huh." After Ryan had dug under five trees and Jessie three, he began thinking for the right words to soothe her when they ended up empty-handed.

"I just don't get it," Jessie said as she sat beneath the bushes.

"Jessie . . ."

"No, don't. Just give me a minute, okay?" She walked back toward the truck. She was mumbling, and her arms were gesturing in their typical way.

Ryan watched as she pulled a book out of her backpack. It looked familiar, but it couldn't be!

Inside the truck, Jessie thumbed through the back of the Book of Mormon. Somewhere within, there were verses highlighted in yellow. She came across them while she was skimming through it the first night she found the book. She found them again within seconds.

And now, my beloved brethren, if this be the case that these things are true which I have spoken unto you, and God will show unto you, with power and great glory at the last day, that they are true, and if they are true has the day of miracles ceased? Or have angels ceased to appear unto the children of men? Or has he withheld the power of the Holy Ghost from them? Or will he, so long as time shall last, or the earth shall stand, or there shall be one man upon the face thereof to be saved?

Behold I say unto you, Nay; for it is by faith that miracles are wrought; and it is by faith that angels appear and minister unto men; wherefore, if these things have ceased wo be unto the children of men, for it is because of unbelief, and all is vain.

"Okay, God. I've heard your angels or your Holy Ghost. I know a voice told me *lilacs* and I know what that meant. What more must I do?" Jessie looked up in time to see Ryan meandering toward the door. She quickly slid Rebecca's Book of Mormon back inside her pack. She opened the door and ventured out.

"Jessie, who were you just talking to?"

"God."

"God? The God that you aren't sure you actually believe in?"

"Yeah."

"Jessie, I'm thinking it may be time to look into some deeper help."

"Just get over here."

She picked up a shovel and began digging under the last two bushes. Ryan followed suit.

"Wait! Ryan, come here. Look! We just didn't dig deep enough. Pull this back." Ryan reached in behind a terribly overgrown tree and held the branches as far back as possible. Jessie stuck her hand down through the dirt and pulled up an old, military-green ammo can. "See! I knew it! Let's fill this last hole and get out of here."

"My thoughts exactly."

Ryan had barely started the engine when Jessie began rummaging through the contents of the can. She pulled out a gold wedding band similar to the one she was wearing. "This must have been my father's when he was married to my mother. And here are his dog tags from World War II."

"Your father was in World War II?" Ryan asked, surprised.

"Yes, he was in his forties when I was born. See, here are his discharge papers." She decided to read those later. "This is strange," she said.

"What?"

"It's a picture I drew when I was young."

Ryan bent to take a closer look. "Wow. How old were you when you did that?"

"I don't remember. Ten, maybe." Jessie had drawn her home with all its surrounding foliage. Inside each window were her stepbrothers, their hands raised and their mouths gaping open. A man and woman, most likely her father and stepmother, were in the kitchen, also with raised arms and mouths open. There were bottles of whiskey strewn across the floor. Outside in the bushes, a girl was hunched over. Jessie had drawn large teardrops falling to the ground. To the side of the bushes was a woman without a face standing very still. And then behind the house was a gravestone engraved with *Katie* on it.

"Look, Ryan, here it is!" Jessie pulled out a wrinkled piece of stationery with a lilac-vine border. She began to read out loud:

> *My dear Samantha,*
>
> *How precious you and Katie look today. When I told you we were going for a long drive in the country, you were both so excited. We packed a big lunch and loaded the car with all your favorite things. We'll be leaving soon, and I have to tell you why I will not be coming home with you.*
>
> *I found out about a month ago that I have a sickness which will take me away from you and Katie. There isn't*

a cure for the kind of cancer I have. I haven't told anyone until now. It's better this way. I don't have much time, Samantha. Neither you nor Katherine need to watch me die. I know you won't read this until you're older, and you'll probably wonder for several years why I left you.

Ryan looked from the road momentarily to see the tears spilling down her cheeks as she gently caressed the gold band on her finger. "Would you like me to pull over?"

She shook her head slowly and continued reading.

> *I've given a will to my lawyer indicating my wish to be cremated. I just want to disappear as quietly as I came into the world. I know all this must make me sound uncaring and uncompassionate, but I hope as you grow older, you can forgive me. It is my prayer that you and Katherine will get to a good home and be taken care of. If there was someone to leave you with, I'd do it, but there just isn't. Your father, in his drunkenness, has threatened my life, Jessie—many times. I fear leaving you two with him. I couldn't bear to have you live the way I have.*
>
> *Your sister will never remember me, so you will be the one left with all the pain.*
>
> *Please know that you and Katherine mean more to me than anything in this world. I don't know why God would take me from my babies, but it is His will. "The Lord gave, and the Lord hath taken away . . ." I used to read Job to you at bedtime, remember? I'll miss your bright, smiling faces. I love you my Samantha and Katie bug. Please forgive me.*
>
> *Ann Smith*

Ryan had to work to control his emotions. He found a back alley that ended in a field.

"I knew it was a letter from her. I just knew it." Jessie suddenly realized by the way her mother had signed the letter that it was she and not her mother who had sealed their fate. She remembered having watched the man in the red vest and the tall woman reading a paper in front of her. She had heard the man say, "Their last name is Smith." And as any intelligent child would do, Jessie had promptly corrected him, not knowing that by signing *Smith,* her mother had tried to disguise who the girls' father was. It had never been her mother's intent for them to live with their father.

Ryan drew near her and pulled her into his arms. She readily accepted. The sun was beginning to rise, and they took in the splendor.

Ryan, it's time. I have to go now. I love you.

The whisper left as quickly as it came, with no lingering scent. Ryan closed his eyes and allowed them to fill with moisture. He wanted to call out to Brecca, to beg her to stay, but he had let go.

"Are you all right?" he asked Jessie tenderly.

"I will be."

"I have to admit that I find it difficult to believe that if the state had that letter in their possession, that they wouldn't have at least investigated your da . . . father before they placed you with him."

"You know as well as I do the system is overworked and understaffed. I'm sure they did. He's very good at lying, remember? They most likely found him when he was sober. He simply told them he'd quit drinking and was going to all the right therapy. He probably threatened all the boys to be on their best behavior, and then he cleaned the house, bought Stella a nice dress, and there's your happy family. I'm sure after they placed us, they made their checkup visits. But after a year, they close the case. You know the process."

"You painted those pictures of Christ in your apartment, didn't you?"

"How did you come up with that?" Jessie didn't move. She realized that she was allowing Ryan to caress her hair, and she accepted the gentle kisses to the back of her head.

"Am I right?"

"Yes, but that doesn't explain how you figured it out."

"It was only a hunch at first, since I never saw a signature. But then the lilacs made it clearer." It was his turn.

"Huh?"

"There were lilacs in the mountain scenes."

"That memory thing of yours is a curse. Painting for me as a child was an escape."

"Named that foal yet?" Ryan grinned as he looked down at her tearstained face.

"Actually, yes, I did."

"Well?"

"Buddy."

"Buddy?"

"Yeah. What's wrong with Buddy?"

"Nothing. It's just been my experience that horse names are usually more, I don't know, majestic."

"Well, she's my horse, right?" She smiled.

"Absolutely."

"Then it's Buddy."

"May I ask where that came from?"

Embarrassed to mention her teddy bear at the moment, she said, "It represents something I once cared for that actually cared back." She gazed out the window at the approaching dawn. "Ryan?"

"Yes?"

"Thanks." Her breathing became shallow as he leaned in slowly. *Oh no, no, no, not ready, not ready . . .* The kiss was gentle, and her eyes remained closed long after he pulled away.

"Ryan?"

"Yeah?"

"I know I just kissed you, but . . ."

"It's all right, Jessie. I know." He would allow her space. Their journey forward would require patience, but someday he would share all that was his.

CHAPTER 37

The path opened about fifty feet from the end of the cabin, leading her into the lush green of the landscaped garden. Jessie walked into the cabin and down the hall entrance to where her room had been.

She had expected the typical aroma of breakfast to meet her at the cabin door, but strangely enough, on this morning, there was none. She listened but heard absolutely nothing. There was no sign of Nelly either. After knocking, Jessie cautiously opened the door and called out. Still nothing. She checked each room on the main floor, but the place seemed abandoned. She decided to make a cursory check upstairs before heading out to the stables. She just couldn't imagine Ryan having risen early enough to be out working yet. Perhaps he was on his morning run.

Jessie reached the balcony that faced the waiting room and proceeded to peek into the adjoining library. There were no sounds from his office, and she had figured that would be the most likely place to find him. She couldn't imagine why he would be in either of the guest bedrooms, but she continued her search anyway simply to rule out the possibility.

The last fathomable place was the loft, so she began the circular climb to the third floor. The loft was empty as well, so she stuck her head around the long radial wall that enclosed the rear of the staircase to check the game room. Silence. The only room left was that huge oversized conference room that Brecca had used years ago. Jessie had never seen him in there. She turned to the staircase, heading down to make some tea. Obviously, he was jogging. She would wait.

A pounding noise invaded the stillness. Stopping, she tilted her head, listening more intently in order to determine its source. There it was again—hammering coming from the conference room.

Jessie leaned into the open doorway. Hammer in hand, facing the opposite wall, Ryan stood straightening a picture. He was wearing headphones, and she could hear the music from where she stood!

Jessie decided to sneak behind and give him the scare of his life. It would go a long way in helping her get even after the dunk tank. She began tiptoeing quietly across the room, although it was hardly necessary with the music blaring in his ears. That's when it hit her. The painting he was straightening was of the rose he'd done for Rebecca! It was refinished, and now there were five lavender roses, intertwined, still on the faded black background. It was stunning.

She continued closing in on him. "Hey!" she yelled, poking him simultaneously in both sides of his ribs. He spun around on his heels, his fist and the hammer drawn up for a fight.

"Whoa there, cowboy, it's just me!" She put her hands up in surrender.

"Sorry about that," Ryan said as he pulled at the headset. "You should know it's dangerous to sneak up on someone holding a hammer."

"I'll keep that in mind."

"Do you like it?" Ryan pointed to the painting.

"Yes, it's beautiful. Hmm, let's see. That one's for you, then Rebecca, Gramps, Ruth, and . . . ?"

"Actually, you're right about Brecca, Gramps, and Ruth, but that one's not me. It's for Joshua, my son. And that one, well, that's for a friend." This he said slowly. He bent over and picked up a couple of flecks of paint that had fallen to the floor below the painting.

"Oh. Well, I like it very much."

"I don't think I'll be hearing anymore voices." There was wistfulness and yet relief in his voice. "So what do you think?" He spread his arms in the air.

"About . . . ?"

"The room."

"It's a bit empty."

"Won't be for long. Did you read your father's discharge papers?"

"Yeah. Apparently he was discharged for disorderly conduct. I'm going to do some research, though. I was always under the impression that his drinking came after his time in the service, not during."

Ryan and Jessie left the room and headed toward the stables. Neither noticed the scent of lilacs that swept through the room for the last time.

Tawny and Joanie were saddled and tied to a post. "I thought a quick ride might be fun," Ryan said.

"Hmm. Well, I'm not really dressed for it."

"Oh, well, in that case, I'll just put Joanie back. Tawny won't mind going out alone." Ryan sported his familiar grin.

"What? Really? Oh, Ryan!" Jessie suddenly wasn't concerned about her lack of appropriate riding attire. She made her way to Joanie and talked softly to her before taking the reins in her hands and pulling herself up. Joanie simply neighed. Ryan was thrilled to see Joanie at her best again.

"Hey, you two," Gramps called, coming up the path.

"Hey, Gramps. Come by to watch Jessie get thrown to the ground?" Ryan teased.

"Nope. Don't think that'll happen. Horse only hates you. By the way Jessie, we're ahead of schedule. You'll be in your place before fall."

"Gramps, that's just great!"

Ryan had pulled himself onto Tawny and nudged the horse alongside Joanie. "I'm going to use Brecca's inheritance the way she would have. Years ago, she and I dreamed of making a summer place here for troubled teens. I'd forgotten all about it till you brought it up."

"Oh, Ryan, that's wonderful!" Jessie said eagerly.

"Which brings me to a question. I'm going to be needing a partner to get it off the ground. Wondered if you'd give it some thought?"

"Couldn't hurt to at least ponder the idea." She was beaming.

"When can you let me know?"

She giggled as Joanie broke into a trot. "Call. Make an appointment."

* * *

Jessie lay in bed with her mother's letter neatly by her side along with Rebecca's Book of Mormon. She was anxious to meet with Milly and Bishop Grant. She wondered if she'd ever be able to tell Ryan about her prayers and her reading. *Will he pull away from me because I'm drawn to the Mormons? What did the Mormons do to make him despise them so? Was it just the loss of Brecca that made him leave the Church?* She knew in time, she'd have answers.

She thought of Ryan's tender kiss. She was falling in love, and she wasn't ready. She still had much healing to do. Would Ryan wait? How long would it take until he would fully gain her trust?

Her thoughts turned to her father's ammo can. At first she figured that it consisted of the things he resented most, but she wondered if somehow they were the things that mattered the most. He was only cruel when he'd been drinking. The few times he was sober, he seemed sad and fragile. He would withdraw from everyone and everything, staying cooped up in his office at home. She wondered what drove him to drinking.

She was sure there was a copy of her mother's letter still in her case file. She'd stolen the original, but the state duplicated everything. It all would have been given to her at age eighteen, but by then she had left and changed her name. Had her mother been waiting outside the theater that day, watching? How could she find her mother's lawyer?

Jessie turned off her light, closed her eyes, and began humming the song she'd sung for Gramps at the hospital. For the first time in years, even amidst her many unanswered questions, she drifted to sleep in peace.

ABOUT THE AUTHOR

Cherrann was born and raised in the shadow of Indiana's Notre Dame Fighting Irish. After serving a mission in Japan for the LDS church, she moved to Utah, and while she missed the mighty oak trees of the Midwest, nothing could take her away from the majestic mountains surrounding her home. She wrote her first story at age seven, a "how-to" book on the art of breaking out of a locked room. Most of her teachers cringed at her essays, but that never stopped her from writing.

Cherrann and her husband own and operate a full-time day care in their home. She enjoys writing and sharing stories with the children and learning from them. She is currently writing an article once a month for a web-based family magazine. She enjoys being active in the LDS church, and she thrives when kept busy. Next to spending time with her husband and two children, writing, and eating chocolate, her favorite pastime is cleaning and organizing.

Cherrann enjoys corresponding with her readers, who can write to her in care of Covenant Communications, P.O. Box 416, American Fork, Utah 84003-0416, or e-mail her via Covenant at info@covenant-lds.com.

Excerpt From

RUNAWAY

Winning a case was not an everyday occurrence for the county's contract defense attorney. Meredith Marchant handled the cases the courts ordered her to take and did the best she could to ensure her clients a fair day in court. She enjoyed her work, and she felt like she was good at it. But winning with a clear finding of "not guilty" by a judge or jury—or even by persuading the prosecutor that his case was weak and he should move the court for a dismissal—just wasn't her fate very often. Most of her *victories* weren't victories at all, just plea bargains.

So why did she feel so empty now as she walked back into the courtroom to join her client? After all, she was about to win. The county attorney had just thrown in the towel on this one. And unlike most of her cases, the man sitting at the defense table waiting for her return was not a typical client. He'd contacted her at her office, dropped two thousand dollars on her desk in hundred dollar bills, and said smugly, "The cops ain't got a case, and it's your job to prove it for me."

She had agreed to defend him, but certainly not because he was a nice man, nor because she was convinced he had been framed by Detectives Osborne and Fauler. The money had been the deciding factor. Any case she took in addition to her court-appointed ones helped her save for the future.

"Well, is he going to drop it?" her client asked with a sneer.

"Of course," she said as brightly as she could muster.

Her client sat back with a satisfied grin on his face, not a word of thanks for her efforts. She glanced at him as she waited for the judge to enter the courtroom. Except for his eyes, her client looked the part of a successful businessman. She supposed he was, but she was almost certain that his business was anything but honest.

The client's eyes caught hers, and once again she was vaguely aware of the impression that there was an evil person within the facade of honesty and integrity he was trying to put on. But those eyes made her skin crawl, and they caused a slight panic in her heart. She silently prayed that after the next few minutes, she would never see this man again in her life.

Desmond R. Devaney was the name his Alabama driver's license gave him. But if Meredith had to guess, she'd say that New England was more likely the area of the country where he'd come from.

The judge entered the courtroom. Meredith and her client stood, as did everyone else. After being seated, the county attorney rose and said, "Your Honor, due to new information that has just come to my attention, I am, in the interest of justice, moving the court to dismiss the state's case of aggravated assault against Mr. Desmond Devaney."

"Is that so?" the judge said as he leaned forward and peered menacingly at the prosecutor. "Twenty minutes ago you talked like you were ready to set the matter for trial. What sort of new information are you basing your motion on?"

"Ms. Marchant, counsel for the defendant, just revealed to me that she has located several witnesses who are prepared to testify that the defendant was at a social gathering in Roosevelt at the time the assault occurred in Duchesne."

"I see," the judge said. His stern gaze turned on Meredith. "How many witnesses?" he asked.

"Six, Your Honor," she said as she rose to her feet.

The judge continued to stare at her for several seconds as if that figure were suspect, then looked in the direction of the prosecutor. "Your motion is granted; the charges are dismissed, and we are adjourned," he said with a shake of his head and rap of his gavel.

There was a groan from behind her, and Meredith turned in her seat. Luke Osborne and the new detective, Enos Fauler, were shaking their heads in dismay. Her client rose to his feet and pushed his chair back. Two men on the second row of seats were looking right at him as he turned toward them. One, a good-looking fellow of maybe twenty-one or twenty-two, grinned at him and gave a thumbs-up. The second, older, sober, and with a surly face, simply nodded. Then they both left the courtroom. Meredith's client turned to her and said, "Maybe those two detectives learned a lesson today," before quickly moving away.

Meredith gathered up her papers and then followed him into the lobby. She spotted the rich, auburn hair of her young daughter and smiled in her direction. Deedee's face was flushed and her hair wind-blown. *She must have ridden her bike up here from town,* Meredith thought to herself. She froze as her client approached Deedee and she heard him say, "Hey, babe, you're very pretty. Need a lift to town?"

Meredith stepped forward quickly and shouted as she neared them, "Get away from her, Desmond!"

He turned around, apparently surprised at her protest, but didn't say a word until she walked up and put a protective arm around Deedee. His attempt at an innocent smile was marred by the slight leer, and he said, "Just being friendly to the girl, Counselor. Know her, do you?"

"She's my daughter," Meredith fumed, "and she doesn't need a ride with you."

Desmond's face grew dark, and he turned to Deedee. "Would you like a lift?" he asked again defiantly.

Meredith was suddenly so angry that she clenched her fists, ready to claw his eyes out if he so much as touched Deedee. Then a tall presence appeared beside her, and Enos Fauler said, "Why don't you just leave, mister? Is this any way to thank the lady who just saved your guilty hide?"

Desmond bristled and looked up at the tall detective. "It won't be any too soon. Not exactly my kind of town." He moved toward the door, but as he pushed it open, he made one last parting shot, looking straight at Meredith's thirteen-year-old daughter. "I'll see you again, beautiful."

For a big man, Enos Fauler moved awfully fast. He had to, or Meredith Marchant would have lit into her former client. Enos deftly stepped in front of her, effectively blocking the way as Desmond smugly left the courthouse.

Everyone in the lobby had been watching the tense drama unfold, and Meredith was suddenly embarrassed. "Thanks," she said to Detective Fauler, whose gaze suddenly dropped to the floor.

"He's not a nice man," the detective said without looking up.

Deedee moved to her mother and clutched her arm. Her eyes were wide. "Who was that horrible man?" she asked with a trembling voice.

Meredith tried to appear calm. "No one you ever want to know. He was a client of mine."

"He scares me," Deedee said.

"He scares me too, sweetheart," Meredith replied even as she was trying to stop her shaking hands.

"I don't dare ride my bike home now," the girl added.

At that moment, Detective Luke Osborne arrived. "Enos and I will see that your bike gets back to your house. You go on home with your mother."

"Thanks, Luke," Meredith said, then added, "I've defended some creepy people over the past few years, but that guy takes the cake."

"You got him off," Luke reminded her with a lopsided grin.

"Well, I did have six signed affidavits from people who are willing to testify that he was in Roosevelt the night your victim got himself beaten up. And you've got to admit that your victim is not exactly a nice guy himself."

Luke nodded in agreement, then turned to Deedee, who was still clinging to her mother. "He'll be out of town in no time. You don't need to worry about him. He knows that if he ever shows up here again, Detective Fauler and I will be on him like glue."

At the mention of the new detective's name, Meredith glanced at Detective Fauler. She met his eyes, and he immediately dropped his gaze. Luke smiled and said, "We'll be seeing you around. We'll get that bike back down to your place in a few minutes."

Just then the sheriff's secretary came in. "Luke," she said breathlessly, "a detective from Los Angeles says he sent you an e-mail you might want to look at. It's about the case you have today. He says it's very important."

Meredith felt a sinking in her stomach as Luke replied, "The case is over, but I'll come have a look anyway. Maybe you'd like to join us, Meredith."

As they walked the few yards to the sheriff's office, Luke couldn't help but notice the way Enos glanced at Meredith. *Maybe I ought to try to line those two up,* he thought. He also thought about Deedee, her young daughter. She was already as pretty as her mother, and even though she was only thirteen, she looked every bit of sixteen. *The boys will be after her long before her mother's ready for it,* he concluded.

Meredith interrupted his thoughts as they entered the lobby of the sheriff's office. "Did you notice those men who were seated two rows behind me in the courtroom, Luke?"

"I did notice, actually. The young one is Stuart something-or-other. I've never seen the older one before. Why?"

"Oh, nothing, I just wondered what they were doing in the courtroom."

"I wondered too," Luke said.

Deedee visited with the sheriff's secretary while Luke, Enos, and Meredith checked Luke's e-mail. None of them looked more distressed than Meredith over what they learned. The man who called himself Desmond R. Devaney looked suspiciously similar to a man the detective in Los Angeles knew as Jim White, a man suspected of international slave trading—women, mostly young prostitutes, who came up missing from time to time. Yet there was no way to know if they were actually the same person.

"Probably not," Luke said when he noticed the anguished look on Meredith's face.

"He saw Deedee," Meredith said softly. "He threatened her."